The Fire Burns

"My beautiful Elizabeth, only you can quench the fire," Como-tan spoke softly.

"Yes..." she felt herself murmuring.

Their bodies became one in a pulsating, cool searing flight that rode her on the billowing crests of passion until desire burst forth like an opening flower and scattered the clouds beneath her into scuttering streams of rain.

Elizabeth woke, lying beside her husband Jason, she realized her inner self had been betrayed. It was only a dream...

PASSAGE TO GLORY

ROBIN LEIGH SMITH

ACE BOOKS, NEW YORK

PASSAGE TO GLORY

An Ace Original

ISBN: 0-441-65219-0

First Ace Printing: January 1983
Published simultaneously in Canada

Manufactured in the United States of America

Ace Books, 200 Madison Avenue, New York, New York 10016

The Beginning

THE FOG THAT rolled in from the channel often made the moor a difficult and treacherous enemy to travelers. Nevertheless, a solitary coach, hurrying along the single, winding road in the early night, moved at a pace that would have been difficult even under better conditions. With the fog, the pace was foolhardy.

The coachman, a large and burly sort, handled his four horses with an experienced if heavy hand, leaning far forward to guess at the road as it materialized in the bouncing light from lanterns hung on either side of the swaying vehicle. His lead horse was an intelligent and surefooted animal, and it was to that one, more than the others, that the coachman gave his commands.

Even so, the animal sensed almost too late a sharp change in the road and shoved a shoulder against the single tree to turn his running mate. The abrupt change caused the coach to lean perilously, rise on the two outside wheels and send the cursing driver into a desperate clutching to remain on his high seat.

"Damn your infernal eyes, man!" came from inside the rocking coach. "I said to hurry, not to kill us!"

The driver was still busy recovering his balance. Damn the man inside, he thought savagely, and damn the mission they were upon in this accursed fog. It would serve the both of them justly if they broke their necks on this Godforsaken moor.

Still, he pulled back on the now recovered reins to slow the horses in their running stride. The change was immediately sensed by his passenger and brought another protest. "I didn't command you to stop, Giles. I called to take more care!"

The coachman was moved to protest at last. "It's the cursed fog, sire! We can't hold a quicker pace!"

The voice from behind him was high in pitch but obviously well used to command. It rose over the loud protest of creaking leather and rubbing wood of the carriage. "We'll serve worse than that if we're not returned to the manor before dawn. The both of us. Remember that!"

The coachman nodded sourly in unseeing agreement and fought against the sudden twist that grabbed at his belly as he urged the lead horse once again. The words were right enough, and although he was only a driver, his own neck could well feel a rope if word of this night found its way to the wrong ears.

An hour later, he was forced to slow the horses to a walk in order to find the dark hut of the peasant.

Lyman Briggs, the owner of the hut, was a man of little imagination. The two years he'd served with the Duke's armies had been the highlight of his otherwise miserable life. Not merely because the life of a soldier had appealed greatly to him, but because he had been required to make absolutely no decisions at all for himself. His unswerving response to command, no matter what it meant, had not gone unnoticed. And when peace was declared, he found himself the tenant for life on this isolated spot as reward. The land's owner was a distant relative of the Duke, and had actually spoken directly to Briggs when he was presented with the right to live here.

But in the years since his arrival, his lack of imagination had made his small crops a continuing failure and kept both him and his barren wife near starvation. Try as he might, Briggs could not succeed. His days saw him always in a bitter mood over his hard existence and gave him a longing for the good life of a soldier.

His thoughts were again upon both subjects as he lay on the straw pallet in the hut, unable to sleep. His wife, lean as a rail and ugly, to his thinking, was having no trouble with her own rest. This only increased his irritation.

Before he could put the words together to give her what for and relieve his irritation, he heard sudden sounds from outside; sounds that replaced his anger with fear. Horses . . . a number of them. And a coach. What would a coach be doing here? And in the middle of the night when decent folk were abed? It could only mean evil . . . perhaps it was Satan's chariot itself! He shivered at the thought.

Straining every muscle to listen, he felt his wife stiffen beside him and knew she heard it too.

The hut contained no windows, but cracks in its flimsy walls and around the door gave quick passage to the glow of lanterns as the sounds of movement halted in front of his door. A horse snorted, and the break in the sudden stillness sent a fresh shiver through his body. Briggs wanted badly to pull the cover over his head.

"What is it?" his wife called in a hoarse whisper.

He could only grip her arm, too frightened himself to reply.

"Briggs! Come out, man!" The voice was that of a human, and he almost cried out in relief.

"Who's there?" he called through a stiffened throat. "Who knows my name?"

"Outside, man! Or I'll soon fetch you out with my whip!"

Briggs moved rapidly, pushing away his wife's clutching hands and throwing back the ragged quilt in the same motion. He slept in the clothes in which he worked and didn't pause to search out his shoes. A moment later he had unbarred the door and stepped out into the frail glow of the lanterns.

The sight that greeted his widened eyes nearly took away his already shallow breath. A coach, appearing black in the dim light and without markings or crest, stood a dozen or so steps away. Its size awed him. Harnessed in front were four magnificent horses with sweat glistening on their flanks. And on the near side, legs propped wide apart, was a coachman half again Briggs's own goodly size.

"Come here," the man demanded as soon as Briggs stepped from the door. He motioned with a hand that held a very large whip.

Briggs moved on fear-weakened legs. The big man, made even taller by a high-crowned, tri-cornered hat, leaned toward him.

"Listen, you scum, and mind you every word I say if you value your worthless skin. If you recognize this coach, be certain you forget you ever saw it!"

The man paused and reached one hand to gather in the front of Briggs's loose smock. "You will receive instructions from someone inside it. Listen to what he says as carefully as your pig's brain can manage, but dare to reply or to look inside and I'll take the meat from your back with this."

The looped whip came up to touch Briggs's shoulder in deadly emphasis. "Mind you what I say?"

Terrified, Briggs could only nod.

"Then listen!" The hand holding his clothes spun him around without apparent effort and his back was shoved hard against the side of the coach.

Above him he heard the whisper of leather as a curtain was drawn back. The sound made him move in spite of himself, but the hard fist against his chest reminded him not to look up. He stared instead into the grim face of his attacker.

"Lyman Briggs," said a thin, muffled voice above his head, "you were once known as a loyal soldier. One who would serve without hesitation, without question. That is why you have been chosen for this work."

The pause that followed was of a length to make Briggs stir if he had dared. But the pressure on his chest had not lessened, and his ribs were already beginning to ache from it.

"You must swear on your life never to mention this duty to anyone, Briggs, no matter who, or under what circumstances," the voice continued at last. "Nor must you even recall to your own mind the events of this night lest a drunken tongue betray you. Do you understand?"

Briggs was torn by indecision. He had been told by the coachman not to reply. But didn't the question require an answer?

The man holding him solved his dilemma. "Nod your worthless head, you dungheap."

He did. Vigorously.

"Good," said the voice. "You will be given a pair of infants in a moment. They are newborn and weak already in health. Give them to the care of your woman. I order you that they are not under any circumstances to be killed. But . . ." another long pause, ". . . it would be far better for all concerned if they do not survive long in this world. Do you understand?"

Briggs nodded his head again. But slowly. He didn't understand. Not at all. Babes? Not to be killed, but not to live either? What did it mean? He didn't dare ask.

The voice above him seemed to understand his puzzlement. "The . . . woman who gave them birth must be told in truth that they died of natural cause for her own peace. You will see that this happens with all your effort. But, I repeat, *they will not be murdered.*"

The hard eyes of the coachman bore into Briggs's own. And the peasant shuddered in spite of himself.

"Take them, shelter them and feed them," the muffled voice continued. "But give them nothing beyond that. No herbs, nor drink that might lessen their chance to die as God surely intends. Or your life is forfeit. Remember, Briggs, *never* mention whence they came, or nothing on earth can save you."

The curtain dropped.

Minutes later, the dumbfounded peasant was standing alone, listening to the sounds of the rapidly departing coach and holding the large basket the coachman had handed him. He was still too frightened and unsure of himself to move. Only when the stricken voice of his wife came from behind him did he allow himself to turn and search uselessly for her in the lightless night.

"Hush your whining, woman," he snarled. "Get your bones inside and build a fire. I must see—I've got something to look at."

He made his way to the hut, carefully holding the basket in front of him, and rebarred the door. He stood and waited as she fumbled around for a few bits of wood and tinder moss with which to build the fire he'd commanded.

He breathed out slowly as the first flickering flames began to create light in the room. A small sound, like the mew of a sick cat, startled him, until he realized it came from the basket he held and remembered the words from the coach. Babes . . . he was holding two infants. What in the world was he to do with them?

His wife rose from her task and stared at him, clutching her arms around her chest to ward off the night chill. Briggs ignored her and walked near the fire to set down the basket.

A blanket was looped about its inside, leaving a small opening in the center. Briggs stroked the material with one calloused hand gently. The cloth was far richer than any he'd ever touched and immediately he thought that it would make a fine jacket for him for the winter. But then he remembered what it covered and drew it aside. There was a touch at his shoulder as his wife crouched beside him.

A fine muslin sheet lay under the blanket. His hand shook as he drew that aside too. Two tiny, wrinkled, naked infants, with eyes closed and small fists clenched, lay foot to foot beneath the sheet.

"Babes!" his wife gasped in surprise. "Briggs! What are—"

"Hush, woman!" he rasped. "Ask me no questions or I'll beat the life from you, I swear!"

"But—"

He hurled a savage look at her. "No questions, I say!"

She was badly frightened, but she was a woman, with a woman's instinct in the matter of babes. She reached for one of the infants, gathered it carefully into her hands with the small head braced on her forearm and pulled it to her breast.

"The poor thing's near death!" she cried. "How could they treat it so?"

Briggs nodded somberly, the words from inside the coach coming back to him. "It's going to die," he said. "And better for us if it does quickly. If both of them do."

His wife looked at him in horror. "But they're babes. We've got to do for them. They need their mother's milk, and I—"

"Are as barren as that damned moor outside," he finished for her sourly. "Worthless to give me the sons I need to grow the food to feed us, much less to take to market."

He watched her balance the one infant carefully and raise the other to join it in her arms. The second child shivered and emitted a tiny bleat.

Holding her burdens gingerly, his wife looked again at him and spoke in a tone that startled him. "They are cold and hungry, Briggs," she said firmly. "I'll take them to bed with me to warm them. You must fetch some goat's milk. There's a crock of it in the well spring. And get me a clean rag I can soak for them to suck. They're much too young to drink properly."

He was astonished to hear her speak so, too surprised not to do as she commanded. Only after he had fetched the crock and found himself searching for a clean rag, did his anger return.

"I told you they were going to die, woman," he said. "What's the use of feeding them milk?"

She was lying in the bed, with the two tiny heads propped across one arm and the blanket drawn up to their necks. "Well they might, husband," she said, "if we do not feed them. Do you want their murder on your conscience?"

Briggs hesitated in the middle of the room, the crock in one hand and the rag in the other. The words he had heard earlier came back to him slowly. Feed them, the man had said. Shelter them. But give them no herbs nor drink to stay their death. Yes, he had been told to feed them. He squatted on the straw pallet beside her and dipped the rag into the milk, handing it to her silently.

As the first dim light from morning fought its way through the fog, he was still sitting on the floor, thinking. Both his wife and the babes were asleep, but for him there had been no rest. His mind was awhirl. The infants were in his care, but they were to die. That much was certain. And soon. It must be soon. He would have no rest until the both of them were buried in the moor. He had been badly frightened by the dreamlike events of the night before, but not too frightened to recognize the coachman. He'd seen the man but once before, driving another coach through the market of the village. And that time there had been a crest upon the side of the carriage he drove....

Briggs forced the thought of the emblem from his mind. To even think upon that was worth his very life, much less to think upon the man and woman who had ridden inside the carriage. Still, his betraying mind returned to the scene: the coach had contained an old man, powdered and wigged, and a young and beautiful woman who was laughing merrily. Briggs had stood and stared at them.

Could that lovely creature be the mother of the two babes now lying in his own wife's arms? It was unbelievable. But the same coachman had been driving her. And the crest was on the side of the carriage.

The babes were to die soon. He didn't want to think of what his life might become if they didn't.

One

ELIZABETH HURRIED BACK from the field as fast as her legs could carry her. Her curls were flying, and her eyes were a clear and shining blue. Tom, her brother, had been grateful for the water she fetched him, pausing to wipe the sweat from his brow and grinning at her before he took a long draught. She was glad she had made the trip for his sake, but she was afraid to be long from the hut. She left the pail with him, knowing he would share it with their father and suffer without complaint the older man's abuse for having taken the time to drink. It was near harvest time and every moment counted. At fourteen, Tom was almost as large as his father and could do a man's work. And she did all the work at the hut herself ever since her mother had taken sick. Still, their father seemed to begrudge their very existence.

It was the way things had always been and they weren't going to change now even if her mother died as she seemed likely to do. When the harvest was finished, they would take the corn to market in the village. This harvest would be better than most, perhaps there would be a bit of money for clothes.

She needed a dress badly; this one was so worn it was beginning to tear for hardly any reason.

The hut held the odor of death when she entered. Her mother lay wan and pale on the straw pallet in one corner. Elizabeth went to a pail near the door for a wet cloth to wash her mother's face.

"How do you feel?" she asked. "Can you drink some water? I have a broth warming on the fire that should make you feel better."

The face under her gaze was thin, with skin drawn so tight across the cheekbones and forehead it resembled little more than a skull. Her mother shook her head slowly. "No," the word floated hollow on a shallow breath. "I cannot eat. It will only increase the pain."

"But you must! You need the strength!"

Her mother shook her head again, a tiny movement. "Child," she whispered, "it is time for me to die. I only worry what will happen to you after I am gone."

Elizabeth's heart jumped at the words and she reached for the hand struggling out from under the quilt. "You must not say that!" she cried. "You will be well again. As soon as the harvest is in we can fetch some medicine from the village. Perhaps even a herb woman."

Her mother coughed long and hard, and Elizabeth wiped away the spittle from her lips. "Don't try to talk," she said. "It is too hard for you."

"I must talk. The time has come," her mother whispered. "Daughter, lean close. And listen. There are things you must know. But you must swear never to mention this to your father. If he knows of what I tell you, he will do terrible things."

Elizabeth frowned in puzzlement. What things? That their father seemed to hate both Tom and herself was apparent. It had always been so and they had come to accept it. He hardly looked at either of them except in anger, and was quick to blows, and both she and Tom avoided him as much as they could in their limited life on the edge of the moor.

The woman on the bed was quiet, gathering strength. "Swear you will never speak of this," she said at last.

The filmed eyes searched for her and surprisingly, the hand in hers tightened. "I must tell you, Elizabeth . . . you are not my own daughter. Nor Thomas of my flesh. You came to me as infants . . . in the night. A long time ago, you were brought to us. Your father was told to take you in."

A strange smile crossed her mother's face. "You were supposed to die but I wouldn't permit it. I nursed you, and loved you, and prayed for you to live."

This was impossible. Elizabeth could not believe the words.

But the thin voice continued relentlessly. "Langlee... Remember the name, child. It belongs to you even if you can never claim it right. But don't ever say it to your father. If you do, he will kill you. I know he will kill you."

Her mother tried to rise in anguish, but fell immediately back. "Don't tell him!"

Elizabeth was frightened. Both for her mother, and suddenly for herself. It was too much to comprehend. She forgot the need for the woman on the bed to rest, forgot everything. She had to know!

"Who are we? What does that name mean?" she whispered, leaning close.

The old woman struggled to reply, her unseeing eyes staring. "He told me once. He was drunk on wine and doesn't remember his words. He would have killed me if he knew."

Slowly, painfully, a word or two at a time, the story was told. Elizabeth listened with her heart beating madly. By the time it was finished, she was shaking as if she had the fever herself. Now she knew why she and Thomas were hated by their father—not their father, she corrected herself. And she knew—nearly knew, she corrected herself again, for the story was not complete—from where they came. The lady, possibly her own mother, had died. Locked in the manor house, she had died unwed. Elizabeth had heard the foul rumors in the village. But she had never suspected she and Thomas could have been the reason behind those rumors!

When Tom and her father returned from the field, she was standing outside, her arms folded across her chest. She had been standing so for most of the afternoon, thinking. Only with the gathering dusk, when she saw them returning, did she remember the meal she had failed to prepare for them. But no matter, there was another task at hand now, and she wanted to cry with the thought of it.

She waited, chin up, until the two of them paused to eye her—Tom with a puzzled look on his young face and her father hard-eyed as usual.

Elizabeth forced herself to meet the older man's gaze. "Mother is dead," she said quietly. "I thought to come and tell you, but I didn't know how best you'd want to hear about it."

His expression failed to change with the news; he merely nodded his head slowly. "She was bound to die," he said. "How long ago?"

"Right after I came with the water," Elizabeth said. "Not much after noon." It had been long after that, but it was necessary to lie to him now, this man who was not her father and who had every reason to hate and to fear her and her brother. Her mother had died with the effort of telling her the truth; it would be a true sin to go against that effort.

Suddenly, looking at the man she had feared for so long, Elizabeth wondered if she hated him. Or if she really felt sorry for him. He had lived with the secret of their birth for fourteen years, a secret that had made him afraid every day. She pitied him for that.

But Lyman Briggs dispelled that feeling with his next words. "Did you not prepare my supper? I see no smoke from a fire."

His indifference to her mother's death made her want to scream out at him, but that would only fetch a blow. "I'm sorry," she said instead. "I was upset because she died."

"Then get you to it," he said. "Your brother and I will see to the burial."

"Father," the word stuck in her throat, "could we not wait a bit? Perhaps Tom could go for the vicar while I see to your supper." She looked to her brother for help, but Thomas was staring out across the moor.

Briggs laughed, a short, harsh explosion of noise. "Are you daft, girl? You think the vicar would make a trip out here for the likes of us? See you to the supper and be quick about it." He shrugged. "We'll wait till after we eat if you're a mind to see her put into the ground."

It was better than nothing. Elizabeth went back into the hut to stir the fire into life, carefully avoiding a look at the still form on the pallet with the quilt pulled above her head.

Late in the evening, Thomas stood beside her and held her hand in his own. They watched their father lower her into the hole Tom had made, and Elizabeth wished they had been able to put her in something other than her own poor dress and a cloth wrapped about her head. But Briggs would not hear of it. Blankets were for the living, he had told her sharply. The dead didn't feel the cold.

She turned her head as he climbed out again and began to shovel dirt in. Tom reached an arm around her and pulled her head to his chest. "Cry if you want, Beth," he whispered. "She was a good mother to us."

Tom tightened his arm and raised his other hand to stroke her hair. The gesture broke down Elizabeth's carefully nurtured strength, and she cried, the sobs wracking her whole body.

Dimly, after what seemed a very long time, she heard her father's voice. "Come back to the hut," he said harshly. "I'll tell you what we'll be about after the harvest is in."

It required the better part of another week to finish the harvest, dreadful days to Elizabeth. She had to help in the field and the heavy work distracted her mind from the secret for a while. But she still had a strong urge to tell Tom that the two of them were actually orphans.

Langlee . . . the name played like the sound of a church bell inside her head, and when she had cooked their supper and sat crosslegged on the floor of the hut to watch the man who occupied the only stool wolf his meal down rapidly, she was sorely tempted to voice it aloud and witness his reaction. But her mother had said he would kill them both if he discovered she knew the name, and she little doubted her mother's word.

He had said he would tell them of his plans as soon as the harvest was in. That too worried her. He obviously intended to make a change of some sort. She was sure it would not be good for her and Tom.

Briggs finished his meal, belched loudly and rose to thrust the tin toward Elizabeth to clean before going outside.

"Good supper, Beth," Tom said from the corner. "You'll make a fair cook for some man before long."

He grinned at her, a tired grin, and she knew he was exhausted from the day. He was only a lad, but he did a man's work in the field.

"I wish for that day soon," she returned, giving him a half smile. Then suddenly, without quite realizing what she was saying, she whispered, "Tom, why don't we leave?"

He looked up from his plate in surprise. "Leave? Where? You think he would want to go elsewhere?"

Elizabeth put her own half eaten plate on the dirt floor beside her. "No, not him. I mean you and me. You can work as well as a man. And I can cook and clean. And I can work in the fields. We could go far away and hire ourselves to someone else."

Astonishment spread over his young face. "You mean run away? Father would search us down and beat the life from both of us. What an idea!"

"Not if we were quick. And ran far away. Tom, come with me!"

Tom shook his head slowly, his eyes upon her face. "We could never do it, Beth. It would only anger him the more."

He was right of course. She got up to gather the plates; he stretched toward her and went out to scrape the three of them clean. Lyman Briggs knew the countryside well and they didn't. He would find them and Tom would stand the worse beating. And, too, they might find an even harder life elsewhere. Still, she thought as she looked into the night, somewhere, somehow, there must be a better life for Tom and her.

Harvesting the corn was slow work. Far better if Tom had a sack of some sort in which to gather the corn, but there was none. He paused at the spot he'd left off and glanced around to find his sister. She was two rows away, gathering the ears into her skirt pulled up to hold them. Her long bare legs were white against the fading green of the cornstalks and he thought the August sun would burn them quickly. He should caution her, but she'd only say she couldn't hold enough ears in her arms. He shrugged, and turned to loosen another ear, breaking it sharply from its stubborn stalk.

Two weeks before, while his mother lay dying, he and his father had worked in the field stripping the protective shuck back to expose the corn to dry. It was still early to harvest the corn now, to his way of thinking, and there had been several days of rain. To gather the harvest now would surely cause a goodly number of them to sour before they had been stored long. He shrugged again. That, of course, was not for him to say.

The work now was tiring, but not as tiring as stripping the ears had been. The corn broke quick enough from the stalk if one knew the correct twist. At any rate, it left Tom's mind free to think, and he had a great deal to think about. There was going to be a change in their lives, of that he was certain. On the night his mother had died, his father had spoken of a change. Now there was a difference in his manner. After the one meal which they ate in the evenings, he'd not fallen immediately into bed and asleep as usual, but had often sat on his stool to stare into the fire.

Tom had watched him without appearing to do so. His father was not a man used to thinking and the effort he was putting into doing it now was apparent. His long face often twisted with the effort. He wished he could have spoken more about it to Elizabeth—he could see it worried her, too—but it wouldn't do to alarm her.

What could his father be planning? Perhaps to hire the two of them out? But then who would cook his supper or help him in his own planting come spring?

Tom shook his head as he finished loading his arms and started once more for the cart. No, that would not be the answer. He winced at his next thought. Once, while in the village, he'd passed near the workhouse and had been sickened at the sight of the people lodged there, those who could not care for themselves. Surely his father couldn't be thinking of sending Elizabeth and him to such a place.

He dumped his load in the cart and started back. Well then, what? Or where? It was a worrisome thing to harbor. If he only had himself to think of, he would not be too frightened, but there was Elizabeth and he couldn't bear the idea of her having to suffer. Somehow he would have to care for her. But how? In spite of his protestations whenever they talked, he realized he was not yet full a man and his experiences were limited to this simple life. He knew naught of the world beyond the village. She spoke of running away, but the thought of that feared him greatly. Too many things could happen to a young lass with no protection.

He sighed and bent once more to his work. With the three of them at it, he calculated they would finish by early afternoon. The time of waiting was nearly over. Surely now his father would tell them of his plans.

He was wrong in the length of time it took to complete his task. It was late afternoon by the time they were finished. With a sense of relief, Tom pulled the last ear from its stalk and made his way back to the cart, glancing about on his way to make sure he'd missed none at all. His father and sister were already there.

"Take hold," his father commanded. "We'll move this to where we'll be ready to leave at dawn."

Tom glanced at his sister, who looked away just as quickly, and then set his shoulder to the cart. It was heavy and took most of the strength he and his father could muster to start it to roll. Once moving, it moved more easily and in a few minutes they had placed it to suit.

His father straightened and put his hands to the small of his back to stretch it. "Good," he said. "We can be well on our way early." His glance took in the both of them significantly. "We've a long way to travel."

"To the village?" Tom asked.

The slow smile his father gave him set his already tight nerves to strumming. "The village is only our first stop," he said. "If Dame Fortune is with us, we'll sell the corn quickly and be well upon the moor by nightfall."

"Where're we going?" Elizabeth burst out. "We're not to return home?"

The smile deepened. But there was no laughter in the eyes above it. "Take a last look around you, girl. This place will never see the likes of you again. Nor me, for that matter, if I have my way."

She started to speak, alarm spreading across her young face, but he cut her off with a wave of his hand. "No more from you now. See to my supper and be quick about it. And make the meal a large one, spare nothing we have left. We'll be eating many a cold meal on the road before we reach the place we're going."

The force of his gesture sent her hurrying toward the hut. Tom followed, a step behind his father. So they were truly leaving then. Never to return. And they would be days on the road to reach their destination.

Tom thought heavily about it as he walked. He was not accustomed to the world, that much was certain. But he did know that to leave the parish in which one lived was a dangerous thing. Neither the Lords who owned most of the land, nor the burghers of the parishes, took kindly to strange faces in their areas. One must have permission, or orders, to move to another parish. Or at least not be of the peasant class. English law required all peasants to be fed by the parish burghers if they could not feed themselves, but that would not be done without requiring some work in return. And the work would be extracted by placing the unfortunate in a workhouse. Surely his father knew he ran a risk by traveling? The few shillings he would earn from this poorly dried corn would not sustain them long.

But then Tom had learned to keep his questions to himself. A trait his more excitable sister had yet to master.

In the hut, Briggs sat upon his stool, his hands resting between his thighs, and Elizabeth knelt before the fire, stirring a pot. Tom crossed to the straw pallet he shared with his sister and sat down to rest his back against the wall. He looked up a moment later to find his father's eyes upon him.

"You've not been wanting to know where we are going?" he asked suddenly.

Tom nodded. "It's a thing we both want to know. When you've a mind to tell us."

"To London." His father said it so quickly, Tom wasn't sure he'd heard correctly.

"To where?" he demanded, in the midst of a gasp from his sister.

"Open your ears, boy. I said we're going to London town. The biggest and grandest city in all of England. What do you think of that?"

"To London town . . ." Tom couldn't believe his ears. He looked at the stricken face of his sister and shook his head slowly. "But we're landed people, father. What can we find to do in such a place? Why must we go there?"

His father laughed, proud of the joke he'd played upon them. "You leave that to me," he said. "I know what I'm about. I've been there before, long years before you were . . . before you came into this world. I'm a man who knows more than this miserable piece of ground, I tell you."

Elizabeth had recovered enough to resume her cooking, but she kept her face turned to watch them both.

Tom forced himself to ignore her look. "London is far from here," he ventured. "And . . . different."

"Aye," his father laughed, slapping his knee. "It's a place for a man to be who has money."

Curiosity replaced Tom's alarm. "But where will we get money?" he asked. "I mean, I did not think the corn would bring—"

"The corn is nothing," his father interrupted sharply. "I only thought to harvest it for the money we would need to travel on. The real money will come in London. A great deal of money. I've thought it all out."

His expression changed, he'd grown tired of teasing them. You leave that part of it to me, boy. Just be sure you do as I say when we get there. And be sharp along the road for there'll be plenty of robbers on the way who would be pleased to knock in our heads for no more than the clothes we wear."

He nodded grimly. "We'll have to keep our wits about us or we might never see the sights you are going to see in London town. And I am a man who intends to enjoy those sights, I tell you. It's only the fool that I am I've waited this long."

Tom could only shake his head in disbelief. To London town! They might as well be going across the sea!

Two

LONDON TOWN. The name lodged in Tom's mind like a smoldering ember, and over the following days—days spent in moving slowly along roads that ranged from packed and smoothed highways to lanes that were little more than rutted trails—the ember had slowly been fanned into a fire of anticipation. He was beside himself at the thought of he, Thomas Briggs, actually being in such a great city.

He was near beside himself when they topped a rise and at last beheld the city sprawling before them, almost as far as he could see. He restrained himself from clapping his hands in glee.

Once inside the city, with a closer look at what he'd anticipated, the fire began to die rapidly. What had been exciting at first gave way to scenes that soured both his eyes and his nose. He felt as if he had stepped into a nest of fleas.

Perhaps he was only seeing the worst of it, he told himself; perhaps the grander side was yet to come. But he had learned to be practical in his life and the practical side of himself said there would be little that was different from what he was seeing, at least not for him.

The city was incredibly dirty. Tom was used to the countryside where nothing was ever wasted, ever thrown away. Here, rubbish of the most foul smell lay everywhere in the rounded stone streets, and even human waste was obvious in a narrow gutter that ran down the middle of the street. There were no raised walkways, only a line of posts to rail off a six-foot path on some of the larger streets, none at all in the lesser ones.

Ancient houses, so old they seemed to totter with the strain of rotting wood, leaned tiredly toward each other, often with space hardly the width of a man's shoulders to separate them. Most of them were of two stories, and then as they drew closer in, there were even three! He couldn't believe his eyes. And the top house was more often than not, larger, jutting out above the lower a foot or more. It made the whole house appear upside down to him.

He paused to look up at one in particular and then was forced to dodge quickly when a woman appeared from a window above his head and threw the contents of a chamber pot in his direction without so much as a look at him.

The sight made his father laugh. "Look to your wits, lad," he chuckled. "You're not in the country now."

Tom grimaced. Not indeed, and already he was regretting the fact. He turned to comment to Elizabeth who stood beside him, but was forced to grasp her quickly instead and jerk her from the path of a horse.

The rider moved rapidly, a seemingly impossible task in a street already teeming with carts, pack horses, hackney coaches of all descriptions and even an occasional carriage. In the midst of all that were people, hundreds of people, men and women alike, all appearing to be peddling something or other at the top of their lungs. The din set Tom's nerves to jangling.

Elizabeth grasped his arm tightly. "Tom, I don't like it."

"Aye. Neither do I, Beth," he said. "It's like being in a pig's sty, except I think the pig's cleaner."

"Move along, you two," his father ordered from a dozen steps ahead of them. "No time to waste here, you can gaggle at the sights after we've found a place to lay our heads."

Tom moved after him, trying to avoid contact with the crowd that ebbed around him as he walked. But that was impossible and he used his shoulder to clear a path for Beth. For her part, she walked so closely on his heels she occasionally tripped him.

There were depressions in the pavement where some of the cobblestones had been dislodged or had sunken below the rest, and for the most part the holes were filled with stagnant water. Tom avoided them as best he could, but after being forced into two in quick succession and soaking his shoes, he decided to ignore the rest and merely plod along after his father.

The people around him were as poor as himself, he judged. Most wore such grimy rags they made his own well-worn clothes seem rich in comparison. Their faces were coarse and pock-marked, their bodies lean but potbellied and, more often than not, their limbs were stunted and backs humped. And the few eyes that would meet his own honest gaze were small and mean.

Tom was more than a little relieved when they at last left the endlessly crowded streets and turned into a narrow lane with far less people. His father paused to allow them to catch up.

"Butcher's Row," he told them when they paused. "I remember it well, though it's been many a year since I stood here. There'll be rooms aplenty for a small price. And a bit of gin, too, I'll wager. More than a bit." He seemed to be talking more to himself than to them.

Tom looked beyond his father to where two men stood silently watching them. Unlike the crowds who'd ignored their presence except to shout their wares at them, these two men seemed to find them of great interest. But the looks came from cruel and calculating faces and made him greatly uneasy.

"Perhaps we had best be finding that room," he told his father without taking his eyes from the men. Elizabeth's grip tightened on his arm and Tom realized she had also seen them. Suddenly, he understood that their interest was less in him and his father than in her. She was a sister to him, but he suddenly was acutely aware that she was also a budding woman.

His father hadn't noticed the men. "There's a tavern near the end that was once familiar to me," he said. "We'll see if it still exists."

He moved and Tom followed, being careful to place Elizabeth on the opposite side of him from the watchers. Looking back, he was relieved to see the two did not follow, and then gave his attention to where they were going.

His father stopped before a three-storied house which sported a sign hanging from an iron pole by only one link, making it swing at an angle. Tom had to cock his head to see its almost vanished markings. There was a faded red rooster on it and beneath that, some sort of lettering. The last brought back an old ache. Once, while in the village, he'd stood in awe and listened as a man read to the crowd from a paper in his hand. On impulse, he'd pushed close enough to see the paper. The little marks made absolutely no sense to him, and he'd wondered that anyone could gather words from that. Afterwards, lying in the night in the hut at home, he'd experienced a burning desire to some day be able to read himself. But it had been a foolish wish, reading was not for the likes of him. Still, the desire had persisted for many a day and this sign brought it back afresh.

If the streets had been an offense to his ears and nose, the inside of this place was worse. It was a small, cramped room, so crowded with shouting, laughing people there seemed no space left in which to stand, much less to sit. The room was low ceilinged and so thick with smoke it made his eyes water. Men were everywhere clutching a mug in one hand and most of them held a woman in the other. As he looked around, his jaw dropped to see a man near him with his entire arm thrust full beneath the skirt of a young girl sitting across his knees. As Tom watched, the man made a sharp movement with his arm and her shattering laugh rang far above the din.

He spun quickly and sought to hide the sight from his sister, but Elizabeth was otherwise occupied. An old man, grizzled and toothless, had grasped her with both hands and she was struggling to free herself.

"Hold still, you pretty wench!" the man shouted in a voice soaked with gin. "I tell you I've a ha'penny for your charms!"

Tom had never struck another in his life. He wasn't aware he was capable of such a thing. As much to his own surprise as the man's, his fist crashed against the bearded face and drove him backward into others. The response brought a roar of laughter from the onlookers.

"By the blood, Yarrow," one man cried through his laughter and at the same time used his foot to thrust the old man aside. "Use your eyes, man! You picked a wench already taken. Drunken fool that you are!"

The man he'd struck struggled to his feet as Tom watched

in amazement, not even grasping the significance of the knife that appeared in his hand as if by magic. He would have been too transfixed to avoid its thrust if his father hadn't stepped forward and swung a heavy forearm to the man's neck to drive him once more to his knees.

His father followed the blow with another one, this time with his knee, and Tom heard bone crunch. A moment later, his shoulder was grasped roughly and he was thrust away from the scene. "Get to the stairs yonder," his father grated in his ear. "You'll learn, boy, when you hit a man you don't stand about and give him a chance to come back at you! You put him down to stay!"

Unable to stop himself from being propelled across the crowded room, Tom twisted his head over his shoulder to search out his sister, terrified that she was being left behind. But his father had a hand on her, too, and dragged her along. Within seconds, they were stumbling up narrow stairs.

They turned on a landing and immediately began climbing more stairs of even less width. There was only room for one person at a time between the wall and a rail that wobbled under his hand and assured Tom it would pitch him to the room below if he allowed his weight to press against it. At the top of this was a short hall with three doors.

His father thrust past him and opened the first, then immediately closed it again. The second suffered a similar fate. However, the third met his approval.

"Inside," he commanded. "It's not as full as the others. Find a corner and stay there until I return." Without another word, he left them to descend the stairs again.

Tom took Elizabeth by the waist and looked around. There were a number of men in the room, lying about on dirty straw, and only two of them were awake. Those two ignored him and Elizabeth as if they didn't exist.

If the ceiling in the tavern had been low, this one was impossible. Tom could hardly stand erect. And it bent even lower across the room until it ended at the outside wall nearly three feet above the floor. But that space was vacant and he led his sister there, being careful not to step upon any of the sleeping men.

They had to drop to their knees to reach the wall and there he turned to sit and Elizabeth moved close to him.

"Tom, it's a horrible place," she whispered. "Must we stay here?"

"Perhaps he's gone to find a better place," Tom told her.

He knew it wasn't true. His father had gone to seek out the owner and pay for their lodging; they would have to sleep here the night at least. But there was no point in telling her that yet. He put his arm around her shoulders and leaned his head against the wall.

Late in the afternoon his father still had not returned, and Tom had become weary with waiting. Elizabeth slept part of the time, more from exhaustion stemming from her fright down-stairs, he reasoned, than the exhaustion of the journey they'd made through the city. His arm was numb from holding her, but he didn't want to move it and cause her to wake. He was glad when she stirred and sat up to rub at her eyes.

"Has he come back?" she wanted to know.

"No." He pulled his arm free and began to rub the muscle to restore circulation.

Elizabeth looked about her and her mouth curled in a gri-mace. The two men who had been awake when they entered were now stretched out themselves. Several others had left. Except for the sounds of drunken sleep, the room was quiet and belonged to them.

"Where do you think he's gone?" she asked. "You really think he's looking for another place?"

Tom shook his head. "Not likely, Beth. He's probably downstairs himself, having the drink he's been talking about." His voice became bitter. "He's spoken of little else for three days."

Elizabeth stretched her dress to cover her legs. "This place is filthy," she said. "I don't like staying here." She turned suddenly to him. "Tom, let's leave."

It made him angry, not so much at her, but at himself. He felt helpless. "You know we can't do that, Beth. Not until he's a mind to. You'll only make him angry to say it."

She stared at him with a strange expression in her brown eyes, her face solemn. "I wasn't speaking of asking him, Tom. I thought of doing it ourselves. You know he hates us. I think he only wants to be rid of us now so that he can do whatever he wants here."

"He'll do as he wants no matter of us," he told her crossly. "What do you want me to do, lead us out into the streets? With no money and nowhere to go? Don't speak so foolishly."

But she refused to be denied. "We can make for ourselves, Tom. Find some kind of work. We can take care of ourselves better without him."

He stared at her but saw instead the scenes he had witnessed throughout the city as they entered. The dirty, shoving people trying to claim their attention over pitiful wares, children half naked and looking as if they were starving, the poorness of it all, and especially the looks the two men outside this tavern had given her. And, too, he remembered the scene downstairs when the man had roughed her and almost killed him. He had no love for his father, and it would be a relief to quit him—but to do so now would be stupid and dangerous.

"Beth, do you remember what happened downstairs?" he asked. "Remember what those people were doing?"

She nodded, but continued to look into his eyes.

He set his jaw. "The women, Beth. Did you see what they were about?" It was painful to speak to her about such things, but she had to understand.

"I'm not like that," she said quietly.

"Aye, I know you're not. But you've a woman's body. And they'll be after you soon enough if we go into the streets. I don't know that I can stop them."

She didn't reply, but her gaze was burning into him.

"Whatever he feels toward us, father will not allow that to happen," he continued. "He has been here before and knows what to do."

"How do you know what he intends?" she said slowly. "Suppose he intends to put me to . . . such things."

He was astonished. "What a thing to say! He's your father!"

"Suppose he is not, Tom," she persisted. "Our father, I mean. Suppose that is why he hates us, because we never belonged to him. Would you quit him then, if you knew that?"

"Wherever did you get an idea like that? Are you denying he's our father? Denying your own dead mother? Are you daft, girl?"

Tom had never seen his sister act so strangely. He could only think this terrible place had loosened her mind. "Beth, don't take on so. We'll not be here for long. Yes, father hates us. But he *is* our father. Were you to say such a thing to him he would give you a beating. Never mention that, do you hear?"

Beth continued to give him the strange look for a time, and then suddenly sighed. "You're right, Tom," she said. "It would serve no purpose. Not yet anyway."

He was relieved. Bad enough to be in this situation. Worse yet to have their father go into one of his rages. He hoped she would put the idea out of her head.

It had been a long night and a longer morning. Briggs came back reeking of gin but with a bit of cold food for them, too drunk to offer any explanation of what he intended even if he had been of a mind to do so.

Elizabeth had lain awake for the better part of the night, worrying. Something terrible was going to happen to them. She knew it without doubt. Briggs not only hated them, he was a man who had lived in fear of the truth being discovered. He had brought them to this city, this place so far from anyone who knew them; a place where no one would give a care as to what happened to them—to be rid of them forever. The only real question was how. What did he intend to do?

The morning was already late when Briggs awoke. Elizabeth was picking lice from the seams of her clothes when he sat up. His eyes were red from drink, but his voice was milder than she'd expected.

"There's a kitchen in the back downstairs," he told her. "I've given money to the woman there. Go down now and she'll give you a bit of bread to eat and some water to clean yourself. Make sure you do a good job of it as I'll be bringing someone to see you later."

"To see me for what?" she demanded, surprising herself with the anger and hatred that was growing within her.

"Never you mind, girl. You do as I say or I'll fetch a proper blow to your sassy head. Now get about it!"

She looked to Tom, who had awakened and was staring at his father. But before he could speak, he was given orders as well. "You go along with her, boy, to see she's left alone. And remember what I said. If you have to fight a man, do a proper job of it right off. Don't stand about like a fool."

With that, he left them again.

She did as he ordered, and the morning went without incident. They were back in the room now. The others who had shared it with them were also gone, leaving one or two at a time until the two of them shared its space with only one other, an old man who appeared more dead than alive, lying in another corner.

With only the cracks in the ancient roof to tell them of the day outside, Elizabeth guessed it to be nearing noon. She wished Briggs would hurry with whatever he was about.

When the door opened, she looked up with relief. Briggs entered, with another man close behind him. She had become accustomed to the roughness of dress the people in this tavern wore and was surprised to see that this man's attire was of a better cut. He wore a frock coat. Although not rich, it was still worth more than any she'd seen either here or in the village back home. A pair of wide breeches were tied close below the knee and woolen stockings without holes in them extended into leather shoes with heavy buckles. He was fat, and perspiration had caused his wig to slip to one side.

The man paused just inside the door to retrieve a large handkerchief from a pocket in the tail of his coat and mop his brow. "Damn, man," he said to Briggs. "You didn't tell me of such a climb. Why in the devil didn't you fetch her downstairs?"

Briggs ignored the question and looked to her instead. "Come here, girl. This man wants to talk to you."

Elizabeth moved reluctantly, crawling forward until she could stand erect, and then paused a few feet from them in indecision.

"Closer," Briggs commanded. "Do as I say."

She did, but was relieved to feel her brother come up behind her.

The man exuded an odor that was more than the sweat that wetted his black hair protruding from under the slipped wig. She was glad she'd had her own bath.

Without a word to her, he stepped forward and grasped her arm roughly, plying thick fingers across the muscle of the upper part. Elizabeth jerked back in anger, only to be caught quickly by Briggs. "Hold still," he commanded in a snarl. "No harm is coming to you!"

The fat man glanced at him. "Does she not know what this is about?"

"She needs to know only what I tell her myself," Briggs said harshly, looking to her rather than to the man. "She belongs to me and will do as I say."

"Father—" Tom protested, but was cut off before he could

begin. "Shut up, boy. Stay out of this if you know what is good for you!"

Tom paused, anger turning his young face red. Elizabeth freed herself from her father's grip and stepped before the man once more.

He nodded in approval. "At least she's the good sense to mind." He reached for her arm again, but this time treated her less roughly, running his fingers over her limbs, then turning her slowly to feel her back and shoulders.

When he had finished, he turned her again and she allowed him to do so, giving a quick, pleading glance to her brother.

"Open your mouth, girl," the man commanded. "I want to look at your teeth."

She did, but couldn't avoid a grimace as he stuck a thick finger in her mouth.

Then, to her relief, he stepped back and eyed her from toe to head, his fists propped upon his wide hips.

He stood so until Briggs grew impatient. "Well?"

The man nodded slowly, reluctantly. "She's in good enough health, I'll warrant you that. But she's smaller than I expected from a country girl. I don't think she's worth the price you ask."

Briggs snorted. "Worth twice the price, and you know it. Make up your mind, man. If you don't want her, I'll seek another. And find one soon enough, no doubt about that."

Still the man hesitated, his small eyes narrowing in the wide face, "I'll give you twenty-six crowns, two. No more."

"Thirty-five, the price I asked," Briggs snapped. "Or you've made a useless trip here."

The man spun to protest but was stopped by an upraised hand that slowly turned into a fist. "Thirty-five. Or get out!"

The threat was enough, she could see he was not a man accustomed to facing danger. "All right," he said hastily. "I don't have the time to waste looking for another. Have her to the ship I spoke to you about by dawn. We're sailing early, the captain says."

The man paused and tried to cover his quick surrender. "But I'll pay you naught until she's there and the papers are signed. I won't have you disappearing with my money."

Briggs laughed. "She'll be there right enough. I keep my word."

With one last glance at her as if to assure himself, the man turned and left, a grinning Briggs watching him go.

The grin disappeared as Tom exploded. "Father! What have you done?"

He spun and pointed a finger at Tom's chest. "Mind your tongue, boy! You're not to question me!"

Tom was trembling and brushed aside the hand Elizabeth put up to restrain him. "You're selling Elizabeth! You can't do that!"

Elizabeth, afraid Briggs was going to hit him, moved to place herself between them, forgetting for the moment what had just happened. But Briggs made no move. Instead, he dropped his hand and a grim look grew on his face. "You're a young fool, boy. But I'll tell you. Your sister will be well off, have no fear. She'll become indentured to that Mr. Cawley for four years where she'll learn to take care of herself right enough. After that, she can do just as she pleases."

Elizabeth turned to stare at him, but it was Tom who spoke. "Indentured! What does that mean?"

The hard look stayed in place. "It means she will be servant to Mr. Cawley and his family. She'll work for him to earn the money he's paying to me. Money that I well deserve for the years I've spent feeding the both of you."

"What will I have to do?" Elizabeth asked as quietly as she could manage.

"You'll do whatever he requires of you," was the short reply. "The cooking, the cleaning, taking care of his children, whatever he demands of you. And I want no argument from you about it."

"I'm not arguing," she insisted. "I merely want to understand. Will I have to live here in this city?" Somehow that worried her more than becoming a servant. In fact, the latter sounded better than some of the things that had been going through her mind the night before. Briggs hesitated, and Elizabeth began to feel alarm rising in her once more.

"All right," he said at last. "You might as well know the truth of it, you'll know in the morning at any rate. But I want no tears or foolish carrying on when you're told. Do you hear?"

She nodded, crossing her arms over her chest and gripping them tightly with her hands.

Briggs narrowed his eyes, watching her closely. "You'll not be staying here in London. Nor either in England for that matter. You'll be taking ship to the Americas."

"To the Americas!" It was a wail from Tom and it echoed the shock thundering through Elizabeth.

"Aye," Briggs said. "Tis a new colony there, he tells me. A new place where a man can be given land, fresh land, to grow crops like has never been. I might be of a mind to go myself if I didn't have other plans."

"If you're bound to do this to her, father, then you must send me as well. I'll not let her go alone," Tom spoke up.

"You'll be telling me what I can and can't do?" Briggs asked with heavy sarcasm.

"I know I'll not let her go alone," Tom repeated, and Elizabeth was surprised at the strength in his voice.

Briggs nodded slowly. "Well, you'll be getting your wish, boy. Perhaps more than you bargain for. You want to go to the Americas? Then go and be damned to you. I intended that all along. Tomorrow when we go down to the ship that'll be taking your sister, I intend to have a word with the captain of it. It's said that he himself buys strong young bucks the likes of you and resells their contract upon reaching the colony. You'll go with your sister, I promise you. And then I'll be rid of the both of you forever."

If Elizabeth had ever felt anything for the man who stood before them, it fled from her now. She hated him with all of her being.

Tom raised a hand to place it on her shoulder. "And we'll be rid of you," he said in a man's voice. "I don't think that will be a hard thing to abide."

Briggs stared at him for a long moment in surprise, then nodded abruptly. "Be you ready the first thing come dawn." He turned and went out the door.

Elizabeth reached for Tom and he put his arms around her. "It'll be all right," he told her softly. "Don't be afraid. I'll be along to see about you."

She kissed his cheek softly. "I know," she said. "I won't be afraid. As long as you are going, too, I'm glad to go. And Tom, when we're away from here, away from him, I have something I want to tell you. It's a thing I think you'll be pleased to know."

"The only thing I'm pleased to know is that we'll not be separated," he told her. "That, and the pleasure of never seeing *him* again."

She rested her head against his chest, grateful for the comfort of his arms. It would be a long journey, full of new things and strange people. But if Tom were to be there none of that would matter greatly. She loved him very much and he loved her in return. As long as that were true, nothing else could be too difficult to manage.

But later, when they sat in the corner and quietly discussed their new fate, another idea grew within her slowly. It was a truth she had to face. She and Tom would have different masters. Men who, like Briggs, would tell them what to do and where to go, at least until they were free of their contracts. The Americas would not be like anything they had ever known, and likely would be a very large place. It was entirely possible that she and Tom would be separated eventually. And he would be able to do nothing about it. Somehow, she would have to find the courage to endure that and to learn to take care of herself alone.

Elizabeth gazed at her brother's face soberly, then forced herself to return the shy smile he gave her.

Three

If the streets of London had seemed crowded, they were nothing in comparison to the riverfront. It was the mass of people hurrying about, pressing and bumping her from all sides, more than the odor of rotting wood, tar and decaying fish that caused Elizabeth's stomach to spin. She clung tightly to her brother's arm.

Tom looked down at her and smiled grimly. "Hold on, Beth," he said. "I promise you'll not be going without me."

Briggs paused to get his bearings and Tom eased Beth against a wooden building where he could stand to protect her. "He'll be looking for the ship we'll take," he told her, looking about himself. "I hope it's not something like that." He indicated a smallish boat rocking gently a few feet away in the river.

She followed his gaze. The boat was rounded on both ends, although one did rise higher than the other. And both were higher than the middle. At the center was placed a little square cabin hard beside a long, smooth pole that had another crossed at its top. A jumble of rope, baskets and other gear she didn't recognize lay about its wooden floor.

"I don't think so," she said slowly. "I think it's too small.

31

What are the poles for? That big one stuck in the floor with the other on top?"

"Masts," he said. "They're called masts and they serve to hold the sheets."

"Sheets?"

"The sails," he explained patiently. "See, they're rolled up now, since this ship is not going anywhere. And you don't call it a floor, you call it a deck."

"How do you know so much?" she asked. "You've been here no more than me and yet you've already learned such things."

Tom shrugged and craned his neck to see above the moving people. Before he could comment, Briggs's voice rose above the hubbub. "This way!" he cried. "Be quick!"

Elizabeth grasped her brother's arm again and followed. *Be quick, he says. Yes, hurry so that I will be rid of you all the sooner.* Well, she and Thomas would be far better off rid of him as well.

If it were wrong to hate another person, as her mother had often repeated to her, then she was committing a great sin. For she truly hated the man they followed down the riverfront. He would, she knew, have been more than happy to see the both of them dead. Would have killed them as babes if he had not been in fear of the deed. Now he thought he was killing them in another way by sending them across the ocean where they would never be heard from again. Well, she had worked out a plan for that. If she were able to bring it about properly, Lyman Briggs would *never* be rid of them!

He paused on a wide quay that like the riverfront itself was crowded with people. But these people wore the clothes of landed people: longer coats, shirts with collars upon them and breeches and stockings instead of the cut-off pants and bare legs of the river people. They would be the ones taking ship to the Americas on the very vessel that floated beside the quay.

It was much larger than the one she and Tom had first seen. Two great masts rose from its wooden deck, with cross beams atop them and such a network of rope she wondered that the rolled up sails would have room to unfurl. The front of the ship wasn't rounded either, as the other boat had been, but came to a point.

Although its wooden sides did not rise all that much above the quay itself, its deck was wide. She trembled a little at the sight of it. That ship would now be her home for weeks. Weeks in which she would be out of sight of any land and at the mercy of the waters beyond this river.

Tom felt her shiver and put his arm around her shoulders. "Remember," he said quickly, "we'll be together."

Elizabeth didn't reply as she spotted Cawley standing with one of the groups. Briggs saw him, too. "This way," he ordered. But she was already moving and Tom followed.

Cawley looked up as they approached. "You're late," he said. "The ship is close to sailing."

"I had the devil's own time in finding it," Briggs complained. "Give me my money; I've other thing· ' '· "

Elizabeth looked beyond the fat man to where a woman and two very young boys stood, eyeing her in return. The woman was lean, with a long, sharp nose and chin, her hair pulled back into her bonnet until it left nothing but skin exposed. She wore a loose overcape that hid most of her dress and the exposed part she held up with both hands to keep it from touching the dirty quay. The two boys were dressed much as their father except for short jackets above their breeches instead of coats.

Cawley reached into the tail of his longcoat and produced a small bag and a piece of paper. "You'll have this to sign before I'll give you any money," he said. "It's the contract. I had it drawn yesterday."

A sneer drew his thick lips aside. "You'll not have time to read it, even if you can. The ship is too near sailing."

Briggs grasped the paper roughly. "Give me a pen."

Cawley nodded to his wife who turned to a small trunk, opened it and produced a quill and bottle. She handed both to her husband, who uncorked the bottle, dipped the quill and extended it to Briggs.

"Where do I make my mark?" Briggs demanded. And Elizabeth looked quickly to Tom. He was going to ask nothing about the contract! It could be for years of her life!

She took a half step forward and stopped. What was the use? He didn't care what the contract said. For her to protest would make no difference.

Cawley showed him with a thick finger and Briggs made his mark with the pen. "Now where's my money?" he said as soon as he'd finished.

The fat man took his time, handing the quill and bottle to his wife again and half turning his back to fish the coins from the bag he held. Slowly he counted them into the eager, out-stretched palm of the man who had just sold his daughter like a cow. Elizabeth watched in silence, but the clink of the coins made her wince.

Briggs turned to go. "You stay with him now," he told her roughly. "Mind you do as he says. Boy, you come with me."

"Wait." She stepped in front of him. "I want to ask—"

He shoved her roughly aside. "I've not time for you now."

But Tom also blocked his path. "Father, she's your own blood! Even if you have sold her, at least hear her out."

Reluctance was in his face as he looked at her; that, and unmistakable hatred. "Make it quick. I have to see the captain of this ship."

Elizabeth looked him directly in the eye. "I ask only a small boon," she said. "The last you'll ever hear from me."

"And what is that?"

She took a deep breath, struggling to keep the loathing from her own face. "I only ask that you not leave this place until the ship is moving away." She paused. "That you stand near enough for a last goodbye when I'm on it."

His hatred changed to amazement. "That's all?"

Elizabeth forced calm into her voice. "It's not much to ask. I've spent my life at your hearth."

She could tell he was suspicious. "I'll stand no crying or wailing from you. What's done is done."

"There'll be none of that," she assured him. "I only want a last word. A farewell."

He nodded slowly. "I'll be here until the ship moves away. Not a moment longer."

She didn't reply and he stared at her for a time until he could shake himself free. "Come, boy," he said gruffly. And Tom, with a look of pure disbelief on his young face, followed him away.

She waited with the Cawleys, the fat man having made no effort to introduce her to his wife, and watched as the sailors from the ship loaded the luggage piled on the quay. She pretended not to listen as his wife complained about her.

"You said she was young," she could hear the woman hiss. "She's much too old to be wearing clothes like that. She's practically naked!"

"I told you her age," he growled. "I don't lie. You can clothe her as you like when we reach the colony."

Elizabeth turned her head, suddenly conscious of how thin and short her dress was and followed with her eyes as, one by one, the groups of people were taken on board, stopping only to be checked by the officer who stood by the plank.

A red-haired lad, not much beyond her own years, suddenly appeared before them. He spoke to Cawley, but his eyes, green and merry above cheeks only slightly marked with pitted scars, slipped quickly beyond him to meet hers. "You'll be ready to board, sir?"

"And about time," Cawley grumbled. "These three trunks." He indicated them with a finger. "But you'll be needing help."

The redhead laughed. "I'm stronger than I look." He bent to demonstrate by easily hoisting the largest of the trunks to his back. "Follow me," he said. "I'll come back for the others." And winked at Elizabeth.

"Not a bit of it," Cawley said quickly. "I'll not leave anything here to the mercy of thieves. Take my family on board and come back for me."

The boy shifted the trunk on his back. "As you will." And set off toward the boarding plank.

Elizabeth followed, but Cawley had to urge his wife. "Go with him, woman! Keep your eye on that trunk!"

They strung out in a line, Elizabeth, the nervous woman and, lastly, her two sons who hardly ceased chattering between themselves. The redhead took them up the plank and onto the ship before pausing to speak to Elizabeth. "Below deck's a stinking mess," he said. "You'll be seeing far too much of it before this voyage is done. If I was you I'd be waiting over there until we're away." He pointed to a vacant spot near the wide wooden rail.

"Then I'll do that." She matched the grin with a smile of her own. "My thanks to you."

He touched his forehead in a gesture and started off for wooden steps leading down through an open doorway with Cawley's wife hurrying at his heels.

The boys, however, tugged at their mother's dress. "We want to stay here, too!"

She waved a nervous hand toward Elizabeth. "Keep them close, girl," she called. "Mind you watch them!" A moment later, she disappeared down the steps.

The two boys were no trouble to Elizabeth, although they ignored her attempts to talk to them, crowding close to the rail instead and competing with each other to point out new and different things. She gave up after a while and stood looking for Tom. He was nowhere in sight although she carefully ran her gaze over every inch of the quay, and up and down the street as far as she could see. A sudden dread that he might not make the voyage after all struck her, but she pushed the fear away. As much as she loved her brother, she was resolved to make her own way now. It was time to grow up. It would be wonderful to have him on this ship with her and to at least share a few more weeks with him, but there could be no knowing what was to happen to them once they reached the Americas. She must learn to be alone.

The redheaded sailor reappeared, went down the plank to fetch the second trunk and she waved to him as he went by. On his third trip up the plank, a sweating Cawley labored after him, and came in her direction. "Where's Mistress Cawley?" he demanded. "Why are you not with her?"

"She went down to watch the trunks as you said," Elizabeth told him. "Your children wanted to stay here so she left me to watch them."

He hesitated, and for a terrible minute she was afraid he was going to insist that she go below and all her plans would be ruined. "Well, see that you watch them closely. And have no thoughts of running away yourself. The man at the plank will not allow you from the ship."

"I'll not move from this place," she told him, but he was already hurrying away.

Beneath her feet, the ship rocked with the movement of the passengers and crew upon its deck, bumping gently against the quay, and echoing the beating of her own heart. She was about to leave England forever and take up a new life in a distant land. What would life be like now for Elizabeth Briggs?

With a sudden surge of newfound freedom, she thought: No, not Elizabeth Briggs. Langlee . . . that was her name. She could use it at least to herself. She and Thomas may well be bastards with no claim to use it properly here in England, but once they were free in the Americas, who was to deny them that name? Tom would agree with her, she was sure of it, once she was able to tell him the story. Like herself, he would be proud to learn they had noble blood in them.

Unconsciously, she straightened herself and lifted her chin.

* * *

Tom hurried after his father, both reluctant to leave his sister and afraid that if arrangements were not made quickly, he would be left behind when the ship sailed. He waited close on his heels as his father spoke to a ship's officer near the boarding plank. "Where can I find the captain?" his father asked.

The officer gave him only a glance and turned away to shout a command to two sailors. "Look lively there! Move your legs, you dolts! Get those barrels on board. We haven't long before the tide!"

He waited a full minute to observe the effect of his words before turning back to them. "Who wants to know? The captain's a busy man."

Briggs's manner was humble. "Tis a matter of business with myself, sir. It's told that the captain purchases the contract of indenture for those who want to go to the Americas."

The officer gave him a sour look. "You're offering yourself in contract?"

Briggs shook his head vigorously. "No, this lad here. He's a strong one and well worth the price I'm asking."

Tom straightened as the eyes of the sailor turned to measure him. He held his breath until the man nodded. "He looks healthy enough, and we're short-handed in crew. Go aboard and aft. Someone will show you the captain's quarters."

The two of them made their way to the rear of the ship. The whole end of it was raised high, with two ladders reaching a deck placed atop. Between the ladders were two doors, a large one to the left and a smaller one. His father stopped a sailor. "Where do we find the captain's quarters?"

"Through there," the sailor said, nodding in the direction of the smaller door.

They opened the door and went down a set of short steps, through a narrow passageway with cupboards fastened with huge padlocks, and found another door. Tom waited as his father knocked.

"Enter," came a muffled voice from behind the door.

Briggs opened it and Tom followed him inside. The room was not deep, but it ran from one side to the other of the ship. Three large openings, filled with heavy glass, gave light into the room, and through them Tom could see wooden shutters spread wide. On the one side was a large bed built into the ship's side with drawers beneath it; on the other, a thick table, fastened to the floor, with a wooden chair behind it. Another heavy chair sat in front and both were roped loosely to the table to prevent them from moving far.

The captain was a slim, erect man, richly dressed in a frock coat and ruffled shirtwaist. He stood near the table, his hand on a roll of maps upon it, and frowned at them. "Who the devil are you?"

Tom's father bowed. "Lyman Briggs, sir. I beg your mercy for coming here, but I've a matter of business to discuss with you."

The captain's lip curled in distaste. "Who allowed you here?"

"The officer at the plank, sir. I hoped to offer you a contract of indenture." Briggs spoke rapidly, as if in fear he would be turned away before he could get the words out. "This lad is in good health. Strong enough from working in the fields, I promise you that. He'll bring a nice profit for you, I'll wager, in the Americas."

"You're not offering yourself?"

"No, sir. Only the boy. And at a fair price."

The captain turned to Tom. A pair of hard blue eyes bore into him. "Is he your son?"

"Yes, sir."

The cold eyes remained on Tom for a long while, making it difficult to meet them. "Are you willing to this contract?" he was asked at last.

Briggs started to object, but was stopped with a hand. "I asked the lad."

"Yes, sir. I'm willing to it." Tom spoke without looking at his father.

"If I buy your contract, you'll belong to me, boy. You'll be part of the crew on this ship until we reach our destination. Once there, I have the right to sell your contract as I see fit. Any refusal on your part to do as you're told will meet with stern punishment. Do you understand that?"

"Yes, sir. I'll give no trouble."

The captain nodded shortly. "Very well." He turned back to Tom's father. "I'll give you thirty crowns. My standard offer."

"Thirty crowns! But that's—"

"That is my offer. Don't waste my time."

Briggs hesitated, and Tom was afraid he was going to refuse. He almost sighed with relief when his father slowly nodded his head instead. "It's not a fair offer, but I've not time to look for better. Give me the money."

Minutes later, the two of them were back on deck, the captain having produced a paper for Briggs to sign. A sailor had been summoned and told to guide Tom to another officer to be put to work. He had only short moments to speak to his father.

"I'll not lie and say I'm sorry to part from you," he told him. "But for the years we lived together and the sake of my dead mother, I'll say goodbye."

Briggs finished stuffing the coins he held in his hand into a bag and then carefully tucked it into the waist of his trousers. When he looked up at Tom, there was neither regret nor anger in the look. It seemed more one of relief. "I'll give you one piece of advice, boy. It has stood me well in the hard life I've led. Remember your place in life and mind your betters. No matter what they be, you carry out the orders given you and you'll stay out of trouble for it."

Tom allowed the words to go past him. He was more than a little surprised at his own lack of feeling. "Remember your promise to Elizabeth," he said. "You were to wait at the quay until we sailed."

"I've no time for such promises."

Tom nodded, suspecting such would be the case. The money his father now had, money for the sale of his own children, was a fire in his gut, waiting to be spent on gin and more in the London alehouses. He didn't understand what it meant to Beth, but damned if he was going to let his father refuse her request, not if he could help it. He'd already thought of what to say about it.

"You'll do what you will," he told the man before him. "But I thought you might make *sure* the two of us are still aboard this ship when it leaves."

"What do you mean?" The look on his father's face told him his words had struck home.

Tom waited in silence.

"You try to jump this ship, boy, and you'll be asking for a hangman's noose." The old anger, so familiar to Tom, had returned. "I'll be having none of that, you hear me!"

"And you'll be losing your money with my hanging," Tom said quietly.

"Damn it, boy!" His father made as if to strike him and Tom braced for the blow.

The sailor beside Tom had grown impatient and suddenly stepped between them. "Come on, man," he said, grasping Tom's arm and shoving a hand into Briggs's chest, "I've orders to take you to Mr. Quinn. He finds we've delayed and the both of us will feel his knout on our backs. Get along now, the both of you."

Tom followed, but cast a last word over his shoulder. "Best you wait!" he called, and grinned to himself as he hurried away.

The ship was near to getting underway; it was obvious even to Elizabeth's inexperienced eyes. The boarding plank near her was still stretched across to the quay, but there was little traffic on it now. Men near either end of the ship were loosening the ropes that secured the vessel to the quay, dropping them into the water, while sailors on board were twisting thick wooden winches to wind the rope aboard. She watched as other sailors scurried aloft in the rope netting, climbing like spiders racing up their webs. In a moment, they dropped three cornered sails, small ones, down the two masts, and the ship immediately moved as the canvas filled.

"Cast away!" The cry from behind her somewhere sent her nerves to singing. She watched the two last ropes cast from the ship, and the gap between it and the quay begin to widen.

Suddenly she remembered her promise to herself and looked across the quay quickly. Her heart sank. Briggs was nowhere in sight! He hadn't heeded her words to wait!

"You looking for somebody, lass?" The voice at her elbow startled her and she spun quickly. The young redheaded sailor stood there, a twisted grin on his face.

"My father," she told him. "He was to be there. To say goodbye."

"Most of those seeing us off will be at the end. We're only moving now to clear it. We'll drift down that way on the tide before the captain steers us to the middle of the river."

She looked, and he was right.. A crowd of people were gathered at the very end of the quay. But she didn't see Briggs. "Which way will we go?" she asked.

He seemed happy she spoke to him. "We'll swing directly around it. The sea is that way."

"Thank you," she said, and his grin widened.

"My name is Hawksley," he said. "What might yours be?"

"Elizabeth. I'm on my way to the Americas."

"Aye. I knew that already. Being as that's where this ship is headed. It's a long hard voyage, but you'll be all right. I'll see to that myself. If you're a mind to let me."

"Thank you," she said again. "But my brother is here, too. At least I think he is; I haven't seen him. Could you find that out?"

"You're not together?" He moved closer to her.

"No. We're indentured. These children belong to the man who bought me."

His smile faded. "Captain Welslip is known to buy indentures and sell them in the colonies. Would that be for your brother?"

"I guess so."

"Then he'll be part of the crew, with little time for his pretty sister."

He glanced over his shoulder. "We're rounding the quay and I've work to be about. Look sharp if you want to see your father."

A moment later he was racing away, his bare feet flying over the wooden deck, and Elizabeth turned back to the rail.

The crowd of people on the quay was thick, watching the ship as it turned slowly around, and to her relief, Briggs stood slightly apart from the rest. He had been hidden from her sight by the others. The distance to the quay was only a dozen or so yards, but she waved to make sure of his attention.

He looked up, directly at her, but he made no attempt to answer her wave.

"Goodbye, Lyman Briggs," she cried, raising her voice and cupping her mouth with her hands to be sure he heard her. "My name is *Langlee!* Do you hear? *Langlee!* I know who I am!"

He staggered like a man suddenly struck. Even at the distance, she could see his face drain of all color.

Elizabeth cried again, the name singing in her own ears. *"Langlee!"*

He could only stare at her, his mouth moving loosely with no sound coming from it, and she returned his stare with pleasure. He had thought his secret safe. Thought he could rest in peace now. But instead, for the rest of his life, Lyman Briggs would have to live in the fear of the secret being told. Elizabeth gave him one last look and, with a smile, turned her back on him.

Four

THE SHIP, NAMED *The Grace,* had been out of sight of land for
only three days, but already Elizabeth had learned a great deal
about it, thanks to Michael Hawksley who seemed to find many
occasions to stop and talk to her.

Elizabeth was grateful for his company, more so for his
quick grin and teasing way of talking away her worries. She
was quick to note, however, that he kept a ready eye out for
any of the ship's officers, especially the third mate, a burly,
sour-faced man called Quinn. The third mate rarely spoke to
any of the passengers, except to order them out of some area
where they might interfere with the work of the crew, and he
habitually carried a thick piece of short rope with a knot in the
end. When she asked Hawksley about the rope, he reluctantly
told her the knot contained a piece of lead and the third mate
was skillful in the use of it. Calculating his blow, he could
leave a bruise on a sailor that would remain painful for days,
crack a rib or knock a man senseless. He was responsible for
the discipline of the crew, Michael said, and carried out his
duties without hesitation.

Further questioning revealed that Michael was forbidden to talk to her or any of the passengers other than in the line of his duty, and that he would suffer punishment if he were caught. It worried her greatly, but the redhead took it like he did everything else, with a grin and the belief it was all part of the great adventure of life.

In fact, he was full of life and he loved to talk. Michael had seen so much more of the world than she had, in spite of being only sixteen. Born to a debtor living in Newgate Prison, he had grown up among thieves, pickpockets and worse, who taught him the ancient art of survival at all costs. It was, he cheerfully admitted to her, the closeness of the King's law on his heels that had sent him to sign on for sea duty where the chronic shortage of seamen in England's vast fleet of merchantmen forbade close questioning of a man's past.

She scoffed at some of his tales of crime and he demonstrated his skill as a pickpocket by lifting the purse of her own master, Thermous Cawley, and presenting it to her. Horrified, and nearly out of her wits with fear, Elizabeth barely managed to sneak it into one of his trunks and then listened with wildly beating heart as he berated his innocent wife for having moved the purse without his permission.

Hawksley had withstood her scolding, promised dutifully never to do such again and she had forgiven him.

With or without his pranks, the redheaded sailor was a relief from her new life, a life already showing signs of being unpleasant. Elizabeth looked forward to the minutes he stole from his duties to be with her. In a short time, she discovered that if she found a place on deck concealed from the rest of the passengers and crew by cargo, Hawksley would soon find her.

The best place was forward, near the ship's bow, where the crew had little reason to go while at sea. There, two large crates were lashed to either side of a shorter one, leaving a niche between them where she could sit on the deck and both feel the sometimes misty spray on her face and watch the endless horizon. She was there when he popped suddenly from nowhere and crowded in beside her.

"Now what is a handsome lass like you doing hiding that beauty of yours where it can't be enjoyed?" he wanted to know, patting her drawn up leg just above the knee. "Tis a mortal sin, it is."

His words picked her up, as they always did, but she shook her head. "I'm not pretty at all," she said.

His face took on mock alarm. "Not pretty, she says! A royal beauty, fit to grace the Queen's Court, and she doesn't even know it! I tell you, it's enough to make a man's head spin."

Elizabeth looked down at his brown hand that had remained on her leg. It was a strong hand, a nice hand, in spite of the hard calluses upon it from the ship's ropes. She liked as well the muscular feel of his leg as it pressed against her own. He was like the sea itself, strong and wild.

She pulled her hair, blown free by the wind, from her face so that she could see him better. "You think I'm fooled by your words, Michael Hawksley, but I know better. You think just because I'm a country girl, I'll believe anything you say."

"Now, now," he said, patting her leg and then resting his hand there. "Haven't I told you nothing but the complete truth about myself? Did I hold anything back? I'm a man who believes in speaking the truth, and when I tell a lass she's pretty, then, by Neptune, it's the truth. And I say you're the prettiest of the lot."

She laughed. "A man who tells the truth," she said, mocking his manner. "You're not a man, Michael Hawksley, you're not much older than I am myself. And I think you'd fail to recognize the truth if it fell on your head."

He leaned closer, his shoulder squeezing her between him and the crate. "Tell me, Elizabeth Briggs, if I were to prove to you, beyond all doubt, that you are the prettiest lass on board *The Grace,* what would it be worth to me? Myself, I believe it would be worth a kiss, no less."

She pushed him back with her shoulder. "I'll have none of that. It's easy for you to prove such a thing since I'm the only girl on this ship. All the other women are older and married to their husbands besides."

"Pretty, and too smart for me. I'll have to settle for only looking at you like a calf that has lost its mama's tit."

Elizabeth laughed again. "What would a lad who's grown up in London town know of cows and their babes? You wouldn't recognize one if you saw it."

He removed his hand from her leg and slipped it around her shoulders, difficult to do in the cramped space. His other hand found the same spot on her leg. "Perhaps not," he said. "But it's the God's own truth that it's the way I feel at this moment, Elizabeth Briggs."

Her face burned quickly, and she became suddenly conscious of his hand on her leg. She removed it with her own and struggled forward to free herself of his arm as well. "I think it's only sailor talk, myself," she said. Her dress had raised as she wiggled forward, and she pulled it back down. "I'll believe none of it."

Michael sighed. "Then what will you believe?"

She turned to face him, holding her hair from blowing. "I'll believe you are my friend if you will do one thing for me," she said.

"And what will that be?"

"Two things." She corrected herself. "One, my name is not Briggs. I hate that name. My real name is Langlee. But you mustn't use it where anyone can hear you. Especially Mr. Cawley. And I can't tell you why. Except that he will think I'm trying to slip my contract and Briggs is the name on that. Will you call me that when we're alone?"

His grin was both puzzled and knowing at the same time. "I'll call you whatever you like. There are some names I could think of to call you that are much sweeter between a man and a lass."

Her face began to burn again, but not as much as before. "There's one other thing," she said.

"Ask away."

She looked at him solemnly. "I have a brother on board *The Grace*. Remember I told you about him? I know he's here since I've seen him twice. But I've not been able to speak to him for that man Quinn seems always near him and rushing him off."

Michael watched her closely. "Quinn is close upon him and one other indentured to Welslip because they're lubbers, they don't know the work of a sailor. But mind me, they will before this voyage is done. Quinn'll see to that."

"Can you talk to him? I mean, could you seek him out?"

His eyes narrowed and a slow, thin smile twisted his lips. "It'll mean running the risk of Quinn's anger, right enough. He won't take well to idle chat from the likes of me interrupting his teaching of a lubber. Disturbing their concentration on their work, so to speak."

Her face fell. "Then you can't do it."

He took her hand and pressed it on his leg. "I didn't say I couldn't do it. Nor that I wouldn't." He grinned. "I'll be risking my skin to Quinn's knot, though, and that ought to be worth something."

His words hurt, and she allowed it to show. She lowered her eyes. "I'm sorry. I thought we were friends. I haven't any money, anything of value to give you."

His hand touched her chin and gently lifted it until she was forced to look into his green eyes. The grin was well back in place again, and relief flooded her as she realized he had been teasing her. "Aye," he said. "I'll do anything for the pleasure of a smile from that pretty face. But for a kiss . . ." He leaned closer. "Now for that I'd throw the man Quinn overboard to feed the sharks."

"You were teasing me," she said. "For shame."

He shook his head. "I'll talk to this great lout of a brother of yours because you no more than asked me to do it. But then if you were a mind later to offer me but a touch of a kiss from those sweet lips in token of the great risk I ran, my joy would fill *The Grace*'s sails and run us to the Americas in a fortnight."

"A kiss from me is no great thing," she said, and her own forwardness caused her to drop her head to avoid his eyes. Though her voice was low, it surprised her to say such a thing, "Nor would I find that such a hard thing to do, I think."

Michael rose to his knees and leaned over, his face only inches from her own and his voice came from deep in his throat. "The bargain is made," he whispered. "Slip out here just as twilight is coming. I'll find a way to see your brother is here. I promise it."

Then he was quickly gone.

She went back to the Cawleys with high hope in her heart and withstood Mr. Cawley's sharp scolding for her long absence with half a mind. Michael would do as he promised, she had great faith in him. At dusk, she would see Tom again. When she did, she would be able to give him her great news at last. She hugged that feeling close.

Cawley's wife, Sarah, was ill again. She had been so almost from the hour *The Grace* slipped from the quay in London. Elizabeth had to bathe her face and clean up her retching. She did so now absently, her mind on Tom. The boys, Robert and Andrew, appeared equally pale from the constant rolling motion of the ship, and their excitement of the first days had subsided.

But they were yet to become really sick, and for that Elizabeth was grateful.

The area the five of them shared below deck put her in mind of cattle pens she had seen in the village back home. It consisted of bare plank walls on two sides, hard against the sloping side of the ship, with nothing to offer privacy across the front from the other passengers. Two wooden bunks on either side took up most of the cramped space, with little room to walk between. Cawley and his wife shared one of the straw beds, while Elizabeth slept with the boys. Their trunks were stored beneath the bunks.

Between the closeness of the space and the smell from the seasickness, Elizabeth preferred to seek the freshness of the open deck as much as possible. Her absence angered her new master, and twice already he had taken her by the shoulders and shook them as he berated her. But his shaking wasn't violent enough to harm her, and she discovered that if she returned his angry look eye to eye with a steady one of her own, it was he that turned away. That part she could stand, it was nothing compared to what Briggs could do when he lost his temper. Far harder for her was to be forced to sit and listen as Cawley regaled all four of them, bible in hand, of their duty as English Christians. He seemed to think that he alone knew the will of their Maker and that God had granted him leave to speak it.

The ship's owners provided no more than passage to those it carried to the new lands; each family was responsible for feeding themselves. That too was part of her job and she used a small pot of burning coal to prepare their single hot meal of the day. That was the time she hated most in the long, low room. Smoke from several fires found its way to the ceiling and eventually out a hatch at one end, making the dark place even darker and making breathing difficult.

Somehow, Cawley seemed to prefer the closeness of the cabin and rarely went on deck, sitting instead on the bed beside his wife and either reading in his bible or writing in his ledger. That, as much as the smell and smoke, made it hard for Elizabeth to remain in the hold. It seemed that anytime she was there, he found reason to climb to his feet and she was forced to brush against his thick body to get between the bunks. The feel of his fat stomach against her and the closeness of his sweat repelled her and increased her desire to go on deck again and allow the wind to cleanse her.

She waited impatiently for this day to pass. Finally it was not yet twilight, but close, and she could stand the wait no longer. She got up from the bed, swung her head to dodge the candle holder hanging from the ceiling and stepped out.

Cawley looked up immediately. "Where're you going, girl?" he demanded, laying his bible aside. "You are constantly running off. Can't you see Mistress Cawley requires your attention?"

Dread stiffened her limbs. She couldn't miss this chance! There might not be another! "I'm afraid I'm going to be sick myself," she said. "My stomach is taking on so. I thought I'd go up and use the side of the ship."

She paused, held her hands to her mouth and noted with satisfaction that he looked at her in alarm. "I'm afraid it would add to her discomfort if I were sick here, too." She glanced toward the woman groaning in the bed.

"Then go," he said, following her look toward the bed. "But be not long about it. You're shirking your duties."

She turned and almost ran toward the steps, leaving him to mutter behind her.

The light was definitely growing dimmer as she emerged from the passenger cabin and brushed past a man in a greatcoat attempting to enter. He turned to look at her appraisingly, but she had become accustomed to that. A number of the men in the cabin and most of the sailors stopped to look at her as she went about the ship and she could only decide it was the simple, thin dress she wore and the frayed short cape she sometimes pulled about her shoulders. They must wonder what a lass so poorly dressed, one without even stockings, could be doing going to the Americas.

She made her way forward to her shelter between the crates and sat down gratefully, doing her best at the same time to quiet her wildly beating heart. Thomas would soon be here! She wanted so badly to see him again, but it was such a risk. Quinn's heavy face loomed before her and made her shiver with more than the night's chill. "Please don't let Thomas be caught," she whispered.

The bow of the ship rose and fell before her, and she looked beyond it to the sea caps, white and foaming. The sea was not frightening as she had thought it might be before she boarded *The Grace*. It was like the sky, neither friendly nor threatening unless one allowed it to be.

He startled her, appearing suddenly with a glance over his shoulder. "Beth?"

"Thomas!" She struggled forward, tangling herself in her own legs and falling forward into his arms.

He caught her roughly, pulled her to his chest and squeezed her breathless. Her pent-up feelings flooded forth in a torrent of tears as she cried, "Thomas!"

"Here now." His voice was rough and gentle at the same time. "Where's the courage my sister promised me?"

Elizabeth continued to cry, like the many times she had when she was little, and her brother of the same age, but bigger and stronger, had comforted her with his child's arms. Now he owned a man's strong arms and held her easily. He gathered her, lifted her even though he was on his knees and swung her around to his lap as he sat down on the deck between the crates.

She held his face between her hands and kissed him between her tears. "I've missed you so!"

"And I've missed you," he said. "But I've little time now, Beth. They'll be looking for me shortly, you can be sure of it. Stop your crying and tell me how it goes with you."

With an effort she held back the tears and pulled herself from his lap, not wanting to appear a babe. But she wiggled around at the same time so that she could be close to his body and pulled his arm around her.

"I've fared well enough," she told him. "I've no complaint. But I wanted to see you, to talk to you, and I couldn't."

Tom nodded. "I know. It couldn't be helped. I'm part of the crew now and they expect me to work most of the day. I've no time for visiting."

"Yes, I know," she said quickly. "Michael told me. But I'm so glad he got you for me."

He lowered his head and frowned. "I wondered what he was about. It was the first time he spoke to me when he told me to come here. Beth, I don't trust him; you be careful around him."

"Oh, Michael's my friend," she said. "He's very nice to me. And he did get you to me when I asked him."

He shook his head and squeezed her hand hard. "Beth, listen

to me. Hawksley may not be much older than we are, but he's a man's way of looking at a lass. He'll want more than friendship from you, believe me when I say it. Watch him!"

She shook her head. "Michael wouldn't do anything to harm me. But we've no time to talk of him. You've got to get back before that Mr. Quinn knows you're gone, and there's something I've got to tell you first. A wonderful thing!"

He nodded reluctantly. "Then tell me, but promise you'll—"

She cut him off with a hand on his lips. "Shh. Stop worrying and listen to me. You remember once I asked you what you'd do if you found out Lyman Briggs was not father to you and me?"

Tom nodded again and this time his brow creased. "I thought you a bit daft then, or crazy with worry."

"Well I wasn't, nor am I now," she said in triumph. "It's the God's own truth. He isn't your father!"

His face was worried. "Perhaps you'd better tell me what you think, Beth," he said slowly. "What this notion—"

"Tom, it's not what I think, but what I know! I heard it from our own mother—only she wasn't our mother. She told me on her death bed. I swear!"

"Tell me," he said again.

Elizabeth gripped his hand. "It was the day she died, Tom. That day you came in from the field and I told you and him she had died right after noon?"

"I remember," he said.

"Well, she didn't! Die near noon, I mean. She died only a little before you returned. And she talked to me through most of the afternoon. Tom, she was dying, and she wanted me to know the truth before she died."

He cocked his head, his eyes hard on hers. "Then it's the truth. Those who are dying don't lie. What did she say?"

Wild elation ran through her. He believed her! Now he would know the truth and be free of Briggs forever.

"Tom," she said, "she told me we were brought to them, Lyman Briggs and herself, as babes. Remember the tale you told me you heard in the village? The one about the grand lady in the manor who died of a strange illness? You said it was whispered that it wasn't an illness that killed her, that she really died for the love of a Frenchman."

He nodded again.

She was breathless with excitement. "It wasn't an illness, Tom! That lady did die in love for him. And she gave him babes...Us! The two of us! Tom, *she* was our true mother!"

"God forbid!" he cried.

"Oh, Tom! It's true! Our mother—only she wasn't our mother—told me from her own dying lips. She said we were the bastards of that lady and were brought to Briggs in the belief we would die too as babes. Only we didn't. And that's why he hated us so. He was afraid the secret would get out and he would suffer for it."

"I can't believe it!" Tom whispered hoarsely. "You and me...of noble blood?"

Elizabeth held his hands in her own, squeezing them tightly. "We are, Tom. We're of noble blood. Our name is Langlee, not Briggs. We're no kin to him. No kin at all!"

"But why?" He shook his head with the wonder of it. "Why would we have been brought to our father's—to his hut?"

"She told me," she said. "She heard it from Briggs's own drunken mouth, only he didn't remember the telling of it else he would have killed all of us. The lady's brother hated the French; had he known his sister had given birth to a Frenchman's bastards, he would have had us killed and locked her in a room forever. Someone, she didn't know who it was and neither did Briggs, took us away no more than a day or so after we were born and placed us with Briggs. They thought we would die since we were so little, and then the secret would end. But we didn't. And Briggs has been afraid all our lives that someone would find out the truth. That's why when his own wife died, he was in such a hurry to be rid of us. That's why we were indentured to the Americas."

Tom leaned back and allowed his head to rest against the crate behind him. "It's too much to take in," he said. "You and I of noble birth."

Elizabeth watched her brother grow older before her eyes. His chin lifted and his jaw grew firmer. "I believe it," he said. "I want to believe it. It does me greatly to know I'm no kin to the likes of him who raised us. I wanted to hate him many a time, but I wouldn't because I thought him our father."

He looked at her, his eyes bright. "Until this day, Elizabeth, I thought of myself as beholding to others. To those who were my betters. But no more. If I'm of noble blood, bastard or not, then I'm as good as any man. And I can do or be as I will. There's dreams I've had . . ."

He jerked his hands free from hers and grasped her shoulders roughly. "Beth, we belong to others now, there's no help for that. Tis the law. But it won't always be so. And when we're free . . ." He shook his head, unable to continue.

"I know," she whispered.

The two of them sat for long moments, looking at each other with love and an unwillingness to break the spell until a shout from behind the crates roused them.

"I've got to go," he said. "But there'll be little sleep for me these next nights, I'll tell you that. Not that there's been much between my working anyway. I'll give this a lot of thought, but already I know I'm different."

"Go," she said urgently. "I don't want to see you in trouble. Take care, Tom. I love you!"

He nodded, and his eyes were wet. "I love you, Beth. Someday I'll be able to take care of you."

Halfway out of the space, he stopped and reached back to cup her chin in his hand. "Mind you, watch out for the men. Especially that Hawksley. You're no longer a girl but a woman, and men will have evil thoughts about you."

He was gone before she could reply, and Elizabeth hugged herself closely, his words in leaving slipping from her mind with the wonderful knowledge that he now knew as she did that they were free to be whatever they would be.

The quarters for the crew of *The Grace* were located in the bow of the ship in a space too low and small to accommodate anything but the miserable sailors themselves. Ship's owners were jealous of cargo space and belowdecks was designed to carry all that it could of profit. The men who manned the vessel had to make for themselves. The part in which they slung their canvas for sleeping, or crowded about its single wooden table for their one meal a day, when they could get it, was three-quarters a normal man's height. The deck under it had been raised for cargo.

Tom stepped across the opening leading into the space and paused to squint in the light from the single lantern. In the short time he'd been a member of the crew, he'd found that, as a lubber, he was afforded the least space close to the bow. It was barely enough to hang his canvas and sleep with his knees drawn up. But it was not to that area that he looked in the dim glow of a single lantern; he looked instead for Hawksley and found him squatting with his back against the bulkhead.

"You find your sister?" The Hawk wanted to know.

"Yes. And it's about her that we need to talk."

"You've no need to thank me," the redhead grinned. "It was for the lass herself that I lied to Quinn about the bilge leak and set his mind from yourself. She wanted to see you, and I made the way for it."

"I thank you for that," Tom said.

Hawksley laughed. "If you're not as dumb as the cattle we've got caught in the hold for shipment, you'll learn there are ways to get around the mates before this voyage is done, Country Boy. You'll learn it or they'll break your peasant's back for you."

"I'll learn my work and do my share," Tom said. "I'll not avoid that. But it's another matter I would have words with you about."

"And what is that?"

He was almost a head taller than the sailor, and he was conscious that his arms were thicker, stronger; his shoulders wider. But he was also aware that his skill at fighting would be less than this lad's, from lack of experience. Still, he would make up for that with purpose.

He lowered his voice for the other's ears alone. "My sister is not wise in the ways of the world," Tom said. "She's most easily fooled because she has too trusting a nature. You'll not take advantage of that fact, or you'll answer to me."

The redhead's grin became a sneer. "I'll answer to you? You who's so clumsy he trips over his own feet in the rigging? Listen, you mud-wallowing peasant, if I become a mind to, I can split your head like a ripe melon. Or spill your guts over the deck before you know your belly's open from my knife. *You'll* be telling me what I can and can't do?"

Tom nodded slowly. "You'll be having your chance to do either of those things if you harm my sister. But you'll not find it as easy to do as you say."

A hard palm suddenly reached for his shirt, grasped a handful and shoved him back. "Lay your country nose to my rosy arse, you mucker!" Hawksley growled. "I've a mind to split your chest right now!"

Tom closed his own hand over Hawksley's fist, squeezed hard and slowly bent the arm back. He applied more pressure and watched as the redhead's eyes widened.

A moment later, he released the hand and rose to a crouch. "Remember my words," Tom said and stepped over the other boy to find his sleeping place.

Behind him, an older man laughed loudly, one who had been lying in a canvas above them. "So the piece you've been chasing has a brother, eh, Hawk? That might be worth your head from more than Quinn if you're caught with her."

"Go roast in hell!" the redhead told him as he got up and went outside.

On the deck, Hawksley instinctively looked about to avoid any of the ship's officers, and seeing he was safe, made his way to the rail. The night's sea breeze did little to cool his anger. He'd done that peasant lout a favor by risking Quinn's anger, and this was the thanks he got. Damn him! He should find a chance to fetch a belaying pin to that stupid lubber's head. Where did he get off, telling Michael Hawksley what he could do!

It was his own fault for getting weak over her. He should have left things as they were and told her there was no chance of getting her brother to see her. That would have been the better of it. But no, he had to play the hero and prove to her what he could do if he wanted; make her the more grateful to him. A damned stupid thing, too, since it could make that farmer set her mind against him.

He swore into the breeze. By Satan's eyes, her brother was right though, she *was* the perfect innocent. And that did as much to set his heart pounding as those sweet limbs of hers set his body on fire.

It was the truth, he'd admit, that he'd first been caught only by his fancy for a pretty lass, and offered his scheming to find a way to lay her on a long and boring passage. No more than for the pleasure of it and the fun of doing the thing under the long nose of Quinn. But this one was so damnable unknowing! She'd look at him with those great brown eyes of hers and actually *trust* him. That had taken away the game.

And then she'd given him a strange new feeling, before he

knew what he was about. He found he didn't want to trick her into the loss of her innocence. Damn it, he'd actually been ashamed of the stiffness between his legs as she sat with her body close against his. So close the warmness of her made him shiver.

What in blazes had happened to him? She was no more than a dumb peasant wench who was servant to that fat bastard who'd bought her. That bloody fool would probably take her to bed soon enough when they reached the Americas, and she'd most likely be willing too! That was the way of all women; they used their charms to make their life easier, just as a man had to use his wits. Why the hell was he, Michael Hawksley, feeling so damn noble toward her? She was no more than a woman he'd see on this voyage and never again!

The thought of her in the fat man's bed agitated him to the extent he danced on his feet and shook a fist to the night sky. No, by Damn! Not her! Not Elizabeth!

It was an hour before he could calm himself down. He knew he'd be up long before the dawn's breaking and would have to work his arse off to stay ahead of Quinn's knout, but still he couldn't drive himself to his bed. He sat instead in the space he'd shared with her and hugged his arms around his shoulders against the chill of the sea and his own wild thoughts. Thoughts that saw him jumping the ship with Elizabeth when they reached the Americas and finding a place where the two of them could live, far from the eyes of any other . . .

The object of Hawksley's thoughts also found it difficult to sleep. She lay on her back, crowded in the bunk by her two young charges, but hardly conscious of the press of the boards against her ribs. Thomas was somewhere on this ship and now knew of the great change in their lives. It had been a deed well done to tell him. She hugged the knowledge to herself, raising her two hands to her cheeks and pressing hard with the pleasure of it.

She wondered if she should tell the whole secret to her friend, Michael. Should she share her truth?

No, perhaps not. He might look at her differently if she did, might even be no longer willing to offer her his friendship. And she needed that friendship. The voyage was still to be so long, and he was such a comfort. She'd never had a friend except for her brother, and Michael was so good just to talk to. No, she'd not run the risk of losing him.

She smiled in the dark and felt her face warm. She'd promised him a kiss for bringing Tom to her. A brazen promise. Would he expect her to keep it?

If he did, she hoped he'd not be disappointed. She'd never kissed anyone but her brother before, never even thought of it. Goodness, she didn't even know *how* to kiss a man!

Five

THE SEA, ALTHOUGH high in swells and already cursed heartily
by the passengers used to a firmness underfoot rather than a
wooden deck that constantly rolled, had been Elizabeth's friend
until now. But suddenly the sea turned on her in savage fury.
Oh, it had given warning enough. In the two days following
her meeting with Tom, she'd noted the gathering clouds, but
she had thought only of possible rain that might keep her from
the deck. She hadn't thought of what a storm at sea might
mean. When it struck, heavy rain squalls racing across the
water to slash at the vessel much as a boarhound might bait
his quarry only to dart away again, she'd ducked below to
reappear as soon as they passed.

But that was merely the opening; the sea had much more
in store for *The Grace*. The squalls gave way to a sky turned
black as night, broken only by the flash of lightning, and the
sea seemed to rise to meet it. What had been waves that rolled
the ship became mountains of water which the now fragile
vessel climbed laboriously only to fall off in fright on the other
side. Waves almost as high as the masts pounded across the

deck. *The Grace* groaned under the impact of each, shook herself free and scurried away like a frightened pup, only to be thundered by another rising wall of water.

Hatches were closed tightly by the crew and cooking fires, if anyone were left with even the slightest interest in food, were forbidden. Within an hour after the full storm struck, all the passengers had taken to their bunks in retching misery. They held on with fear-stricken arms to keep from being pitched to the floor and gave no thought to where their sickness spewed.

The storm wouldn't last forever, Elizabeth told herself over and over, and surely this ship had been through such storms before. The captain and crew must know what they were about and how best to keep the ship afloat.

The room around her was filled with groans from the men and gagging screams from terror-filled women and children. Elizabeth closed her ears to the sounds and prayed. But the cries grew until fear became a live thing in her own breast. She could no longer keep away the doubt that *The Grace* might not withstand the onslaught and would be forced in the end to give up the fight and seek its eternal peace beneath the pounding waves.

Death was a thing of which she'd never given thought, but she was faced with it now, and it was a terrible thing to consider. Never to look upon a blue sky again, never to grow to be a full woman and know the joy of being wife to a man, nor feel the softness of her own babe in her arms . . . She discovered she had screamed out her own fear.

She would never see Thomas again. Thomas! He was part of the crew! He wouldn't be lying in a pitching bunk, in a stinking cabin below the deck, not him. He would be topside, struggling to keep the ship righted.

Oh, God in Heaven! He wasn't a sailor. What would he know of how to survive in such a storm!

She whimpered, forgetting her own fear and half-rising from the bed in a useless attempt to see in the darkness. Even now, at this moment, Thomas could be swept away by the sea, his cries unheard in the howling of the wind. "Oh please, God! Don't take him. Don't take him without taking me as well!"

She fell back on the sheets, twisting her head from side to side with the agony of her thoughts until at last exhaustion overcame her and she slept.

* * *

The storm lasted two full days. Although the ship rose and fell to a degree that was twice that prior to the storm, Elizabeth knew it was over from the lack of the sound of water rushing over the deck above her.

The stench in the room was unbearable. Although her limbs rebeled with the effort, she forced them to work and drag her to the ladder and fresh air. She had hardly made it when the hatch was thrust aside and a man entered: one of the ship's officers.

He stared at her, his face obscured by the light behind him, a light that made her own poor eyes blink from its brightness. Elizabeth could hardly blame him, she knew she must look much as a swine that had been wallowing in its pen. Her hair was tangled about her face, one or both of the Cawley boys had soiled her dress and it was twisted about her body from her own thrashing in the bunk. She wanted to hide her head.

"Are you injured?" he wanted to know in a voice that carried neither interest nor pity, only duty.

"No," she said. "I need to get some air."

He sniffed. "I should think so. This place smells as a sty. Is anyone injured?"

Elizabeth turned. The silence behind her was startling; she'd not noticed until now. "I don't think so—I mean, I don't know. I hadn't thought to look." She shook her head. "I don't think I can look just now. I've got to have some air. Will you see?"

He sniffed again. "Nay, woman. I'll not set foot in the place. But I'll send men with buckets of sea water and some of you can wash down the whole of it. If any have broken bones, the ship's carpenter is skilled at resetting them. You may tell the rest that."

It was not a clear blue sky outside; heavy clouds still crowded about as far as she could see and some of them were black in the center. But it was a beautiful sight after the closeness of the cabin, and she was grateful for it. She leaned back her head and breathed deeply of the salt-laden air.

"Whist!"

The hissing cry brought her head down and made her look. It took a full minute to find its source. Michael stood near the rail, partly hidden from her by the ladder leading to the steersman's deck, his red head darting first to her and then swiftly around again. When he saw she was looking his way, he jerked his head for her to come.

Elizabeth was torn between a desire to go to him and to dart back into the darkness behind her. She looked such a fright!

The first won out, urged by his bobbing head. She walked quickly toward him and was stopped only by his frantic motion. "Stand by the rail," he whispered hoarsely. "It'll not do for me to be seen talking to you. Stand with your back this way."

She did as she was told, grateful that she didn't have to face him.

"Are you all right?" he wanted to know. "I was afeared for you, lass."

She nodded, realized it was not enough and spoke, her own voice low enough to match his. "I'm well enough, Michael. But terribly weak. And I was afraid for you, too. Was it powerful bad for you during the storm?"

Michael chuckled. "Bad enough, I'll tell you. Time or two there I gave us up to the deep. But Welslip knows what he's about, right enough. He's steered a storm before, our captain."

"I'm glad you're all right," she said, and then had to force her words. "Tom . . . my brother . . . is he alive?"

"Aye, he is that. Though wishing he were somewhere else even if it be hell itself, I'll wager. He's learned what it's like to be a sailor, Quinn saw to that. Tis no easy thing to be swinging in the ropes with the wind tearing at you from the top and that bastard threatening you from below."

Pain washed over her for the moment, but it was a pleasing pain. Thomas was alive. That was all that mattered.

"Are you sure you're all right?" Michael asked again. "You look like you're hurt."

She risked a glance at him, a grateful one. "I'm all right, but I know I look a mess. I wish you wouldn't look at me."

His voice was low and throaty. "You look the world to me, lass. If I thought you injured, I'd not be able to stand it."

Elizabeth wanted to reach out to him with her arms and had to force herself to grip the rail. "I want to talk to you," she said instead. "Can we find a place?"

"Later, lass. And I'll not be able to stand the wait. We'll make it soon, if the wind doesn't start afresh. But now I've got to go. If I'm caught, it won't stand well for either of us."

"Michael, I—" But he brushed by her quickly, his hand sliding across her waist, and was gone.

* * *

The sailors brought buckets of sea water for those passengers able to stir enough to clean themselves. Only a few did, the rest lying still abed and moaning. The room remained fetid, although leaving the door open at one end and a large hatch open at the other to allow the sea breeze to flow through helped. Even without the feeble orders from a miserable Cawley, Elizabeth would have worked throughout the day.

She removed the top clothes from the children and her mistress and dropped them in a bucket to soak, along with her own dress. With no other to put on, she was forced to wear a blanket wrapped about her, secured with a piece of rope.

With the other bucket and a piece of cloth, she cleaned the beds and the floor between, then washed the clothes and hung them to dry. Cooking a meal would be a waste, no one would be able to eat, not even herself. Except for Cawley—the fat man surprised her by recovering rapidly. By late afternoon, he was up and ordering her to brush his coat and clean his shoes.

She was busy with the last, sitting crosslegged on the floor and conscious of his eyes upon her when three men crowded the opening of the crib.

"Thermous Cawley," one of them said, "we would have a word with you."

Cawley looked up in surprise. "How do you know my name? I know none of you."

The man who spoke was lean and tall, with a sharp face in which a drooping nose and pointed chin seemed determined to meet.

"We know who you are, Mister Cawley, because the ship's list of passengers has been made known to me." The lean man assumed a pose of importance. "My name is Thomas Potts. I've been chosen by the Trustees to deliver the papers for those on this passage to the commissioners in the colony."

Cawley nodded, his face now registering suspicion. "That's naught to me. I'm a man who's paying his own way. The Trustees have no call on me."

"Aye," was the quick reply, "we're aware of that. So's the truth for Mr. Bottle here." Potts indicated one of the others, a thickset man with a face scarred from pox. "But the two of you and four others of like passage are aboard the same ship with the rest of us. We think you should have a say in the decisions."

"What decisions?" Cawley said. "I've no decisions to make

before we reach land. And then it will be none of your business what I do."

"If we reach the land," the third man cut in. He was short and ugly. Elizabeth thought his great head much too large for the rest of him. She stared at him in curiosity, quite forgetting to clean the shoes.

His statement, however, had angered her master. She saw Cawley's face turn crimson. "What do you mean, man?" he demanded. "We're bound for the Georgia colony in the Americas. What else is there about it?"

The lean man held up a placating hand. "Tis of that we would talk, Mr. Cawley. But not where the womenfolk can hear and become frightened. Come with us."

Cawley stared at him. "Frightened of what? The storm is over and done."

"Aye, and that's what I told them myself," Bottle said quickly. "But they're bound to do this talk. Sailor's tales, if you ask me. And should be ignored."

"What talk?" Cawley demanded. "What's this?"

"Will you come on deck?" Potts asked.

Cawley turned to look at his wife, nearly covered completely with the blankets, no more than her nose showing. "My wife is ill," he said. "I'll not leave her. She's sleeping and will hear nothing at any rate. Speak here if you will, but be quick about it."

Potts nodded at Elizabeth. "There's the girl."

"She's a servant. Indentured to me. She's of no matter."

Potts looked again at the short man and the latter nodded reluctantly.

"Who might you be?" Cawley interrupted during the exchange. "What did you mean, *if* we reach land?"

The short man was slow to answer and Potts beat him to it. "His name is Watson, and like myself, he's brought his family under agreement to the Trustees."

"Charity, you mean," Cawley said with contempt.

Potts reddened. "It's an honest agreement we've made. And no disgrace. We'll earn our rights by the honest sweat of our brow. But that's not the matter we're here to discuss."

"Then state your matter," Cawley told him shortly.

Elizabeth could well see that the both of them were growing angry. And so could Bottle. She was grateful to him for taking a turn in the conversation. "Tis not a matter of the colony, Mr.

Cawley, that worries them," he said in a soothing voice. "They're of the belief this ship might sink under us. They want to turn back."

"Turn back!" Her master's face expressed his shock. "Are you daft, man? We're four weeks out of London!"

"Aye," Watson said sourly. "And twice that to the Americas. Our only chance of saving ourselves is to turn back."

Watching Cawley's face, Elizabeth could see fear creep into his eyes, much the same as when he'd faced Briggs in the tavern. But his voice remained the same. Contemptuous. *"The Grace* has a sound bottom," he said. "I've Captain Welslip's word on that."

"That's not what the sailors say," Watson told him in triumph. "I've spoken to them myself."

"Sailor's talk!" Cawley spat the words out. "Idle chat from stupid seamen. I'll see that Captain Welslip knows of this. He'll have the man who told you put in irons."

"It's not only one man," Watson countered. "I spoke to more. They say the ship is taking water because the storm loosened its timbers. If we don't turn back, we'll never see land again."

"I don't believe this rot," Cawley told him. "If you do, then you're more the fool for it. Take your nonsense to Captain Welslip. He'll set you straight quick enough."

"That is our intention," Potts said. "But we intend to tell him for all of us so he'll have no choice but to turn back. That's why we're speaking to you. So that you'll join us."

Cawley stood up, and Elizabeth could see the fear was gone from his face. "I will do no such thing," he told them. "Captain Welslip is in command of this vessel and will make all the decisions necessary. And so it should be. If you go to him with your demands, you may well find yourself in irons, mark my words. Now I insist you leave me in peace."

"I believe you're right, Mr. Cawley," Bottle put in quickly. "I've done my best to talk them away from this notion, but they insist. That's why I got them to come to you first, I thought you'd be a man to set them straight."

"He's set no one straight!" Potts said with heat. "We'll see the captain with or without him!"

"Then be prepared for the consequences," Cawley told him grimly. "Captain Welslip will brook no interference from the likes of you."

The fat man stared at their retreating backs, then sat back down on the bed. "Damnable fools!" he muttered. "Turn back indeed!"

He looked at Elizabeth. "Mind your tongue, girl. I'll not have you speaking of anything you've heard."

"Yes, sir," she said. Then, because he continued to stare at her, she decided to risk a question that had been on her mind. She wasn't worried about the ship sinking, no matter what those men had said. If God had allowed them to come through that terrible storm, then He fully intended them to go to the Americas. And it was of that place she was curious.

"I'll not speak a word," she assured him. "But I would ask about where we're going. If you're a mind to tell me."

He was taken aback, and Elizabeth realized it was the first time she'd done more than reply to him. But he seemed pleased that she'd spoken.

"Why, we're going to the Americas, girl," he said. "Didn't you know that?"

"Yes, sir. But it seems such a large place from what I've heard. A moment ago, you mentioned something about the Georgia colony. What is that?"

"You know very little of anything, do you, girl?" His voice didn't match the harshness of the question, however, and she was encouraged.

"No, sir," she said truthfully. "I'm afraid I've little experience in any but the place I grew up."

"That's the way our Lord and Master intends servants to be," Cawley told her pompously. "Too much knowledge clutters their heads and distracts them from serving their betters. But I see little harm in telling you of your new home to be."

He nodded in agreement with himself and Elizabeth leaned forward eagerly to listen.

"The Americas are a huge land," he told her, "stretching hundreds of thousands of miles and split by giant rivers. Most of the land is made of great forests, inhabited by savage cannibals and strange animals, some a hundred-foot tall and most fearsome."

Elizabeth shuttered. "It sounds a horrible place!"

He chuckled. The very first time she'd seen him laugh. "That's the interior of the land, girl. On the sea coasts, there are civilized towns such as in our own England. You'll not be seeing anything such as I've described."

"But don't the cannibals attempt to come into the towns?" she wanted to know.

"Only those who have been saved to our Lord by missionaries," he said. "The ones who have given up their pagan ways. Soldiers keep the rest at bay. You'll be safe enough."

"Is this Georgia one of the towns?" she asked.

He shook his head slowly from side to side. "Such ignorance. No, girl. Listen to me carefully and see if you can understand. There are certain areas in the Americas that are called colonies. Set up for the most part by the Crown. Each of these areas includes several towns and villages. There are thirteen of them to be exact, and Georgia is the thirteenth and newest. Therefore, there is still land aplenty in it to be distributed among those wise enough to go there. Land in which fortunes can be made in rice and other such crops. Myself, I intend to go into the silk trade. In a few short years, I'll be rich beyond my wildest dreams."

He was suddenly talking more to himself than to her, and Elizabeth was wise enough to remain silent, though a dozen questions plagued her.

"Rich, black earth," he went on, his voice taking on a dreaming quality. "I've read the books describing it. Many of them. I tell you, a fortune is to be made in such a place."

He was silent a long time, no longer looking at her. Finally, when she could hardly sit still, he began talking again, "Benjamin Martyn's book, that's the one with the truth to it. Trade with the mother country. When we reach the Georgia colony, I'll be granted a lot in Savannah for my house and a garden. But most of all, I'll be given a number of acres shortly outside that town. Acres on which I'll plant thousands of mulberry trees to feed my silkworms."

"Worms?" she said, not being able to stop herself. "You'll be raising earthworms?"

Cawley's attention returned to her reluctantly. "Silkworms, girl! The tiny creatures who spin the finest of silk. Where did you think that grand material came from?"

"I confess I didn't know," Elizabeth said in apology. "I've never seen any up close."

She was sorry she'd spoken. His attention was full upon her of a sudden, and there was a different light in his eyes. But she decided to risk another question anyway. "Who are the Trustees that Mr. Potts spoke to you about?" she asked.

He seemed to shake away another thought in order to answer her. "They're men who secured a grant from the King to establish the colony," he said. "They're chartered to administer Georgia."

She wished he would turn his gaze away from her. "And Mr. Potts and the others are beholden to these men?"

"Yes. The Trustees choose people who are in debt, or who have no work in their trade, and send them to the colony. They pay passage for them and will give them land when they arrive, although for their kind it will amount to no more than fifty acres to the man."

Again he seemed to drift and had to force his words back to her. "The Trustees will also provide them with food and clothing, tools and other things from their stores until such people are able to do for themselves. Then they must pay it back."

"I see," she said. "But you're not one of those people?" She hoped her question would draw him back to himself.

It didn't work. He continued to stare at her with an odd look in his eye. "No," he said slowly. "I was a peruke maker in London, with a good business. I come at my own expense and will be beholden to no one. I merely believe the raising of silk for gentlemen's and ladies' clothing will pay me far more than the making of their wigs. That's why I've chosen to come."

He leaned over to peer directly down at her. "Do you know what indenture means, girl?" he asked suddenly. "Do you understand its complete meaning?"

His eyes were bright. They worried her. "Yes, sir," she said slowly. "It means I'm to be servant to you and Mistress Cawley for a time. I don't know how long."

"Four years," he said, extending a hand to grasp her shoulder and pull her toward him. "You're to do my bidding for four years before you're released. All of my bidding, no matter what it means. Do you understand?"

She was now a little frightened. His look was so strange, and his hand on her shoulder hurt. "I'll do whatever work you choose to give me without complaint," she said. "And do it the best I can."

Suddenly she realized he wasn't looking at her face, but beneath it. She followed his gaze downward and discovered to her horror that the blanket had loosened and most of her breasts were showing. Shame rushed to her face as she covered them quickly.

Cawley shoved her back harshly. "Cover your nakedness, girl!" he hissed. "The fact that you are ignorant is no excuse for lewdness!"

"I'm sorry!" She wanted to hide from his eyes. "I didn't mean to—"

"Hush!" His voice was strangled with rage. "Get yourself from me, girl! At once! Go and pray to God to forgive you your wickedness. I'm not a man to be tempted. You'll not make your service the easier for all your sly ways!"

"But I didn't—"

"Go!"

She scrambled to her feet, snatched her dress from the rope and fled. What a terrible, shameful feeling!

Elizabeth found another place to dress, then hurried out again. Her dress was damp but she would have worn it were it sopping wet. Even an hour later, after standing on the deck to allow her dress to be dried by the wind, she still felt hot with shame.

She walked about restlessly, wanting to go to her hiding place in the bow, but there were two sailors working close by there and she was afraid they'd chase her away. And, too, she had to move about constantly because it seemed that more and more of the men passengers were coming on deck and gathering in close discussion.

She knew they were talking of the danger of sinking, of whether the ship was leaking or not. She didn't believe it was. Mr. Cawley had been right about one thing: the captain of this ship would decide on their course and nothing the passengers could do or say would change that.

She looked for Tom, hoping for a chance to at least see him even if she couldn't talk to him, but he wasn't in sight.

The hour was growing late and the sky, already heavily clouded when she came on deck, seemed more so. Still, it would be some time before she would have to return to Cawley.

She moved through the standing passengers toward the bow and discovered the sailors had gone. At last! With several glances behind her to be certain she wasn't noticed, she moved around the crates to slip gratefully into her niche where she could lean back against the sheltering wood and be alone once more.

Her solitude lasted only a short time. Michael appeared from out of nowhere, cast one quick glance behind him and dropped beside her.

"Well, lass," he grinned, "I thought you'd never come here. I've watched you wander about this deck for an hour. Twas all I could do to keep myself from singing out for you to hurry."

Elizabeth returned his smile as best she could with the weight in her heart. "You've been watching me? How? I didn't see you."

He slipped an arm around her shoulders. "In the rigging, lass. You never look up to the rigging above your pretty head. If you had, you'd of seen me right enough."

She was suddenly grateful for the warmth of his arm and leaned against him. In her haste to get away from Cawley, she'd taken only her dress and left her cape behind. The damp dress had brought her a small chill in its drying, and the chill had remained.

But she knew it was more than the warmth of his arm and body close beside her that made her feel better; it was his strength and his regard for her that she needed.

"Don't call me lass," she said. "Call me Elizabeth."

Michael tightened his arm to draw her closer to him and lowered his face into her hair for a moment. "Sure I will," he said gently. "Elizabeth Langlee, not Briggs. See, I remembered. It's a beautiful name. Fit for the princess you are."

It was wonderful to be with him. Especially now. She wanted to reach around him and hold him close to her, to hug him so tightly he would never get away, but she couldn't. The knowledge that she couldn't hold him long made her want to cry and she had to struggle against it.

Michael sensed her change. "What's the matter, Elizabeth? What's wrong?"

She shook her head. "I can't tell you, Michael. It's terrible." She fought against the tears forming in her eyes.

He took her chin in his fingers. Hard fingers, but gentle to the touch, and he used them to make her look at him. "Tell me," he commanded. "You've been hurt and I want to know about it. Who is it—Cawley? I'll ring that fat bastard's belly with my knife if he's laid a hand to you."

His green eyes looked deeply into hers. Elizabeth tried to shake her head but his hand wouldn't allow it. "Tell me," he said again.

Still, she couldn't answer, and he leaned forward slowly and kissed her. Very gently at first, only a touch of his lips on hers, and then, as she waited breathlessly, he kissed her again. Much harder.

She was glad he did, knowing suddenly that she had wanted him to badly. It was the first time she had ever been kissed on the lips and it was a tender, wonderful sensation. Nothing like she had ever dreamed. She closed her eyes, wanting to hold the feeling forever.

Michael's voice, his face still close to hers, brought her back reluctantly. "You didn't mind?" he whispered. "You didn't mind my kissing you?"

She opened her eyes and looked into his. "I fair wanted you to do it," she whispered back. "Please do it again."

He was quick, almost rough, in his holding her, one arm around her shoulders, the other reaching swiftly under her arm and pressing her toward him. His lips were hard against hers, demanding a response. And she did respond, straining against him. Her head began to swim with the wonder of it; she seemed to be lifted up to float on the wind, with only the hard pressure of his chest against her breasts to give her awareness of her being.

The kiss lasted a long time; she was breathless when he released her.

"Elizabeth," he whispered. "I love you, lass. Gor, it's such a feeling I have for you."

Elizabeth tightened her own arms. His shirt was open, only the thinness of her own dress separating her suddenly sensitive breasts from his smooth skin. Still, she couldn't get close enough.

"Michael!" It was difficult to make her voice work through the surge of emotion that was penetrating every portion of her body. The long weeks since she had left the hut on the moor had built a great void of uncertainty in her, an aching, dark void that had threatened at times to smother her. Now the emptiness was filling rapidly. Michael was filling it with the pressure of his body against her. She was so grateful to him. So very grateful . . .

"Tell me you love me, Elizabeth," he said. "Please tell me."

"I do love you. Oh, Michael . . ."

He slid forward, pulling her with him, until they could lie, their bodies touching from chest to knee. A wonderful touching . . .

His kiss was long, painful in the pleasure of it. She parted her lips under the force of his kiss and trembled at the sensitive touch of his tongue.

It was more than she could bear. "Michael!"

He broke away. Forced himself away. His whole body trembled against her.

"Michael, what's wrong?"

His trembling increased. "I can't! Elizabeth . . . my love . . . My sweet Elizabeth. . . . It's a true feeling I have for you. Please believe me!"

She was frightened, in spite of his words. "Michael, I believe you." She tried to pull close to him again.

But Michael stopped her. He was straining to hold back and her fear increased. He couldn't change! Not now! Please not now, when she needed him so!

His head was shaking slowly, his arms still holding her away in spite of her own urgency. "No . . ." His voice was a gasp. "I will not! I love you too dear for that. Hold, Elizabeth. Hold a minute!"

She was losing him. He was behaving so strangely. "Michael, please!"

He shook away her plea and turned his head.

"Michael." She was growing desperate. "Please don't leave me. I need you so!"

He was crying suddenly, great tears streaming down his face. "Oh, lass! I need you, too! I want you! Gor, I want you! But I can't! You're the only one I've loved!"

For a moment she didn't understand, and then she did. In his agitation, Michael had twisted his hips full against hers and she felt the hardness there. A pressure between her leg and his . . . and she understood.

She knew nothing of the mating between a man and a woman, only what she had seen between animals and the night grunting of Briggs. Thomas had refused to talk of such things when she asked, and she suspected he really knew as little as she.

But she had seen her brother naked and knew what caused the pressure between her leg and Michael's; knew, without knowing how she knew, that its hardness came from his love for her. She kissed him as deeply as she could.

"Elizabeth!"

"Love me," she cried. "Michael, love me . . ."

His whole body shook as with a fever, but the joy of his

kiss chased away her fears. Her body blazed alive with the roughness of his hand as he stroked her.

Michael was crying and clumsy, and she held him tightly to have him know it was right between them. This joy, this love, was theirs...

Suddenly, he was gone, snatched away by the wind. She heard its angry howl as it penetrated her throbbing senses, the rage in its voice shattering the sweetness between her and Michael.

The shock of it jerked her up. Elizabeth opened her eyes— and screamed.

Michael was locked in combat with her brother. The two of them struggled back and forth with their arms locked around each other.

She screamed again as Thomas freed one arm and smashed his fist against Michael's face, driving him to his knees. Blood spurted from Michael's mouth, bright red and spreading, but he shook it away and drove his head into her brother's stomach, butting him backwards toward the rail and the foaming sea beyond.

Thomas grunted with pain as his back struck the rail, but brought his knee into Michael's chest, shoving at his head at the same time.

The redhead staggered backwards, his arms torn away from their grip, and Thomas stepped forward quickly to swing his fist in a great arc. Michael's feet slipped with the blow and he went on his back to slide across the deck. Elizabeth screamed, but neither boy stopped. Michael scrambled to his feet and dodged as Thomas aimed a kick at his head, a kick that never reached its target as men—including Quinn—were suddenly around the two of them. The big mate swung an object in his hand to Thomas's head and the boy went down in a heap.

She gasped for breath, and blocked the sight from her eyes with her hands.

She waited, trembling, and when she uncovered her eyes at last, expecting to see him dead, the sailors were dragging his limp body away.

Thomas! Her dress was up to her thighs, she struggled to bring it down and make her shuddering limbs function at the same time. But she had to see. He had to be alive!

It seemed hours before she could get around the crates to the deck beyond, a deck that was full of people, more than she'd seen upon it since it sailed. Tom was crumpled in the middle of them, in a cleared space. She watched in horror and relief as he slowly climbed to his feet and stood there swaying.

Elizabeth wanted to run to him, but she didn't dare. Her trembling legs threatened to collapse and she had to use all her strength to cling to one of the crates.

Dimly, through the roaring in her ears, she heard the captain speak from the steersman's deck. "Mister Quinn! What is the meaning of this?"

The mate stepped clear and pointed. "Fighting, captain, between the crew. I had to brain one of 'em to keep him from killing t'other."

She looked quickly for Michael, and found him standing alone, wiping the blood slowly from his face.

The captain's voice snapped like a whip. "Fighting, is it? First a mutiny among my passengers, and now fighting in my crew!" His voice trembled with rage. "By God, I'll have an end to this!"

It was a dream. A terrible dream. She wanted it to end. But it would not, she watched in pain as Thomas stood erect and turned to look up at the captain above him. Even from the distance, she could see blood matting his hair.

"Who started the fighting?" the captain demanded.

"This one, sir." Quinn pointed to Thomas.

"Then lay him to a hatch, Mister Quinn. Let him feel the lash to his back."

"Aye, sir."

Quinn gestured to the sailors around him. "You heard the order!" he bawled. "Fetch a hatch to the mast and lash this dog to it! Be quick!"

She wanted to cry out to them, to stop them, but she could only watch in horror as the seamen pushed the standing, fascinated people aside and raised a hatch to lean against the mast. It took only moments for them to tie her dazed and unresisting brother to it, his arms spread wide, and then strip his shirt from his back.

Quinn stepped up beside him to look to the captain. "How many lashes, sir?"

The captain didn't hesitate. "Ten lashes, Mister Quinn. And lay them on well. I will have discipline on my ship!"

Dimly, the blood pounding in her ears and bringing her near a faint, Elizabeth watched as the big mate drew back his arm.

The whip in his hand swung forward, wrapped around Thomas's bare back and brought forth bright, red blood.

Thomas screamed.

The crowd of people on the deck murmured as the whip rose and fell relentlessly, bringing as it did a shuddering cry from her brother each time. Elizabeth her hair flying loose in the breeze, her cheeks pink, experienced the terrible lash of each blow, and sank to her knees.

By the time it was ended, the last strike accomplished, she was barely conscious. Thomas, too, had sagged against the hatch, his legs no longer supporting him. As if in a haze, she heard the mate call, "Ten lashes, captain!"

"You passengers mark this well! I'm in sole command of this brig! As captain, I'll stand for no resistance from you nor from my crew," the captain called out.

He paused and leaned over the rail, his hands spread wide. *The Grace* will put into Savannah and no other port. Any man of you who offers to prevent that will suffer the same fate you've witnessed."

Beneath him, the passengers moved nervously and looked at each other.

"Let this be my last warning," the man on the steersman's deck said, and turned his back in contempt.

She hardly heard the last words; the ship, the man who spoke and all the rest disappeared in a reddish haze as she lost consciousness.

Six

EVER SINCE THE public whipping of her brother, the voyage had been nothing but misery for Elizabeth. Sarah Cawley had seemingly recovered from her sickness, at least to the point she could sit up in the bed, and in a shrill, complaining voice, she demanded Elizabeth's constant attention. Between that and Cawley's strict orders not to leave the crib lest she offer herself to further disgrace, Elizabeth hardly saw the sun anymore. Not that she wanted to; the deck was but a reminder of the beating, and of her own shame.

She had believed in Michael Hawksley, believed that she loved him and that he loved her. How foolish she had been. She'd merely *needed* someone, and the sailor had used her need to his own ends. Her face burned when she remembered his whispered words and the effect they'd had on her.

Thomas had forgiven her weakness, at least she knew that. It was only because she lacked knowledge of the world, he told her. That, and the ways of men. He'd sought her out, risked another whipping in order to see her, and the two of them had talked, not as long as she would have wished, but enough for her to learn from him of her foolishness.

She'd never dreamed that Michael might have been laughing at her behind her back. That he'd even boasted of his conquest to his fellow sailors and of how easy the ignorant country girl had been. Well, Tom had set her straight. She'd never again allow herself to be so easily fooled. She needed to be loved, that much was true and she would admit it. But the love she would accept must be true love, and then she would have much to give in return. Never again would she allow herself to be tricked by soft but meaningless words.

Suddenly there was a small commotion. "Land Away!" She thought she was dreaming, yet she heard the words clearly.

The cry came from outside and was rapidly repeated all across the room the passengers shared. There was an immediate rush for the door, and Elizabeth joined them, quite forgetting to ask permission to leave.

The sky was a clear blue, the water again reasonably calm as she emerged on deck. The forward press of passengers carried her all the way to the side of the ship, and she was forced to hold on and brace herself to keep from being crushed.

She scanned the sea, but there was nothing to break the horizontal line between it and the sky. She had decided it was a false warning when the captain appeared on the steersman's deck.

The officer held a looking glass under one arm, but didn't immediately put it to his eye. Instead, he spoke quietly to one of his officers standing by. That man looked up to the rigging. "Where oh?" he called.

Elizabeth followed his gaze. There was a sailor at the very top of the main mast, perched there like a crow at the top of a cornstalk.

The sailor swung an arm, pointed to the right of the bow and cupped his mouth with his other hand. "There away!" His voice held an echo, riding on the breeze that filled *The Grace*'s sails. "Two points to starboard!"

She looked hard, saw nothing and turned back to watch the captain at last put up his glass. He looked through it only a moment, then lowered it briskly. Then Captain Welslip, his mouth set in a thin line, nodded to his officer.

That man took a step forward and raised a hand for quiet. "Land is in sight," he called loudly. "It'll be the coast of the Americas off the South Carolina colony. We're half a day's sail away."

He paused, said something to the captain in a low tone and received a quiet reply.

"We'll turn and follow the coast to our destination," the officer then told the crowd. "Savannah will be reached on the morrow. You passengers see to your belongings and be ready to depart when we anchor." He held up a hand to still the murmur. "Bringing this brig to land will be a close business. All passengers are to remain clear of the deck tomorrow morning. The captain orders it so."

The people broke into excited chatter, relief apparent in their faces. Many had not been convinced the ship wouldn't sink in spite of what the captain had told them; now that the tense voyage was nearly done and they knew they would set foot on land again, they were almost childlike in their joy.

It would be a relief for Elizabeth as well. No matter what she faced in this new and strange land, it could be no worse than the past weeks of confinement in the ship. She closed her eyes and raised her face to the wind. She needed this moment to breathe the fresh air and savor the end to their journey.

Left alone for the moment from Quinn and any duty, Tom hung in the rigging, one foot on a rope, the other on a wooden rail, and watched the scene before him. John Crosse, the ship's Cooper, was sprawled across bent elbows beneath him, puffing contently on a clay pipe.

It was sheer fascination. *The Grace* had come within a hail's distance of land late the evening before and had been close hauling the shoreline ever since under no more than top sails and spanker. Now she was turning before an island, a sandy expanse of small brush and marsh, and slowly entering what appeared to be the mouth of a river. To his left lay another island, at least he thought it so since it looked much like the first in vegetation.

He glanced down at Crosse, but the older man anticipated his question. "Tis Tybee Island, lad," he said with a broad smile. "We're entering the river called Savannah. No great shakes of a place if you ask me."

Tom dropped lightly to the deck beside Crosse. "You've been here before, John?"

"Aye. Crewed the *Anne* herself back in thirty-three when we crossed with the first of the poor fools who began this colony. A bunch of prattling idiots, if you ask me, wanting to live ashore in such a Godforsaken place."

He glanced at Tom to assure himself of an audience and Tom made sure his face was attentive. The Cooper liked to talk and would do so at length. But let him suspect he was being ignored or disbelieved, and he would grumble sourly into silence.

Satisfied Tom was listening properly, Crosse placed the pipe between his teeth once more and talked around its thick stem. "Of course on that voyage we didn't put into here right off," he said. "We held up in Charles Town in the Carolinas. Waited there for Oglethorpe—he's the leader in this Georgia colony— to hie himself down this way and pick a site for his town. Him and a Carolinian—Bull was his name, as I recall—picked this place, and then we brought the rest down. The town he built is called Savannah, just like the river."

"Where is it?" Tom asked. "Can we reach it by ship?"

"Aye, lad. Tis tricky, but it can be done. The river's fresh water of course, and damn full of sand bars, but our draft's such we can manage it. A bigger vessel might drag her bottom. They'd have to unload here on Tybee and cutter the goods on up."

"Up to where?"

Crosse chuckled. "Anxious pup, ain't you? Well, you'll be there soon enough. It's about seventeen miles as the river turns. Soon as we clear this island and turn into the mouth of it proper, you can scoot up the rigging and see it, you look sharp. Town sits on a bluff, rising a good bit above the river."

"A bluff?" Tom looked about himself dubiously.

Crosse nodded. "Damn good thing too. At least they get a bit of wind across. Holds down the musketoes. Damnable little critters would fair eat a man alive otherwise."

Crosse suddenly lost his audience. Tom was staring in sheer fascination at the land. A man had appeared on the shore, a man almost completely naked, holding a net of sorts in one hand.

It was a savage; it had to be, Tom decided. His skin was the color of dark berries, his hair jet black. A native of the Americas, the very first he'd ever seen. But the longer he looked, the more disappointed he became. This was no fierce warmaker; he was no more than a stooped and bent old man.

Crosse followed his gaze with amusement. "Well, what did

you expect, lad? Paint on his face and arrows flying at you?"

Tom grinned self-consciously. "It's only that I heard—"

The Cooper exploded with laughter. "And heard aright. You'll see enough of that other kind, I'll wager, before you've sense enough to set foot to a sea deck again. Best you be sure you have dry powder when you wander about in these parts."

Tom changed the subject and tried not to look at the Indian again. "You say Savannah Town is on a bluff?"

Crosse nodded. "Called Yammacraw Bluff. Named after the savages that had a town of their own on it. Or whatever they call the places they live. Oglethorpe got permission from their head man to settle there with his people. I'm told him and that savage is thicker'n thieves. Past me though, why a white man would want to do such with a savage, unless they figure to need each other to hold off the Dons from the south."

"The Dons?"

"The Spanish, lad. Castillians. Bloody papists! They claim the rights of discovery to this land the same as they do in the Floridas. And you can mark my words, they'll make an attempt to take this land from England before too many months are past. You still sure you want to go ashore? Between the savages and the papists, your throat's as good as cut already."

Tom grinned. "Do I have a choice?"

But the Cooper didn't smile back. "Listen, Briggs. You're a good lad, better by far than many I've shipped with. Given another voyage under a good captain, you'll make a fair sailor. I'd be the one who'd like to see that."

He reached out and tapped Tom on the arm. "You think because you're indentured you've got no choice but to go ashore and work your time for one of those grubbing farmers. But I'm telling you, if you go to the captain in a proper manner and ask, he might well be a mind to let you work your debt out on this ship. There's never enough good hands."

Tom shook his head. "I'll not want to ask anything from a man who's had me whipped like a dog," he said stiffly.

"There's rules to the sea," Crosse told him. "If the captain wasn't a hard man, you think this pack of mongrels would act anything like a crew? He done you no more than you deserved. I didn't see the fight you had, but from the tale of it, you'd of killed the Hawk right enough if they hadn't stopped you. And then Welslip would be short a hand. He couldn't have that."

Tom didn't answer. He was watching the shoreline as *The Grace,* well into the river now, heeled completely around the island and slowly made her way upstream.

"Aye," Crosse went on as if he'd been answered. "I know all about it, tis not a thing that can be kept from a ship's crew. You would have killed the Hawk because of your sister."

"He had no right," Tom finally said. "She's too young to know the difference."

"She's the right to make her own decisions about a man or any other thing," Crosse said shortly. "I've looked at the girl and I think it time you did with clear eyes yourself. She may be blood to you, Briggs, but she's fair a woman to others and the Hawk won't be the first to hang his tongue out after her skirt. You try to kill every man who wants to bed your sister and you'll be taking on the colony ahead of you."

"She's just a child," Tom said.

Crosse turned and spat. "And you're a bloody fool!"

Construction for a dock was underway at Savannah but not yet complete. *The Grace* anchored offshore and shuttled its cargo and passengers by boat to the bottom of a wide path cut into the bluff. Tom was kept busy with the unloading and missed seeing the boat that carried his sister ashore with the Cawley family. He only knew she was gone when the unloading was nearly finished.

He hadn't time to think about how he might see her again when he was told to report to Captain Welslip on the steersman's deck. He arrived, hurrying up the ladder, to find Andrew Platt, the other man indentured to the captain, already there. Platt was a man twice Tom's own age, a sour, clumsy individual with extremely bad teeth.

Welslip stood near the rail, watching the unloading, and ignored both of them until he was satisfied the last load was gone. Tom was restless and glad when the captain finally turned, taking some documents from his coat. He held the rolled papers in one hand and tapped them into the palm of the other.

"Platt and Briggs," he said officially. "By those names you are under agreement for four years of indenture to myself or to whomever I choose to sell these papers. Do you mind that well, the both of you?"

"Aye, Sir," Platt muttered. And Tom nodded.

Four years. . . . It was the first Tom knew of the time. Four years was a long time, but still he'd be young enough to start a new life. It could have been much worse; he'd heard tales aboard ship of men indentured for twenty years.

Welslip then offered him even better news. "I'm going to give both of you an opportunity to lessen that time if you can," he said, and Tom's heart jumped.

Welslip waited—an agonizingly long time. "I'm going to offer you the chance to secure a new contract in town for yourself," he said at last. "A better one. The two of you will have until dusk on this eve to find a buyer for your contract. I believe if you look lively and show your worth, it shouldn't prove difficult."

Tom strained not to miss a word. Could it be possible? A shorter time? It was too good to be true.

"This colony has hardly begun," Welslip continued. "Many hands are needed to build it. The fact that no black slaves are allowed in Georgia means that labor must be done for the most part by indentures such as yourself. You should be much in demand. If you present yourself properly, I expect you'll have many vying with each other to purchase your contract."

Welslip waited again for his words to take hold, then: "Now, I want the both of you to go ashore and do as I say. My terms are these: I will accept ten pounds for this contract. The length of time you serve to repay those ten pounds is for you to negotiate. But the money is to be paid me in sterling today. If either of you fail to place your contract, I will be forced to place it on the market tomorrow for whatever is offered in terms of service to recoup my money."

His voice became hard. "Mind you well, the both of you, don't think to flee once you are off this vessel. Any attempt to escape indenture is a capital crime in this or any other colony in the Americas. You will be caught no matter where you go. And when you're caught, you'll be hanged. Do you understand?"

They both nodded. Tom vigorously. He couldn't believe it! He might reduce his indenture to three years. Perhaps even two! If labor was a market in demand, he had much to offer. He wasn't afraid of work, no matter what it was. He could hardly wait to get into Savannah!

But Welslip wasn't finished. "Mind you. Return before dusk with or without a purchaser. Be late and not only will I have the town bailiffs in search of you, but the most of my crew as well. Your punishment for failing to return will be severe."

He dismissed them with a wave of his hand. "Now get you ashore."

He was afire with anxiety, the skin of his entire body tingled with it, and the slowness of the boat made him want to jump out and try his hand at swimming ashore. Platt, however, sat beside him with his long chin resting in one horny palm. Tom couldn't believe him. "Well, what do you think?" he demanded at last.

Platt's gaze remained fixed on the bluff ahead of them. "I think we'll be the worse for what just happened," he said. "Nothing goes well for the likes of us."

"What goes well, does so for those who seek it," Tom told him. "We have a chance to see for ourselves for a change and not have someone else do for us."

This time Platt's head did turn. He eyed Tom sourly. "You're young yet, Briggs, and subject to believing in such nonsense. But I'm a man what knows the world is set for the ones what has money. For those of noble blood and the like. You and me, we're the bottom of the pile and will always have their boots wiped on us."

Noble blood. The thought struck him like a blow. The world is set for those of noble blood . . . well, his was noble, he knew it now. And by that blood, he'd make his way in this new world!

"You've a chance to do for yourself, Platt," he said. "I intend to take that chance and make the best of it. You should be looking to it as well."

Only a few more feet of river separated them from the land and Platt watched the dwindling distance sourly. "You think Welslip is doing us a favor, boy? He ain't the type to do for those beneath him. There's some trick to his offer. I don't know what it is, but I know that bastard is only looking out for himself. He don't care a fig for the likes of you and me."

Tom started to answer, but the boat ground into sand. He stood up instead to leap ashore. "Have it your way, Platt," he called over his shoulder, his feet already moving him up the path. "I intend to succeed!"

The town of Savannah was a new experience. He stood on the edge of the bluff and looked about him in fascination. Below him the river wound about in a half moon to partly encircle the town, the southern part of which lay forty or more feet down. Along the riverfront, the activity was normal for any English seacoast town, but as he turned to look into the heart of the place, he knew there was none like this in England in spite of his limited experience.

The town was fortified, palisaded around its entirety as far as he could see, and contained two high blockhouses with cannon thrusting forth their black mouths. More cannon, he counted a battery of six, were along the riverside. He shook his head in wonder. Protection against the Spanish? Or against the savages? At either rate, it was exciting.

More surprising was the town itself. It was laid out in perfect lines and squares, he could stand in one street and look to the end of it. Amazing. But then he remembered this place was but a few years old and had been deliberately begun and not helter-skelter grown as those in England. Still, it was a marvel to see houses constructed on a line instead of a wandering lane.

The houses themselves, at least the first few he passed, did remind him of England. They were of yeoman design, a single room, much as those of his own village, with a peaked roof that would contain a sleeping loft. The difference was that these houses were covered with feather-edged boards, irregular in shape, and the roof was covered with tarred shingles.

He stopped to examine one. It was set on a log foundation about two and a half feet above the ground, but as he looked close, he could see the ground logs had started to decay, one more than the other so that the house actually tilted a bit to one side. One man not seeing properly to the upkeep of his living quarters, he thought, shaking his head. There would be lazy ones, even here in this place of opportunity.

The single door on the front stood slightly ajar and he risked a quick look, fully expecting a sharp and sudden scolding from the mistress of the house for his intrusion. To his surprise, the house stood empty. He entered it curiously.

The floor was made of planks, but planks that had been milled smooth and were held down by puncheons tapered to fit into holes. He was right about the loft for sleeping, it covered the entire length of the single room, about twenty-four to twenty-five feet, he judged. The width, from wall to wall, couldn't be more than sixteen feet, still a good size compared to the hut where he'd grown up. The best of all, however, was a great stone fireplace taking most of the opposite end from the door. He examined it with pleasure. It would be a comfort on a cold night, and its roominess would make cooking a pleasure for some mistress.

But he shook his head at the emptiness of the space: That someone would give up such a house was beyond his reasoning. Why? For a better? Then truly the rest of the houses, the two- and three-storied ones he could see waiting farther down, must be grand indeed.

He went out again and paused to look back toward the riverfront. Along its length, men were busy loading the goods from *The Grace* onto sleds and hauling them away with the help of horses. A few others were working at different tasks, but many seemed to be idle, standing about in groups to talk.

Tom looked them all over, his eye ready for any who seemed well enough in wealth to afford a strong young indenture. None seemed likely. He decided to turn into the town proper. An idea would come to him there, he was sure of it.

Before he had time to do that thinking, an opportunity presented itself in the form of a man hurrying toward him. The hurrier wore a woolen coat, long in the tails, and quite obviously of a good cut. His tri-cornered hat, too, was of good wool and showed no evidence of fray or fall. But the best indication was his stockings; they were not of wool, but a shiny material, and Tom knew they must be silk.

"Excuse me, sir." He stepped across the man's path as boldly as he could manage.

The man was startled into pausing. "What? What is this?"

Tom pulled his cap to his side. "I'd like very much a word with you, sir. With your permission."

The man had a wide face upon which a long, thin, hooked nose seemed out of place. The nose climbed a fraction, and two close-set eyes peered down it at Tom suspiciously. "What do you want? Alms? I've none for you. You're a sailor, are you not? What are you doing here?"

"Yes, sir, I'm a sailor—or I was a sailor. I arrived on *The Grace* still now in the river. But I'm no longer a sailor. I'm indentured and here to place my contract. I hoped you might be looking for a strong man to help you on your farm."

The man's suspicious look slipped into sly mirth. "You're indentured to the captain of that vessel, I take it?"

"Yes, sir. But he's given me leave to place my contract

here in town. If you'd be interested, I guarantee you an honest hardworker for your money."

He got a knowing nod in reply. "For a shorter term, I take it?"

"I'll work very hard, sir. And I'm in good health. You'd not regret it, I swear."

This time he received a thin, hard smile. "Perhaps you would, young man. Perhaps you would. But not at the price your captain would ask. At least not today. Methinks I'll be at the river for his sailing, however."

"Sir, I—" But the man was already hurrying away.

What did he mean by being at the sailing? What did that have to do with indenture? But then Captain Welslip had said if he weren't successful in placing his contract, he'd do it himself. At whatever price. Could that be what this man had made reference to? For the first time since leaving ship, Tom had his doubts.

There was a tavern ahead of him, and it struck him as a good place to present himself; there'd likely be men there who could afford to spend part of the morning away from their work. And even if there weren't, the keeper would certainly know of them. His hopes rose again.

The interior of the room was far different from the one Briggs had taken them to in London. Here the ceiling rose two feet above his head, and the room was well lighted from the sun glinting through three large windows. The tables with their benches were not pressed close but spread around the large room to give space to the men who used them.

The room was half full, its patrons sitting about with clay mugs in front of them or long-stemmed pipes in their hands. A few looked to him as he entered, but most seemed not to see him. Tom spotted the innkeeper near a thick table in one corner upon which two heavy barrels lay on their sides. He crossed the room quickly. "Excuse me, sir."

The keeper was near as thick as his barrels of ale. Shorter than Tom by nearly half a foot, he had to peer up from beneath heavy brows. "Sailor, eh? Have you permission to leave your ship, lad? I want no trouble here."

"No, sir, no trouble. I've permission from the captain. I'd like to speak to you about it."

"About what?"

He took a deep breath. "About myself. I'm indentured to the captain of *The Grace,* but have his permission to place my contract here in Savannah. I hoped you might know of someone who needs my work."

The keeper stepped back to regard him from head to toe for a long moment, then nodded. "And you would be a good buy at that, lad, from the looks of you. You're wide enough in the shoulder to do a good day's work. But you're about a useless quest, I fear."

His voice was roughly sympathetic and brought the doubts back quickly. "Why?" Tom asked him. "Isn't there work? I thought there'd be plenty."

The other nodded again. "Work aplenty for those who are willing to do it, but precious little in the way of money. No one will buy your contract, lad. Not in the way you want. It'd be foolish of them."

"I don't understand what you mean. I only know I'd be worth the cost to the man who buys my contract," Tom persisted.

The keeper smiled. "Well spoken, I'll grant you that. Come, let's give it a try and see for ourselves about the truth." He grasped Tom by the arm and propelled him to the center of the room.

"Gentlemen, your attention!" he boomed. "A moment of your time for a matter of this lad here!"

Tom felt like a cow on the selling block as the voices about him fell silent and every head turned his way. He straightened his shoulders and took a deep breath to swell his chest.

"This lad is indentured," the keeper went on in a more normal voice. "He's here to offer his contract to any man who's willing to pay for it. He promises handsome work in exchange. Any of you the will for it?"

To Tom's surprise, there were chuckles scattered about the room and broad smiles on the rest. He felt his ears burn.

The short silence was painful. A man directly in front of him broke it with a laugh. "Good work, eh? But for a high price and a quick time. I thank you no for meself."

"Aye," came from behind him and Tom spun to find the speaker. "I suppose you'd want it for two years, lad? Or perhaps one?"

The laughter increased.

Tom's face was now aflame. "I'm an honest man," he declared. "My work will be worth its cost to the man who buys it!"

"Not when it can be had for less," someone said.

Tom started to reply, his fists clenched, but the innkeeper took him by the arm and drew him away. "Come, lad. There's no point in embarrassing yourself more. I only wanted to prove to you the truth of what I said."

Tom shook his head. "I don't understand."

The keeper moved him back to the barrels and the conversation began again in the room with only a few still looking at them.

"It's like this, lad," the innkeeper told him. "Those in this room, like those about the whole town, know your circumstance better than you do yourself. There are other indentures brought here by seamen, and the people quickly learned that they are offered first at a high price. But if they wait until the ship is about to sail, the owner will bargain. Such is your own case. Perhaps there will be a few interested in buying you, perhaps not. But they'll wait until your ship is about to sail and offer a lower price for a longer service. Your captain will be forced to accept or lose the money he has in you."

That made horrible sense to Tom. "Do you know for how long the service might be?" he asked, his voice cracking.

"That depends, lad, on whether there's more than one bidder. I've heard of services bought for as much as ten years."

He noted the quick look of despair in Tom's eyes and shook his head quickly. "But that was for an old man, hardly of any use at all and feared to die soon anyway. It's a surprise he sold at all."

Tom couldn't reply.

"Be of good heart, lad." The heavy hand patted his shoulder. "Perhaps it'll not be as bad as you think! This colony is suffering from want of good men now. We've lost a goodly number to the sickness and to fear of the Spanish invading us at any moment. Tis a raw young land, and when your freedom comes, you'll be the equal to any in opportunity."

"Aye," Tom said bitterly. "When it comes." He turned to walk slowly out, trying to ignore the knowing smiles that fell upon him on his way.

As evening approached, Tom was tired and hungry and sick of being laughed at. It had been a foolish thought that he might find a man unaware of the situation. Now he had but one small hope left. Several had been interested in spite of their words; he could read the intent in their eyes. If enough came with the ship's sailing, they might well bid against each other. They would bid first in money, of course, not in time served, and Welslip would be interested in the money. Would he bother to allow them to bid in time? Doubtful, but it was the only hope he held.

He walked slowly along the waterfront, stepping aside occasionally to avoid men carrying loads. Reluctant as he was to regain the ship, he was even more reluctant to try again and face the laughter. There was no point to it. He stopped and allowed his eyes to sweep the river, cross its width and roam over the forests in the distance. What would it be like to be a free man and wander those forests at will? To stop in a place, clear the ground with a sweet singing axe and till the land. . . .

He felt a leaden hardness grip his chest and turned away from the scene. Tears were not for him; he was no longer a boy. Feeling sorry for himself would be of little help. Still, it was difficult to ignore the ache in his throat or the prickle to his eyes.

To rid himself of both, he stopped to watch a group of men working under the watchful eye of a broad, scarlet-faced man wearing a gentleman's coat and fanning himself with his hat. The coat looked well-cut, but it was worn with much use as though the wearer was too busy a man to give thought to its keep.

Tom moved closer in order to hear him. "Pick it up, you louts!" the man shouted. "Heave it to your shoulders and cease standing about so! Do you believe we've the night to work as well as the day?"

His efforts bore little fruit. The men moved reluctantly in the hot sun, and Tom noted with surprise that one of them wore leg irons. A prisoner?

The man in the well-cut coat rushed forward and thrust his own shoulder under a load, pushing it into the wagon. Tom then had an idea. Everyone else he'd seen today had been using loading sleds, long wooden logs supporting a platform of rough planks. Sleds that could haul much lesser loads. But this man had a wagon with true spokes in its wheels rather than the solid ones used in his old village. A wagon like that meant the man had wealth.

He started forward to speak, but before he could open his mouth, the man shoved him aside and hurried away to another group. As Tom watched, he waved his hat in a gesture, and two of the three men to whom he spoke moved reluctantly away. In a moment, the leader was back.

"Wilkins," he cried, "go with Ellis. You'll be needed in town. Come back to me as soon as possible."

The man to whom he spoke stopped his work to protest. "But Mr. Jones, we're not but half loaded here!"

The man called Jones waved his hat again. "It can't be helped. You're needed there. Thomas will tell you what it's about. Hurry, man, he's to report to Mr. Stevens."

Wilkins turned away, but moved too slowly for Jones. "Hurry, I said! There's much to be done yet!"

The other picked up his speed under Jones's sharp gaze and Tom chose that moment to step forward again. "Excuse me, sir."

"What? Who are you?" The scarlet face contained two deep-set eyes that locked on him quickly.

Tom straightened his shoulders. "You're short of hands, sir," he said. "I'd like to offer my own."

One thick eyebrow rose in question. "You're offering to work? I find that damned interesting and seldom heard. But at what price, young man?"

Tom was gambling, but the stakes weren't all that high, at least not in cost for him. An hour's work against a lifetime. "At only the price of a few minutes of your time, sir. To hear me out."

The eyes seemed to penetrate to his very thoughts, as if the man was reading them himself. "I've no time for games, young man. What do you want?"

Tom raised a hand. "Let me work first, sir. Then listen to me for only a little."

Jones was a man used to decision. He gave a short nod. "A cheap enough price at that. Heave to with the others and when the wagon's loaded, you'll have my attention for a few minutes."

Tom turned quickly, a surge of new strength coming to his legs. He grasped a barrel, waved off the man who already had his hands upon it and heaved it into the wagon alone. He didn't stop to see if Jones was watching, but hurried over to another and repeated the process.

The man in the wagon stacking the load as it came grumbled a protest. "Hold on there! Not so damnable fast!"

"Look lively, Travers!" came from Jones, and Tom grinned as he bent down to help with a crate. "You've a lad there who's not asleep like the rest of you!"

Tom increased his pace amid angry looks from the other men working. Twice a rough shoulder was thrust into his to slow him, but he was well used to working with the crew of *The Grace*, and merely shoved back to show he would take care of himself. It required only a short time to complete the loading as the others were forced to keep pace with him, and when it was done, he stepped back in satisfaction.

Jones motioned him over. "All right, lad. You've proved yourself a worker and I keep my bargains. What will you say to me?"

Tom took a deep breath. "Sir, my name is Thomas. I'm indentured to Captain Welslip of the brig, *The Grace*. "He's—"

"Sent you into Savannah to try to place your contract," Jones interrupted. "'Tis a common thing."

"Yes, sir. I know that now." He matched the eyes with a direct look of his own. "I know I stand little chance. But I thought you seemed a man who would appreciate others who are willing to work and give me leave to prove myself. If you think not, then I've lost little but my time."

Jones stared at him for a long moment. "What are the terms of your contract with this Captain Welslip?"

"He desires ten pounds, sir." Tom hesitated. "The length is to be decided."

"Ten pounds, indeed." Jones gave a wicked laugh. "Unless he's a fool, he knows he'll get no more than eight. And be fortunate to receive that."

Tom waited, fighting between hope and disappointment.

The hat came off again and Jones used a wide handkerchief to wipe his brow. Suddenly he bobbed his head again. "If I purchase your contract, Thomas, do you vow to serve me honestly? Or will I see you soon as lazy as the louts now around you?"

Tom's hopes soared. "Sir, I ask only a chance!"

"I promise you, fail me and it'll go hard for you."

His voice rose in spite of himself. "Give me that chance, sir. You'll not be sorry."

Jones smiled. "I've learned to read a man's eyes, Thomas. And I like what I see in yours. Very well. Get you back to your ship and tell its captain that Noble Jones will call on him within the hour." He paused, and then the wicked little laugh returned. "He will not find me an easy mark, however. But you needn't tell him that."

Tom had to restrain himself from shouting. "Yes, sir."

"We'll bargain with him and he'll come to our terms," Jones went on. "At least in monies. The bargain between you and me will be one of time. Serve me honestly, as I ask, and both of us will be satisfied with its length. Fail me and you'll regret it."

"Thank you, sir. Thank you."

"Get to your ship. I'll be there to collect you within the hour."

The rest of the men were watching Tom and the one with the leg irons regarded him with amusement. But he didn't mind. He was learning to measure a man by his eyes, too, and Noble Jones was a man he could respect. He felt good for the first time since setting foot in Savannah.

Minutes later, he was hurrying down the riverfront to where he could descend the bluff. He hoped a boat from *The Grace* would be there and he wouldn't have to hail one. He was in a great hurry to face the man who'd had him whipped and tell him he no longer owned Thomas Langlee.

Seven

THOMAS CAUSTON, the first bailiff, was a fat man. Or rather, a man with a fat stomach. It seemed much the greater part of him, the rest of his body merely serving to move it about. He also had great lumps of cheeks, a mouth like a fish and tiny black eyes that jumped out hotly at you. Elizabeth decided she didn't like the man. Besides being ugly, he seemed to carry an urgency to convince everyone around him of his very great importance. His every manner, including a constant laying of his finger on his nose and rubbing it about, indicated his large opinion of himself.

Standing with the Cawleys—as indeed with every member of the passenger list of *The Grace*, men, women and children— Elizabeth was treated to a long discourse on exactly *how* important Mr. Thomas Causton was to the colony. He was, she discovered, the first law enforcement officer, and along with two other bailiffs and the recorder of the Court, Mr. Thomas Christie, made up the governing body of the colony, known as the Magistrates. He was also keeper of the Trustee Store, from whence the new colonists would draw their supplies until their farms were producing on their own.

For those listening to him who came "on the charity," as he put it arrogantly, that is, the ones who had their passage paid for by the Trustees, the Store would be their only lifeline, but their accounts there would be monitored most closely.

Elizabeth grew bored listening to him. It was of no account to her, she was indentured and had no say in what happened, no matter what. And, too, her own master, Thermous Cawley, wasn't on the charity and could make decisions to please himself. So there really was little point in her listening.

She allowed her gaze to wander around the people assembled on the square, both the new arrivals and the curious few older settlers who had gathered to observe. There was little difference between the two groups that she could see; if any, the passengers from *The Grace* were dressed in clothes showing the lesser wear. That struck her as odd. She began to look more closely. Perhaps these were all indentures, wearing cast-off clothes of their masters and mistresses. But then, if they were indentured, would they be able to stand about and watch others rather than go about their duties?

It didn't seem right. Her attention centered on the one passerby she noticed who seemed concerned with his work and only mildly interested in the newcomers. He was a slim youth, a year or two past her own age, with brown hair that dropped over a rather handsome face. He wore a short coat without tails, being sewn all around, and his woolen stockings were without holes and fit quite snugly around his calves. All in all, an interesting boy.

He was carrying a sack of something loose over his shoulder, bracing it with an encircling arm. As he walked by the crowd, he turned several times to see, but didn't stop.

An explosion of questions brought her attention back to the group and Mr. Causton for the moment—but only for the moment. She looked again for the boy, couldn't find him and stepped back from the crowd for a better view.

Stepping back brought her right into his path. He'd been making a circle around the rest in order to come down the street on which she was standing. She was suddenly face to face with him.

He stopped, and Elizabeth found herself looking into deep but lively brown eyes. She met his startled gaze with curiosity, and it was only after he touched his forehead with his free hand and moved around her that she realized what she was doing.

She spun away without answering his shy smile and didn't look back as he passed behind her.

Whenever was she going to learn not to be so open? Here was a young man she had happened to like the looks of and she'd played the brazen hussy and practically thrown herself at him. Whenever would she remember!

She moved forward to lose herself in the crowd and tried to pay attention to what was going on once more. She couldn't, and had to risk a peek over her shoulder. To her dismay, he had stopped only a few feet away and was watching her closely. She jerked her head back and walked even faster.

Her first night in Savannah wasn't a pleasant one. Cawley had spent most of the day looking at houses that were for sale before deciding on one at last, and then he'd discovered he'd lost the opportunity to purchase food due to the lateness of the hour. They'd have a roof over their heads, but nothing to eat except some hard bread, mouldy from its journey across the sea. His anger at his own mistake had directed him in a tirade toward his wife at first, but she had retreated quickly in a sickly swoon and left Elizabeth to bear the brunt of it.

Her master's mistake took away his pleasure in the bargain he'd made in purchasing the house so cheaply. It was a much better house than some they'd looked at, she had to admit. Those had been for the most part of a single room, with a fireplace on one end and a sleeping loft above. And the walls had been constructed of thin planks. This house consisted of two rooms, side by side, with a smaller fireplace in both. Only one had a sleeping loft over it, a loft that covered it entirely and was reachable from a ladder in the other. She'd had trouble in hiding her pleasure when she was told she would have the loft to herself, the children would share the sleeping room below it with their parents.

The roof was low, for half this area she could call hers she would have to move in a crouch, but it would be a place to be alone, and she treasured that part of it.

Still in all, it was a puzzle. Why was a house this large and so well built empty in the first place? And why would it be sold so cheaply?

She had given it a great deal of thought through the night, finding it hard to sleep anyway from the lack of anything between her own body and the hardness of the loft boards.

Sometime this morning she would have to find some straw to make her bed, and perhaps by tonight she'd be accustomed to the non-movement of the land rather than the rocking of the ship.

She smiled at the thought, only to be startled out of it by Andrew, who burst through the door. "Mother! Come quick!"

She stopped her sweeping as Sarah Cawley rushed in from the other room. "What is it?"

Andrew was joined by his brother. "Indians!" they screamed together. Both ran to clutch at their mother's skirts and pull her toward the door.

"Two of them!" Robert, the oldest urged. "They just passed our house. And they were almost naked!"

Her heart jumped. She wanted badly to see for herself. Savages: Walking by the house like any passerby. Oh, she would love to see them!

But any attempt on her part would irritate her mistress the more and already today she'd experienced the lash of her tongue. She sighed and went back to sweeping, though she did sweep toward the door.

Sarah Cawley clutched each of her sons to her with a hand around the side of their heads and hurried to the door to peer out. "Where?" she said.

Andrew, younger but bolder, slipped free of his mother's grasp and bounced the single step to the ground in front of the door. "That way!" Elizabeth heard him call. "They went that way. Around the corner!" Then his brother joined him at the door.

She couldn't help herself. She moved to the door and tried to see over the woman in it.

"Come back inside," her mistress told her sons sharply. "You don't know what might happen. Stay inside until your father returns. We don't know what those people might do."

Andrew's wail of protest was joined by his brother's, but their mother was firm, until she noticed Elizabeth beside her. Her expression changed suddenly from worry to distaste. "Very well," she told the boys to their obvious surprise. "But no more than a few feet from this door. And if you see anyone approaching, come in immediately. Immediately, do you hear?"

"Yes, mother!" It was a happy chorus from both.

Sarah turned to Elizabeth. "I want them out of the house anyway," she said shortly. "It's time I had a talk with you, girl, where the men can't hear. Master Cawley will return shortly and I want this settled between us before he does. Come with me."

She turned and headed for the sleeping room, and Elizabeth had no choice but to follow, laying the broom aside as she went.

The room contained a single bed, left there by the previous owners; blankets brought by the Cawleys and spread on the floor for the boys to sleep on; and the trunks of their possessions. One of these stood open and most of its contents were spread across the bed. There were several gowns, petticoats, shifts and bodices, as well as a pile of stockings and garters. Elizabeth stared. It was hard to imagine anyone having more than one dress at a time, much less all of this. She drew her gaze reluctantly to the woman beside her.

Sarah Cawley could read her thoughts, or at least thought she could. "It's proper clothes, girl. Clothes that any moral woman would wear. Smallclothes as well, you'll notice. I'm quite sure having been brought up in the immoral way you've been, these are of no interest to you. You'd prefer to go around nearly naked under that single dress of yours."

She paused and pursed her lips. "But let me tell you, girl, from this moment on you will not. I'm going to give you one of these dresses and a shift to wear under it. You'll take needle and thread and adjust them both to fit yourself. As soon as I can get to a store in this town, I intend to purchase stockings for you and a belt to hold them. To say nothing of an apron and cap to wear over the lot. From now on, you'll dress as I say. Do you understand?"

Elizabeth was overwhelmed. A real dress! Never mind that it was one used by someone else, that was all she'd ever had at any rate, purchased reluctantly by Briggs when the one she wore had fallen to pieces. But those had been near rags themselves when she got them. And smallclothes! All she'd ever owned were made of his old smocks, worn through with holes. She'd never owned a shift in her whole life!

She was unable to answer, and Sarah Cawley grew impatient. "Do you hear me?"

"Yes, ma'am."

Sarah shuffled through the pile for a moment and then brought out a dress of calico print and held it up. It had long sleeves and a ruffled collar that would fit tightly around the throat. "Stand close," she told Elizabeth. "Let me see."

She moved closer and Sarah held the dress across her, her hands resting on Elizabeth's shoulders. Then she shook her head. "It's too short. Your ankles will show."

Elizabeth was disappointed. It was such a pretty dress. But she held her peace.

Sarah turned back to the other gowns on the bed, but then straightened again. "Oh nonsense! All of them will be the same! If you can't let it out enough, then you'll just have to sew a piece around the bottom. Take this one." She thrust the calico toward Elizabeth.

She took it and tried not to show her pleasure. "Yes, ma'am. I'm sure I can make it fit."

The hard little eyes of her mistress came around to meet her own. "You will make it fit, girl," she stated flatly. "But you will *not* make it fit too tightly. And you'll wear a shift under it at all times. I'll not have you flaunting your unholy body at my husband again."

Flaunting! Her face turned crimson. "But I wasn't—I haven't—"

"Yes you have! Don't attempt to lie to me! I know your whorish ways. My husband told me!"

The words stung her with the force of a slap across her face. That, and the hatred in the older woman's eyes caused her to fall back a step. She shook her head violently. "I didn't! It was the blanket . . . I didn't know it had—"

"Temptress! Don't lie to me! You took advantage of my being sick to tempt a man without the comforts of a wife! And when he refused you, you made to lay in open sin with a common sailor!"

Shame burned in her. Burned brightly, and just as suddenly it was gone. Anger replaced it. Deep, wrenching anger, she'd never felt such in her life, not even with Briggs. She had to grasp her face to keep from screaming. Slowly she fought for calm.

"It's your husband that's mistaken in his belief, mistress," she said, and her voice shook. "I made no tempting of him, not in my intention."

Sarah slapped her hard across her face and drove her backwards from the blow. She caught herself and raised her arms to ward off a second, but the effort was too much for the older woman, still pale from her illness aboard ship. She sat down in a heap on the bed.

"I'll not have it," she gasped. "I'll not have your insolence toward your master. Do you hear me?"

"I mean no insolence." She was calmer now, in spite of the slap. "I must do as the two of you tell me, and I'll work my best. But I'm an honest girl, not a whore." She paused to take a deep breath, and her own anger caught her off guard. "I want *nothing* from your husband!" she blurted.

"How dare you speak to me like that?"

Suddenly she was trembling, trembling all over. It was all she could do to keep from fleeing from the room, from the house itself. She crossed her arms and held herself to keep from shaking. "I'm sorry, mistress. I mean no disrespect. I only want you to know that you have nothing to fear from me toward Mr. Cawley."

The face of the woman sitting on the bed turned livid. "You arrogant little bitch," she hissed. "You think because you have a body that tempts men, you'll have it all your own way, don't you? Well, I'll tell you right now, you will not! Not in this house. You're indentured for four years and in that time you'll do as I say, not as you want."

She had to stop to get her breath, leaning forward and drawing it deeply. Her eyes bore into Elizabeth's. "I tell you this, girl. If I see any part of your Jezebel flesh exposed again, I'll have your master take the whip to your back. Do you understand me?"

She nodded slowly. "Yes, mistress."

Sarah stared at her a moment longer, then turned and grasped the nearest shift to her to fling it in her direction. "Go and clothe yourself!"

She picked up the garment and fled.

Thermous Cawley was angry. Angry as much at the slowness of the officials in Savannah as he was at the small, gnawing fear that had appeared in the back of his mind in the two days he'd been in the colony. It was true he'd placed a roof over the heads of his family, an excellent roof, better than he'd expected so soon. He had expected to take whatever accommodations available and build his house later. He'd heard that was done regularly in the colony before he left England and looked forward to owning his first dwelling. The fact that he found a good house at a ridiculous price had delighted him at first, until he began to wonder why. Then in his two days here, he'd begun to suspect the reason. There were many empty houses in Savannah, and precious little market to sell them in. The town, indeed the colony, was losing inhabitants weekly, either through shipping back to England, those who could afford it, or in moving across the river into the older colony of South Carolina.

The exodus had been easy to discover, his own eyes had told him of it, but finding out why the others were leaving had been more difficult. Now he thought he knew at least two reasons. Sickness had done in many of the first to arrive in Savannah, a plague that destroyed whole families. And even now there were many who became mysteriously ill for no good reason. He was told Mr. Oglethorpe, the leader of the colony, blamed the deaths on too much consumption of rum punch and was trying to ban the liquor from the colony completely. With little success, his informer told him with a sly smile. But others blamed it on the lack of a pure water supply, saying the people drank river water polluted with putrid marshes and numberless insects that deposited their eggs there. To say nothing of the rotting carcasses of animals and corrupted vegetables in the waters.

Some of the ones leaving still feared a return of the plague that had wiped out half of those who came over on the first ship, *The Anne*. They left, saying the area was too unhealthy for men, at least white men.

Others were leaving, it was strongly hinted, out of fear of war. They had been told that they were forming a new colony for the Crown and glory of England. But they began to suspect that both England and the South Carolina colony wanted a buffer zone between that prosperous area and the Spanish to the south. The Spanish, they discovered, lay claim to all the territory the Georgians now occupied, all the way to the Savannah river.

If the Spanish governor at St. Augustine decided to move his troops in force, the weak colony spreading out from Savannah would be quickly overrun and the papists were not known to be kind to their prisoners.

It was true that Oglethorpe had planted a group of Highland Scots, excellent fighting men, at New Inverness to the south, and was now engaged in creating a strong fort at Frederica on one of the islands barring the waterway from Florida, but those, Cawley was told, would stand little chance against the might the Dons could bring against them whenever they chose. The island of Cuba was a Spanish stronghold from which two to three thousand soldiers could be brought, more than enough to sweep the tiny garrisons of a few hundred men. Savannah, in spite of its cannon and closeness to South Carolina, would most likely suffer the same fate.

Two excellent reasons for leaving the colony, and two reasons of which he'd been carefully not informed in the glowing accounts that had drawn him from England. Still, he reasoned as he made his way to his house, not enough to deter him. He understood enough of royal politics to know that England and Spain would remain at their differences over much of the world for some time. If the war came here, to the Americas, England would be forced to defend its people. Good, stout English troops would be sent not only from the home country but from the northern colonies.

As far as the plague was concerned, he was told there were doctors now in Savannah. Several, in fact. One man, a Mr. Noble Jones, had an excellent reputation, although he had other duties to perform as well. The sickness would be controlled.

He turned the corner to leave Bull Street and started down the one which led to his house. The thought of Noble Jones brought back his original anger and thrust away his doubts. That man stood between him and his beginning to make his fortune. He had been given his land, although they would allow him only a hundred and fifty acres rather than the five hundred he had wanted, because he held no male indentures, but even that was to be kept from him until Jones could survey it.

Besides being a surgeon and the chief surveyor, as well as head carpenter and architect of Savannah, Cawley was informed that Jones had responsibilities for the defense of the city. Did they have no other man who could do some of those tasks? He could be weeks waiting for Jones to get around to surveying his land!

He turned to enter his door. Well, at least the plot he had in town in which to raise vegetables for his family's consumption was ready. It was already surveyed since it had belonged to the inhabitants of this house. When they left, it reverted to the Trustees and Mr. Christie had merely assigned it to him.

The girl was sitting on a low stool by the fireplace and reached to stir a broth cooking in a pot swung from a hook as he entered. She wore the dress his wife had given her, as well as a long apron and a white cap. He looked to see that she allowed none of her leg to show and was irritated to note that she caught his look and pulled her feet under her.

"Where's your mistress?" he demanded.

"She was invited to a house down the street," Elizabeth told him. "A Mrs. Habersham, I think. She took Robert and Andrew with her."

Cawley walked close enough to stand over her and look down. Her dress was tight around her throat and loose enough below so that he could no longer see the outline of her breasts. His nerves tingled with the remembrance of that curving young flesh, but he put the thought away just as quickly. The Devil put flesh such as that on young women to tempt a man. Only the strong refused to succumb to it.

"I would have my tea," he told her roughly. "Make a pot."

"Yes, sir." She made as if to stand, but he was too close; she would have to brush against him to get to her feet. He waited a moment, and when she didn't get up, turned and moved to the table and his chair at the head of it.

From that point, his thoughts, dark and competing with each other, ran from his frustrations with the Magistrates and his beginning fear that he might have made a mistake in giving up a good trade in making wigs in England to come here and his persistent dreams of becoming wealthy in the silk trade.

He watched her move as he brooded. Young and effortless, not the least like Sarah who for as long as he had known her had been in complaint of one thing or another. His wife had not even been fair of limb and face when he married her, but her father had been in the trade and he could see the advantage to himself.

The girl had the tea in the pot now and leaned forward to place it on the stone niche provided for it at the rear of the fireplace. Cawley looked at her bottom when she leaned over, the skirt tightening against it, and the tingle returned.

He forced his thoughts back to the land he would soon receive. It lay to the west, at least he knew that much.

The Trustees required with the granting of the land that a thousand mulberry trees be planted within each hundred acres, but that was no problem. He intended to plant many more than one thousand. Let the others plant corn, peas and whatever to sell, *he* was interested in the production of silk. And silkworms required the tender leaves of mulberry trees to thrive on. He would plant his acres tenfold in mulberry trees. He could see it now: A filature of his own—no, two. Large ones, with dozens of young women inside them unwinding the threads from the cocoons after they had been removed from cooking basins. Bales of the finest silk shipped back to England, Cawley silk on the back of the Queen herself . . .

The girl, with hardly a glance in his direction, resumed her seat by the fire. Silk fled from his head as he watched her; slowly, against his wishes, he remembered lying beside his wife in the darkness of his sleeping room and listening to this girl's movements over his head. Remembered, although he struggled against the remembrance, of his visions of her clad only in a shift for sleeping—even the possibility that she slept without the shift . . . naked under a blanket.

She reached forward with her left hand to stir the broth she was cooking and the action stretched the fabric of her dress. Finally he could see the definite outline of her young breast.

He looked away quickly. The Lord would punish him severely for such thoughts. He was a man with a wife, a good and true wife. But—the thought persisted wickedly—a wife who lay cold and stiff whenever he was upon her, interested in performing no more than her duty to him.

The girl was a temptress. Had she not deliberately shown her breasts to him? She would not lie so coldly, she would . . . With a great effort he thrust the image away.

Her gasping intake of breath jerked him back. Elizabeth was staring not at him but at the door, and when he turned to see, his own nerves screamed in alarm. A savage stood in the doorway, a giant savage whose bulk filled it completely.

Cawley jumped to his feet, but before he could move, the savage stepped inside the room and was followed by a grinning Mr. Henry Parker, one of the bailiffs, and another Indian.

Relieved by the presence of the white man, Cawley stared at the first savage in awe. He was old, apparent in the long clefts of his face, deep crevices that gave it a look of whithered oak. But he stood erect, over six feet tall, and the naked skin that covered his broad shoulders and thick chest was unwrinkled and gave evidence of powerful muscles underneath. His head was shaved except for a lock of long hair tucked over his left ear. He wore a breechcloth over his waist and thighs, buckskin boots and leggings.

Black eyes regarded Cawley from the mahogany-skinned face for a long moment and then to his immense relief, the savage smiled, a broad, friendly smile showing wide white teeth.

He spoke, a liquid though guttural sound that rose and fell, and at the same time raised a palm twice the width of Cawley's own.

Cawley had no idea how to respond. He could only stare at the Indian stupidly. It was a long and embarrassing moment before Parker rescued him.

"Mr. Thermous Cawley, it is my pleasure to present Mr. Oglethorpe's dearest friend, Tomochichi, Mico of the Yamacraws. He has asked to welcome all the new arrivals to Savannah."

Cawley could still not regain his speech, and with a look of condescending amusement, Parker continued. "The Mico was gracious enough to negotiate the very land this town lies upon for Mr. Oglethorpe. He's been a good friend to the colony. We consider him the greatest of help to Georgia."

Cawley recovered his voice at last. "Uh, how do you do."

The giant savage increased his grin and stepped forward to place a hand on Cawley's shoulder. A heavy hand. He spoke again in his own language, patted the shoulder twice and stepped back to wait.

The third man spoke for the first time, moving around Parker in order to make himself seen. "Tomochichi says he welcomes you, Mr. Cawley, as he does all Englishmen who come to his land."

This man was also an Indian, obvious in the color of his skin, but he was dressed in civilized clothing, trousers of wool that extended into boots and a linen shirt.

Cawley turned to face him but was pulled away again when Tomochichi boomed once more. He listened until he was finished and looked to the interpreter.

"Tomochichi says he has had the pleasure of visiting your country and considers himself a friend to your king," the man said. "He wants you to be happy in this land." Unlike the other two, the tall Indian and the Englishman, he didn't smile when he spoke.

Cawley nodded slowly. "Tell him I thank him for his good wishes. I . . . I hope we can become good friends."

The interpreter translated his words into the same language the savage had used and Tomochichi's face beamed. "Good," he said in understandable English. And repeated it, "Good."

Parker touched his arm. "Come, chief. We've a few more families to visit." He glanced at Cawley. "I thank you for welcoming us into your home, Mr. Cawley. I'm sure both the Mico and Mr. Musgrove here appreciate your attitude. Sorry we can't stay longer."

His smile was no longer condescending, but wicked. "I hope we didn't startle you?"

Cawley felt his face flush. "Not in the least, Mr. Parker. I welcome your friends at any time. In fact, I was about to have this girl prepare tea. Are you sure you can't stay for some?"

"I'm afraid not, sir. Time is pressing, and I must escort the Mico about. You understand, of course."

"Of course." Cawley bowed.

To his surprise, the tall savage did, too, as good a bow as he'd ever seen, incongruous in buckskin and leggings. A moment later, all three men exited the door.

"My goodness!" The servant girl had evidently been struggling to hold herself back. "He was so big!"

Cawley spun around. "A savage! An unchurched savage! They're stupid for allowing such as that to walk the streets. By Heaven, the way that man Parker acted, you'd think the Indian a prince!"

She looked at him wide-eyed. "He called him a Mico. Does that mean he's a leader? I mean of the savages?"

"How in thunder would I know?" The question fueled his anger. "He's a pagan! Serve my tea!"

He stalked back to his seat at the table. *Stupid girl. To be impressed by a savage! Such ignorance!*

Eight

THE COAST OF the Georgia colony, Tom learned, was guarded
by numerous islands, creating in effect an inland waterway in
which even good-sized ships could make their way up the coast
without standing out to sea. One of the islands, located a dozen
miles below Savannah, was the Isle of Hope, and his new
master, Noble Jones owned a large part of it. In fact, he and
two others, Tom was told, Mr. Henry Parker and Mr. John
Fallowfield, owned the entire island.

All three men planned to build plantations there, but so far
only Jones had begun construction. He had built a small fort
on the island in his responsibilities as Captain of Georgia Rangers, but now was engaged in the beginning of a house for
himself. The log fort, being empty at the moment, would house
Tom and the six other men brought by Noble Jones to begin
the work.

It was a pleasant place, green with oak trees and low shrub-
bery, and even in the hottest part of the day sea breezes dried
the sweat on his brow as he worked.

The house was being built of tabby construction, a process
that Tom found fascinating. They began by setting two boards

on edge as wide as they intended for the walls of the house, then poured in lime-shell mortar mixed with sand, and lastly pounded oyster shells, of which the salt water creeks of all the islands were literally covered, into the mixture. Then the process was repeated. In the periods of waiting, more lime-shell mortar was made by gathering and calcinating oyster shells.

Of the six men working, three were indentured to Jones besides himself and the other two hired for their experience in tabby construction. One of the indentures was the man he'd noticed wearing chains the day Jones had bought his contract. His name was Lawrence, and Tom was told by one of the others that he wore the leg chains because he and another had run away once before. Not only had the two of them tried to escape their indenture by fleeing into the forests, but they had robbed Jones and others in the attempt.

Lawrence was a big man, a few inches taller than Tom, and inclined to be rough speaking to the men who worked around him. But to the newcomer's surprise, the roughness didn't extend to him. Rather, Lawrence seemed overly friendly, smiling at him often and being quick to lend a hand in anything he was doing.

Tom was suspicious. The difference in the man's attitude toward him and the others was too clear to be an accident. Still, he had no cause to take offense and responded in the same manner. His suspicions were confirmed, however, when William Coar, another indenture who was left in charge during Jones's absence, drew him aside.

"This way, lad," he ordered, laying a hand on Tom's shoulder. "I've a task for you."

Tom put down his shovel and followed as Coar led him down a short path, around a large oak, and then stopped. He glanced around, but they stood in long grass with no sign of construction disturbing it. He looked a question to the other.

Coar nodded. "'Tis naught here to do. I said that so not to have the others take note that the two of us were having a talk."

"Why?" Tom asked. "What difference would it make?"

Coar was a stocky man with wide shoulders and thick arms that indicated strength, but his face was old, his hair gray and standing out from his head like tufts of cotton. He reached up with the fingers of one hand and smoothed down one of the tufts, a gesture Tom had noticed he made often.

"The difference it would make, lad, is that of your own good. In speaking to Mr. Jones, I've come to think he is some taken with you. He says right out that you might be a cut above the usual."

Tom started to reply but was cut off as the hand Coar was using to smooth his hair turned palm out in his direction. "You need say nothing now. Mr. Jones is a man who knows his own mind and if he's wrong about a thing, or a man, he'll find it out soon enough. What I want to speak to you about is preventing him from thinking he's made a mistake about you."

"About me? Why? What have I done?"

Again the palm waved. "Don't get ahead of me, lad. You've done nothing wrong yet, I just don't want you to do so. What I mean to say is for you to watch out for Lawrence. I've noted he's taken a liking to you and is trying to get inside your own liking. But I warn you, it means that bastard is moving about his own ends. He's a man who really likes nobody but himself, you remember that."

"Aye. I had thought it as much myself, Mr. Coar. He seemed a bit too quick. A man takes more time to pick his friends, I'd think." He shrugged his shoulders. "But then I don't know what he's got in mind, I've nothing to offer him. I own no more than these clothes on my back."

Coar nodded. "I understand that, and his actions are a puzzle to me right enough. But I do know that man, Tom. He's cunning and as low as a sand crab's belly. He's got in mind using you some way, and I want you to be knowing it."

"Yes, sir. I'll be on my guard."

Coar smiled, a pulling apart in a straight line of his thick lips. "And you'll not be calling me sir, lad. I'm no more than a working man like yourself. William's good enough."

Tom answered the grin. "William, it is. I thank you for your words to warn me."

"If you're as smart as I think you are, you'll pay close heed to them," Coar said. "Now best you get back to work."

"Yes si—William." He laughed and started back.

He was enjoying himself. The work was hard but not as driving as learning to be a sailor under Quinn had been, and the Georgia sun though hot, was not disagreeable. Best of all, the constant breeze across the island kept away the musketoes that seemed to plague Savannah. Tom took pleasure in waking to the dawn and the smell of the seacoast, and in knowing he was alive and a man of his own. Elizabeth was right, once he found out Briggs wasn't his father, he was well able to put both that man and the hard years spent under him aside.

As usual, he finished breakfast before the others, an event caused, he suspected, by the fact that he was the only one of the men who actually enjoyed the work, and walked over to inspect the progress of their labors.

He was looking closely at the construction of the house where the break would begin when Rodriguez, the man most knowledgeable in this construction, spoke from beside him. "Well, what do you think of this so far, Briggs?"

The Spaniard had a harsh, unpleasant voice which coupled with his accent had taken Tom several days to be able to understand. But he managed, learning as he had on board *The Grace* to listen to the rhythm of how a man talked and adjust his ear to that rather than try to fit the other's speech into his own pattern.

"It seems to be going well," he said. "We'll be leaving the openings for the windows today?"

The Spaniard nodded, his black eyes watching Tom closely. "Yes. But what do you think of the wall? Is it not thick and strong to you? Good for a house? Yes?"

"Good enough, I suppose," Tom said. He turned to study the long line of it again. "Strong enough to last, too, I think. But I don't know if I'd like it for myself or not."

Rodriguez's expression changed quickly and Tom realized it had been the wrong answer. The man didn't want opinions, he wanted compliments. He was exceedingly vain about being more knowledgeable of the construction techniques than the other, a South Carolinian, brought to show them how to build the house.

"You would rather live in a wooden house?" he demanded. "That is stupid! Have you not seen how quickly they rot in this climate? This house will last a hundred years. And it is cool from the hot sun, its thickness keeps the heat out. Can you not see that?"

"Aye." He didn't want to argue. It wasn't his house at any rate. But he had found a new freedom in having his own opinions and he would retain them. "I suppose you're right. Still, it's what a man gets used to himself."

But the other man obviously felt challenged and was bent

on having his way. "What do you know of houses? You are but a boy. I have seen houses in St. Augustine that were already two hundred years old! That is strength! That is correctness! Wood is for savages in the forests."

"Made of tabby?" Tom asked, more to divert the other than out of curiosity.

"Out of stone and mortar. But there is no stone here and this 'tabbee' is just as good." Rodriguez set his jaw. "Why do you not like it? Give me a reason."

Tom shrugged. "No great reason, I suppose. Except maybe it's pretty rough. This oyster shell could cut you if you brush against it. A man would have to be pretty careful living in a house made of it."

Rodriguez's sudden laugh was triumphant. "So! That is your objection? A stupid one! Do you not know that the inside walls will be plastered over? That they will be made smooth? Ah, you know nothing! Nothing at all!"

It made him angry, but before he could speak he was shoved aside by Lawrence who had come up without either of them knowing it.

"And you know everything there is in this world, you bloody renegade papist?" the blond man sneered. "Just what the hell do you know, Rodriguez?"

"What is it to you?" the other said quickly. "I was talking to the boy."

Lawrence laughed, a short, ugly laugh. "You were showing off your bloody brown ass, you mean," he said. "So you think this lad knows nothing, eh? Well tell me, my intelligent friend, who was the king who signed the Magna Carta? John? Or Richard?"

"What do I know of your English tales?" Rodriguez said sourly, taking a step backwards as if to turn away. "I was born in Spain."

"Aye," Lawrence barked, and used a hand to prevent the other from moving farther. "Born a bloody papist and then decided to switch, did you? Soon's you denied that anti-Christ in Rome, you had to run for your life, didn't you?"

He laughed again. "And that makes you so damn wise, does it? Well, since you were born in Spain as you say, you can surely tell me of your reading of Cervantes's *Don Quixote*, can't you? A learned man such as yourself could discuss fully one of your country's most famous writers?"

There was an eagle look of hate in the Spaniard's face. Rodriguez tried again to turn away. "I've no time to talk nonsense to you," he growled. "There is work to be done."

But Lawrence refused to let him go. One large hand closed on Rodriguez's arm and nearly pulled him from his feet.

"Let me go!" Rodriguez demanded. "What is this to you? Who says you yourself are so intelligent? A man with chains on his legs!"

Lawrence released him with a push that shoved him backwards, then quickly leaned to scoop up a shovel in one hand. "I'm twenty times the man you are, you stupid donkey, and so's this lad here. And you'll apologize to him or I'll split your skull and spill what little brains you have."

"I'll apologize to no one!"

The shovel rose.

"Lawrence!" It was Coar, the rest of the men close behind him.

But the blond man ignored him. "Show your regrets, you bloody bastard." His voice was the growl of a dog baiting a bull as he shifted the shovel to both hands. "Or try to outrun this."

Rodriguez was backed into a corner and Tom knew it. The blond man was half the Spaniard's size and Coar and the rest had stopped where they were. They would offer him no help since all of them feared the temper of the man with the shovel. He tried to stop it himself. "No apology needed to me," he said. "I take no offense."

Lawrence didn't look at him. "I damn well do. Speak, you cat's piss!"

Rodriguez's voice was forced and edged with hatred. "I meant no offense to the boy," he said. "It was but talk between us."

"Apologize, damn you!"

The Spaniard's head came up as if it had been jerked on a rope. His black eyes flashed and he trembled with anger. But he answered, "I am sorry."

"To the lad," Lawrence said scornfully.

"That's enough." Coar finally decided to take a hand. "Enough, I say. Get to work, Lawrence."

"Go to hell." The blond man didn't bother to look. "Well, Rodriguez?"

The Spaniard whirled to face Tom. "I am sorry!" He screamed the words.

But Lawrence was relentless. "And to me, you bastard."

"I am sorry." Tom had never witnessed such a look in a man's face before. Fear and hatred, coupled with shame. He had been thoroughly whipped without being touched. Humiliated in front of those whom he had lorded it over these last days, and Tom knew it would gnaw at his gut forever. He decided that the blond man with his chains had better sleep lightly in the coming days.

But Lawrence certainly didn't care. He tossed the shovel to the ground and laughed. "Just what I thought all along," he said. "A bloody coward. An ignorant, bloody coward. And you want to call others stupid."

He turned, still chuckling, and strolled away.

Tom answered Rodriguez's look with a direct one of his own and mentally shrugged. The blond man had proved little, he thought, except that he could make an enemy for the both of them. That had been the real stupidity of this encounter.

He walked away himself, realizing that after this the work would be far from pleasant for him. The Spaniard would see to that if he could. But then it couldn't be helped now.

One thing he did know, however. He was going to find time to talk to Lawrence now, in spite of Coar's warning and his own dislike of the man. Lawrence had surprised him with his questions, questions that only a learned man would know to ask. Where and how had he received such an education? How did a man become indentured if he had an education?

He'd asked Rodriguez to discuss a famous writer. That meant he could read that which the man wrote himself. It brought back the old ache. To be able to read . . . Good Lord, that must be wonderful!

A thought nagged at him, a foolish one that he discarded quickly only to have it come sneaking back. How long had Lawrence been indentured? Could it be possible that he had been taught his education while a servant for some reason? It didn't seem likely anyone would go to the trouble for a servant. But then neither did it seem possible that a man with an education could allow himself to be sold into servanthood.

At any rate, he had to find out, or putting up with the hatred of Rodriguez would be the least of things to gnaw at his mind.

* * *

Coar and the others seemed to think he'd taken a more direct
part in the affair with Rodriguez. In the days following, he
found himself being more and more isolated by them. They
spoke to him little, and Coar, when he gave Tom orders, did
so with a note of reproach in his voice.

He had an urge to protest, to tell them the argument was
none of his doing, but put it aside as little use. A man did not
whine like a pup, he took what life handed to him and made
the best of it. If he continued to do his work well and held his
peace, perhaps they would come to know he wasn't a trouble-
maker. And if they didn't, then so be it.

Surprisingly, Lawrence also let him be, although the blond
man remained friendly and laughed when he spoke to Tom, he
ceased being always around and offering a hand. Given the
both, being cut away from the rest of the men and left alone
by Lawrence, Tom had time to think while he worked. And
his thoughts rolled often to his sister. He didn't mind being a
servant himself, especially to a man like Noble Jones who
seemed most fair. But Cawley was different. A fat pig who
lorded it over those he could, he was bound to make her life
miserable. He would probably treat her worse than Briggs had.

It was a fair shame, he thought. Cawley was a pig who
thought he was a better, and Elizabeth was his servant though
she was born to the ranks.

The woman who gave them birth, their true mother, must
have been beautiful, for his sister was beautiful. He could
recognize that even if he were her brother, and by the Furies,
it was apparent to other men the way he saw them look at her.
Did his true mother once have that brown hair? Or the smoothness of Beth's face?

He tried to picture his sister a few years older and wearing
a grand gown, with her hair done up in the fashion of ladies
and her face powdered. But it didn't seem to fit. Beth was his
sweet sister and his dead mother was another person. Someday,
when he was free and had made his way in the world, he would
return to England and visit the manor to see her grave.

"You seem to be deep into your mind, lad. Far away from
here in your thoughts. Or is it that you're only listening to your
stomach complain of the salt beef and Indian peas we had for
this sup?"

He turned as Lawrence dropped beside him to the ground.

"Aye," he said. "I was thinking about something that happened a long time ago. My stomach has yet to complain about the food we eat here. Not after suffering a sailor's fare at sea."

Lawrence chuckled. "Wormy bread and saltier beef. I suppose even this slop would seem good at that."

He filled a pipe from a leather pouch and offered the latter to Tom. "Have you a pipe, lad?"

Tom shook his head. "No, I've not yet taken the habit of tobacco. I don't own a pipe." He grinned. "I don't own two coppers to rub together, much less the cost of one of those." He indicated the long-stemmed clay pipe in Lawrence's hand with a bob of his head.

"That's no problem," the blond man said. "If you care to enjoy tobacco, I can make you a pipe easily enough without a cost to you."

"You can mold a pipe?"

Lawrence shook his head. "Not a pipe of clay, Tom. There's more than one way to do a thing if a man uses his eyes and his brain. I can make you one of dried corncob and a reed from the marsh. Tis a common thing in the colonies, at least among those who haven't the pretense of gentlemen."

He held his own pipe in his hand without attempting to light it. "This is different land that you're sitting on, Tom. Far different from England where a man keeps his station in life and never has an independent thought for himself. Most of these dullards we're surrounded by don't realize that fact yet and act accordingly, but men like myself, and you soon enough, recognize the truth of what I say. In the Americas, you don't wait for so and so to make such and such for you at a price in coin or trade. You make it for yourself, or if you can't because the materials or skill isn't at hand, you substitute something else."

Tom was silent for a moment. "It's a thing I hadn't thought on," he said slowly. "I like the sound of it, building or doing for yourself. Whatever you want."

He turned to look full at the man beside him, into the ruddy face with its deep-set eyes, so heavily lidded it was nigh impossible to tell the color. "You're a different man, Lawrence. You make me think. And that's a puzzle to me."

Lawrence chuckled. "Making you think, as man was intended to do, is a puzzle to you?"

Tom shook his head. "Nay. I meant that you yourself are

the puzzle. I would ask about you, but I don't want to pry into your business. A man's life is his own."

The blond man lay the pipe aside, still unlit. "It's also his business who he shares it with. Ask away, young Briggs. I'll answer any questions you have since I've nothing to hide."

Still he was hesitant. His long silence was broken by Lawrence. "Shy about the asking, eh? What you really want to know, Tom, is why a man like me is indentured. Isn't that it? Indentured, and in chains to boot?"

"Aye," Tom said. "I know you've an education, that you're learned. Those questions you asked Rodriguez the other day, they could be questions a man had heard from another I know, but the way you asked them I knew that wasn't the case with you. I knew you held the answers and more."

Lawrence nodded, and the smile was faint on his face. "You're quick, lad. Quick as any I've met. You've a good head on your young shoulders, it lacks only experience and a bit of book learning. Not many men without both those things would have understood what you just did."

"How did you learn to read?" Tom asked suddenly. "Were you already a man at the time?"

"No. I was taught as a child. Almost from the time I was a babe. My father was a schoolmaster, and by the time I was your age, I could read as well in Greek and Latin as in English. The classics were as much a part of my roaming as the quays of Boston. I found plenty of time to nose about in both."

"Classics?"

"Books, Tom. Books written by men dead hundreds of years before you were born. Their flesh long turned to dust, but their ideas living forever. Books, the printing of words on paper, the soul and essence of man's being, and the quality of doing that raises him above the animal."

The deep-set eyes probed Tom's own and though the evening was darkening around them, he felt their presence and restrained a shiver.

"A man who cannot read has fastened a shell around his mind, Tom," Lawrence went on in a low voice. "His thoughts are like a fowl who has had its wings clipped so that it cannot fly free of the fence that limits its movements. There are forever boundaries upon that man."

It was true. By the Heavens above him, it was true. The

blond man's words made him ache with pain from his head to his toes. He closed his eyes tightly.

Lawrence's voice dropped even lower with sympathy. "I can see the hurt in you, Tom. I suspected that case was true with you, you're one of those rare men who seek after knowledge and have the misfortune to be denied it. Am I correct?"

Tom nodded, not looking at him. "For as long as I can remember, I've wanted to read. But there was never the chance."

"There is now."

This time he did turn. Quickly. "What do you mean?"

Lawrence smiled. "I said my father was a schoolmaster, but I didn't say that I was one myself as well. I'm trained to take the minds of youth and round them into intelligence. Teaching one as quick as yours would be an easy task."

"You could teach me to read? You were a schoolmaster?" His words tumbled over each other in his eagerness. "I don't understand."

This time the blond man chuckled. "Back to your original question, is it? How could a man like myself become indentured. If I were so smart, why am I now owned body and soul by another?"

He cut the chuckle short and his face hardened. "Well, I tell you, my young friend, I am *not* owned body and soul by our arrogant Mr. Jones or any other man who called himself master to me. Physically, yes. I must do their labor though it galls me deeply. But my soul is my own. And so is my brain."

"Then how—"

"How did I become indentured? Through the perfidy of another, that's how." Lawrence was angry now, the low rage Tom had witnessed in him before came to surface. "A partnership between the two of us. A shipping venture that was to make us rich. It did him, but left me in debt when he disappeared. Debt that could only be paid with the selling of the only thing I had left—my body."

His angry stare held Tom for a long, painful moment before Lawrence shook free of it himself. "There will yet come the day when I break the chains that tie me here, Briggs. And when I do, I'll find that man and I will kill him."

"I'm sorry," Tom said. "Sorry that happened to you."

His words seemed to wipe the rage away. It shocked him that a man could change so rapidly. The smile burst again on

Lawrence's face, but Tom suspected it went no further; that beneath the smile there was not and never would be any real mirth.

"But then that's another thing, Tom," Lawrence said. "We were talking of your learning to read. I can teach you as I said."

"How?"

The blond man glanced around. The others were a distance from the two of them and almost obscured by the gathering shadows. Still he lowered his voice to a whisper. "As I said, a man who cannot read has chains on his mind. But a man who has chains on his body is equally in pain. The two of us can help each other."

"What can I do for you?" He was wary, but the promise was strong in its appeal. To learn to read . . . to gain knowledge and be the equal of those with the power. . . . That would be worth almost anything.

"More than you think," Lawrence told him, still in a whisper. "There's a cockle lying hidden no more than two hundred yards from where we sit. Jones, or someone else must have put it there some time ago. None of these dolts know it exists. It's a small boat, but big enough for the two of us."

He reached a large hand and gripped Tom's shoulder hard. "Easy enough for a man to manage himself in such a cockle even with chains on his legs. But afterwards, when we're free of these islands and moving through the forests, I'll need your strong arm until we find a means of striking these." He pointed with his other hand to the links between his legs.

"You want to escape again?" The thought was hard for Tom to embrace. "But if you're caught, it'll mean more years to your servitude. And you've—"

"More than aplenty!" Lawrence's harsh whisper cut him off. "Once you show these bastards with their small minds that you're a man, they want to hold you in bondage the longer. But it's because they're afraid of people like us, Tom. Afraid of those with the ability to read through them."

This was going too fast for him. The hand gripping his shoulder hurt. "I don't like being a servant," he said slowly. "But it's the law and I'm bound to it. When my time is served, I'll be free for the rest of my life. I have to honor the law."

"The law is made by those who would keep their foot on

the neck of others!" Lawrence hissed. "For those who are afraid! You and I, we don't have to be bound by their laws." The hand holding Tom's shoulder pulled him toward him until he could feel the other's breath. "Did you receive the money that was paid to place you in bondage?"

Tom pulled away. "Nay. It was paid to my fa—to the man who raised me."

"See? You owe them nothing. Not to that bastard, whoever he was, nor to Jones who bought your contract. You're a man, Tom Briggs. A man who should make his own destiny."

Slowly, reluctantly, Tom shook his head. "I can't go against it." He looked at the chains. "I've only a few years."

"Don't be a fool, lad," Lawrence said. "They'll find a way to extend it. Your time, I mean. I know of men in South Carolina and Virginia who are indentured for twenty, thirty years. Come with me now. I promise you, once we're free in the forests beyond their reach we can become rich in the fur and deerskin trade with the Indians. And when I'm through with you, you'll be able to read Homer in the language in which he wrote. I swear it."

"I cannot." He fought against the longing in himself. That Lawrence could do exactly what he promised in the learning he had no doubt. But he could not be an outlaw. Not and help his sister.

William Coar's voice rescued him from the intensity between the two of them. "Time for sleep," he called. "A hard day for us on the morrow."

Lawrence leaned close once more. "Think on it, Tom. You'll be a free man. A rich man. And," his voice was drawn and teasing, "you'll be of better education than any in the colony of Georgia."

A moment later he was up and gone.

Despite Coar's orders to go to his bed in the log house, Tom sat for a long time and stared out across the water he couldn't see. Lawrence could teach him the one thing he desired above all other things. But at what a cost! He couldn't do it. Lawrence was the devil himself, sent to tempt him!

He got up and walked swiftly to the log structure.

The blond man was smart enough to leave him alone for awhile, but it was no decision to make. The quarrel that had raged in his mind these last days had been only a losing action

against giving up the hope of learning. He'd never really thought
he could become an outlaw.

Now they were finally face to face. Even in the dim of the
moonlight, he could see the rage build quickly in the blond
man's face. "You're a fool, Tom Briggs!"

He met the other's eyes with his own. "I may be that," he
said. "But I'll be free one day, Lawrence. If you do this thing
again, you'll never be free."

"You damn young pup! Rodriguez was right. You *are* stupid! You think Jones gives a whit about such as you? You'll
work your back to breaking for him and when your time's up,
he'll free you right enough—free you with a kick in your
backside and not a farthing to go with it. You could be rich
with me!"

Tom shook his head doggedly. "Mr. Jones is a fair man.
At least he's been fair with me. I'm bound to him in my word
as well as in the law. I'll not go against that."

He turned to leave but Lawrence grasped his shirt with both
hands. "Then keep your stupidity," he hissed, his face inches
from Tom's own. "But you keep your silence as well or I'll
kill you. You hear?"

Tom gripped his wrists and tried to push him away. He was
strong in his hands, but the blond man was stronger. He couldn't
move him. He was afraid. But he couldn't let the fear rule him.
If he did, he would always be afraid.

"I'll not do either," he said, trying to keep his voice steady.
"You belong to Mr. Jones as well as myself. I'm bound to
protect his property."

"Damn you!" Lawrence flung him backwards suddenly and
pulled up his own shirt. For the second time in his life, Tom
was faced with a man holding a knife. He looked desperately
for something to defend himself with, a shovel, a tree limb,
anything. But if it were there, the darkness hid it.

Lawrence held his knife up and ready. "You'll sing no songs
with your throat slit, Pup."

He raised his own hands to defend himself.

"Hold! Drop the blade, Lawrence, or I'll put a ball through
your head."

Both of them spun to see, but the shadows hit the owner of
the voice for a moment. Then Noble Jones stepped from the

trees into the moonlight. He held a cocked flintlock pistol steady, its muzzle pointing at Lawrence.

The blond man cursed, a rapid flow of obscenity. But he had no choice and he knew it. He dropped the knife at his feet.

Jones was without hat or wig, but he was an imposing sight to a relieved Tom. He moved closer to them without causing the pistol to waver in the least. "So you would escape me again, eh, Lawrence? And once more you would rob me. Not of goods, but of this young man. I think it high time you be placed where you can't run away."

"Go to hell!"

Jones nodded. "Perhaps, in due time. But I'll likely find you there afore. You speak of stupidity, Lawrence, but for all your education, you're the most stupid."

He paused, then without removing his eyes from the blond man, he said, "Thomas, I'm pleased with you this night. I heard most of the conversation from where I stood. You give me cause, good cause, to believe I can trust you. I'll have more to say to you on that later when I've time to think about it. What did he promise you if you went with him, riches from the Indian trade?"

"Sir, he was going to teach me to read."

Jones shot him a quick glance. "And that tempted you?"

"No, sir. I was never that tempted."

Jones nodded slowly. "I see. Well, as I said, we'll have more to say to each other later. Meanwhile, suppose you fetch William Coar and the rest out here. And tell him to bring some rope. I think Lawrence will have a most uncomfortable night before our boat trip on the morrow."

"Yes, sir." He turned to do as he was told and ignored the glare from the standing blond man.

Nine

HESTER PULLAM WAS a tiny young woman with an elfin face and twin reeds for arms, but there was a surprising strength in her small body. Elizabeth could never get over this visual deception. She stood and watched as the other cranked the well rope handle with only one hand to raise a full bucket of water and talked at the same time.

"My brother would take a stick to my backside, Elizabeth, if he knew what I just told you. So don't you dare mention it around him. But it's the King's own truth, I vow it. Douglas talks of you all the time. Of how fair you are—and that's the truth, more's the envy for someone who looks like me—and what a grand way you have of walking. He says he likes the way you take a fair stride instead of a mincing step like most women do, but you do it and walk like a lady at the same time. My goodness, you should hear him talk about you sometimes."

Elizabeth smiled. "I should think your brother wouldn't say such things if I were around, Hester. But it's nice to know he thinks well of me. Not many in Savannah do, I suppose."

"But they do!" The other girl paused in her cranking the

handle. "Everyone likes you. I know they do. Mistress Long-footte—do you know her?—spoke to me just the other day in asking if I knew you well. And what kind of girl did I think you were."

"Surely," Elizabeth said. "That's what they all want to know. If I'm as bad as the Cawleys say I am."

"No, no. It's not true. Not true at all." In trying to talk to her, Hester was in danger of losing her grip on the handle and allowing the bucket to fall back into the well. Elizabeth stepped forward and grasped it herself.

"Nobody believes the Cawleys." Hester allowed herself to be helped, but continued to protest. "At least nobody I've talked to. They don't like them. Why, I heard Mistress Habersham say just the other day that Sarah Cawley owned a snake's hiss for a tongue. She said she'd never seen such a spiteful woman in her life."

Elizabeth nodded but continued to help crank the handle until the bucket was free of the well top and then reached to swing it to the side. When she had it seated on the rock lip, she motioned with her head for Hester to hold her own bucket close, then tilted the well bucket to fill it.

"You probably have more friends in this town than you can imagine," Hester told her as she sat her bucket aside and reached for Elizabeth's to move it close for the next draw. "I know when the two of us walk down the street together, many people turn to look. And I know they ain't looking at me."

Elizabeth dropped the well bucket back, allowing the rope to slide through her hand to slow its fall. She waited until it reached the bottom and tilted to fill before she spoke again. "Yes, they turn to look at me," she said slowly. "And I know why."

"You mean because Sarah Cawley tells everyone you're lazy and won't do your work?" Hester said. "Nobody believes that."

"No, that's not what I meant, Hester Pullam, and you know it. It's the other things she says. I'm not going to discuss it, but I know what some of the men in this town think about me, and about what their wives think as well. I've seen the way those women look down their noses at me."

"The men don't look down their noses." Hester was smiling at her, a tight little smile with a great deal of mischief in it.

Elizabeth didn't know whether to be angry or to laugh. She

decided on the latter. "Stop your teasing, Hester. You know perfectly well what I mean."

Hester's smile eased, but continued to hang around the corner of her mouth. "Yes, I do. More's the pity for me. The men look at you because you're beautiful, Elizabeth Briggs. Far prettier than any woman in Savannah. And their wives don't like that. At least some of them don't. But I still say you have many friends here."

"In spite of what their husbands are thinking?" Elizabeth asked.

"I told you most people don't like the Cawleys," Hester reassured her. "They don't believe the tales. They see you going about your work in all modesty. They'll believe their eyes, not something the Cawleys say."

"I wish I could be sure of that," Elizabeth said. "I really do."

"All right. Suppose I can prove it to you?" Hester moved Elizabeth's hand from the well crank and began to turn it again herself.

"And just how will you do that?"

The grin came back in full to Hester's face. "I'll tell you something Douglas said. But Lord, you've got to promise never to reveal it; if he found out I'd told you, he'd thrash me within an inch of my life."

"Good Heavens. What in the world could he have said?"

Hester stopped cranking and leaned over the handle conspiringly although the two of them were quite alone in the square, not another soul in sight. "He said," she whispered, "that only a fool would believe that a pretty lass such as yourself would want as foul and fat a body as Mr. Cawley has." She paused and then nodded in emphasis. "He says that you could have any man in Savannah for the asking."

Elizabeth turned scarlet. "How could he talk like that about me!"

Hester hadn't expected her reaction and stared at her in alarm. "I thought you'd be pleased to hear it, Elizabeth! Oh, Lordy, I'm sorry!"

The shock was gone as quickly as it had come, and she lowered her eyes. "That's what I mean, Hester. Everyone talks about me as if I were a fallen woman and only interested in— you know, that sort of thing."

She raised her head and looked at her friend directly. "But I never have in my entire life. I swear it."

Hester was driven to tears. "I know you haven't, Elizabeth. And Douglas knows it—oh I shouldn't have told you what he said! I just wanted you to know what he thought!"

"Your brother is a good man," Elizabeth told her. "Stop crying. There's no harm done. I still admire Douglas Pullam; he's taken on a fair burden to keep you and Tod since your parents died. I know he meant well when he spoke of me. But don't you see, Hester, that's all anyone talks about when they mention my name. And the more dirt that's blown on a hanging wash, the more that will stick to it. One of these days, everyone in Savannah will believe I'm . . ." She paused and took a deep breath, "a whore."

Hester shook her head vigorously. "No they won't. I know Douglas shouldn't have said that to me, but he didn't mean it to be foul. He's crude sometimes and he lacks in manners, but that's because he's had to work so hard ever since he was ten years old. He hasn't had time to learn how to speak."

She clutched Elizabeth's arm. "What I really meant to tell you when I started talking about him was that he spoke of wishing he had the money to buy your freedom. If he had, he said he'd ask you to marry him quick enough." Her look was pleading. "Now does that sound like a man who thinks bad of you?"

She sighed. "No, I suppose not. I'm sorry, Hester. I guess I feel too sorry for myself at times. I keep telling myself not to do it, but I forget. Your brother was nice to say such a thing."

"Would you?" Hester asked quickly. "Marry Douglas, I mean, if it could be done?"

Elizabeth shook her head. "No. Not that I don't respect him, but I've thought much about marrying, Hester. I hope to do so when I'm free of indenture, but it's got to be a man I love truly. Perhaps I'll never find him, I don't know. But I intend to try."

She paused for a moment, then went on slowly, as much to herself as to the girl standing beside her. "I may not even recognize love, might not ever know what it is. I made a terrible mistake in thinking I'd found it when I was on the ship coming here, and I was wrong—but I intend to try."

Hester patted her arm. "I told Douglas I thought that would be the way you'd be. I said you wouldn't marry a man for comfort or security as many do here. That you'd want more from a man than that."

She turned and began to crank the well rope again. "But I'll confess I do wish you liked Douglas. I think we'd make fine sisters-in-law. But if it's not the case, so be it. At least then I can tell you the other thing I had in mind."

"What was that?"

"You know I said Mistress Longfootte asked about you?" Hester waited until she got a curious nod from Elizabeth before she went on. "Well, I suspect she had more in mind than wondering for herself. She and Mr. Longfootte think Jason Welburn's more their son than their indenture. I really think she was asking on his behalf."

Elizabeth's heart jumped, but she tried not to show her interest. It had been a month or so after her arrival in Savannah before she'd met him, days in which she'd often seen him from a distance. If she had met him sooner she'd been too embarrassed to speak anyway. After practically throwing herself in front of him that first day on the square, she wouldn't have been able to face him.

But she had spoken to him; actually, she'd had no choice in the matter. Walking home from the store, she'd been forced to stop when he stepped out of nowhere to say hello. But as soon as she'd replied, he'd touched that forelock of hair again and walked on his way to leave her standing alone.

"Well? What do you think of that?" Hester brought her back to the present.

"What should I think of it?" She tried to make the question casual. "He's just another man."

"Just another man." Hester was her old self again and mimicked her. "Except that you forget that not long after you and I became friends, you asked me everything in the world about him. Who he was, if he were indentured, how long had he been in Savannah, all that sort of thing. You've a short memory, Elizabeth Briggs."

She shook her head. "I was merely curious at the time. He'd spoken to me and I wondered who he was. It meant nothing."

Hester had the well bucket to the top and the two of them paused to pour its contents into Elizabeth's bucket. She was sorry they had, the conversation had taken an interesting turn and she wanted to hear more about it. But Hester would tease her again if she asked questions, and she was late already. Sarah Cawley would be in a tiff—not that she wasn't most of the time anyway, but Elizabeth tried to do as much as possible to keep from giving her cause.

"I've got to go," she told Hester. "I'm late."

"You don't want to know if Jason Welburn asked Mistress Longfootte about you?" Hester wanted to know, the grin firmly in place once more.

"If I did or if I didn't, Hester Pullam, I'm quite sure you'll tell me anyway." She picked up her bucket. "But you'll have to do it later. Goodbye."

"You're a spoilsport," Hester told her. "Here I've news that any sensible maid would want to know, news about a handsome young man who just might have his cap set for her, and you want to run off and not hear it. I don't believe it."

"Goodbye, Hester." She set off resolutely on her way.

Sarah Cawley was abed when she returned to the house. Her mistress had taken the habit of lying down through most of the afternoon in the last few weeks when there were just the two of them at home. The boys were packed off to study their lessons with a half dozen other children under Martin Milgreen, an anemic looking young man whom Elizabeth thought should wash his shirt, and Mr. Cawley was usually off on his business which consisted mostly of lamenting loudly to any in the colony who would listen that he was months here and still didn't have his land surveyed. Until his grant was laid out, he could do very little else.

This gave Sarah Cawley plenty of time to indulge in her two favorite pastimes: complaining of how sick she was and how she should have never left England in the first place, and scolding Elizabeth. She did the latter by constantly calling her to appear in the bedroom, voicing a complaint loudly and then dismissing her abruptly. Only to repeat the process a few minutes later. The interruptions made it difficult for Elizabeth to get her work done, much less give thought to Hester's news of Jason Welburn.

She managed the latter only after her mistress fell asleep and she sat by the hearth to shell the peas for the evening meal. He was handsome, she decided, in a boyish way, with a chin not really square enough for his long forehead. It tended to point a bit and cause a half-moon wrinkle in the skin between it and his curved mouth. But his mouth was nice. He had the kind of mouth that looked as if it would laugh at a moment's notice. But then, she'd yet to see him laugh.

His eyes were deep and clear, brown as her own. And when he'd spoken to her that day, he'd looked directly into her eyes, not shifting away awkwardly as so many did. His gaze said I'm an honest man and need not turn away from anyone.

Fie! If you're such an honest man, Jason Welburn, why didn't you say your name to me that day and ask of mine? Why do you have to go sneaking about asking others. And why does your mistress want to know if I'm a decent girl? Is she afraid I'll sully this young indenture she thinks of as her own son?

Fie indeed! Who am I to care what Jason Welburn asks about me or who he gets to do the asking? He's probably just like the others, believing the stories about me and hoping to talk me into a quick walk into the bushes as that poor widow Hartwell did with one of General Oglethorpe's soldiers. And paid for it with the skin of her bare back when the Magistrates had her whipped in the public square.

But then why was she getting so angry? She didn't even *know* Jason Welburn. He could well be a kind and gentle man, one with no wrong thought in his head. *He also could be a man who doesn't care a fig for one Elizabeth Briggs!*

Oh how she hated that name. If only there was a way for her to change it now, before she was free. "Langlee." She said it aloud. "Elizabeth Langlee is my name, good sir. And how do you do?"

The peas were finished. She threw the pods into the ashes and crossed the room to soak them in a pot, noticing as she did that the beer hogshead was missing. Mr. Cawley probably had taken it with him to be refilled.

Anyhow, she wasn't being fair to Jason Welburn. Hester said he was one of the hardest workers in the colony, a rare trait for an indenture. Perhaps that was why the Longfoottes favored him so. Hard work was certainly what it took if a man were to be successful in this Georgia colony. He just might go far.

She got out the cabbage leaves and began to scrub them in another pot to clean away the dirt. What would it be like to live on a farm with a man such as Jason Welburn who could raise fine crops? To be mistress of her own house?

She stopped and stared at the wall behind the table. It wouldn't have to be a large house, not the size of this one, for she'd have no indentures to share it with and her children would sleep in the same—Good Heavens! What in the world was she thinking?

Ten

TOMOCHICHI, MICO OF the Yamacraws, held influence in the Creek nations well beyond the small size of his own tribe. He was related to many great Creeks: Coweta, Kasihta, Cheehaw, Palachocolas, Oconas, all of these he could call his blood. His brother was King of the Etiahitas, and King Oueekachumpa, the White King, was his cousin. Fierce in warfare, Tomochichi could have been one of the most powerful had he so chosen.

But Tomochichi was a philosopher, a dreamer of dreams. As his years advanced, he led a small group of followers away from the other Creeks and settled them on Yamacraw Bluff near the mouth of the Savannah river to live peacefully and quietly, away from the struggles of war. It had been there, through the influence of Mary Musgrove, Indian princess and wife of the trader, John Musgrove, Tomochichi met and became the close friend of James Oglethorpe. He was already ninety years old when they met.

Like most Creeks, Tomochichi held an intense hatred for the Spanish who had invaded his lands three hundred years before. Advancing with their sword and cross, claiming to teach their new religion of mercy and forgiveness on the one hand, but showing unyielding cruelty and death on the other, they had made eternal enemies of the Creeks. Also, along with the other Micos, Tomochichi had been surprised and pleased to discover that the English were more interested in trade with the Indians than in conquering them to make them slaves. Where he differed with the other leaders was in his wise understanding that the Creek way of life was doomed. No matter whether it be for trade or conquest, the white man's way would eventually overcome that of the red man. The Indian must adapt to those ways or perish.

With this in mind, Tomochichi had used his influence to persuade any Creek who would listen to learn the ways of the English, to study their language and learn their amazing manner of communicating with little marks upon white paper. Far too few had listened, but he sat now with one who had, a young man, tall and straight, strong of limb and clear of eye, Como-tan, son of Chekilli and grand nephew of Tomochichi. This man had listened and learned from the old Mico, and now could meet the white men on their own terms. As always, the sight of him was a pleasure to Tomochichi.

The Mico's house consisted of three rooms built of clay and covered with planks. One room was kept locked always, for in it were his two treasures, the picture of the lion which the Trustees had sent him after his trip to England, and the picture of James Oglethorpe, his very good friend. Only those whom Tomochichi held in the highest regard were allowed to share this room with him.

Como-tan was one of these, and the young man sat attentively on a low stool covered with deerskin and listened as Tomochichi spoke, his words liquid in the language of their ancestors.

"Soon there will be a great battle between the English and the hated ones to the south," he said. "James Oglethorpe is expecting this. Only two mornings ago, he came from the place called Frederica to see me. Then he told me this battle would come."

Como-tan nodded, but remained respectfully silent.

The old Mico rested his eyes for a moment in the pleasure of regarding his nephew's finely chiseled features, then brought himself back reluctantly. "Many of our people will come to the aid of James Oglethorpe, but that will not be enough. The brown ones will bring large ships, filled with many warriors.

Enough, I think, to cover the ground as swarming ants. Only if enough white warriors come from South Carolina with their cannon, will my friend be able to defeat his enemies."

Again he received a nod from his nephew.

"That is why I have asked you to come here to talk," the Mico went on. "In your work for the trade between the Creek nation and the South Carolinians, you have come to know them well. Will they send these men to aid my friend?"

This time, slowly and reluctantly, Como-tan shook his head. "I do not feel it to be so, Great Uncle," he said. "Those in that colony, the ones in power, have come to hard feelings against your friend, James Oglethorpe. It is true they want to see this colony survive, but only because it serves as a wall between them and the Spanish. But they do not wish it to become strong in trade, for then it will take away from them. Also they do not like the fact that your friend has been made a general and placed in command over all the English, both here and in South Carolina. They would like to see him defeated because of this."

The words angered Tomochichi. "They are fools! Do they not see what will happen if James Oglethorpe is defeated? The brown ones will destroy this colony, kill or make slaves of all and come to live in this land. Then where will their trade and protection be?"

Como-tan nodded. "Wisdom is often overcome by jealousy, Great Uncle. There are few men who can look beyond it."

"They must be changed in their minds. How can this be done?"

"I am on my way there now, Great Uncle. My influence goes little beyond the traders, but I will do what I can. If I speak of the loss of trade, some one of them will go to their governor. How soon do you believe this battle will come?"

Tomochichi shook his head. "Soon, I fear. Perhaps this season."

"Then perhaps it would be best if Tomochichi led his people to safety deep in the forests. If the others fail to help your friend, all are doomed here as you say. There is no need for you to die with the whites here."

Tomochichi stared long at his nephew, then released a long sigh. "I fear for my people, but I can no longer lead them for my own days are numbered. No more than a few are left. I grow more tired with the setting of each sun. Very soon I will depart."

He took another deep breath. "My people have come to trust James Oglethorpe and look to him to protect them. Their fate will be the same as the English in Georgia."

"Then the Spanish must be defeated," Como-tan said. "I will do all that I can."

There was no more to be said. Senouki, the wife of Tom-ochichi brought roast pork, fowl, pancakes and tea, but Como-tan could see that his uncle ate little and thought to himself that this might well be the last time he would see him alive. It was a sad thing, but it was the way of all life and regret would not change it. All that he could do was to try his best to save his uncle's people.

An ebullient Thermous Cawley insisted both his ailing wife and his servant girl accompany him on an inspection of his new farming land. Two days before, the surveyor, Noble Jones, had laid it out for him at last. Now, the ex-peruke maker was convinced he was halfway to his fortune. He was so excited, he fairly danced as they walked the three miles from Savannah to his land. When the three of them reached the site and he was able to look over his very own land, his glee increased. It was not as heavily wooded as he had feared. In fact, the pines were for the most part short and spindly.

"Look, look!" he told Sarah, ignoring the fact that she held her side with both hands and grimaced with pain. "Isn't it beautiful? Why, in a few days we can have a good part of those trees cut down and begin planting the mulberrys from the Trustee Garden."

His wife didn't answer, but he hardly noticed. "They say I must plant at least one hundred mulberry trees for each ten acres, but I'll plant a hundred times that! Let those other fools plant their corn and tobacco and such nonsense. I intend to plant nothing but mulberry trees! Silk is where the money lies. In a few years I'll have hundreds of thousands of silkworms feeding on those trees and spinning their silk threads for me."

He took a couple of skipping steps across the ground, kicking at the pine needles as he went. "Come, Sarah! I want to walk over its entirety!"

"Mr. Cawley, please." Her voice forced him to stop and look at her. "I'm not well," she said. "Not well at all. And it was such a distance from town. I shouldn't have come!"

"All right," he said, making his voice as reasonable as

possible. "Perhaps you'd better sit down for a while. You can rest until I'm through. Elizabeth, make her a place. Gather some of these needles to make the ground soft for her."

"Yes sir." The girl did as she was told and he watched her, pleased that he'd not lost his temper. It would be better at any rate to look over his land without his whining wife along to spoil it. And if it looked as if he showed some concern for her well-being, perhaps she'd keep her damn mouth shut on the way back.

Elizabeth chose wisely, piling a soft blanket of pine needles in a small depression at the base of a tree where Sarah could lean back. He waited until she had helped her down on the bed and then waved a hand toward her. "You come with me, Elizabeth."

This brought an immediate protest from his wife. "She must stay here! I feel faint, husband. Suppose I go into a swoon?"

"I need the girl with me to give her instructions," he said as patiently as he could. "She's going to have to help me plant the trees."

Sarah looked at him in horror. "Help here? But what about the work in the house? I can't do any of that now. My illness—"

"Damn your infernal illness!" he shouted, losing his temper at last. "Don't you understand this work comes first, woman? We've been months waiting already, spending our savings and growing poorer by the day. It'll be months yet before we can start making a profit from silk. There's no time to waste!"

"But I can't do the cooking. The cleaning. I—"

"Should have stayed in England where you could constantly whine to your relatives," he finished for her. "I know!"

He took a deep breath. He was doing what he didn't want to do—lose his temper and look the fool in front of the girl. "Elizabeth will work in the fields during the day, but she'll have time to prepare our supper when she returns. I'll see to it. The rest of her chores she can do when there's time. But this work *must* come first. When the silk is sold, I'll be able to afford a dozen servants for you, don't you see that?"

The change in his voice was enough to mollify her. Sarah leaned back against the tree and rested her hands in her lap limply. "Very well, husband. I suppose you're right. But I do feel I might swoon at any time."

"You'll be fine," he told her. "We'll not be far away. Come, Elizabeth."

He turned and walked away quickly to prevent her from saying more and was pleased to see the servant girl followed directly on his heels.

Jones had given him instructions as to what to look for and he found the stakes easily that laid out the boundaries of his property. It wasn't square, as he'd expected, but held a long and a short side, giving one end of it a point. That would make the trees he intended to plant less, regular and more crowded at that end. He stood and frowned as he looked at the last stake.

Too, the land he saw didn't seem to make up the great size he had fixed in his mind. Was it possible that fool Jones had given him less than he was allotted? He had expected to walk for hours to cover his property and here he was at the back side of it and hardly out of sight of Sarah. He must find a way to check it somehow. He'd heard that there were other surveyors in the colony, not officially designated by the Trustees of course, but if he could prove Jones had made an error, he could be forced to change his plat. And he had heard that Jones wasn't in good favor with the Trustees at any rate. With any luck, he could help bring that man down to size.

The girl was standing a few feet from him, gazing about her with a great deal of interest it seemed to him. She appeared very relaxed and at ease with herself. Thermous was aware of his own breath coming heavily from his effort in moving over the rough ground, although he prided himself on the fact that he'd lost weight since he arrived in the colony.

She naturally showed no signs of strain. Youth. She owned a supple body, young enough to run, not walk, across these acres. How long had it been since he was that young?

"Well, what do you think of it?" He was suddenly feeling very good.

His question surprised her; he could see it in the quick way she glanced at him. "It's fine, sir," she said.

"Oh no." He raised a finger to admonish her, and gave her a smile at the same time. "You can be truthful with me, Elizabeth. I know I'm your master but today I'm in a fine mood. I want you to treat me as a friend. A good friend."

He watched her eyes narrow and increased his smile. "I also know you grew up in the countryside and must have learned how to raise crops. Since I did not, I may well have to depend on your knowledge at first. To learn from you as it were. So you see, you must be truthful."

"Yes, sir."

She still seemed unsure of herself so he stepped forward and patted her on the shoulder. "That's the way. Now tell me what you think of the land."

He would have left his hand in place, but she bent quickly from under it and brushed back some of the pine needles. He watched curiously as she swept the ground clean with her hands and then used her fingers to dig a small pile of soil. She gathered the pile into her hands and stood up again to look at it.

He stepped near to look himself. "What is it?"

She gave him a cautious look. "I wanted to see the dirt, sir," she said slowly. Much too slowly, he thought. "It's true I grew up with a man who made his living from the soil, but I only know what I heard him speak of it. That, and what my brother would tell me."

His impatience was growing. "I understand that, Elizabeth. But you do know something, I can tell it. What of this soil?"

The girl looked down at her hands, shifted the dirt into one palm and poked at it with the finger of her other hand. The dirt moved easily. Cawley watched, fascinated, as she raised her palm even with her lips and blew gently. Her action raised a small brown cloud and she continued to blow until her hand was bare.

Her silence drove him mad. "Well?"

"Perhaps I'm wrong, sir. I really don't know that much about the soil."

"What in the blazes do you mean? Wrong? What about?" He had a sudden sinking in the pit of his stomach.

She gave him a wary look. "Mr. Cawley, this soil seems most dry to me. I do know that you need moisture to grow crops. The ground where I lived contained a great deal, sometimes too much my brother told me. But this contains almost none."

He sighed with relief. "Of course, you foolish girl! Exactly! This soil *is* dry. I was aware of that already. More's the reason the others are fools to try to plant crops in it. But I'm not planting crops, don't you see? I'm planting *trees*. Mulberry trees. Look around you, Elizabeth. What do you see?"

She nodded, but the wary look stayed in place. "Trees, sir."

He gloated in satisfaction. "Precisely! This soil grows trees very well. It should be just right for my mulberries."

"But these are pines, Mr. Cawley. And they aren't very big."

He refused to be deterred. "Have you seen the mulberry trees at the Trustee Garden? Of course you haven't! Well, let me tell you, they aren't large either. Very small and delicate. Half as large as some of these."

"But will they grow—" she cut herself off. "I'm sure you're right."

He patted her shoulder again until she moved away. "Of course I'm right, Elizabeth. You'll soon see."

A brown forest creature chose that moment to dart at their feet and startled her into a gasp of surprise. It made his own heart leap but he quickly settled it down. A creature that size couldn't be dangerous, and besides, it had already run a dozen yards away from where they stood before it stopped again.

He placed an arm around her shoulders to draw her close to him. "Stand still," he said. "There may be more of them."

She did as she was told and he was highly conscious of the pressure of her body against his side. He tightened his grip to increase the feeling. "We'll wait a moment to see," he said.

She attempted to pull away and he was forced to place a hand on her stomach to hold her still. "Wait, Elizabeth. If there are a lot of them, we might startle them into an attack."

Her voice was harder than he'd ever heard. "I don't think so, Mr. Cawley. That creature doesn't look dangerous; it looks frightened."

"But we don't know that." He increased the pressure in his arm, aware that she was struggling to free herself without appearing to do so. The movement of the muscles of her stomach under his hand caused a shiver through his thighs.

"Please let me go," she said in a tight voice.

He had no choice. Reluctantly he released her, loosening his arm around her shoulders first and only losing the touch of her stomach when she broke completely away. The memory of that touch clouded his mind. He felt very warm toward her.

"Elizabeth, Elizabeth." His own voice was soothing to his ear. "You mustn't fear me, child. I'm not a difficult man. Not at all."

She was watching him closely. Good.

"I understand life must seem hard to you in your circumstances. Terribly difficult for a young woman of your perception."

He raised a hand. *Move it slowly. Don't frighten her.*

"But I can make it easier, you see. Much, much easier."

She hadn't moved far—he was pleased with that—and she was listening. He lowered his voice.

"We must become friends, Elizabeth." A haze had settled delightfully over his vision. She was floating in front of his eyes—a beautiful, delicate nymph with soft, young flesh. "We can help each other."

Without conscious effort he moved forward. "Don't you see that, Elizabeth? I can make life so much better for you. And you could . . . as you see, Mistress Cawley is ill. Elizabeth, a man needs—"

"No!"

The word was sharp and hurled directly into his face. It hit with the force of winter water. The pleasure in his limbs fled with the shock.

He couldn't gather himself. "I don't—"

She cut him off. "I said *No!* Never! You're my master, but you don't *own* me!"

What did she mean? He was Thermous Cawley! Not to be spoken to like this by a servant! It was difficult to find words. "Now listen, girl. You misunderstand—"

"I understand full well!" Her small fists were clenched at her sides. "I know what you want. But you'll never have it from me. I'll *never* share your bed!"

Rage choked him. It burned his brain. "You think . . . you believe I . . . you stupid girl! Do you think that I, Thermous Cawley, would stoop so low? That I would break my Christian vows of marriage made before the *Lord?* You're evil, girl! A temptress who throws herself at an honest man and then mocks him when he refuses her! You accuse *me?*"

"No!" She grasped her head and shook it violently, backing away from him at the same time. "You won't *do* that again! I won't let you! You made it my fault before, but it wasn't! You won't shame me again!"

His control was gone. He stepped forward and slapped her across the face, sending her full length on the ground. But she immediately scrambled up again.

"Beat me!" She screamed the words. "But you won't *have* me! You can't! I won't *let* you!"

He wanted to strike her again. Wanted it badly. But she was younger than he, she could run away. Dodge. He'd only appear foolish. A foolish, fat man...

He forced himself to be still. But he allowed the rage full rein in his words. "I shall beat you, girl. I'll beat you often until you learn respect for your betters."

He was forced to take a deep breath. "You'll learn that I'm a Christian man and in no way interested in your harlot's body! If you ever mention that again to me, or to anyone, I'll charge you before the Magistrates and have you whipped naked in the public square. Do you *understand?*"

But she had suddenly stopped being frightened. She returned his stare. And when she answered, it wasn't a frightened plea as he expected. Her words chilled him and drove away his own anger in a puff.

"If you do that, Mr. Cawley," she said. "My brother will kill you. I know he will."

He could only stare as she walked away.

Eleven

THE SPRING SUN was warm but friendly overhead; a fresh young sun, friskily playing hide and seek with her from behind conspiring small but fluffy clouds. A spring breeze was on her side however, and quickly whisked away even the tiniest drop of perspiration the teasing sun managed to bring out as Elizabeth worked. It was a good day to be outside and working. A better day since she was alone. After several days of trying, Thermous Cawley had managed to hire two sawyers to cut down the pines on his land. Since the area she was in was already clear, he left her there to plant his mulberry trees while staying with the men himself to see that they didn't rob him of any of the time he paid them. All of them were far enough away that she couldn't see them and only occasionally, with the help of the breeze, could she hear one of them shout.

She pulled the hand cart along behind her, carefully stepping off the distances between planting with wide strides as Cawley had told her. The measurement correct, she would stop and take the shovel to dig in the hard ground until she had a hole halfway up to her knee and twice as wide. Then she would kneel to mix a little of the dry dirt with water from her bucket until she had a muddy bottom in the hole. With that right, she would carefully place one of the young white mulberry trees in the hole and even more carefully push the rest of the dirt in around it. Lastly, she would take a little more of the water and pour it gently around the tree to both wet and pack the soil.

She straightened from the last planting and looked at her bucket. It was nearly empty and she debated with herself whether to try to stretch it to plant one more tree or to stop and walk the quarter mile it took to fetch some more from the low creek. She decided the water wouldn't stretch.

It wasn't a bad walk, but coming back the bucket would be heavy and it would be necessary to switch it constantly from one hand to the other since this one was much larger than the one she used to fetch water to the house in Savannah. Perhaps she would wait and rest a moment before starting for the creek, it would be pleasant to just stand and listen to the quiet of the morning.

The white mulberry trees stretched out prettily behind her, for all the world like short rounded green soldiers lined up in a row. They were nice trees, with bright green heart shaped leaves. She didn't yet understand what they had to do with the silkworms, that is, exactly how the worms got on them, but she hoped the action wouldn't destroy the trees.

But then, unless she was mistaken, these poor young trees would be destroyed long before any worms got to them. It was too hard to believe that anything but the hardy pines could live in this soil. However, that wasn't her worry. Except . . . suppose she were right and all the trees died? Then Mr. Cawley would be in trouble. She'd heard him complain to his wife that already their funds were running low with the delay getting this farm started. If his crop of silk failed, he might be out of funds entirely and could possibly sell her contract to buy food for his family. She might even be sold to a family as nice as the Longfoottes. That lady had stopped her on the street and chatted with her as if she were as good as anyone else. But then she was being uncharitable. It was wicked for her to hope for misfortune for anyone, even Thermous and Sarah Cawley. Anyhow, she'd dawdled long enough. It was time to go and fetch the water. She picked up the bucket and began to walk.

The creek lay between her own master's property and someone else's. She strolled along side until she could find a deep enough spot to lower her bucket.

The sun had grown hot, and impulsively, she reached up to remove her cap and allow her hair to fall free. She shook her head enjoying her new found freedom.

"Very nice." The voice startled her so, coming as it did from nowhere, she nearly stepped into the water.

No one! She spun all the way around.

"I've wondered many a time why women wear their hair all bunched up under those caps. Seems like it would be powerfully hot."

This time she found him. He was across the creek from her and sitting with his back against a pine. It was the shade of the tree blending him into its shadow that had kept him hidden.

It made her angry. "Jason Welburn! You've no right to spy on a person that way!"

He rose, shoving himself forward with one hand and standing erect in one continuous movement. "You call it spying? I was sitting here, tending to my own business, when you walked up. I paid you a compliment, but instead of receiving a thank you, I'm accused of spying. Now that's unfair."

She couldn't decide on a reply and stood watching as he waded the creek, unmindful of it wetting his shoes.

He stopped beside her. "And how, may I ask, did you know my name? I'd begun to think that after that day you came to Savannah and stepped out to look me over, you'd decided I wasn't worth knowing."

"I did no such thing," she said.

"You didn't decide I wasn't worth knowing? Well now, I'm happy for that."

She gathered her wits quickly. He wasn't smiling, but there was a humorous glint to his eye as he regarded her. Well, she would not be teased.

She tossed her head. "I did not step out to look at you or any other that day. I was merely bored with the talk and wanted to look at the town. It was my first day, you know."

He nodded, thrusting both hands in his wide pockets and leaning back. His shirt, she noticed, was open down to his waist, showing the smoothness of his chest.

"Yes I know, Mistress Elizabeth Briggs," he said. "And to tell the truth about it, I've given little thought to anything else since that day. I was sorry the next time I saw you and you were wearing your cap. But even then you were the most beautiful girl I've seen. Until now, when you took it off again."

She refused to be embarrassed. "And how do you know my name?" she asked in the same tone he'd used.

The glint in his eye increased, but he still didn't smile. "I asked immediately, of course," he said. "As soon as I got a chance to talk to one of the ladies who came over on the ship with you, I asked who that beautiful young creature might be."

"You did no such thing. I'll not listen to such nonsense."

He placed a hand on his chest and swung the other wide in a gesture. "I swear. Unfortunately, that poor woman thought I had gone quite mad in the heat and refused to answer me. Have you noticed that it gets very hot in Savannah?"

He was teasing her. The look in his eye, the tone of his voice, everything about him told her he was. But he still didn't smile.

"I believe I've noticed," she said. "Do you ever smile?"

"Often. I've a lot to be happy about."

"Then why are you not smiling now? Since I know full well you're teasing me."

He was taller than she was by half a head, but leaned over to bring his face on a level with hers. "I will if you will," he said. And pulled down the corners of his mouth.

It was too much. She laughed in spite of herself at his droll face and he immediately gave a whoop. *"Aieee!* She can do it! I knew she could do it!"

He pranced around her like an Indian, kicking his heels together and clapping his hands, making her turn to follow him until she was dizzy.

"Stop it," she laughed. "Stop it! You *are* daft!"

He stopped in front of her and this time the grin was wide on his young face. "I couldn't smile before, Elizabeth Briggs, because you wouldn't. I said to myself, Jason, if that charming creature has a mysterious disease that allows her to own no more than a solemn face, it would be a fair shame for you to smile at her. Much as you would like to."

She laughed again. "Do you always make up such tall tales? You didn't think any such thing."

He shrugged. "Why was there reason for me not to think it? You absolutely refused to smile at me. Everytime I saw you, you seemed bent on going in another direction so you wouldn't have to pass me by. And when I went to great effort and plans to place myself where you would have to look at me, all I got for my trouble was a wicked frown."

"I didn't frown."

"Oh but you did! It was a definite frown, a terrible frown. I felt as if a knife had been driven into my poor heart."

She shook her head and laughed again. "Poor, poor fellow. But I really didn't frown; I remember. You surprised me, that's all. If you hadn't gone rushing off as you did, I would have recovered."

"And then you would have smiled at me?"

"Of course."

He clapped a hand to his head in mock despair. "Fool that I was! Lovesick, stupid fool!"

"Now stop that," she said, and felt her own smile leave her face. "That isn't funny."

The smile remained on his lips, but it was a different expression, a small twist that hung at the corner of his mouth as he looked at her. "No," he said gently, "it isn't funny. But it is true, Elizabeth Briggs. I am in love with you. I think I've been in love with you every hour since that day I first saw you—a beautiful girl who looked so free and graceful when all the others were bound up in caps and aprons."

She stared at him and he nodded slowly. "Yes, now that I look at you, I know it's true. I'm very much in love with you."

His words were a shock, she knew he wasn't teasing her. A surge of warmth made her want to reach out and touch his face with her hand, but a numbing fear held her back. She didn't want to be hurt again.

"You don't know me." It was difficult to get the words out. "We've not met . . . nor even spoke . . ."

She wished he would look away. His eyes, locked into hers, made her feel she was spinning.

"I knew all I needed to know," he said quietly. "All except to speak to you and hear you speak in return. I'm going to marry you, Elizabeth Briggs. You may as well make up your mind to that. There can be no other way about it."

She had to force her eyes away from his. To make her head turn from the spell he was casting. It was difficult to speak. "I would think to have something to say about that myself," she managed at last, though she could hardly hear the words herself.

"Aye." He moved very close to her, but still did not touch her. She could feel his presence almost overwhelming her.

"You'll have something to say about it, Elizabeth. I know you've a mind of your own. But I intend to spend my time until I'm free of indenture in giving you reason to set that mind of yours to wanting to marry me."

He dropped into silence for a long time. Still, he didn't move and she was afraid to look at him. Afraid of what she might see in his brown eyes.

"I'm a man who knows what he wants, Elizabeth. A man who's willing to work hard for it. I thought the greatest thing I wanted in this life was land to work for myself, and I still want that. But even more I want you. For the rest of my life."

He seemed to be waiting for her to speak, but she didn't know what to say. Didn't know what she *wanted* to say. This had come on so quickly. A moment ago she was scolding him for surprising her. What had happened?

His voice, slow and soothing, rescued her. "We'll speak no more of it for now, Elizabeth Briggs. But I must ask that you give it some thought. Will you from time to time say to yourself, would I not like to marry that Jason Welburn? A man who will work his heart out to make me happy? A man who will do his best to bring me laughter in all my days as well as care for me forever?"

His words were a heady wine. But she had drunk that wine before. She stood silent, not daring to look at him.

"Will you give it thought, Elizabeth?"

She had to answer. "I will give it thought. I promise no more than that."

"Good." His voice was magic. "Then I do believe the lady was planting trees this morn. And carrying water for them as well. May this strong-backed lout be of assistance?"

She drew a long, deep breath and turned to face him. It was as if she had shaken off a net that enclosed her, and she found herself able to match his tone. "Aye, sir. If the lout will be so willing to aid this poor lady. But don't you have chores of your own to do?"

He grinned. "None. I came out early this morning, before the dawn, in fact, and finished. I've time now to spare."

A sudden suspicion crossed her mind. "You knew I was here, didn't you? You weren't under that tree by accident?"

"Of course not. I was delighted to discover that your Mr. Cawley had land but a short distance from Mr. Longfootte's, even more so to find out he was bringing you out here. More's the chance, I say to myself, the beautiful Mistress Briggs might be found alone for once."

She placed her hands on her hips. "And how did you know I'd come to this creek?"

Jason swept low in a mock bow. "Easily enough, m'lady. Tis the only one about. And besides, I sat on the top of that little rise yonder and watched you work. When you started for the creek, I merely made sure to place myself at your stopping."

"Jason Welburn! You *were* spying on me!"

"Aye." He picked up her bucket. "So we're back to that, are we?"

She was forced to move too as he started off. "What do you mean?"

He slowed only a pace for her to catch up. "Don't you remember? That was what you accused me of when I first spoke."

She nodded and smiled. "And I was right."

"Absolutely. But aren't you glad I was?"

She didn't answer. She wasn't going to tell him a thing like that. Even if it were true.

The weeks following her meeting with Jason Welburn went swiftly. One day followed on the heels of the other and she enjoyed meeting each. Time has wings when you're happy, she told herself, it's only burdensome when you're miserable.

And she was happy, as happy as she could ever remember being in her entire life. Even Sarah Cawley's shrill voice failed to break through the skein of lightheartedness she'd pulled around herself ever since that day.

It was wonderful. Thermous Cawley had promised to make her life miserable and perhaps he would when he got over his own excitement of his planting. But he'd have a hard time of it. She was certain of that. Jason Welburn's smile and light words could take her mind off any troubles her master could bring to her.

She saw him often in the fields now. He spent a lot of time helping her work so that they could have time to sit and talk and Cawley wouldn't know the difference. Even when she had to work beside her master, she could make some excuse to go to the creek at a certain time during the day and find him waiting. It was a good life, and she was beginning to be pleased with herself again.

If she had a care, it was the two young boys she was charged with watching over when she wasn't in the fields. As summer began and the sun turned hot, deadening the air in town and making it harder to breathe, both of the Cawley children seemed to wilt. More often than not, they didn't want to play after their schooling was over and then they began to miss some of the schooling as well, complaining of being hot and tired even when the air was cool in the early morning.

She worried about them, but Sarah Cawley hardly noticed and her husband's mind was on his fields. He did send for a doctor, one of the Jews who lived in Savannah, saying he'd rather a Jew tend his son than that damned Noble Jones, but the man told them it was only the summer doldrums that most newcomers experienced. Both boys would recover as they became used to the Georgia climate, he said.

Elizabeth gave them the herbs he left, boiling them as he directed and straining off the water into a bottle, but it didn't seem to help. Robert and Andrew continued to decline.

She asked Hester Pullam about it, but the other was of little help. "I don't know, Elizabeth. That man is highly thought of even if he is a Jew. He's cured a lot of people. But what you describe, sounds a lot like my parents before they died. It seemed as if they would be very sick for a time and then get better. But then they'd get worse again. And then they died."

"What did they die from?"

The smaller girl shook her head. "We don't know. We were all children, even Douglas was hardly more than a child himself. We couldn't afford to summon a doctor and there didn't seem to be any point to it after they were dead."

"You had a hard time, didn't you?" Elizabeth said. It was late in the evening, supper was done and the Cawleys already in bed, so she had time to visit before darkness set in.

"I would have had a worse time if it had happened later," Hester told her. "That all happened before the Reverend Mr. Whitefield came here to start his orphanage. The people back then gave Douglas work and donated food to us so we could stay together. If Reverend Whitefield had been here he'd of made us go to his orphanage."

"Wouldn't that have been better for you?"

Hester looked at her sharply. "Goodness no! Haven't you heard about that place? They work those poor children to death in there and give them no time at all to themselves. They teach them some schooling, I know, but it's mostly about the Bible, and they make the poor dears pray aloud four or five times a day. And if that weren't enough, they must constantly confess their sins. As if children have any real sins to confess!" She shook her head. "They're at them from dawn to dusk, I understand. Those poor children are miserable."

"I didn't know all that," Elizabeth said.

"Well it's true," Hester said. "I know of one boy who ran away and told—My goodness, who in the world might that be?"

Elizabeth turned to see. Halfway down the street and walking briskly toward them was a tall young man wearing a short-tailed coat and a tricorn. As she watched, he waved.

"I don't know," she said slowly. "But he acts as if he knows—Tom!"

He'd swept the tricorn from his head and left her no doubt as to his identity. A second later she was running as fast as she could, lifting her skirt to keep from tripping. She didn't even slow as she reached him, but flung herself full tilt into his open arms and drove him backwards with the force of her rush.

Her brother swept her up and swung her around in a circle. "Hey! You'd knock the breath clear from a body!"

But she was hugging him, kissing him and crying all at the same time. He tried to grasp her arms and hold her back to look at her, but she'd have no part of it, jumping against him until, laughing, he gave up and lifted her once more to squeeze his arms around her until her ribs hurt. When he sat her down again, Elizabeth gasped for breath.

"Well, I see my little sister hasn't forgotten me." His smile was teasing, but his eyes were tender.

She was having great trouble stopping her crying and reached forward to lock both her fists in his coat. Tom pulled her head close to his chest for a moment and then gently moved her away again. "I'm happy to see you again, Beth," he said. "But I need to talk to you and we can't talk if you're going to do all of that bawling, can we?"

She nodded her head, shook it quickly and reached up to wipe her eyes. "No," she blubbered. "But I'm just so happy to see you! It's been such a long time and I didn't think I ever would again."

"It has been that, Beth," he agreed. "A great long time. But come, is there a place we can talk?"

"Yes." She turned and found a curious Hester Pullam standing a few feet from them. "Oh, Hester! I almost forgot about you!"

"I see you did," was the dry reply. "And I can't say that I blame you. But I do wonder what Jason Welburn will think of this?"

Elizabeth laughed. It felt good to laugh. "Don't be silly," she said. "This is my brother. Thomas, this is Hester Pullam."

He nodded forward. "A pleasure, Mistress Pullam. I'd take my hat off to you but my sister seems to have knocked it about somewhere."

"Oh I did, didn't I?" Elizabeth looked around, found it on the ground even as he did and beat him to retrieving it. "Here— Oh, it's a nice hat! Wherever did you get it?"

Tom chuckled. "From the same place I got these clothes. Mr. Noble Jones provided them for me. He's the man I'm indentured to."

"Oh, I know him! I mean I know of him. Mr. Cawley doesn't like him."

"More's the reason to recommend him," Tom said flatly. "He's probably too much a gentleman for that fat prig you have to work for." His face settled into a frown. "How are you faring, Beth? Does he treat you badly?"

She started to speak, but Hester-interrupted. "I know you both want to talk and I'm only in the way. I'll just go along home. Goodnight, Elizabeth." She looked at Tom. "It was goodly to meet you, Mr. Briggs."

"My own good fortune, Mistress Pullam." He gave her a short bow.

Elizabeth watched the look on her friend's face, a look of pleasure and high interest, before the other girl turned reluctantly and walked slowly away. Then she moved her gaze to her brother's face with a new realization. He wasn't just Thomas, her brother who had grown up with her, he was a *very* handsome young man. She shook her head in amazement. Tall, with strong shoulders, a sturdy chest and a trim waist that tapered into flat hips. His hair was neatly drawn into a bagwig, pulled away to emphasize the high bones of his cheeks.

He would, she decided, interest any lass, much less poor Hester.

Tom dropped his gaze from watching the departing girl in time to catch her shaking head. "What's wrong?"

Elizabeth smiled broadly at him. "I've only just discovered what a handsome brother I have," she said. "I can assure you, you just set that poor girl's heart aflame."

He grinned self-consciously. "I don't know about that. But I didn't come here to talk about my looks; I came to find out how you're doing. You said there was a place we could talk?"

"Yes. The log seat where Hester and I were." She pointed. "But where will you spend the night? I can't ask you in to my room, the Cawleys wouldn't allow it."

"I didn't expect they would," he said. "It's of no matter though. I planned to get a place to sleep at a tavern. I've the money for it. And in the morning, I have to catch the boat for Frederica."

They had been walking as he talked and she waited until they reached the log seat before she spoke again. "You're going to catch the packet boat? You can travel around just as you please?" She was amazed.

He slipped an arm around her shoulders and hugged her lightly, then released her. "Not as I please, Beth. But I do a good deal of traveling now. Mr. Jones is responsible for many things in this colony and he must keep in company with a lot of people. He decided I would make a good messenger, so that's what I do for him. Carry messages."

"That must be interesting."

"Yes it is. I've already come to know the area around here well. I've even met some Indians."

"Oh I did, too," she said, then added quickly, "I mean I didn't get to meet him exactly, but one came to Mr. Cawley's house. He was a big man. Mr. Tomi—something or other. Anyhow, he died and they had a big funeral for him here in Savannah."

"Tomochichi," Tom said. "He was General Oglethorpe's friend."

"Have you met General Oglethorpe?" she wanted to know.

"I've seen him twice, and once he spoke to me. I'm on my way now to take a message to him from Mr. Jones."

"My goodness. My brother is a very important man these days." She regarded him for a moment. "And you know, it shows. You don't act the same. I mean, you act—let's see—like a gentleman. I'm very proud of you."

He nodded. "It's what I'm trying to do, Beth. I study Mr. Jones's manners whenever I'm around him. And I observe others as well—General Oglethorpe for instance. Ever since the day you told me of our heritage, I've tried to learn to be true to it. We're of noble blood, you and I. Someday I'll claim the name Langlee, and I'll be a gentleman, too."

"I hate the name Briggs also," she said. "But only because of him. Sometimes I feel guilty about that because of mother. I mean the one who raised us. In her eyes we were her own and she did the best she could for us. I still love her."

He nodded again, and she went on. "But can you *ever* claim the name? And if you do, will it make you a gentleman? What difference does it make here in the Americas?"

"It makes a great difference to me, Beth. If I had come here truly owning the name Briggs, and had no more blood in me but that, I'd be different, I know. But since I'm who I am, no matter if no one but myself knows it, I feel I can advance to any station. Don't you see?"

"I think you can be anything you want because you're Thomas my brother whom I love very much," she said quietly.

He sighed. "And I love you too, Beth. But I worry much about you. You didn't say how you were faring. Is he cruel to you?"

"Oh goodness no," she said lightly. "He huffs and puffs, but he doesn't treat me badly. Nor my mistress. You probably got the wrong impression of them that last day we were in England."

His look of relief was reward enough for her lie. "Good!" he exploded. "You don't know how glad I am to know that. How long is your indenture?"

"Four years," she said. "And yours?"

"The same. That's good. I'll be able to take care of you then. Mr. Jones hasn't mentioned it, but I'm sure he'll give me employment. There are some things I want to do, but I can do them and care for you at the same time."

She regarded him with a smile. "And do you still think I'm a helpless girl, dear brother? That I can't take care of myself? Or," she allowed the smile to reach her eyes, "that I can't find *another* man to take care of me? I'm not exactly ugly, I think. Surely there's someone . . ."

He looked at her sternly. The old Thomas look. "That's just the problem. You're much too pretty a girl. Men will take advantage of you without me to—"

"Question them," she interrupted, laughing. "Dear Thomas! I'm not the foolish young girl you remember. I've grown up fast."

Her laughter broke through his brotherly look and made him smile ruefully. "I suppose you have at that. Still, we'll see when the time comes and we're free. Tell me, who is this Jason that girl mentioned?"

"Jason Welburn. He's a very nice man and my stiff brother would approve of him. He's indentured, too, but he works very hard and he has less than three years to go to be free." She moved her face close to his. "And—he doesn't take liberties with your innocent little sister."

This time he laughed and reached to hug her again. "Well, he'd better not. That's all I can say. But I would like to meet him. Perhaps I can when I come back through Savannah."

"You'll be back soon?"

"No more than a few days. In fact I might make several trips through here now, Beth. I hope to see you more often."

"Oh I hope so. I've missed you terribly." A sudden thought struck her. "Tom, do these messages you're carrying have anything to do with the Spanish?"

He looked at her quickly and there was no longer laughter in his eyes. "Why do you ask that?"

"Because there's so much talk in town now about it. Most of the people here think the Spanish will attack soon. They say that General Oglethorpe is driving them to have to do it."

"James Oglethorpe is doing his best to hold the Spanish at bay," he said. "But if they decide to invade us, we've got to be ready. Mr. Jones says if the South Carolinians help us enough we can defeat the Spanish no matter how many men they bring. He's been charged with manning a gunboat himself, out of the island."

"But if there's a fight, will you be in it?"

"Every man will have to be in it, whether he wants to or not," he said shortly. "I'll do my part. But when they come, as soon as you hear of it, you find a way to get across the river into South Carolina. I'm sure that fat man who owns your contract will run for his own life when the Spanish appear, and

I hope he does so you can go with him and his family. But if he doesn't, you do. You hear me?"

"But then I'd be a runaway. And they're very badly treated when they're caught."

"Better than what the Spanish will do to you, Beth, if we can't keep them out. You do as I say. I'll find you somehow and protect you."

She nodded slowly and was glad when he changed the subject. They sat until nightfall and talked together, she allowing him to do most of it since his life had become more adventurous and she could only talk about her housework. It was only when it became too dark to see his face that she reluctantly allowed him to leave.

She kissed him on the cheek, held him close and then stood and waited until she could no longer make out his shadowy figure going down the street before slipping silently into the house to avoid waking the Cawleys.

She looked forward for days afterwards for Tom's return, hating the time she had to spend in the fields tending the trees for fear he would pass through when she was out of town and wouldn't have time to find her. But after three long weeks had dragged by, she was forced to admit that he wouldn't be back as quickly as he said he would. It wasn't his fault, of course, still it hurt to expect to see him again and be disappointed each day.

That disappointment, as much as a growing need to be with Jason Welburn, made her take a great risk. The growing season for crops had begun to take most of his time during the day and he could no longer slip away to find her. So he had asked her, and she had first refused, to slip away just after nightfall and meet him in town. But as her loneliness increased, she agreed.

It put her heart in her throat to hurry through the shadows in the streets, pausing whenever she heard movement in fear of being seen. The Magistrates in Savannah were very stern and if any woman was caught out alone after nightfall they would assume she was out for only one purpose. If she were caught and turned over to one of the constables, the least she could expect was the pain and humiliation of spending a day in the stocks. At worse, she could be publicly whipped or even branded on the hand.

Was it worth the risk? She told herself no. But when she met Jason the first time and they sat on the ground in Percival Square near the mound where the Indian chief was buried and he held her hand and talked to her, he chased away both the emptiness and the fear.

A week later, she went again, lying stiffly in her own bed until heavy snoring from Thermous Cawley below and the lack of sound from his wife or children told her they were all asleep. She crept down the ladder holding her breath and prayed that the animal fat with which she had greased the door hinges that morning would do their work.

They did, and quickly she was flying down the street. Jason was waiting for her in the shadow of the trees and before she could object, he gathered her into his arms and kissed her. She tried to protest, but he continued to hold her and she lacked the strength to pull away.

"Elizabeth," he whispered. "I love you so. Don't you see that? I'm going crazy for the want of you. These arms of mine ache to hold you. Tell me you love me, lass."

Elizabeth rested her head against his neck, allowing herself to lean against him. "Jason, I just don't know. Sometimes I think I do, but—"

"You will!" he told her fiercely, his arms tight around her. "I know you will, Elizabeth. I'll *make* you love me. I swear it!"

He was too demanding. She wasn't ready. Not yet . . . so much to think about . . . so much to learn . . . She had to *know!*

Anyway, they were indentured. Their lives, both hers and Jason's, weren't their own. Not yet . . .

She allowed him to hold her, but left him after a short time in spite of his protests. To remain with him longer would be more than the danger of being discovered, it threatened her own good sense.

But she did permit him to kiss her again. And found herself responding to his hunger more than she willed. She had to struggle to free herself and hurried away, trying not to hear his groaning, "Elizabeth!"

The moon was low in quarter as she made her way back to the house, dark enough to make finding her way difficult in the rutted street; she had to sense more than see where to place her feet. She was greatly relieved to step from the lane into the darker shadow of the house and feel for the latchstring.

A hand came from nowhere to snatch her shoulder and fling her hard against the wall. Elizabeth screamed in fright.

He slammed her hard against the wood of the house with one hand on her chest and reached with his other to choke off her screams. "Silence, damn you! Be quiet!"

Elizabeth fought desperately, but he grasped her wrists and held her, his overpowering body pressing hers against the wall until she was struggling for breath.

His own rapid breathing was hot against her cheek. "Where've you been, you whore? Harlot of hell, who have you been laying with?"

Cawley! The realization hurt more than his hard grasp of her wrists or the pressure of his body. *He would have her punished! Oh Lord above! She would be whipped!*

"Answer me!" His rage drummed in her ear.

"I've not!" Fear choked her words. "No! I was only—"

"You laid with a man!" He ground his body against hers until she gasped with the pressure.

"No! I swear!"

"Liar! Whore!"

He was choking her with his body. She couldn't breathe! "I swear it!"

"Swear on the book!"

"I swear!" She wailed her answer.

"Quiet!" His voice hissed in her ear. "I would not have your shame known!"

Slowly, a little at a time, he lessened the pressure against her until he was clear. If it weren't for his holding her wrists, she would have collapsed. She sucked in air in great gulps.

He leaned his face near. "Tell me!" he commanded.

"I was visiting—"

"Who? And don't lie to me!"

She fought down her fear, struggled to bring back her shattered sanity and think again. It seemed a long time. An image of Jason appeared in her mind and she shook her head. If she were to be punished, she must suffer it alone. It had been her own choice to go this night."

"I won't say his name." Her voice nearly betrayed her in its shaking. "I don't care what you do to me, I won't say his name."

"Swear that you didn't lie with him!" In spite of her fear she realized his own voice was trembling.

"I swear it," she said, and her voice was stronger. "I swore it already. I'm a *virgin*."

His voice was obsessed. "Did he touch you? Here?" He loosened one of her wrists and grasped her breast cruelly.

Elizabeth fought away his hand. "No! No one has touched me! And you should not!"

He snatched his hand away from hers and thrust hard below her waist. "Here?"

"Stop it!" She screamed the words breathlessly.

Suddenly he released her and moved back, but no more than inches away, his presence overwhelming her. "Listen, you strumpet!" he hissed. "Don't you ever! Do you hear me? You will never let another man touch you. Do you hear? If you do, I'll beat you senseless!"

He was insane. His rage was much more than a master's anger with his servant. Suddenly she understood, and the understanding made her afraid.

Breathing hard, she forced herself to look into his face, so close to her own. It *was* the face of a madman: twisted, grotesque, bloated, it made her more afraid than she'd been in her life. But as she stared, the face began to change, his cheeks quivered with effort and the insanity began to die at last. Long moments later, he was Cawley again.

"God put you on this earth to tempt men," he said in a voice that strained with the effort. "Beg his forgiveness, girl. Go to your loft and kneel. Fall on your knees and cry your shame. Pray throughout this night that you might be forgiven."

She shoved both hands against his chest suddenly and pushed him away enough to flee. A moment later she was through the door and climbing her ladder, slipping twice in her haste, to where she could fling herself on her straw pallet and hug her arms around herself, shuddering against the awful touch of *him*.

A long, long time later—it seemed an eternity of waiting to see what he would do—she heard him enter and make his way back to his own room.

Elizabeth could not overcome the feeling of being dirty during the next days. Bath night was on Sunday evening when she would haul extra water to the house for all of them and take a bucket to her own loft to bathe with a cloth. But she couldn't wait for that and sneaked a wetted towel with her to sponge her body each evening before she lay down. And once, when the feeling became overpowering in the field, she slipped away to strip to her shift and bathe in the stream. It didn't help, none of it did, she could not be rid of the feeling of his body, his tremendous, bloated, overpowering body thrust hard against her own...

His name was Peter Abercromby and he was a brickmaker. One, it was rumored, of the few men in Savannah who was on his way to wealth. It was also rumored that he was so close with his money he'd allowed his frail wife to die rather than risk the cost of paying a doctor to see her. Elizabeth had begun to know almost everyone in Savannah from her coming and going about the town on errands, either through actually speaking to them herself or being told who they were by Hester, who seemed to know everyone. But Abercromby was one she was just as glad not to know. From what Hester told her, the ferret-faced man who walked with both a cane and a stoop to his shoulders held as sharp a tongue as Sarah Cawley.

She did know he was one of the "Malcontents," so named because they were forever complaining against the rules laid down for the Georgia colony by the Trustees and petitioning them in long writs to change those rules. A lowland Scot, he was far away from the sturdy fighters who inhabited the town of New Inverness to the south.

Elizabeth was surprised when he stopped her on the street, stepping in front of her to block her path. "Mistress Briggs, I would have a word with you."

His voice was thin, high and unpleasant. It reminded her of the squeak of the rats she often had to chase out of the house.

She started to step around him, but decided it would be both rude and useless. Anyway, he held his cane off the ground as if to stop her.

"What do you want from me?" she said in irritation.

"Now, now." To her astonishment, he smiled, a thin smile that hardly disturbed his lips. "'Tis a friendly greeting I offer, girl. I would expect a bit of consideration for my trouble."

"I'm in a hurry," she told him. "I've many chores to do at home."

"Well I know that, young lass," he said. "It's an excellent job you do of your work, I've been aware of that for some time."

Elizabeth didn't like him, didn't like the way he looked at

her as if appraising a pig in a market he intended to buy. His eyes were small and mean. "I don't know why my work would be of interest to you," she said. "Please allow me to pass, my mistress is waiting for me."

He raised his cane higher as she made to move. "Hold a minute. Hold a minute. What I have to say to you will take no longer." He nodded his head in agreement with his own words. "No more than a minute of your time."

"A minute," she agreed. "That's all I have to spare."

He peered closely at her and if the thin smile stayed in place, his eyes turned more shrewd. "I believe you have three more years to go in your indenture? Is that correct?"

She nodded.

"Three years is a long time to work for someone else," he continued. "Especially if the one who owns you is unhappy with your work. A very long time."

"Why do you think my master unhappy with me?" she asked, knowing full well it was Sarah Cawley's tongue that left no part of Savannah unknowing about her.

He chuckled, a harsh sound coming from the back of his throat. "Now, now, my dear. Let's not bandy words about. We were to be brief at your request. We both know of your reputation, but what you don't know is that to a man such as myself, your past history doesn't matter in the least. I'm a man who cares little what others think."

She colored, more from anger than embarrassment. "I don't care what kind of man you are," she said in heat. "It's nothing to me."

"Oh, but it is. It is. Or it could be if you are as smart a lass as I think you be." He paused a moment significantly. "You see, I intend to offer myself in marriage to you."

"Marriage!"

"Yes. I know it's a shock to you, Mistress Briggs. Since you've never met me. But I'm a man who doesn't believe in the waste of time. Never. I need a wife at the present, and you badly need a way out of your present unpleasant circumstances. An ideal solution for the both of us is for me to buy the rest of your indenture from Thermous Cawley and marry you."

Elizabeth could only stare at him in astonishment.

He misunderstood her look to be consideration of his offer. "I see the idea interests you. Good, good. Give it thought through this coming night and I shall call on Mr. Cawley on the morrow to discuss the terms. I'm a man quite well off as I'm certain you're aware; you'll be married to a man as well-to-do as any in this Georgia colony. Quite a feather in your cap I should think."

He paused again and allowed the thin smile back to his lips. "And, if you're wondering, Mistress Briggs, if I'm a man capable of satisfying a younger woman's, ah, needs . . . let me assure you I am. Quite able."

"I don't—" she started, but he cut her off with a quick wave of his hand. "It doesn't matter to me what you might have done in the past; just as long as you're loyal to me in the future. I will insist on the rights of a husband."

"Are you finished," she said, controlling an urge to scream at him with difficulty.

Her tone surprised him. His eyebrows went up. "Why, yes. I believe I've said it as I wished. You have an answer already?"

"Yes, Mr. Abercromby, I do. And my answer is this. I would not, under any circumstances, agree to marry you. Not today, nor any day. I think you're . . . you're . . . loathsome!"

She could have done no more if she'd slapped him in the face. "How dare you! To speak to me like that! A snippet! I can buy your contract anyway, girl! I can become master to you!"

"You can do that," she told him grimly. "But all you'll own is my work. You can't own *me*."

Quickly she stepped around him and hurried on her way, leaving him to splutter aloud behind her.

To recover from the incident took her most of the day. Bad enough the fact that he thought her already soiled, proving she was right in assuming that most of Savannah did, but he also thought her so easily bought, that was worse. He assumed she would fall over herself with the opportunity to become his wife, that she was stupid enough not to realize that doing so would only mean she would become his unpaid slave for life.

Bad enough that others . . . but to have a man like him . . . she hoped she'd set him straight with her words. Hoped he would be angry for a very long time.

Two days later, she was almost over her own anger and debating whether to speak of the incident to Hester, when it became very much alive again. Thermous Cawley, with a light of triumph in his eyes, told her Abercromby had approached him to buy her contract. He was, he said, giving it his consideration.

Elizabeth could only look at him and he nodded his head in satisfaction. "You'd be much worse off, girl, with the likes of him than with me. He'd be much more apt to take a stick to your back. Much more."

He waited a long time. "I shall give it thought, I assure you. And in the meanwhile, if I were you, I'd see that my attitude changed considerably. I'd become much more pleasant to my *present* master."

With that, he turned and walked away.

Twelve

HE WAS TALLER than his father and leaner in the face, although his eyes and mouth were the same. Tom knew he was near his own age, despite the worldly mannerism he affected. For this, their first meeting, Tom tried to maintain his reserve, but failed, and returned the one-sided smile the other wore with a near grin of his own. He started to speak, but then decided to wait and allow his master's son to begin the conversation.

"So you're Thomas Briggs that I've been hearing about." The lopsided smile remained in place. "Do you happen to know who I am?"

Tom nodded. "Noble Wimberly Jones. Mr. Jones's son."

The young man shook his head immediately. "Wrong. Right in the name, but wrong in the identification at the present."

"You're not Mr. Jones's son?"

"Oh yes. Wimberly to my friends, Thomas, or Tom, whichever you prefer. But more than that, I'm your new teacher. Schoolmaster of one, as it were. Unless you object. Which would be rather foolish of you since I'm a very good teacher. And besides, it will get you out of a great deal of work, I'll see to that myself."

Tom didn't understand. He'd been working on the patrol boat tied up on the island and under constant use by Noble Jones to guard the approaches to Savannah on General Oglethorpe's orders, when he'd been told Jones wanted to see him at the blockhouse. But when he arrived, Noble Jones wasn't in sight, only this young man was there, dressed fashionably in boots, frock coat, laced shirt and wool tricorn. The servant had recognized his master's son easily, a difference in build, but with features that were unmistakably the same. However, this strange beginning to their conversation left him at a loss.

The crooked smile increased. "May I assume, Master Briggs, you don't know what the devil I'm talking about?"

"I'm sorry," he said. "I was told Mr. Jones wanted to see me."

"Mr. Jones being my rather busy father," Jones nodded. "Not too busy to assign you to me for a time, but too busy to tell you why in advance. I'm not surprised. I suppose he left that to me also."

"You spoke of being a teacher," Tom said. "Were you supposed to teach me some new task? Your father has another job for me?"

Jones laughed aloud. "No, my friend, not a new task. My father expects you to continue in the work you're doing. Except he wants you to take time to learn to read. And I'm assigned by him to teach you that little trick."

He was stunned. Here was his life's desire—like a bolt of lightning. Such a thing! But this other suggested it so lightly he couldn't believe his ears. Could it be possible?

"Well," Jones said. "You *are* interested, aren't you? You do want to learn to read as my father said?"

"Aye—I mean, yes. Yes, indeed! I just don't—I mean, why? Why would you do such for me?"

"I just told you, Thomas. My father has assigned you to me. Or me to you. I'm really not sure which. Anyhow, he said he wanted me to teach you to read. And to cipher as well. Just as he once did for me. We're to start right away, I'm told we might be interrupted by the bloody Spanish knocking on our door at any minute. Do you read at all? Any words or letters?"

Tom slowly shook his head, overwhelmed by the turn of events. "No, nothing. I recognize signs that have been read to me and remember what they mean. But I've no training beyond that." He paused, his mind still whirling. "Why would your father want to do this? I don't understand."

The other shrugged casually. "I've learned in life to raise a question to everything since nothing ever is as it seems, and nothing is ever permanent. The one exception to that rule of mine is my father. I never question my father. Disagree with him, yes, but not so that he might know it. You don't have an idea of why he wants you to learn to read yourself?"

It came back to him in a rush. The night of the escape. The attempted escape . . . Jones holding the pistol on Lawrence but directing his questions toward Tom: *"What did he promise you, Tom?"*

He'd answered, and his master's eyes had narrowed as he turned to look at him hard. He remembered . . . Noble Jones had remembered, and he'd understood.

"Your father is a fine man," he said softly. "A gentleman. I'm in debt to him more than I can say. And my name is Tom, if you care to use it, sir."

The other had caught his change of mood and shook his head. "Not sir. Wimberly, Tom. To my friends as I said. I trust we'll become friends—no, I know we'll become friends. Life is too dull around here, I need a co-conspirator to liven it up." He leaned forward suddenly and placed an arm around Tom's shoulders, turned and started to walk away, forcing Tom to come with him.

"We'll spend a great deal of time together. Studying, of course, I shall justify my father's wishes by having you reading in no time at all. Not just the common reading, say of that fool's prattle run off by the locals here in their paper, but of the great English classics as well. But reading and mathematics will not be all the learning we shall pursue. Not by the beards of the prophets!"

He allowed his arm to slide from Tom's shoulders as they walked, but left his hand to rest on the nearest. "Do you hunt? Fish? Play cards?"

Tom shook his head.

"None of that? Good Heavens. I've a real task on my hands. Cards I can understand. It's called a gentleman's game, but I've always thought it a foolish way to waste good coin. But to hunt! Now that's a thrill you shouldn't be missing."

"I've not had the time since I've been here," Tom told him.

He was surprised that although he was slightly taller, Wimberly's stride, done in his calf high boots, was hard to match.

"Nor in England, I suppose?"

Tom laughed grimly. "Nor in England."

His new companion missed his change in tone entirely, seemingly lost in his plans. "We'll remedy that quick enough, my friend. Father said to aid you in acquiring an education and I choose to interpret that as I will. I've paper and pen in my baggage at the house and this very evening we'll begin your lessons with them. But tomorrow . . . ah, tomorrow . . . we shall procure fowling pieces and take to the forests. Good enough?"

"You're the schoolmaster," Tom told him. "I'll be the best learner I can."

"Student," was the quick reply. "Pupil. Not learner. I see, young Tom, I've a task with your speech as well. You know, this is going to be fascinating. I'm going to be able to watch myself create a gentleman." He stopped suddenly and looked at Tom. "Do you know where I've been? Or why?"

"No. I was told Mr. Jones had a son, but I didn't know where you were."

Jones nodded in satisfaction. "In Charles Town, my friend. Sent there for the last two years by my father to mix and mingle with the gentry. To learn the polish of a gentleman by being in the association of gentlemen. He was afraid that in growing up in this young and raw colony I would have neglected that art."

He threw back his head and laughed. "Manners and morés that I shall now pass along to you, good Tom. I vow I shall make of you a prancing dandy!"

Tom grinned. "Perhaps not that far, if you please. I'll settle for knowing what's proper. So that I can look any man in the eye."

Jones shook his head slowly. "You know that already, Tom. I can see it. You're not afraid of any man. All I can do is put a bit of polish on it."

He waited a moment and then laughed again. "And see that both of us have a bit of fun in the process. Do you agree?"

"Agreed. And my thanks to you." Tom extended his hand and Jones took it heartily. "Then let's find that paper and ink. I'm anxious to see how fertile that mind of yours is."

The weeks following his introduction to Noble Wimberly Jones flew by in rapid succession. Tom was hardly conscious of their passage. Wimberly was both intelligent and likable, as well as a whirlwind of energy. He plunged Tom immediately into the world of letters; in one evening he memorized the alphabet and understood its function; by the second, he was reading short words; and in a week, he was putting those words into sentences himself until his hand ached from holding the quill over paper.

Still it wasn't enough. Tom felt as a blind man suddenly given sight and unable to drink in enough of the world around him. Wimberly marveled at his quickness of mind and became caught up in his thirst. The two of them sat hunched over a table under lantern light until far into the night, but then, after no more than a few hours sleep, he was up and urging Tom to his feet as well. With hardly time for breakfast of bread, salt pork and coffee, the latter Wimberly's favorite drink, they would be off to the woods to hunt deer or turkey. Or to one of the many streams to fish for bass or perch.

It was a busy, headlong time, and the indentured servant forgot his station in becoming close friends with his teacher. If the elder Jones noticed that he now received little in the way of work from his servant, he held his peace. Tom and Wimberly pursued their interests undisturbed.

"What an absolutely beautiful day." Wimberly lay his back against a scrub oak tree, folded his hands behind his head and glanced briefly at Tom before returning to the scene. Like Tom, he had removed his coat, rolled up his long sleeves and unhooked his shirt down to his waist.

Tom nodded sleepily. The two of them had been up later than usual last night, first studying and then Wimberly had read to him from John Bunyan's book, *Pilgrim's Progress*, with great eloquence. Then he had been dragged from his bed at little after the first light of dawn and found himself wading through the salt marshes of Skidaway Island in search of an elusive horned reptile that Wimberly had been told of only yesterday. It was, Wimberly assured him, extremely hard to find but when boiled, its skin produced a remarkable cure for flux. He had to find one and discover for himself if the tale were true.

They had walked and hunted for miles, and he felt it. He was more than happy to lean back himself and look out to the open sea.

"It's a good day for those working in the fields," he said. "Not as hot as the last few have been. A man could get much done today."

Wimberly grunted. "There you go again. Always talking about accomplishing something. Don't you ever think of just relaxing and enjoying a day for itself?"

"I wasn't the one who insisted we climb out of bed in the middle of the night and fight our way through all the marshes between here and the river," Tom reminded him.

"That was research. An aid to my becoming a surgeon. Besides, it was fun."

Wimberly stretched his arms above his head and yawned. "But not for old Tom Briggs here," he continued after he'd settled himself again. "Got to be at work at something that is productive. Otherwise, time is wasted. What a bore you are!"

"You don't intend to make something of yourself?" Tom asked him. His eyelids were beginning to get heavy; he allowed them to close for a moment to rest them.

"I intend to become a doctor," Wimberly said, and yawned again. "I'm studying, and will continue to study, until I've mastered all that's possible of that trade, more than my father has taught himself, I trust. But I'm young yet, and there's time enough ahead of me to accomplish my purpose. I intend to enjoy life along the way. At least for the present."

"Good," Tom told him. "I'm happy you're going to do something. I was beginning to believe you'd spend your life doing only what amused you. To say nothing of dragging me along at the same time."

An insect buzzed its way past Wimberly's nose and he brushed it away. "I'll become the best doctor in the colony of Georgia," he said. "Probably the best south of Boston. But as I said, there's no reason to hurry. Have you ever done *anything* merely to amuse yourself?"

"I suppose so. I don't remember. Nothing important."

"What about when you were younger, I mean, very young. Back in England." Wimberly rolled his head to look at him.

"I worked," Tom said shortly. "The man who raised me didn't believe in my doing anything else."

"Even as a child?"

"As long as I can remember."

Wimberly heaved a sigh. "Terrible. Even the black slaves

in South Carolina are given a day off each week. How about holidays?"

"Nothing," Tom told him. "It wasn't his way."

"I'm sorry for you," Wimberly said. "You've missed out on a lot. No wonder you act so serious all the time. You know, I think I'm going to have to find an amusement that will unbend that reserve of yours, Thomas Briggs. Something that will make you more aware of yourself."

Tom laughed. "Some one of your pranks, no doubt. And I'm apt to find myself trying to explain my doings to your father."

"No." Wimberly leaned back and closed his eyes. "No pranks. Nothing as childish as that. Give me time, my friend. I must find the proper way to knight Sir Thomas Briggs into the royal world of true living."

Tom waited, curious as to what his friend intended. But the other was silent for so long he fell asleep.

A week later he had forgotten the incident, caught up still in his pursuit of knowledge. He was reading, slowly but with accuracy, pausing when he reached an unfamiliar word and then attempting it at least once before Wimberly corrected him. He was engaged in trying to read by himself in late afternoon, Wimberly having gone off to do something or other, when the latter reappeared.

"Did my father find you," Wimberly wanted to know.

Tom closed the book and stood up. "No. Does he want me for something? I haven't seen him in the last two days."

"Doesn't matter," Wimberly said. "He was in a hurry at any rate. He gave me instructions for you in case he didn't find you himself. He wants you to go into Savannah and see a Mr. Grayson."

"Of course." Tom lay the book on the table and reached for his hat. "I'll go at once. What am I to say to him?"

Wimberly stroked his jaw thoughtfully. "I'm not really certain what it's about myself. Something about furthering your education, I believe. You'll probably understand when you reach Mr. Grayson's house."

Tom was filled with a rush of gratitude. "Your father has done more than enough for me already. I don't understand why he's being so generous. Nor how I can ever repay him."

Wimberly grinned. A wicked grin. "Probably you already have, to his thinking, by keeping his son out of trouble. Go on now, get into Savannah this evening. The Grayson house is the last one on Queen's Street. It sits apart by itself. Oh yes, I wouldn't stop to talk to anyone else if I were you, I believe my father intends this meeting to be quiet."

"Surely. I'll waste no time." He hurried to leave. If he walked as rapidly as he could and took a short cut he knew of through the forest, he could be in Savannah before nightfall. Where he spent the night was unimportant, it was warm enough to sleep on one of the greens if necessary. The important thing was to show his responsibility to Noble Jones.

"Good luck!" Wimberly called after him, and Tom waved in response.

He made good time as he'd hoped and was in Savannah before dusk. Finding the right house was no problem, he knew the street and the house had to be the last. Wimberly had said it was set apart and this one looked as if it had been shunned by its neighbors, being at least three lots away from the nearest. He paused before the door and knocked.

He waited, got no reply and knocked again, louder. A few seconds later, it opened and he was faced with a young woman, a pretty young woman, a few years older than himself, with strands of blonde hair pushing from beneath her cap. "Yes?"

"Good eve, mistress. I'm Tom Briggs. Sent here to see Mr. Grayson."

She had a smooth face, unmarked by sickness scars as so many were, and deep blue eyes resting above cheeks that were near to a rose in color. A *very* pretty young woman. "Tom Briggs?" she echoed slowly.

He nodded and waited, but she didn't move, merely stood looking at him in a quizzical manner.

"Mr. Jones sent me," he said at last. "Mr. Noble Jones."

She smiled then, a very nice smile, he thought, relieved that she had finally understood. "I see," she said. "Do come in Mr. Briggs."

She stepped back and held the door for him to enter. Tom stopped a few feet inside and looked around. It was furnished as most houses were, with a large table and chairs made in the South Carolina colony, muslin curtains over the open-shuttered front windows, a wash stand with pitcher by one wall and the end taken up by cupboards and a hearth. Suspended over the low fire in the back of the hearth was a cooking pot and sitting near it a bread warming pan. Through a doorless opening he could see a bed in the near room. There seemed to be, however, no one else in the house.

The young woman closed the door behind him and dropped the latch in place. "Won't you have a chair, Mr. Briggs? I've some tea brewing, I'll be happy to serve you a cup."

"Thank you," he said. "But I'm here to see Mr. Grayson. Is he not in?"

She shook her head, the blue eyes never releasing his face and containing, he thought, more than a bit of humor. He wondered what there was about himself that seemed to amuse her. Suddenly he felt extremely awkward.

"I'm sorry," she said, after he was certain she'd thoroughly inspected every part of him. "Mr. Grayson is not in Savannah at all. He took my mistress to Charles Town the day before yesterday. I expect them to be gone a fortnight."

"Gone? But I don't understand. Mr. Jones told me to come to see him tonight. At least that's what I understood him to mean."

"Mr. Jones told you," she echoed. "Are you quite certain?"

He felt even more awkward, not knowing full well what to do with his hands. "It must have been a mistake on my part," he said at last. "I'll not trouble you longer, mistress. My apologies."

"Oh, none needed, Mr. Briggs. None at all. I'm happy you're here in fact."

He cocked his head in surprise. "You're happy what?"

"Happy you're here," she assured him and reached to take his arm just above his elbow. "Come and sit down. I'll serve you that tea. I was preparing myself a meal and I do so hate to eat alone. It will pleasure me greatly if you'll sup with me."

Tom found himself being moved before he could object and was only able to protest when he was halfway down to his seat in a chair. "But I couldn't," he argued. "I couldn't take advantage of your—"

She gave him a push, a surprisingly strong one, to complete his journey to the chair. "And why not, pray tell? You would deprive this poor maid from supper with a handsome young man? I find that most cruel, sir."

"But that's the point. The very point." He put up his hands. "You're alone and you don't even know me. It wouldn't be proper for me to—"

"Fiddle-dee-dee!" she said, interrupting him again. She was laughing at him, he realized with embarrassment. "I do know you; you're Tom Briggs and you're servant to Mr. Noble Jones. Now will you have a bit of sugar to your tea?"

Tom sighed, growing tired of both his awkwardness and his embarrassment. "I'll have the sugar," he said. "And thank you. What's your name?"

She fetched him a cup, smiled over it at him and went back for the teapot. As she poured, she glanced over it at him again. "My name is Charity Lorne. I'm indentured to Mr. Grayson. Actually more to his wife. He purchased me as maid to her."

"I see." He watched as she poured her own tea and replaced the pot in its niche over the hearth. "I'm happy to meet you, Mistress Lorne." He liked the way she moved, quick but graceful, an economy of effort. "But why aren't you with them now in Charles Town?"

She sat down opposite him at the table and spooned sugar from a bowl into each cup. "Mr. Grayson left me here apurpose to receive some goods he expects in the next few days. I'm to see they're stored in this house properly. He's thinking of setting up trade in Savannah."

"Then he's not been here long?"

"Little over a month. We came from the Virginia colony. To my mistress's regret, I'm afraid. She wishes very much to go back. She thinks Georgia too wild for her tastes."

He sipped the tea. "And what does Mistress Lorne think of the colony?" The tea was excellent. So was her smile. He was beginning to relax.

"I long ago decided to enjoy wherever I am, Tom," she said through the smile. "Since I can do little about it, why not? Will you please call me Charity?"

"Charity," he said. "It's a nice name. And you're . . . a nice person."

"A nice person." She gave him a mock frown. "Surely you can do better than that, Tom Briggs. How about 'a lovely young lady'? Or at least, 'pretty'? Could you not say that?"

He could feel his face redden, but not uncomfortably so. "Yes, I could say that readily enough," he told her. "T'would be no more than true, I think."

"Then you must say it."

He returned her smile, feeling at ease with himself again. "Mistress—no, Charity Lorne—you are the most beautiful and charming young lady it has been my good fortune to meet. I'm overcome by the loveliness of your delightful blue eyes, your delicate face and the promise of that little bit of golden hair I see peeking from under your cap. I'm a man transfixed."

Charity laughed and clapped her hands together. "Excellent! You did that more than well! Thank you."

He smiled and bowed, as much as he could from a sitting position. "True, every word," he said. He was enjoying himself, she was most easy to like.

"It calls for a reward," she told him. "You've earned both your sup and more than a peek, as you say." She reached up and quickly undid the strings beneath her chin and swept her cap from her head, allowing long blonde hair to drop to her shoulders.

Tom was stunned. It was most unseemly. But she had done it with such naturalness he could find no room to object. And she was right, it was a reward. Her hair was the color of gold reflected in the light from the hearthfire.

Charity rose from the table and tossed her head to spread her hair about. "Do you like it?"

"Lovely," he said, not knowing what else to add.

"Thank you. And now for your sup. I'll be but a moment."

"Are you certain?" he wanted to know. "I really don't want to impose. Nor to give you trouble from Mr. Grayson."

"Who's to know?" she asked, turning from the hearth to look at him. "Or, for that matter, to care?"

"Well, I don't know. But I thought your neighbors . . ."

"The neighbors likely did not notice your arrival," she said. "None are close. And if you wait until after nightfall, they will be unlikely to notice your departure. Now will you please relax a bit and allow me to enjoy myself?"

He shrugged and gave up. "No more to enjoy than myself, Charity. I suddenly find I'm most hungry."

"Good, that's the more as it should be."

She fed him well, he was surprised at the amount she had cooked for herself. Fresh beef, stewed to tenderness in the pot, Indian peas, cabbage and baked bread—there was more than enough for them both.

They talked as they ate, facing each other. She was easy to

talk to, he told her more about himself than he'd told anyone, even Wimberly, leaving out, however, a good bit of his life before arriving at the colony. In return, he learned she had been married at sixteen in Virginia. A few years later, her husband had died of smallpox, leaving her their farm to run alone. She'd tried to manage it by herself, hiring the use of a neighbor's slave to help her, but slowly she'd sunk deeper and deeper into debt until she had lost both the farm and her own freedom. She had been sold into indenture by the Virginia courts to pay her debts. Her indenture to Grayson would last for several more years.

"I'm sorry," he said, genuinely feeling so. "That must have been terrible for you."

Her blue eyes lacked the least bit of self pity. "It's the way of life, Tom. There's no need to look back on it. And my life now isn't all that unhappy. Except..." She paused and looked at the low flames flickering in the hearth.

"Except?" he asked, and then regretted the impulse. It was none of his business.

Charity turned her head again and looked thoughtfully at him. "I miss my husband," she said. "He was a good and kind man. A man who was strong in his desire for me but gentle in the doing. Do you understand what I mean?"

"I think so," he said slowly. "I know what it is to love someone. As I told you, my sister and I are close. I should hate much to lose her to death."

Charity continued to look directly into his eyes as her mouth moved into a very slight smile. "I don't think you do understand," she said softly. "It's not the same as love for your sister."

"I'm sure it's not," he said quickly. "Exactly the same, I mean. I'm certain having a mate, that is, someone you're married to—"

"Someone to touch you," she interrupted. "Someone to tell you you're still pretty. And desirable. Someone to take the ache of emptiness from you, at least for a moment. Do you understand *that*, Tom?"

"I'm not sure I do," he said slowly.

Charity rose and walked around the table to stop near him. "Stand up," she commanded. "Please."

He did, puzzled. "I hope I didn't say anything to displease

you," he said. "If you mean for me to leave, I will of course. I merely hope I haven't—"

"Hush." She placed cool fingers against his lips. "Talk not of leaving. Tell me instead that you find me attractive."

"I do," he said, his confusion growing. "I find you most attractive."

She stepped closer to him, her body almost touching his, to look up into his face. "Tell me that you want to kiss me, Tom."

He stared down at her. So close . . . and so desirable. But . . . "It wouldn't be right," he managed, his throat tightening. "I would be no gentleman to take advantage of you this way."

Both her hands reached up to touch his cheeks, to glide smoothly over them, and then encircle his neck, there to tighten her fingers. "Forget your instincts," she whispered in a low, soothing voice. "Or at least forget the gentlemanly ones. Listen to the others, Tom. Your instincts as a man."

He couldn't stop himself. His hands reached for her waist of their own accord, his head leaned to meet her upturned face. He kissed her, gently at first, then harder as her hands tightened even more on his neck.

A moment later his arms were about her, pulling her close to him, and the pressure of her breasts against his chest made him giddy.

He moved away. Tried to move away, but she clung to him and he couldn't. "Charity," he whispered, his throat thick. "I can't. It isn't right—"

Her cool lips shushed his, then moved away to brush across his cheek and touch the tip of his ear. "Do you want me, Tom?" the soft voice whispered into his ear.

Her body was a glowing flame touching his. He could feel his manhood strain rapidly against the confines of his breeches. The nerves across his back and down his arms began to play like lightning flashes. "Charity . . ." It was a moan from somewhere deep within him.

The flame kissed him again, moving her body from side to side against his as she did. Tom trembled with an exploding urgency, a feeling he'd never experienced before. A feeling he didn't know how to control.

"Come," the voice whispered through the roaring in his blood. "Come with me, Tom."

He was helpless to do anything but follow. To refuse would require a strength he didn't possess. Right and wrong faded from his consciousness, he knew only the soft press of her body as it still lingered on his own though she moved away. She held his hands in her own as she led him to the bedroom.

This room was nearly dark, lit solely by the reflected glow of the fire from the hearth in the other, flickering splashes of yellow-red against one back wall. It heightened the sheen to her blonde hair.

Charity stopped and turned to face him, reached to unhook his shirt with sure, soft hands and then rubbed them over his bare chest.

Tom put his hands on her back and pulled her to him to kiss her again, slowly, drawing an intense pleasure from her lips as they parted under his.

She raised her hands as she kissed him, spread them over his shoulders under his shirt and drew it away. He shivered as he aided her, drawing his arms from the sleeves and pulling the material free from his waistband. Naked from the waist, his skin burned hotly from the touch of the muslin fabric over her high breasts as Charity slowly moved them from side to side against his chest kissing him.

"Charity . . . I cannot endure this long."

"And you shall not, my love," she whispered. "Do you wish to remove my clothing, or shall I?"

He was inside a giant bell, its soundless ringing vibrating his soul to its very depths. His fingers shook as he reached for her, fumbled hopelessly in indecision as to how her garment was fastened and dropped willingly as she pushed his hands to her hips. Charity did quick magic with her own hands, her dress parted at her throat and then continued as if opening of its own accord. She stepped back a pace, and the garment fell around her feet to leave her in a soft, linen shift.

Tom moved to take her again, but she stopped him with a hand to his chest. She wiggled quickly and then stood before him in nothing at all, her body glowing in the light from the fire, a blonde vision beyond his most secret of dreams. He feared to touch her lest she vanish before his eyes.

"Charity . . ."

"Do you like me, Tom?" she whispered. "Do you *want* me?"

"Charity . . ." It was no more than a strangled groan as he

reached to take her into his arms. The fire from the hearth was real in the pressure of her breasts when they touched his naked chest, real enough to sear him. Then her vibrant body molded completely against his own. He was completely aroused by her.

Charity kissed him hard, pressing against him, then turned inside his arms and without allowing their bodies to part, led him to the bed. Only there did she allow him to part from her, moving away reluctantly and lying partly down with her eyes large upon him. "Hurry, Tom," she whispered. "Please hurry."

He bent quickly to remove his shoes, his stockings and then his breeches. The beauty on the bed watched him with open, unashamed interest, then reached her arms for him as he moved toward her.

Tom lay her back, stretched beside her and then drew her into his arms to stroke the smoothness of her back as he kissed her again. Tenderly, as much as he could manage with the great need for her that raged inside him, he explored her firm body, silken under his touch. Encircled her breast with his palm, touched with a shiver of pleasure the erect, hard nipple and then slowly traced the soft curve of her hip.

Charity shivered under his questioning touch, kissed him harder, her lips parting to allow the thrust of a delicate, delicious tongue and moved his hand to her stomach.

He was soaring. Waves of desire moving him higher and higher until he was aware of nothing but the two of them. His hand slipped downward from the movement of her stomach, guided by her own, and Charity parted her legs to accommodate it.

Then, quickly, her small hand left his to encircle his manhood and Tom was certain he was about to explode.

"Charity!"

Her voice was warm and alive, penetrating through his singing senses and echoing the same desire that had him aflame. "Now, Tom," the throbbing voice whispered, "Come into me. But slowly, my love. Let me show you how best . . ."

He was lost in the immensity of his feeling, his body no longer belonged to him but to the moving sensation that was the two of them. "Slowly," the voice whispered through sweet lips against his ear. "Let it be long in lasting . . ."

But his youth would not be held back, and his desire burst forth as a shooting star.

But that was only the first time, and he learned, then, how to pleasure her and did so for a long, long time. It was nearly morning when he left. Charity saw him to the door and kissed him a last time before she opened it.

"Thank you," he said. "I hope I'll see you again soon."

She smiled. "If it be so, Tom Briggs, I hope it, too. But if it be not, then we have the memory of this night between us."

"For as long as I live," he said. "It was my—" He stopped, embarrassed.

Charity laughed. "I know," she said. "And I'm glad it was me. You'll make some fortunate woman very happy, Tom. Be good to her."

"But not you," he said.

She laughed again. "No. Not me. For I do not love you, nor you me. But we both will love—you for the first time, and I again. I promise you that. Goodbye, Tom Briggs."

"Good night, Charity," he said and made as if to kiss her again, but she pushed him away. "Go on with you now, whilst I will allow it."

He did, glancing back as she closed the door and then swinging his arms as he strolled down the street. It was a good feeling to be alive. A good feeling to know you were a man. She was a beautiful, desirable woman. A woman not ashamed to allow a man to know she wanted him, too. It was foolish to lay sin to that; why should not a maid have the same thoughts as a man?

He laughed aloud with it. To think that he, Thomas Langlee, would have such a thought! By the Heavens, a day ago he was certainly much more rigid in his thinking. Charity Lorne had done more for him than help him lose his virginity, she had set him to a right mind.

He walked on, not caring where he was going, then decided he felt so well he would walk all the way back to the Isle of Hope now. He was, after all, a different man.

Halfway back, he stopped congratulating himself as a thought suddenly hit him. He *had* become a new man, a man less rigid in his thinking. And Noble Wimberly Jones had recently said he would come up with a way to unbend him—the same Noble Wimberly Jones who had sent him to see a Mr. Grayson who was out of town and told him it was his father's doing.

Damn! It was intentional! He had been—but Charity? Surely

she wouldn't have been a party to it on purpose! She was not—
he didn't know whether he'd been made a fool of or not.

By the time he reached the island and started across it for
the site of the still building home of Noble Jones, he knew the
truth of it however. Wimberly had met Charity and had been
smart enough to understand her loneliness. He'd set him up
rightly enough, but not through any conspiring on her part,
merely expecting nature to take its course. And it had.

At least he hoped that had been the case.

Thirteen

SUMMER WAS DRAWING to a close. It had been a harsh summer
for Elizabeth for reasons greater than the dry heat that had
prevailed through the many cloudless days. The lack of rain
had sucked away at the marshes, leaving areas open where no
one had been able to trod before, and it had sucked as well at
the vitality of the people in the young colony. Elizabeth felt
it, suffered both the heat that chafed her skin, and the end-
lessness of an unchanging sky. Bad enough to endure such a
summer, but Cawley had succeeded at last in his boast of
making her life miserable. He'd done it not by the occasional
push he gave her to speed moving, nor by the numberless tasks
he assigned her, although she fell into her bed late each night
numb from work. The fat man had succeeded in his intention
by his constant, everlasting presence. Few were the hours that
she was not within the range of his vision, his small eyes
following her every move. After weeks of being watched constantly, her nerves were screaming for relief and she sought
any means to get away.

Water in the wells was low and being conserved for drinking
and cooking, so the washing of clothes was now being done

by most in the river instead of hauling water to the houses. Elizabeth was glad even though it meant a long trip and extra work. At least it got her away from the Cawley house. And it gave her a chance to visit and talk with Hester and others.

But it didn't, she discovered, completely take her away from Cawley's suspicion. Twice in the few short hours she'd been working near the river this morning he'd shown up, pausing on the bluff above her and the others and standing for a long time to watch them. Elizabeth had tried to ignore it, but the others had noticed.

"There he is again," Hester whispered, moving close to her.

Elizabeth used the wooden paddle to lift some clothes from the boiling pot and transfer them to a rinse pot. She nodded without looking up. "I know," she said. "I saw him coming."

Hester's voice held a tinge of worry. "Why, Elizabeth? That's the third time. Why is he doing it?"

Ann Barlow, an older woman indentured at a late age, was near enough to hear and Elizabeth glanced her way, met the other woman's direct gaze and shrugged. "I really don't know," she said to Hester. "Perhaps he thinks I should have been done by now. When I get home he'll see the large load I've washed and be satisfied."

Hester caught her look at Ann and understood its significance. Barlow was a gossip, one of the worst in the town of Savannah. "I suppose," she said, and changed the subject. "Have you seen Tom again?"

Elizabeth had her sleeves rolled back to keep them out of the water and plunged both arms deep into the rinse to slosh the clothes in it up and down. She talked as she worked. "No, not since the last time three weeks ago."

"I remember. But I thought he might have come through here again."

Elizabeth smiled to herself. That Hester had a feather set for her brother was obvious. But it was a useless one. Tom was much too busy to notice and besides, he probably still didn't care anything for girls.

She glanced up to the top of the bluff without appearing to do so and was glad to find *he'd* gone again. A relief for a time, but she was almost through here and soon would have to return to his house. Return and place herself once more under his accusing eyes and listen to the sound of his voice.

She forced the thought away and returned to thinking of

Tom. He was different now, still the same brother who loved her and treated her as if she were years younger than he instead of the exact same age, but his manner of speaking, of acting, was different. He had never spoken as slowly as Briggs, nor drawn out his thoughts as if struggling with them as that man had, but his words now were even crisper. He was, she decided, surely acquiring the manners of a gentleman.

Elizabeth paused to stretch her back. It must be nice to learn to read books, but she wasn't certain she had the patience to accomplish such a task. Anyhow, she was happy for Tom, it was what he had always wanted.

A nudge in her ribs turned her attention back to the present. Hester stood beside her and nodded with her head to where Ann Barlow had moved off to join in a conversation with some of the other women. "Now tell me the real reason," she said.

"I can't."

Hester's face creased instantly. "You've got to, Elizabeth. You're my best friend and I'll die if something happens to you. And you look so terrible of late! I want to know what's wrong."

Elizabeth sighed. "I didn't know I looked *that* bad. I'm just tired. And the summer's been so hot."

Hester shook her head firmly. "No, that won't do, Elizabeth Briggs and you know it. That man has come by here to look at you three times now. And several days ago when I stopped to speak to you, he made me leave. What's wrong with him? And what's wrong with you? Has he been mistreating you?"

Elizabeth pulled the last of the clothes from the rinse pot and wrung them out before tossing them into her basket. She was tempted to tell the whole story to Hester—it would be such a relief to share her worry and fear of Cawley with some-one—but she must not. Hester could do nothing to help her, indeed no one could help her until she finished her indenture. Telling the other girl the truth would only make her miserable, too.

She shook her head. "No, he doesn't mistreat me. Not badly anyway. But he does demand a lot of work from me. With Mistress Cawley ill, and the boys, too, much of the time, there's a great deal to do."

"And that's why he has come by here three times? To see if you're working hard enough. Elizabeth, I don't believe that." Hester waited to see if she would get a reply and when she didn't, continued. "I think he's jealous of you. That's what I think."

So it was obvious even to Hester. The reason for Cawley's action, a reason that she wouldn't admit even to herself, was so apparent that even her friend had noticed it. What could the rest of the town think?

"Hester," she said, "he has a wife of his own. I'm only his servant girl."

"A man doesn't act that way about his horse, or something else he owns," Hester told her grimly. "Has he—you know—attempted—"

"Hester! What a thing to ask!"

Hester brushed her protest aside. "I know. It's wicked to think of such things. But, Elizabeth, I worry so!"

"Well then stop worrying. No, he hasn't."

"Then he's heard about Jason." Hester spoke with finality.

It was of no use. She'd have to tell her friend enough to quiet her curiosity or she'd never get any peace. "Yes he has," she said. "He doesn't want me to see Jason anymore. But only because he thinks it will take away from my work; Mr. Cawley is a close man with his money."

"From what I've heard," Hester said, "his money is running out. He's had to ask for credit against his silk crop at the stores."

Elizabeth was finished. All the clothes she'd brought to wash were in her basket and ready to be taken home. There was no need to stay and help remove the boiling pots or put out the fires under them as several women had come late and were still using them.

"I'm sure that's worrying Mr. Cawley," she told Hester. "That, and the fact that my mistress is ill places a burden on his mind. But it doesn't make him abuse me, so stop worrying about it."

"Will you continue to see Jason Welburn?" Hester asked.

She paused and shifted her basket to a more comfortable position on her hip. "I like Jason," she said slowly. "Perhaps more than I thought at first. It isn't fair for Mr. Cawley to forbid me to see him if I do my work well."

She turned and looked at her friend and nodded. "Yes. I intend to see him whenever I can."

"I'm glad," Hester told her quickly. "He's good for you. Please take care of yourself, Elizabeth."

"I will. Goodbye, Hester." She waved as some of the other women looked up and received several waves in return.

"Goodbye, Elizabeth." Hester was watching her thoughtfully. "I'll see you when I can."

She nodded and walked away but paused with the younger girl's sudden words, "If you see Tom, tell him I send a greeting."

"I will." She hid a smile as she walked.

The streets of Savannah were mostly of sand and the stirring of horses' hooves or the occasional cows being driven through from the cowpens caused the sand to settle over everything. She had taken the precaution to bring a cloth to cover her basket since the sand on her wet clothes would have undone the whole morning's work.

It would have been quicker to take a couple of back streets home, but although the basket of wash was heavy, she went the longer way through a busier part of town. She passed the storehouse for received Indian goods, the gaol and finally the combination courthouse and church, the latter in front of which Mr. Stephens, the secretary appointed by the Trustees to the colony, spoke a greeting to her. He was an old man with a bad leg who needed the help of a cane. Elizabeth felt a little sorry for him, he always seemed so unhappy with himself.

A bit farther on, she passed one of the ale houses in Savannah and wondered briefly what it must be like inside. Her only experience with taverns was one she would prefer to forget, the horrible days she'd spent in that one in London. She decided she'd ask Tom if these were the same.

Briggs must have long ago drunk up the money he received for her and Tom. She hoped he choked on it.

A man she didn't recognize rode by on a beautiful bay horse. Dressed as a gentleman, his boots turned back at the top and wearing a powdered wig, he held her rapt attention as he passed. The wig was unusual, at least in its being powdered white. Most men wore wigs colored much to their own hair, and more and more were defying custom by going without one entirely. It was rare indeed to see a wig so carefully done.

Cawley had worn such when he first arrived in Savannah, she remembered. But then he owned many wigs, since his occupation in England was that of making them. Even he, however, had discovered its uncomfortableness in the heat of the Georgia colony and had gone to plainer ones.

Cawley... what was she to do about him? It had taken her weeks to overcome the revulsion she felt the night he had assaulted her. Weeks of lying alone in her bed and feeling as if her skin were crawling. Suppose he did it again? How would she stand it?

As an indentured servant, she had little rights in the court. It was true that if he beat her badly he could be fined by the Magistrates the same as if he mistreated an animal he owned. But first she would have to prove that the beating was unjustified by her own actions, and Elizabeth suspected strongly that it was rare that any trial had ever gone in the favor of the servant. No, she had little recourse in that direction. The best she could do was to bear her burdens and wait for the day she would be free of him.

Working in his fields of mulberry trees was hard, but Elizabeth was glad nonetheless when Cawley summoned her to do it. It gave her a chance to get away from Sarah Cawley and often, Thermous Cawley himself as well. He seemed to feel that by bringing her out there, she was out of harm's way, or at least the harm he envisioned, that of seeing any other man. More often than not, he would merely assign her a section of trees to tend and move to another himself, leaving her alone and out of his sight.

A better reason for being glad of the move was that she knew it was only a matter of time until Jason Welburn discovered she was back in the fields and she would see him again.

A belief that proved itself right in no more than three short days. On her fourth trip to the creek in midmorning to refill her two buckets of water for the dying trees, her heart leaped to see him waiting for her.

Jason allowed her to reach him before he spoke. "I know where he is," he said without other greeting. "I checked before I came to see you. He's not that far away but moving in another direction. We've plenty of time."

He reached to take her into his arms but Elizabeth pushed away. "Why did you do that?" she asked. "Look for Mr. Cawley, I mean."

Jason placed his hands on her shoulders. "Hester told me,"

he said. "I couldn't understand why I never got the chance to see you anymore, until she told me about him. What's he said to you?"

"It's no matter," she said. "Let's sit under that tree; it's hot out here."

He followed her to the tree, a low branched pine whose falling needles had formed a blanket beneath it over the years. It was a comfortable place to sit, especially with him beside her.

"It matters to me, Elizabeth," he said, taking one of her hands into his own. "I know he's your master and would refuse to allow you to marry me if I were to ask, but he has no right not to let me see you. No right at all."

"Jason, he can do as he likes. There's no need to discuss it. Tell me what you've been doing."

"Dreaming of you." He dropped her hand and placed his arm around her. "That's all I ever do anymore. A bit of work now and then, Mr. Longfootte has begun to call me lazy, but he's joking. He knows I'm in love with you."

"Well you shouldn't be." She turned to look at him. "We're not certain of anything yet, and we've still over two years to go in our service. Or rather, I have." She corrected herself. "You have less."

"I'm certain," he said. Her movement had pulled her from under his arm, but Jason left his hand on her shoulder and placed his other on the opposite one. "I know full well I love you, Elizabeth. I also know I want to marry you. I've no doubts of my own, and I wish most sorely you didn't."

As she continued to look at him, his expression changed to concern. "You don't look well," he said. "Are you all right? You shouldn't be out here if you're ill."

"I'm fine, Jason. It's just the heat."

He reached to hold her face in one hand. "No, it isn't. He's been working you too much, hasn't he? And Hester told me she thought—does he mistreat you?"

"Hester talks too much," she said wearily and tried to look away from him.

"No she doesn't." He held her face and made her look at him. "She was concerned about you and told me for that reason. No more than that. Hester thinks he's tried to have his way with you, Elizabeth. Has he? Tell me the truth."

"No, Jason." But she didn't have the will to move away from his hand. "It's not that at all."

He shook his head slowly and his hand tightened until it hurt. She'd never seen him act so. "It is that way," he said flatly. "I think that fat bastard wants you for himself. That's what I think. And him with a wife of his own!"

"Jason . . ."

"Don't lie to me, Elizabeth! I want to know! Has he touched you?"

"No."

His hand holding her face hurt. "Elizabeth! I've got to know! Tell me the truth!"

She was frightened. For herself, and for him. But she could hold back no longer, she jerked her face from his hand and buried it in his shoulder and sobbed, great wrenching sobs. Jason wrapped both arms around her tightly, trying to talk to her and failing, and suddenly Elizabeth knew he was crying too.

Knowing he was crying created a surge of warmth for him; she'd never known a man could cry, not even Thomas.

"Elizabeth . . ."

Her shame and her fear began to leave her in the comfort of his arms. She forgot where she was and drifted slowly with the peace of it, conscious only of Jason holding her. It was a shock when he jarred her back with a shout. "Damn him!"

He shook her by the shoulders. "What's he done to you? Tell me!"

"Jason, I—"

"Tell me, Elizabeth!"

She couldn't refuse. She wanted to desperately but his eyes locked with hers and broke her will. Slowly, with a great deal of hesitation, she told him everything: the beginning on board the ship when she wore the blanket; the many times Cawley had found reason to place his hands on her; and finally, she described the night she had returned from seeing Jason himself. As she spoke, all the horror she'd felt that night came out in her words.

Jason listened, his young face working in fury, barely able to contain himself until she'd finished. When she did, he cursed. "Damn him! Damn his soul to hell! I'll kill him! I'll kill him now! This very day!"

He was halfway to his feet and Elizabeth clung to him frantically. She shouldn't have broken her silence. If he did anything—if he attempted to harm Cawley—they'd hang him!

"Jason, no! Please!" She grasped his arms and used her weight to pull him back to her. "Don't! They'll hang you! Jason!"

It required all her strength, more than she knew she had, but she held him, falling on her back and dragging him atop her. Jason struggled to rise and she clung to him in desperation. "Please, Jason!"

He paused for the briefest of seconds and then his mood changed again, as rapidly as the first. Suddenly he was crushing her to himself and covering her face with hungry kisses. Demanding kisses. With both relief and joy she matched them with a rush of her own.

She needed him. She loved him! She *had* to love him to feel this way. He was so good. So kind. And he loved her so much! Jason . . . Jason . . . his name sang over and over inside her.

Time and place became unimportant. She no longer existed in a world of earth and sky, of trees, straw or shadow. Only she and Jason existed, she could know nothing but the crush of his arms around her . . . the pressure of his lips demanding her own . . .

In the swirl of her feeling she was aware of him loosening the strings to her cap, of his pulling it free and burying his face in her hair, his breath hot against her neck. "Elizabeth, I love you so!"

She struggled to free her arms from his embrace, succeeded with difficulty and then held his face in her hands to kiss him frantically. She loved him, too . . . she knew she did . . . it was so good to be loved . . . so good to be able to respond to him without holding back . . . she'd been so alone!

Jason lay still, his body so close to hers became stiff and unbending. Then, slowly, he brought his mouth to her ear and whispered, his voice muffled by her hair but sending joy through her with its truth, "Elizabeth . . . I need you . . ."

"I know, Jason." Her own voice trembled. "I know, my darling."

His hand shook as he reached to fumble with the buttons that held her dress about her throat. Shook so that she was forced to aid him, stilling his fingers and freeing the buttons herself while tears of love for him flowed freely down her cheeks.

Jason drew the open dress aside and quickly moved his head to her exposed throat where his excited, *needing* mouth raised her to a new wave of feeling for him. She grasped his head and pressed it downward, downward until she could feel its loving touch against the beginning swell of her breasts.

She drew in her breath sharply. And shivered with the joy of it.

Jason's hand moved and she strained against his touch, then pushed back his head long enough to release the remainder of the buttons to allow him full play. The questioning hand found her breast, brushed aside her thin shift and lifted her flesh to his lips. Elizabeth cried aloud, held his head in her two hands and arched her back to press even closer to him. To the exciting *demand* of him.

She opened her eyes to the shadow of the tree sheltering them. To the bits of blue beyond its embracing branches. The world beyond didn't exist. There was the now for only the two of them—herself and Jason—and no more...

He trembled fiercely as his mouth left her breast and moved up across her throat, touched her lips and then her cheek, her ear... "I love you, Elizabeth. God, how I love you!"

His hand stroking her body was heavy, clumsy in its touch, but it didn't matter. Not in the way she felt for him. Nothing mattered except being in his arms.

"Elizabeth..."

She reached to shush him with her mouth boldly against his. "Jason. It's all right..."

He was awkward, hurrying and fearful in the same moment, and she knew his love for her was crossed with his great need. Elizabeth aided him, adjusting her dress and waiting patiently as he fumbled with his own clothing.

It was managed at last and he rose above her, closed downward, and she moved gladly to meet him. To meet her love...

There was a brief pain, quick and sharp, but just as quickly lost in the pleasure of him as the two of them became one. The knowledge was a drumbeat to her rising senses as he moved. She and Jason were one. She would never be alone again...

Afterward, Jason lay spent in her arms and Elizabeth was content to hold him, marveling at the great upheaval that had occurred in him, an unheaval that had brought a near shout to his lips as he completed his doing. What a wondrous thing it had been, for the two of them to love so; she still thrilled with the pleasure of it. The excitement of love reached a great peak for a man, that had been obvious in her dear Jason, but it must continue much longer for a woman. She would, she knew, feel that excitement for some time yet today, her limbs would ache with it.

Jason moved, like a man asleep, brought his face near hers with his eyes closed, and she kissed him gently. His hand reached to stroke her back as she held him. Softly it moved up and down.

"Are you content?" she whispered. "Was our love the way it should be?"

His eyes came open. "I can't give you up again," he said, and Elizabeth felt she could drown in the softness of his look.

"You don't have to," she said. "I love you."

Jason shook his head slowly. "But we'll be apart. Except for what moments we can steal to be together, we'll live separate lives until we're free. I don't think I can stand that, Elizabeth."

She kissed his cheek. "As long as you love me and I love you, we can abide anything. I don't care what happens in these days, Jason. Not as long as I know someday we'll be together."

He raised to his elbow to look down on her. "But the thought of that bastard—if he touches you again, I'll kill him. I swear it."

She placed her fingers on his mouth. "Hush now. He'll not bother me. He'll only watch me closely and make it more difficult for me to see you. That will be the hard part, dear Jason. That I will see you so little until it's over and we can be together."

Jason threw back his head, his face a grimace. "If only it were to be soon! But it's so long away!"

Elizabeth moved from under the pressure of his body, aware suddenly that her dress was still awry, and smoothed it down. Then she sat up and turned her back to rebutton the top of it.

But Jason grasped her shoulders and turned her around roughly. "Elizabeth, let's run away! To South Carolina! Or farther! They'll never catch us, I'll see to it!"

"No, Jason." She was calmer than she would have believed. "I'll not begin my life with you in fear. I've waited too long for freedom, I'll not live it afraid of everyone I meet. If you love me, you must be patient."

His breath went out in an explosion. "You're right. Damn, I know you're right." His look told her more than his words. "It'll be hard, Elizabeth. God, it'll be so hard!"

She leaned over to kiss him lightly and then finished her buttons. When she reached for her cap as well, he stopped her. "Not yet," he said. "Don't go."

"I've got to go, Jason. He might be looking for me by now."

Jason fell to his back and looked up at her. "You're right again. And if he finds you gone, it'll make it even harder for me to see you. Tell me, Elizabeth Briggs, are you always right?"

She laughed. "When you become husband to me, Jason Welburn, *you* will always be right. I promise it."

He returned her smile with a grin of his own and Elizabeth started to rise, then sat down again to look at him seriously. "But you're wrong about one thing now," she said. "About my name. It isn't Briggs. I want you to know that."

Jason sat up quickly. "It isn't?"

"No. That's the name on my papers, and I've no help for it. But my real name is Langlee. Elizabeth Langlee. I want you to know that, especially I want *you* to know it, Jason."

He shook his head in puzzlement. "I don't understand. Why have you changed your name?"

"I didn't," she told him. "Someone else did. I'll explain it to you the next time we can be together, when I have more time. Please don't say anything about it to anyone, even to Hester. It's just that it's important to me for you not to know me by the name Briggs. Will you promise?"

He nodded, and the crease in his brow faded. "I need know only that I love you, Elizabeth. By whatever name it might be. Until it becomes Welburn."

Elizabeth leaned swiftly to kiss him one last time. Hard, for she didn't know when she might again. Then she had to force herself to leave, to hurry away to the creek without looking back, for if she did she might not be able to leave him.

Fourteen

LONG BEFORE James Oglethorpe had brought the first settlers, including Tom's own master, Noble Jones, to Yamacraw Bluff to build the town of Savannah and begin the Georgia colony, the Empire of Spain had lain claim to the territory. The Spanish, in fact, even disputed a large part of South Carolina. Spain had never forgiven England for either her unwelcomed settlements in Spanish territory in the Americas or for the years English pirates had preyed on Spanish galleons carrying their golden wealth from the new lands to the old.

Tom had been made aware of these facts in his long conversations with Wimberly Jones. The discussion of world events had grown to become part of his education. As his awareness grew, so did his curiosity. He learned of other great powers, the Kingdom of France, the Holy Roman Empire and even of dark kingdoms of yellow men in the far corners of the earth. Tales of which as a peasant boy in England he would have scoffed, but with the magic of logic and training in thought, plus a growing ability to read, he readily understood the truth.

The history of the world was interesting, but not more so than the few years of his own Georgia's existence. Politics on a royal level held his attention more when they affected the colony. And this last was why he had followed so closely Wimberly's description of Oglethorpe's struggle with the Spanish from the south.

From their stronghold, Castillo De San Marcos, at St. Augustine in the Floridas, the Spanish had constantly harassed the Georgia colony. They did all they could to stir the Creeks, Cherokees and Choctaws against the English, encouraged the Negro slaves in South Carolina to flee or revolt and even led raiding parties against isolated settlements themselves.

Many people, Tom learned, even some of them English, thought the Spanish had a just claim to the territory and that James Oglethorpe brought his own troubles upon himself by extending his line of forts deep into that part still occupied by the Spanish, thereby provoking their wrath. But Tom didn't agree. The only claim to any of this land the Spanish held that he could judge, came from their exploration and attempted conquest two centuries before. They had entered the region with soldiers, looking for gold. Following the soldiers were Jesuit priests, and later Franciscan monks, both establishing missions to convert the natives. But the ruthlessness of both, the soldiers and the priests, had raised rebellion among the Indians and the Spanish were finally driven out, retreating into the Floridas. Tom thought the territory belonged rightly to its original inhabitants and Oglethorpe was correct to negotiate with the Indians, not with the Spanish, to begin his settlements.

Wimberly, who had lived through the early troubles along with his father, told him of Oglethorpe's dueling with the Spanish and, though he wasn't aware of it at the time, that shortly before his own arrival in Savannah aboard *The Grace,* England herself had declared war on Spain.

He did know, however, that the following year, James Oglethorpe had led an army of Georgians, Indians and some reluctant South Carolinians to lay siege to St. Augustine. He'd failed, however, in his attempt to conquer that stronghold or to starve its garrison into surrender, and nearly lost his life in the process. Contracting a sickness, Oglethorpe had lain near death for two months following his return to Frederica.

Since that time, until the spring of this year, the war between the Spanish and the English colonists had been dormant. But that condition was drawing rapidly to a close. He heard the rumors of invasion a day before he was summoned to report to his master, Noble Jones.

The big house was still not yet finished and Jones, along with the rest of his family, lived in a palmetto log structure roofed with wattles. A temporary place, meant to last only until the tabby house was completed. Tom stood, his hat in one hand, and waited for the older man to finish writing at his desk.

It was a long wait, but at last he watched Jones scrawl his signature across the bottom of the papers and then reach for the sand bottle to blot it. He looked up only after he was satisfied.

"Tom, I've a task for you. An urgent one."

"Yes sir."

"It may well be dangerous."

He resisted the temptation to straighten his shoulders and throw out his chest. "Sir, I'll do whatever I can."

Jones nodded. "I know you will. What I wish you to do is to take this letter to General Oglethorpe in Frederica. It contains my report on the military status here. It also contains my best information on what he can expect from Carolina."

He paused, but his eyes didn't leave Tom's own. "It would be quicker to send the gunboat to Frederica but it's needed here. And I've no men to spare to send an armed escort. A single man, who knows the land well, has a better chance of not being encountered."

"I know the land, sir. Wimberly and I have hunted most of the way to Frederica."

A slight smile crossed the older man's face, no more than a twitch at the corner of his mouth as he nodded again. "I'm somewhat aware of that, Tom. It seems you might have spent more time at that than in my service."

"Sir, I—" But he was cut off with a wave of the hand. "You were doing precisely what I wanted you to do, Tom. You see, I've been expecting just this situation to arise, this need for a messenger who knows the countryside. No better way of doing that than by hunting it and wandering about it freely with my inquisitive son."

So that's why he'd been left alone. Well, so be it. It was a good exchange and he'd carry his part through now. "I'm ready for whatever you want, sir."

"All right. Take this letter to General Oglethorpe as quickly as you can get there. But be careful, Tom. The Spanish and their allies, the Yamassees, will have spies about. I don't want you captured."

"Yes, sir." He hesitated. "Are the rumors true then, Mr. Jones?"

"What have you heard?"

"That they're on their way here in a thousand ships, with a dozen armies."

The dry smile returned to Jones's lips. "Hardly that many, Tom. But it might as well be. To the best of our information, there are but fifty or so ships and three to four thousand men. They're under the command of Monteano, the governor of Florida. He also controls a thousand or so Yamassee warriors, though I'm not sure just how many of those will take part willingly."

"There will be a battle then, sir?"

Jones nodded. "There will be a battle. No retreat, if that's what you mean. General Oglethorpe plans to stop them at Frederica, or at least somewhere between there and here. God be with him."

"Yes, sir. What about here? Will Savannah be evacuated?"

"Why do you ask that? Oh, never mind, I know. You have a sister in Savannah, don't you."

"Yes, sir."

"Well I shouldn't worry about her if I were you. I understand there has already been panic in Savannah. Most of the women and children, and a lot of men who should have shown more gumption, have fled to Carolina. I would assume she was one of those."

"Yes, sir. I hope so. Should I leave now?"

Jones nodded. "Get a knapsack from my cook and tell her to provision it well. And secure yourself a musket."

"Sir, I could travel much faster without one I think. It would burden me and be of little use except against one other man. My best defense is not to be seen."

"I see. You're correct, of course. It proves I've chosen wisely. Get about it, Tom, and God be with you."

"Thank you, sir. But should I return immediately? Or stay?"

"Stay there until General Oglethorpe wants to send instructions to me."

"Yes, sir." He turned and went out the door, hurrying to the kitchen. The thought of it being dangerous to travel to Frederica alone seemed of no importance. He was certain of his ability to get there no matter what. It did concern him that Noble Jones didn't appear confident of victory. A Spanish

Georgia, indeed, the possibility of Spain conquering South Carolina as well, would delay if not entirely do away with his own future. Oglethorpe had to succeed!

The trip to Frederica proved far easier than he had expected. He took a horse to New Inverness, the town founded by the Highland Scots a few years before. From there to St. Simons Island was another story. He left the horse in town and traveled on foot, borrowing a cockle to negotiate the Altamaha River to the north shore of St. Simons. Fort Frederica was half way down the island, fronting on the inland waterway, placed there by General Oglethorpe for that very purpose. Any invading ships would have to pass under its guns or stand out to sea in order to reach Savannah.

His passage on the island itself was the most dangerous. Except for the forts at Frederica, and a battery placed at the southern tip called Fort St. Simon, the island was sparsely inhabited, a place of dense forests, creeks and impassable marshes, but shot through with open glades surrounded by ancient oaks, cedars and pines, festooned with hanging moss and vines. A place beautiful in its wildness, he would have liked to slow his pace and explore it, but he had a mission.

He moved with great care, both to avoid the possibility of meeting hostile Indians and to watch for the "Serpent Logs," the common name given by most Georgians to the large-mouthed reptiles Wimberly Jones called alligators. These creatures had first been discovered by Englishmen on this very island and were considered extremely dangerous.

The town lay on a bluff where the Lower Altamaha made two right-angle turns and was enclosed on the landward side by a fence of cedar stakes ten feet high, at the foot of which was a wide moat almost dry of water. The river side of the town was guarded by the fort and Tom paused for a moment to admire the latter from his vantage point at the edge of the forest.

It contained thick-timbered platforms, laid on four high and solid appearing bastions, and a large spur work thrusting well out into the river, all of which bristled with cannon. A far cry from the little fort with its meager two pounders on the Isle of Hope behind him. But then, all of this and more would be needed if Mr. Jones was correct in the number of invaders they faced.

A raised plank walkway carried him across the dry moat and into the landside port of Frederica, though he hardly set foot on it before he was challenged by the guards. They were, he thought, understandably nervous in their questioning; he tried to answer without giving the appearance of a spy, then wondered to himself just how a spy would act. He told them of his mission and showed them the letter he carried, but even so, he was taken under armed escort through the town and into the fort itself.

Minutes later, he was standing in a room in one of the two large storehouses in the fort, facing a young officer.

The first guard knuckled his forehead. "Lieutenant, sir. Prisoner here claims he's a messenger to see the general."

The officer was less than ten years older than himself, Tom judged, a slender man with a strong jaw set in a handsome face. His black wig was tied neatly in the rear and his uniform gave the appearance of just being donned. His intelligent eyes rested on Tom for a long moment, and by the time the lieutenant spoke, he knew he'd been properly sized up.

"Who's the message from?" he asked. His voice and manner was easily that of a gentleman.

"Captain Noble Jones, sir," Tom said. "Commander of Rangers at Savannah. My name is Tom Briggs."

"Well, Mr. Briggs, what is the message?"

He didn't hesitate. "My apologies, sir. The message is for General Oglethorpe. It's a letter."

The face before him didn't change, but Tom was sure he read approval in the other's eyes. "General Oglethorpe is away at the moment, Briggs. He may not be back for a day or so. If your message is urgent then we'll find a way to get it to him."

"It concerns the defense of Savannah, sir. And information on the Carolinians. I'm not aware fully of what it contains, but if you'll tell me where I can find the general, I'll deliver it to him as quickly as I can. And I'd be most obliged."

This time the officer allowed himself a short nod of approval. "He's at Fort St. Simon. That's a battery works at the extreme end of this island and about nine miles from here. My men will show you the road, but I can't spare any to go with you, we're short handed enough as it is."

"Thank you, sir. I travel well enough alone. If you please, I'll be on my way."

The officer stood up. "Have you eaten? You've time to sup first."

"My thanks, sir. But I'd prefer to be on my way. I've provisions left in my pack to carry me."

"As you wish." The lieutenant reached for his hat and stepped around Tom to lead him outside. He followed and was followed in turn by the soldiers who had brought him in.

"Be careful, Briggs," he was told as the lieutenant placed his hat upon his head. "We know the Spanish have spies on the island, both Indian and white."

"Yes, sir, I'll be careful."

"Merrow," the eyes left his face and switched to the first soldier, "show Mr. Briggs to the road."

"Yes, sir."

Another quick trip through the town and he was placed on the road to the south. Merrow, the soldier, had little to say other than to answer his question as to the identity of the officer. "Lieutenant Sutherland," he growled. "One of the damn few real officers in this place."

The others, he continued grudgingly under Tom's persistent questioning, spent far too much of their time in drinking and dueling for this soldier's tastes, to say nothing of prancing about in front of the womenfolk. A condition that would not have been allowed to occur in Merrow's old Guards Regiment of Foot in England.

Curious as always, Tom continued to ply him with questions as they walked back to the gate on the other side of town. But Merrow evidently decided he'd spoken too much and refused to answer further, even turning away without a word when he left him on the road outside.

The woods south of Frederica were, if anything, even more dense than those through which he'd already passed. The road was narrow, and hardly cleared the first wood until it skirted a heavy marsh. Tom debated briefly whether to leave the road altogether for safety's sake, then decided it would be best to continue on it for a time. A mile or two more, and he'd leave it to travel through whatever lay beside it under cover.

A bad decision, he should have realized it earlier. Any spies lurking in the woods or marshes would be close to the fort at Frederica, not miles away where there was nothing to gain. He'd traveled no more than two when he almost ran into them where the road opened into a savannah of knee-high grass, devoid of trees.

Only a movement at the opposite end of the meadow, caught because he was nervously alert, stopped Tom from exposing himself. He paused, his heart pounding, and fought the impulse to jump to his left behind a tree. He may not have been seen by whoever was on the other side of the clear space, probably hadn't been seen or he wouldn't have caught their own movement. But if he stirred now he ran the risk.

Slowly, to decrease the chance of being seen, he dropped into a crouch and waited.

A heart-stopping moment later they appeared, four of them, three Indians in breechcloths and leggings led by a dark-skinned white man in buckskin. They crossed the road quickly and disappeared into the woods on the other side. Smarter than himself, Tom thought with a grimace, they weren't ambling along the road like some country bumpkin.

He had to move now. Although they had crossed the road, it was obvious they were coming in his direction. He'd be discovered soon enough if he didn't move.

He eased to his hands and knees and crawled to one side, trying not to disturb the grass more than necessary, and allowed himself to breathe only after he was behind the tree.

Time was growing short, but he had to move with more intelligence than speed if he weren't to be caught. He'd learned a great deal in his wanderings with Wimberly Jones and considered himself a woodsman now, but he was no match for the Indians. One wrong move and he was as good as dead.

The savannah was fairly wide, and the side through which the enemy had gone was guarded by a crescent-shaped hedge of palmettoes and underwood. On the other lay a marsh, thick, and from all appearances, impassable. But he really had no choice. He couldn't take the side the Indians were on, even if he could cross the road unseen. And he couldn't go back to Frederica with them so close behind him. The marsh was his only chance.

He moved quickly and carefully through the trees, always trying to keep some between him and the men somewhere on the other side of the meadow. As the trees thinned, the ground became soft underfoot and he had trouble lifting his feet without an accompanying sucking sound in the bright stillness. The difficulty lasted only a few yards, then he was wading in the marsh proper, and the heavy, reed-filled water rapidly approached his chest.

His knapsack was being soaked, but the letter was in his hat and safe. But when the water reached his neck, he knew he couldn't continue, he'd have to back up and find another way.

Tom moved to his left, still away from the road, suddenly more concerned with drowning in the sullen water than with the Indians. He felt a surge of relief when the slippery bottom under his feet began to climb abruptly. He struggled ahead and the bottom rose sharply until he was no more than waist deep, then just as suddenly dropped off again. He had crossed an underwater ridge. A ridge that was going in the direction he wanted to go. *If it would only continue to the other side!*

It did, rising at times until he appeared to be walking on top of the water before dropping down again. When he reached the end of the marsh, he looked back and adjudged the hidden ridge lay in near a straight line according to where he'd entered and where he now stood. A good fact to know when he returned, for he'd not be damn fool enough to walk along the road. Not unless he was accompanied by most of the troops at Fort St. Simon.

That fort turned out to be little more than earthworks thrown up to face the entrance to Jekyll Sound; earthworks that were protection for a battery of cannon. Well to the rear of the mounds were huts to house the soldiers who manned the guns and a watchtower for early warning. In the sound itself, and lying under the protection of the fort, was a cutter and five larger boats, mounted with smaller cannon and swivel guns.

Tom's initial impression, however, was that this place was a fort in name only. It was obviously weak.

General James Oglethorpe was a tall man with a well-filled frame. A handsome man, Tom had heard many tales of the women who had set their cap for him only to find themselves virtually ignored for all their trouble. He had a bold face, a large, Roman nose and a cupid's bow of an upper lip that would have been feminine on most any other man. But the long jaw and the sloping planes of his cheeks, as well as the forward jut of his chin, gave an immediate impression of masculine strength.

He read Tom's letter quickly, his eyes traveling over it at a speed that made the latter wonder that he read it at all. However, his remarks quickly dispelled that notion.

"The Carolinians will rally," he said contemptuously. "But far too late to be of service to us here. They'll argue and dicker with each other and finally send us a troop or two." His hazel eyes, under bushy brows, bore into Tom's own suddenly. "But by that time, young man, we'll either be victorious or defeated."

Tom didn't know whether to speak or not, then decided the general seemed to be waiting. "I'm sure it'll be victory, sir."

"I wish I were as sure, messenger," Oglethorpe grunted. "At any rate, we'll know the answer shortly."

"The Spanish have arrived then, sir?" he asked. But the general only gave him a short nod and abruptly strode away, raising an arm to signal others to his side.

The Spanish ships were a grand sight when they came. If the situation had not been so desperate, if they weren't the enemy, Tom would have exulted in their sleek-lined beauty. As it was, they were more dangerous than scorpions, for their deadly stingers were the hundreds of armed men he knew were being transported in their trim hulls.

They came on in a rush, favored by a strong wind and the flood tide for which they had been waiting, thirty-six in all as he counted. Tom measured their strength from a vantage point behind the earthworks where he could see the battle but not place himself in the way of the cannoneers. The first ship contained twenty-four guns, two more held twenty guns and these leaders were followed by two large scows of fourteen guns apiece, then four schooners, four sloops and the remainder made up of half-gallies mounting two-to-four-pounders in their bows. He'd never seen such a formidable array in his life!

Opposing the Spanish were the guns of the fort, eighteen-pounders on the rampart and a water battery of four-pounders. General Oglethorpe had also armed his one merchant ship with twenty-two guns and protected it with two guard schooners and a few small trading vessels. It was pitiful strength against the firepower of the Spanish. Tom was aware of it even before the cannon began to roar around him.

The English were determined to make a fight of it, however,

and their small force more than held its own for nearly four hours. Tom watched in pride and amazement as the tiny vessels harried the Spanish ships like hounds worrying a boar. It was only after most of them had been damaged and one of the guard schooners sunk that the enemy fleet forced its way past the fort and moved up the channel behind a leading breeze, its battle flags flying in triumph. Tom stood with the others around the suddenly useless guns of the fort and watched them go.

The silence didn't last long. Oglethorpe moved rapidly, his orders repeated by shouting officers, and in far less time than Tom could imagine, the guns of the fort were spiked to prevent their use by the Spanish, the cohorns burst and he found himself, along with every defender there, racing up the road to the safety of Frederica.

He didn't understand the need for such haste and put a hand on the arm of the man hurrying beside him, one of the gunners and a man whose quickness afoot belied the heavy gray in his hair. "Why are we retreating? They haven't attacked us ashore yet."

The man hardly glanced his way. "The general figures the Dons to put ashore below Frederica, lad. If we don't pass the point first, we'll be cut off." He spat aside without slackening his pace. "And then they'll do us in quick enough. No doubt of it."

"Where do you think, Page? Another soldier had overheard the comments. "Reckon the cove?"

The old man shook his head. "Gascoigne's Bluff, I figure. It's nearer the fort and a better landing."

The second soldier continued without replying for a time, and Tom matched their stride in silence. The three of them had covered half a mile or more before the man decided to speak again. "Reckon you're right at that, Page. Gascoigne's plantation would be the best spot. We'd damn well best rush if we're to beat them past there, I think."

Page merely grunted and Tom wished he knew how far ahead the spot lay. He'd dodged one Spaniard and three Indians on the way down this road, he'd surely hate to face a few thousand on the return.

The others obviously shared his worry as the pace increased, most of the men afoot and in a half run with the general leading the way on horseback. Well before dawn they reached Frederica and poured through its land port, down the nearly deserted main street and into the fort itself. It had been a grim run that succeeded, but Tom knew worse was on its way.

He was tired, but too much on edge to sleep. He ate with the others, but while they sought out places to lie down, he went in search of the officer who'd talked to him when he first arrived and found him standing near the entrance to the powder magazine, talking to another officer. Tom stopped quietly near them until he was acknowledged.

Lieutenant Sutherland broke off his conversation abruptly as he noticed him. "You wanted to see me, messenger?"

"Yes, sir. But only for myself, sir. I've no message to deliver."

The lieutenant frowned, caught at the same time a questioning look from his brother officer and nodded in Tom's direction. "This man fetched a message from Savannah to the general," he said. "Carried it on to St. Simon."

The man to whom he spoke was a large man, wearing the tartar of a Scot. Hanging on his side was one of the large broad swords Tom had heard called a claymore. It was a wicked looking blade, even at rest. "You were in the fort for the fight, were you?" its owner asked him.

Tom nodded. "Yes, sir."

"Then you should be finding your rest, man. You'll not be worth that much in the next fight without it."

It was a rebuke and probably deserved. But he couldn't join the next fight without both permission and a weapon. "Yes, sir. I'll do that soon. But it's about the fighting that I'm here. I'd hoped to ask Lieutenant Sutherland to give me a musket and allow me to serve under him. Unless I'm needed as a messenger again."

The Scot's frown broke into an immediate smile, a broad smile, full across his wide face. "By Harry! A man who *wants* to fight! What do you think of that, lieutenant? Not a lot like this one around, eh?"

Sutherland refused to join in his laughter and looked at Tom skeptically. "Can you fire a musket... Briggs, wasn't it?"

"Yes, sir. Briggs. I've done a good bit of hunting since I've been here in Georgia, sir. I'm a fair shot with a musket, I think."

The officer's eyebrows rose sharply. "A good bit of hunting?

How've you found the leisure for that? I should think you had
work to do; or does no one bother to work in Savannah now,
as I've heard?"

"I did as I was told to do, sir," Tom answered quietly. "I'm
also fair at that."

The Scot laughed again and this time Sutherland joined him
with a wry smile of his own. "Well said, Briggs. Perhaps you'll
make a fighter at that." He turned to the other. "Mackay, you
think I should give this man a musket?"

"By God, Sutherland, if you don't, I will myself. I truly
like this lad's spirit."

The faint smile on Sutherland's face disappeared as he turned
back to Tom. "Find yourself some rest, Briggs. Then report
to me in five hours. No more and no less, mind you. Unless,
of course, the fort comes under attack before then. Dismissed."

"Yes sir." He fought down the urge to knuckle his forehead.
That was a peasant's gesture and he was not a peasant, indentured or not. "Thank you, sir."

Including among the planters he had called to aid the fort, the
regular soldiers under his command, and the Georgia Rangers,
General Oglethorpe had ninety Indian allies, and he used the
latter in the way they knew best. They roamed the woods
between Fort Frederica and the main Spanish camp now set up
on the site of Fort St. Simon, harassed their pickets, watched
their movements, and even occasionally captured an unwary
Spaniard. A few at a time and sometimes singly, the Indians
filtered back to Frederica to report to its commander and immediately left again. Not, however, any quicker than fresh
rumors, sparked by their arrival, had spread among the fort's
defenders.

Tom had discovered that Oglethorpe had little more than
six hundred men, including his Indian allies. The rumors tended
to confirm Noble Jones's words that the Spanish had brought
three to five thousand soldiers. It seemed hopeless odds even
with the protection of the fort. But he kept his doubts to himself
and listened to the others until slowly his hope grew. There
was one large fact in favor of the defenders. The heavy woods
and marshes along the road between them and the Spanish
would confine any march in strength. The enemy would be
forced to advance in columns rather than in ranks and therefore
would be unable to exploit their numbers to the fullest. It was

this, he learned, that the general was counting on.

Tom hoped he was right. At any rate, there was little to do now but wait for the Spanish to attack, and waiting wasn't an easy thing to do. He cleaned his musket for the third time since morning, measured each shot from his bag against the muzzle once more and checked his powder horn for tightness. Minutes later, Lieutenant Sutherland appeared on a dead run.

"To arms, men!" he shouted. "They're coming!"

Tom broke after him nearly forgetting to resling his powder horn, as all around him men scrambled to follow.

Sutherland didn't wait to see how many were obeying, he went through the fort gates still running and only outside, in the town proper, did he pause to take stock. His men were experienced, they quickly formed ranks, and Tom found a place near the end for himself. Sutherland didn't give the last stragglers time to catch up before he waved his bare sword. "Forward! At the trot!"

Excitement flashed through him like a thousand stinging needles. He—Tom Langlee—was going into battle! He was actually to fight other men—to fire a musket at them and be fired on in return. Perhaps even to face them at knifepoint! Was it fear—or anticipation—that set him atremble? No matter. He'd give good account of himself! By the Furies, he'd promise himself that!

They were moving down the road at a run, the same road he'd traveled twice in the last days, and ahead of them he could see a troop of soldiers already disappearing around the first bend. Within seconds, the sounds of rapidly fired muskets mixed with wild cries, told him the battle was already joined.

The noise increased as they drew near the bend and Sutherland raised his sword for a halt. "Prime and load!" he shouted.

The fight ahead seemed to change in sound as he approached and it took a moment for him to realize it was suddenly both dying and moving away. When he rounded the bend he could see why. Oglethorpe himself had charged the Spaniards full force with his Rangers and a Highland company, and the enemy had melted under that first fierce assault. Dozens of them lay dead or wounded and the rest were in full flight down the road. Tom stopped with the rest to watch, feeling both disappointment and relief. In the center of the site, Oglethorpe reared in his stirrups and waved his men on.

Hours later, Tom was waiting again, squatting at the edge

of a savannah and peering out across its long grass to the south where the Spaniards might appear once more. They had pursued the detachment the general's charge had routed for a mile or so before halting on orders. Oglethorpe then left three platoons of the regiment and a company of Highland foot soldiers in the woods at the edge of this savannah to ambush the enemy should he return in force. Theirs was to be a delaying tactic while the general returned to ready the rest of his troops.

Tom crouched a few paces away from both Lieutenant Sutherland and Lieutenant Mackay and listened to their guarded whispers as they spoke of feints, landing parties, flanking movements and other things he didn't understand. A light rain had begun and he hunched over his musket in an attempt to keep its prime dry.

The savannah was the same one in which he'd almost allowed himself to be caught by the Indians a few days ago, he realized suddenly as he waited. On his left, the marsh appeared quite as impassable as it had that time. Finding that ridge had been incredible luck; luck that had saved his life, he had no doubt of it.

He turned to point it out to the man nearest him when the opposite side of the meadow suddenly erupted with screaming men at a full run, firing weapons wildly as they came.

Tom stared in amazement. The ambush was discovered! The Spanish knew they were there!

Panic set in as the English realized it was themselves that had been caught by surprise. And caught by a much superior force. Spanish, Indians, and to Tom's astonishment, Negroes poured out of the woods on the other side of the savannah. There were hundreds of them!

A ragged firing was going off around him and Tom threw up his own musket, took aim on a running Spaniard and felt the hammer fall—uselessly. His powder was damp!

Frantically he cleared the chamber and poured fresh powder in, looked up and found the first of the attackers had passed the center of the meadow and was nearly upon them. And more were still pouring from the woods!

He jammed wadding home, jerked the ramrod free, primed, leveled and fired, the small explosion before his face followed by a hard jar against his shoulder. As soon as his smoke cleared he looked hard, but the man at whom he aimed was still on his feet unhurt. Damn!

He cleared the barrel and rammed more powder and shot down it, then primed as a cry went up around him. "Fall back! Retreat!"

Suddenly he was alone. The men on either side of him were gone. But he had missed his shot! He leveled the musket on the chest of a running Negro and squeezed the trigger more slowly than the first time. When the smoke cleared he shouted aloud. The man was down!

A moment later he was running himself.

The English rallied and fought desperately, but they were badly outnumbered and were being forced through the woods. They slowed the attackers by the sheer rapidity of their firing, but couldn't hold them long.

Tom knelt to reload and found himself at the side of Lieutenant Sutherland who gripped his sword in one hand and a pistol in the other as he cursed steadily. "Damn my blood," he said aloud, "If there was only a way to get behind them!"

Mackay appeared from nowhere. "We're beaten, Sutherland!" he shouted. "Pull back to the fort!"

"Don't give in!" Sutherland spat. "We can hold them!"

"Don't be a fool, man!" The Scot grasped him by the shoulder. "They've got us outnumbered! We stand no chance!"

Tom moved forward without realizing what he was doing. "Sir, I know a way around them!"

Both officers stared at him in astonishment.

"You just said if you knew a way around the Spanish," he told the look on Sutherland's face and fought to keep his voice from rising. "I do! I can take you through the marsh to the left!"

He was seized roughly, his feet nearly leaving the ground, as the big Scot gathered in his coat at the collar. "Tell us, lad! And it'll be worth your life to be lying, I swear!"

"We can wade the marsh," Tom said quickly. "I know a ridge through it. It can't be seen, but it's there. I used it only a few days ago."

"How'd you find it?" Sutherland too put his hand on Tom.

"Does it matter?" Tom asked him quickly. "I swear, sir, I can lead you to it and around the Spaniards."

"Then go, lad! Lead us!" Mackay made the decision for his brother officer, turning at the same time to bawl for his men to follow him.

Sutherland's dark eyes swept Tom's face only briefly, and

then he, too, began to shout orders.

Tom led both of them along with dozens of men through the woods, trying to ignore the whistle of musket balls around his head and the lump lying in his belly. The thought grew in his mind that if somehow he missed the ridge, these men would be helpless in the deep marsh. They would either drown or be killed one by one by the Spaniards as they attempted to fight their way out of the reeds and water.

But it worked. Under cover of the rain he found the ridge more quickly than he'd expected and led them across the marsh. At the other side, behind the Spanish who were still pursuing their fellow soldiers, the Englishmen once more crouched in ambush and fought to dry their powder.

This time Tom knew they wouldn't be discovered by Indian scouts. The Spanish wouldn't dream of them being behind them, not when the only route was through an impassable marsh.

He looked at the two officers who squatted behind palmetto logs and measured the brightness of battle in their eyes. The Dons would succeed in driving the rest of the Englishmen into Fort Frederica, no doubt. But then their guard would be down, and that would be the moment when these waiting men would strike. He took a deep breath, and waited . . .

It became almost *too* quiet. The men in ambush were doing such a good job of it even the birds were making their normal sounds in the trees around the savannah. And the rain had stopped, an even better sign. He was afraid it couldn't be true. That something would go wrong at the last minute.

Tom eased his bottom to a fallen log and stretched his legs to break the strain at his kness. But in a moment he was back again at a crouch as new sounds came from the woods before them. The enemy was returning, returning noisily, with a great deal of laughter and shouting. He slowly raised his musket and rested the barrel over the stump in front of him.

They came through the trees in open ranks, carrying their arms carelessly over their shoulders and joking loudly with each other. Dozens of them at first, and then a hundred or more, he quickly lost count as he waited, holding his breath.

On they came, Spanish soldiers, Indians in full war paint, and Negroes in uniform who were officered by men of their own race. They sauntered out of the woods and into the broad meadow as if they hadn't a care in the world.

Tom set his jaw and lay an eye to the barrel of his musket. This would be far different from the last battle. There would be a surprise this time. And no rain to misfire a musket.

He grew tired of waiting for a signal. Straining. Why didn't the order come?

Slowly the Spanish came to a halt, gathered in the middle of the meadow and, to his great surprise, stacked their arms and flung themselves on the ground to rest.

Tom held his weapon steady but eased an eye around to the two officers. Mackay held a grin on his face as the Scot nodded to a Highlander. The soldier answered the grin and raised his cap on a stick for a signal.

It quickly became a slaughter. The men lying on the grass held no chance against the murderous fire from the woods. Some died as they lay, others tried to seize their weapons, but most tried to run from the deadly swarm of musket balls.

Tom fired, reloaded and fired again, the second time deliberately picking a Spanish officer trying vainly to rally his men. The Spaniard spun about as if hammered with a sledge and pitched face-forward to the ground.

"At them, men!" Mackay's deep bellow rose above both the rattle of muskets and the screams of the dying. "No quarter!"

Tom scarcely knew what he was doing anymore, only that the blood was pounding in his veins, its rush driving him to his feet in a charge forward.

He ran, reversing the musket in his hands to use as a club, swung it in a wide arc and drove a whirling Spaniard to his knees.

Another thrust a sword in his direction and Tom evaded it by getting his musket up in time to cause it to slide harmlessly along the barrel. He brought the heel of the weapon up instinctively and crashed it against the man's jaw, flinging him backwards. Then spun as a warning cry bearing his name sounded, only to pitch forward into blackness as the world exploded around his head...

Noble Jones stared long at the young man standing in front of him and then nodded at the chair across the room from his desk. "I think you'd best seat yourself, Thomas. You've had a long boat ride for a man in that condition."

He waited, his jaw propped on the folded fists of his two hands as the other made his way, very unsteadily, he thought, to the chair indicated and sat down slowly and carefully.

"How do you feel?" he asked after the maneuver was completed. "That head wound appears serious."

"I'll be all right, sir," Briggs said. "The surgeon at Frederica says my head isn't broken; I've only a concussion."

"I see. Well, I trust he's right. But I'd prefer to see for myself, if you don't mind. But later, after you've had a rest. Right now I think I'll prescribe a brandy and whatever comfort that chair might bring to you while I read this letter you've fetched me."

He paused to shake his head. "I'm surprised that General Oglethorpe sent it by you, surely he had men in better condition? But then, I suppose they were needed to defend Frederica."

The young man failed to answer and Jones's worry increased. He was most fond of Thomas Briggs. Almost as much as he was of his own son, if the truth were known. He'd had very little luck with indentured servants in his lifetime, but this lad was different, as if reflecting the drive of his own youth. He smiled to himself at that. It could very well be that in Thomas Briggs he saw the desires of a young Noble Jones.

He rose and crossed to a sideboard, opened it and produced a bottle. Pouring a glass full, he returned and extended it to the man in the chair.

"Sir, I've only experience for beer," Briggs said.

"Then it's time you learned a gentleman's drink, Thomas. Sip it slowly. Tis a strong drink, but comforting if not overdone." He smiled. "I speak as a surgeon, of course."

He waited, watched as the boy drank a whisper and then returned to his chair to open and read the letter from Oglethorpe. When he was done, he lifted his eyes and looked at young Thomas Briggs with new interest.

The boy was in bad shape, it was obvious even from this distance. Well, he'd examine his wound himself shortly and then see that he was put to bed. But first there were things to be talked of, things that couldn't wait.

"Do you know how you came to be hurt?" he asked.

"Yes sir. A tomahawk, I was told. I was lucky it wasn't a straight on blow according to Lieutenant Sutherland. He's the officer I was assigned to in the battle. He's also the man who killed the Indian who struck me or I might've been finished. I owe him my life."

Jones nodded. "From what I understand in this letter, Thomas, this officer and others owe a great deal to you. That must have been quite a trick you performed, leading them around the enemy to strike in the rear."

"I guess I was lucky there too, sir." Briggs shifted under his look and sipped at his brandy.

"Luck, perhaps, Thomas. But I think intelligence played a greater part. Tell me, did General Oglethorpe speak to you? I mean, after you were brought to Frederica?"

Briggs looked up in surprise. "No, sir. He was much too busy chasing the Spanish. They've now left the Georgia coast completely, you know."

"Yes I know. The general fooled them into thinking he had reinforcements coming. Thanks more than a little to the defeat you and the others put to them at that marsh." He leaned back in his chair. "I understand they're already calling it Bloody Marsh because so many Spaniards were killed there."

Briggs nodded slowly, painfully. "I wouldn't know about that, sir."

"Well, they're gone and we'll have peace for a time. At least until they lick their wounds and decide to try again. But back to the general. He may not have spoken to you, but he took time to write me this letter and it concerns you. Did you know that?"

"No, sir. No one mentioned it to me. I was merely told to bring it to you."

Jones had been thinking as he spoke and now he sat up again in his chair, well satisfied with what he had decided. "Thomas, General Oglethorpe speaks in the letter of your playing the hero's part in the battle at the marsh. He was, or rather is, very impressed with both your courage and your intelligence."

He reached again for the letter, glanced at it and then looked back at Briggs. "In his words, 'Georgia badly needs young men such as Thomas Briggs.'"

He waited and Briggs slowly inclined his head. "I thank the general for those words, sir."

Jones couldn't resist a small smile. "There's more, Thomas. General Oglethorpe has asked me to sell him your contract of indenture. If I will do so, he says, he intends to immediately release you from its obligation. He wants you a free man."

As he watched, the pain fled from the young man's eyes,

to be replaced by something else. Hope? No—desire. Strong, passionate desire . . .

"That's most generous of him, sir," Briggs said slowly.

"But I cannot allow him to do that," Jones said quietly, and before the desire could flee from the eyes he was watching so closely, "For I intend to free you myself. As of this day, Thomas, you're free of all debt to me."

He paused. "I think you've more than repaid me with your service to this colony."

The boy turned his head quickly, obviously to hide a sudden choking, and Noble felt it best to continue talking. "As a free man, however, you'll need some means of supporting yourself. If you choose to farm, then I'll see about getting you some land from the Trustees. But if you prefer to work at something else, Thomas, I'd be most happy to have you in my employment. I need help in my position as surveyor. Would you like to learn that trade?"

"Sir, you do me great honor. Your generosity . . ." Thomas couldn't continue.

He felt a stiffness in his own throat and cleared it sharply. "Nonsense. If you come to work for me, I'll get my wages out of you, have no doubt of that. I'm not a man to waste good coin. Well, do you agree?"

Briggs was silent for a long time, staring first at the floor and then raising his head to look even longer out the open door. Jones could imagine what was going on in his mind, but when he spoke at last, the words were startling.

"No, sir." Briggs turned to look directly at him. "I don't wish to be a surveyor. Nor do I wish to farm. But I do desire to work for you, and I'll give you more than a fair share of my labor."

He paused and Jones started to speak, thought better of it and waited.

"Sir, I have a great desire to be a surgeon such as yourself. The same calling you're giving your own son. I know I've no right to ask, but if you'll consider giving me that training in exchange for my work, I promise you'll not regret it."

Jones stared at him in astonishment. Then suddenly wondered why he was astonished. He knew Briggs was intelligent, he'd known that from the start and told Wimberly to teach him so that he might someday become a valuable assistant. But it'd never occurred to him that the lad would want to become a doctor.

Thomas mistook his silence. "I'm sorry, sir. I shouldn't have asked. It would be unfair to Wimberly."

Jones shook away his thoughts. "Nonsense, Thomas. My training Wimberly has nothing to do with it. Georgia is going to grow again; many people will come here eventually. There'll be the need for many doctors. Yes, I'll be pleased to strike that bargain with you. I intend to start a plantation here on the island, you'll help me manage it, and in exchange I'll teach you along with Wimberly. An excellent idea."

"Sir, I don't know what to say."

Noble Jones was delighted with himself. "Say nothing. Nothing to be said. A fair exchange between us; I told you I'll get my money's worth from you. Now, we'll find a bed for you to mend in. You'll get your first taste of what it means to be a doctor by becoming the patient."

"Thank you, sir." Briggs stood up as he did, but a bit slower. Before Jones could cross the room, however, he spoke again. "Sir, could I ask another boon?"

Noble's eyebrows raised. It was unlike the boy to ask favors, especially after he'd just been granted two very large ones. Large ones indeed. Had he misjudged him after all?

"What would that be?" he asked nevertheless.

"That I be able to change my name, sir, now that I'll be free. The name Briggs isn't really mine. It belonged to the man who took me in as a babe and raised me and my sister. I'd like very much to claim my own."

This young man was full of surprises. "You were adopted?"

"No, sir. I was taken in because the man was ordered to do so. Not because he wanted me or my sister. He held no love for either of us."

Jones nodded slowly. "I see. Well, there's no reason you can't regain your name of birth. I can see to the papers. What is it?"

"Langlee, sir. Thomas Langlee." He pronounced the name slowly, as if he were savoring it. And Noble Jones suddenly knew that he had been waiting a long time to do so.

He extended his hand on impulse. "Very well, Thomas *Langlee*. So shall it be. I look forward to our new relationship."

He shook hands, felt the coldness of it and immediately

became worried again. "Good Heavens, lad! I nearly forgot you're a sick man. Come, lean on my arm; we've got to get you to bed no matter what your name might be."

He glanced up and the pale face was struggling to grin. "I'll not argue with that, sir. Under either name."

Fifteen

SHE NOW OWNED two dresses, the first time in her life she'd ever owned more than one at a time. Cawley had given her the second, and Elizabeth didn't know whether he'd discussed it with her mistress or not. Probably not. Sarah Cawley had little to say to anyone of late, her shrill voice had lessened almost to the point of silence since their return from South Carolina, her complaints had become fewer and fewer until they ceased entirely. She now spent most of her days lying in bed with her face turned to the wall. Elizabeth no longer doubted that she was sick, though she didn't show the same signs as her two sons in their illness. She bore neither the sudden sweating for no reason, nor did she return the little she ate in green bile that so often stained their lips in spite of the best care their servant-nurse could manage.

Cawley had handed Elizabeth the dress two evenings ago, telling her that she needed to change to prevent wearing out the older one. He'd waited, staring at her, but Elizabeth merely nodded and accepted the garment, knowing she fared better by her silence even though that too would anger him. Any answer from her would lead to further words until he would work himself into a rage. Painful silence between them was better than his tirades.

She thought about that as she sat on a stool pulled close to Andrew's bed, alternating between watching the child and mending a slight tear in her old dress with very small stitches. Cawley hated her at times, that was more than obvious in his manner, but it was because he despised himself for the thoughts he harbored toward her. For all his high talk of religion, it was sin he had on his mind at times when he looked at her, and he couldn't stand not being in control of himself.

Why didn't he just sell her contract and be rid of her? He certainly needed the money the sale would bring him, and more than once he'd reminded her that Peter Abercromby still wished to buy her. But then, if he did sell her, who would tend his sick wife and children while he worked his fields of trees? Who, indeed, would keep his house for him and cook his meals, poor fare that he provided now for the latter. No, she could answer her own question. Cawley might hate the sight of her, but he couldn't afford to be rid of her. Not until his wife recovered or his silkworms finally began to spin.

Andrew stirred, coughed heavily enough to raise his head and then fell back again. His head hardly touched the pillow before she was at his side, wetting a small towel in a pan by the bed and wiping his face with it. The cool of the cloth seemed to soothe him and she wet it again and bathed his neck above the blanket. It pained Elizabeth to look down on the sunken cheeks and the closed but nearly transparent eyelids.

Poor little creature. He rarely opened those eyelids now. He'd been sick before, but nothing like the way he'd become since their flight across the river into South Carolina at the news of the Spanish invasion. The nights of sleeping on the open ground had been more than his frail body could stand. He was dying now, dying slowly, but dying nonetheless. She knew it and she was young enough herself for the fact to pain her. The Cawleys, like many English parents she had noted, seemed to love their children well enough in life but did not suffer greatly their death. The loss of a child was a thing they accepted as the will of God. For herself, it seemed more the parents neglect, or ignorance, than God's doing. A thought she was wise enough to keep entirely to herself.

Andrew coughed again, a weaker sound, more the mew of

a sick cat. Elizabeth bathed his face again, pulled back the bed clothes and did his chest as well all the way to his stomach. It hurt not to take him into her arms and hold him close, but to do so seemed to pain his body the more. He didn't like to be touched. If only Cawley would summon the doctor again. If only that man when he came could do more than shake his head and say it was something the boy had to overcome.

The thought of Andrew's dying was too much for her of a sudden; she turned, picked up her candleholder from the table and crossed the room to where her mistress lay. For once, Sarah Cawley had her eyes open and looked back at her unblinking in the glow of the candle.

"Are you better, mistress?" Elizabeth asked. "Would you care to eat something? There's some peas and bread I'm keeping warm for Mr. Cawley."

The eyes remained on her face, but they were lifeless eyes— as if the woman in the bed made no attempt at all to understand.

Elizabeth waited another moment, then turned away from that bed as well. Sarah Cawley could speak if she wanted to do so, there was little need to worry about it. Whatever the sickness she had, it was as much in her mind as her body, Elizabeth was convinced of it. She was also convinced that her mistress had made up her mind to die—to rid herself of a world she didn't want. And there was nothing anyone could do about that either.

She had to get out for a time. Being alone in this room of the dying, one who had no choice of it and one who did, was suddenly more than she could stand. Robert was in the loft, she had placed him in her own bed several days ago to spare him the sight and sounds of his dying brother. During the day she sat him in a chair and covered him with a blanket and talked to him. The boy wasn't as sick as his brother and lying in a bed all day troubled him greatly.

She held the candle and climbed the ladder, only to find him sitting up on her pallet for all the world as if he had been expecting her. Which he most probably had.

"What in the world are you doing?" She used a playful, scolding tone, one she often employed with him, knowing he liked being mothered.

"Beth, I couldn't sleep. Really I couldn't, though I tried." He grinned. "I guess I slept too much today."

Elizabeth crossed on her hands and knees to sit beside him on the pallet. "I ordered you to go to sleep, young man. I do not like to be disobeyed. The only reason you haven't done so is that you knew full well I'd come up here to check on you and then you'd coax me to play a game with you. Now isn't that so?"

He nodded, watching her, and his grin widened. "You will, won't you?"

She couldn't hold the mock frown and laughed. "Of course I will, you little tease. But you must pull that blanket around you or you'll catch cold. Here, I'll do it."

"But it's hot, Beth. I get so tired of it."

His words sent a new alarm through her and she reached to feel his brow with her hand. He was warm, but not overly so. Still, with his brother so sick and no one knowing the reason for either of them being the way they were, she should take no chance at all. "Well pull it to your shoulders anyway. That is if you want me to play."

She did it herself, adjusting it carefully. "There. Now what shall we play?"

"Let's play the cat and mouse," he said quickly. "You used to play that with Andrew and me a lot."

Gently she shook her head. "We can't. Not with you sick, it'll tire you too much. How about making shadows?"

Robert looked at her in puzzlement. "What do you mean?"

"Like this." She moved the candleholder around to the other side and then held her hands before it so their shadow would reflect on the wall below the roof.

Robert looked, then shook his head. "Your hands make a shadow, but that's no fun."

"Just wait a moment, Mr. Impatience. You have to make something out of the shadow. Like a turkey gobbler."

She folded the fingers of one hand to meet her thumb and extended the tips of the other above the first. "There, you see? Mr. Turkey with his comb. And he talks, too. Gobble, gobble!"

Robert laughed as she moved her fingers. "I see him! Do another!"

"All right. How about a hawk flying high in the sky?" She crossed her hands and waved her fingers. "See?"

He pushed the blanket aside and clapped his hands. "That's good! Show me how!"

"Oh, but that's part of the game," she told him: "You must use your imagination. See if you can't think of something to make."

He squinted his eyes in hard thought and she waited patiently until he slowly shook his head. "I can't think of anything to make, Beth."

"Of course you can." She reached to take his two hands in her own. "For instance, you surely know that if you held your arms close together like this, and waved your fingers at the top of them, it would be a tree being blown by a hard wind?"

Robert laughed again. "It is, isn't it?"

Before she could reply, the door in the room below them slammed suddenly and loudly, startling them both. Quickly she grasped his hands and lay him back in the bed. "Your father has come home. You go to sleep while I see to his supper."

He started to protest as she expected him to do, but stopped when she held a finger to his lips. "Hush now. Or I'll not allow you to sleep up here anymore."

Robert closed his eyes immediately and she moved quickly to the ladder.

Cawley stood in the middle of the room and watched her descend. She tried to ignore the stare, looking away, but her mind's eye could readily see him. The difficulties of the past few months were leaving their mark heavily on her master; Cawley had lost much of his weight and hard lines now crossed the planes of cheeks that were no longer rounded. His clothes hung much too loosely, and his wig was seldom in proper place. He seemed to Elizabeth a haunted man.

Worse than his appearance was his temper. In spite of her resolve, she knew she now feared him.

"What were you doing up there?" he demanded. "Don't you know the hour's early? Or did you not care that your master was still out?"

"I was seeing to Robert, Mr. Cawley," she said, and hurried to the hearth where she'd left the meal warming. "You know I asked if I could put him in my bed to separate him from Andrew."

"Lying wench. The boy should have been asleep by now. You were slacking about yourself, knowing I wouldn't be home."

She didn't reply. There was no point in denying his words nor defending herself in any way. He would think as he pleased no matter what she said. She bent over the pot of Indian peas and lifted the cover with one hand to stir them with a spoon.

Cawley waited to see if she would answer, then stalked across the room to sit down heavily at the table. "What's that you're cooking?"

"Peas, sir. And some bread of corn to go with it. I'll be but a minute."

"Bah! You've served that for the last three days, girl. Can't you think of any better?"

"It's all we have, Mr. Cawley. The only thing left in your garden. The rest went bad from lack of watering while we were across the river."

"It went bad from your neglect, you mean. As everything else here seems to do. With your mistress sick abed and myself away during the day, you've no one to answer for your lazy way, have you?

But his voice dropped off at the end, and Elizabeth wondered if he realized himself how often he uttered the complaint. His silence lasted but a moment, however, before he roused himself again. "Fetch me a mug of beer now. Don't wait until you serve my plate of your cursed peas."

She replaced the lid on the pot and crossed to the hogshead in the corner to draw his mug full of the dark brown liquid. Returning to the table, she placed it in front of him while avoiding the eyes watching her at the same time. Then she turned back to the hearth to fill his plate with peas and bread.

She remained by the hearth, standing while he ate. As bad as she hated to speak to him, she must make herself do it. His son was dying before her eyes. "Mr. Cawley, have you thought of fetching the doctor again? Andrew is much worse. I fear for his life."

Cawley took a large bite of the bread and washed it down with beer before replying. "The doctor can't do anything. He said so himself. A waste of money—I don't have to fetch him back to tell it to me again."

"But he also said he thought Andrew would recover. But he's getting worse. I can see it. I'm afraid—"

"Leave it be!" He slammed his open palm on the table and glared at her. "You'll not be telling me what I should do. The Lord will decide the boy's fate and so be it. Mind your tongue."

"Yes, sir."

"You've listened to the gossip in this town too much," he

continued, his anger rising again. "Tongue waggers, all of
them. Most of the women in this town should be placed in the
dunking chair and cured of their gossip! Just because I've had
bad luck with my silkworms, I'm accused of both poor management and neglecting my family. Well I tell you now, girl,
there's never a man who's tried harder. But the Lord is punishing me. I know it. He's punishing me by causing my worms
to die in this cursed weather as well as by making my family
sick."

He half rose and extended his arm in her direction, finger
pointing. "And you're the cause of my downfall! Temptress!
But I'm too strong for you. Soon He'll see that and all will be
well again. I know that, too!"

Elizabeth stared at him. Watched his face turn from crimson
to near white, his eyes bulging from his head. *He was going
mad!* The thought struck her with the force of a blow.

Saliva escaped the corner of his mouth, sputtering out as
he leaned over the table to hiss at her. "You'll see, harlot! I'll
win! I swear to you I'll win. And when I have, I'll sell your
contract to the devil to be rid of you!"

Elizabeth was afraid he intended to come around the table
and attack her and gripped the large wooden spoon for defense.
But just as suddenly, Cawley sat down again, slumped back
in the chair and looked at her from beneath a lowered brow.
"You'll see," he muttered.

She turned and with shaking hands began to remove the pot
from the fire and prepare it to save for the morrow. The silence
now in the room seemed like a heavy blanket—a thick and
evil blanket.

Morning usually began in the darkness for her, a creeping
awareness that although it had not yet penetrated to her loft,
dawn was breaking its light over Savannah. She had long been
trained to wake herself at dawn, even before she became a
servant. As long as her mother was well, Elizabeth had held
the luxury of a few minutes beyond first light to lay abed and
stave off her day's work the longer. But as that poor woman
had failed, Briggs had expected Elizabeth to take her place.
And now, as servant to the Cawleys, she was expected to be
the first one up.

She didn't really mind, it was a good time for her, a time
she could hold to herself and a time when she could enjoy

being alone. She would descend her ladder, stir the banked fire in the hearth to life, adding wood to it at the same time, and then partially bathe herself in front of it before beginning her duties. If Cawley were late in arising, she might even have time to step outside and enjoy the morning, breathing the fresh air and listening to the stirrings about her. All in all, it was the best time of the day.

This morning she was having difficulty in beginning, however. Light was already penetrating the cracks in the dried wood of the shutters downstairs and finding its way even to her pallet in the loft, and she still lay abed. Cawley had kept her late into the night, sometimes muttering, sometimes cursing and sometimes merely staring blankly at a corner of the room. But when she tried to leave, he roused himself and made her stay. It was only after he'd drunk a half dozen mugs of beer and lurched off to his own bed that she was able to creep to the loft.

That was a new worry for her, she'd never known him to drink to excess before. And, too, she suspected he'd consumed something stronger than beer before he came home. Rum was still banned officially in the colony, but even she knew the rule was widely ignored. It was easy enough to get the drink if a man could pay the price.

Still, he was not the same as Briggs used to be when he got his hands on gin. At least Cawley's drunkenness didn't lead him to violence. Not yet, anyway.

He knew he was failing in his silk making. There could be little doubt of it in the way he was now acting. But it seemed to her that he was trying to hide from that failure, or at least to find someone else to blame for his troubles.

She allowed a long sigh to escape. No matter, there was nothing she could do about it. Her life for the months she still had left on her contract was tied to the fate of the Cawleys, to whatever decisions that man might make. That was the truth of it and all the worrying she could do wouldn't change a part.

She threw back the blanket and rolled over to rise to her knees.

But there she stopped and allowed herself a small smile as she looked at the sleeping child on the other half of the pallet. Robert lay curled into a half ball and had threshed the blanket fully from himself during the night. All her commands to cover himself well had gone to naught in his sleep. Elizabeth reached to feel his brow, hoping the fever was gone.

It had more than gone. In fact, his skin was cold to her touch. She quickly drew the blanket around him, tucking it close to his body down his entire length.

But something was wrong—badly wrong. His small form moved much too readily under her hands, offering not even the resistance of a sleeper.

Panic began in her throat, stiffened it and then moved rapidly to her chest until she was laboring for breath. She fought against it as she grasped his small face in both her hands. "Robert! Wake up!"

His head rolled uselessly in her grasp and his eyelids failed to move. *"Robert!"*

She thrust her cheek close to his partly open mouth and felt nothing. . . . Dropped her ear to his chest, pressing it tightly in hope—nothing . . .

Elizabeth rose, holding him in her arms and closing her eyes as she threw back her head in the pain of it. This was wrong! Andrew was the sickest! This child was doing better—she knew he was! She'd played a game with him only last night!

The tears burned her cheeks as she rocked his body back and forth. Hugged him close, and rocked . . .

Dimly, after a very long time, she heard his father stir below, walk heavily out of the bedroom and out the front door. Gently she replaced the limp body on her pallet and covered him again with the blanket. She couldn't bring herself to cover his face.

Then she went down the ladder to wait for Cawley to come back inside so that she could tell him his son was dead.

The earth had hardly been spaded over the body of Robert Cawley before he was joined by his brother. Elizabeth, with her mistress unable to rise from her bed, bore the responsibility of preparing both boys for the simple services held at the grave sites. A dozen, perhaps more, neighbors attended each rite, more from sympathy to the two children than respect for their parents, she suspected. Then, watching her master's abrupt manner when they offered words to him, she knew she was right. Life in the colony was difficult enough if a man had the help of his neighbors, but Thermous Cawley seemed bent on driving his away.

With the second service over, she dreaded the return to his house now that both boys were gone. The terrible silence that would exist there during the day would be as bad if not worse than her master's constant eyes upon her in the evening. Elizabeth watched the spademen replace the dirt over the small pine box and thought of the child beneath. They had both been good children, a pleasure even in their sickness. She was going to miss them greatly. She cried, then, once again.

If only Cawley would take her to his farm again. Let her tend to his trees and help in the sheds where he kept his silkworms. But he wouldn't. He expected her to remain with the woman who refused to live—and refused to die. And Elizabeth suspected he didn't want *anyone* to see his failures. Not even her.

Cawley turned and walked away and she followed him a step or so, as he made his way back to the town. His pace was slower than usual; she noticed it by the time they entered the streets and she had put her own thoughts aside. When they had first arrived in Savannah that long time ago, he had surprised her with the quickness in which he moved, astonishing for one of his bulk. He had tired easily in those days, and she thought it because he moved about so rapidly without pausing to pace himself. But as he lost weight from hard work and poor fare at his table, the quickness had disappeared. He began to move with more deliberation. This morning, however, he walked without even that deliberation, more as a man unaware, or uncaring, where he was going. Had the death of his children, coming one after another as it did, affected him more than she had thought?

He stopped suddenly in the street and faced her. "Wait here."

Elizabeth looked up in surprise, but he offered no further word and she was left to wonder until he crossed the street and entered a tavern. She was ill at ease, standing there in the street with no apparent reason. Why couldn't he have ordered her to go home alone? She was sorely tempted to do so anyway and accept the consequences when he got home.

But Cawley reappeared in only a moment, tucking an object in his coat as he walked. She followed him as he continued down the street.

When they reached the house, he entered ahead of her and crossed to sit at the table while she went to see about his wife.

Sarah Cawley was alseep, her narrow chin, made even more pointed by sunken cheeks and a drawn mouth, rested on her chest as if she were in prayer. Elizabeth looked at her. The woman on the bed had little life left.

The object he'd purchased in the tavern had been rum instead of the wine she'd hoped. It sat now on the table in front of him, cork beside it and a generous portion poured into his mug. Cawley looked up as she re-entered the room. "Come here, Elizabeth. Sit down."

It was as long as she could remember since he'd used her given name. And his voice lacked its usual anger. She hesitated.

"Come and sit as I tell you," he said, still in the same level voice. "You've time aplenty to tend to your chores later."

She had little choice, and so she removed her cloak, hung it on a peg and came to sit in a chair across from him with her hands folded together in her lap.

Cawley watched her as he took a long draught from the mug and returned it to the table. He wiped his lips with the back of his hand and then nodded to her. "I give you thanks, Elizabeth, for the care you've shown my sons these last weeks. You did as much as possible for them."

She was caught off guard. His words, the sincere tone that carried them . . . she'd never seen him quite this way.

Cawley waited, saw she wasn't going to reply and nodded again solemnly. "I know. You thought I didn't notice—that I didn't care—but I did, Elizabeth. I loved both my sons. I held great plans for them to join me in my silk business."

His eyes drifted away and his tone became hollow. "Great plans . . ."

"Mr. Cawley, I'm truly sorry Robert and Andrew are gone. I loved them both very much."

He made a gesture with his hand. "I know you did, Elizabeth." His eyes drifted back to her. "You're a person capable of much love. I know that as well."

He lifted his mug, looked at it for a moment, then set it down again. "Why don't you make yourself some tea," he said.

"Thank you. But I really should go about my work."

His hand moved in the gesture again, an open sweep that spread his fingers. "You may do as you like, I won't insist." He looked away. "But if you're willing, I'd like to talk to you. It would help me . . . overcome today."

Could she actually feel sorry for him? What a strange sensation. "I don't want the tea, Mr. Cawley. But I will stay and listen to whatever you want to say, of course."

"Thank you. You do understand I'm not ordering you?"

"Yes, sir."

"Good." He paused to take another long draught of rum, then seemed not to know what else to say. The silence grew between them.

"Was it about my duties?" she prompted him when she could hold still no longer.

The question roused him. "No, no. Your work is fine. As I said, you took such good care of my sons. And Mistress Cawley—you do know she's dying, don't you?" His eyes came around with the sudden question and stared at her intently.

"Yes, sir. I believe she is. I'm sorry."

"Truth," he muttered, looking away again. "No need to be sorry about God's own truth."

The eyes came back, he seemed unable to keep them on her face nor away from it. "What do you think of me, Elizabeth?"

Careful. She must be careful. "I think of you as my master, Mr. Cawley. I'm debted to you by contract."

"Nothing else? You don't hate me? I've been . . . unpleasant to you at times."

"I hold nothing against you, Mr. Cawley." *Why on earth was he asking this?*

He took another drink as she watched, holding the mug long to his lips. "I'm glad of that," he said when he put it down again. "I shouldn't want you to feel harsh toward me, not when you loved my children."

He waited, but Elizabeth could think of nothing to say.

"I understand your life has been hard till now, Elizabeth," he went on after a while. "That fellow, Briggs, your father, must have been a cruel man. Most peasants are—through ignorance of course, not necessarily because they want to be so."

Again a pause, as if he were selecting his words carefully. "What you don't know is how I understand what your life has been. I understand it because my own youth was hard. Very hard, Elizabeth."

"I didn't know that," she said.

"'Tis true. Very true. My parents were impoverished. Became that way while I was a child. Bad investments, a poor time for business moves, that sort of thing, nearly put all of us into debtor's prison. Those were hard days for me, Elizabeth."

"Yes, sir. I understand."

He shook his head. "No, I think not. You come from peasant stock and have never known better. It would be difficult for you to understand the pain of being well-to-do and then losing that status."

The lines of his mouth tightened. "As I seem to be doing once more here in the colony."

"Yes, you're right," Elizabeth said. "I've never known any but a poor life. It's not something that I concern myself with."

She tried to change his mood. "But you didn't remain that way yourself. You became important again."

He nodded. "I did that. Did it on my own, with no help. But I paid a price for it, Elizabeth. A terrible price."

He lifted his mug, paused to look into it, then poured more rum from the bottle before drinking again. "I was apprenticed to a peruke maker for years. Years of hard work and much abuse from my master. He was a cruel man who enjoyed taking his cane to my back. A man who begrudged the crumbs he fed me and the few hours he allowed me to sleep."

His mouth tightened again and the red-rimmed eyes brightened with a strange glint. "I suffered his abuse in silence because I knew I was learning a trade that would bring me eventually to my proper station again. I learned that trade well. Better than most."

He chuckled suddenly, a nearly soundless laugh. "And I had my revenge on him as well, for I ended up owning both his business and his daughter."

"I see," she said.

"That's all over now, of course." He spoke as if he hadn't heard her, as if he were speaking to himself. "The profits from selling the business are gone entirely. All I worked so hard for . . ."

He whirled to look hard at her. "But I did it once. I can do it again."

"Yes, sir. I'm sure you can."

Cawley trembled, then stood up quickly and walked swiftly back and forth, his hands locked behind his back beneath his coattails. "I can! I will do it again!"

He stopped just as suddenly and stared at her. "With your help."

"My help?"

"Yes, Elizabeth. Your help. My wife is dying. You know that as well as I. I'll need another wife. New babes with which to share my silk business, as I had planned for my dead sons. Do you understand what I'm saying?"

Slowly she shook her head. Not wanting to understand.

"You, Elizabeth." Both hands came free of his coat to extend toward her. "I want you to be my wife when she's gone. A man needs a wife, and you must realize your opportunities are limited as a single woman in this colony."

She was aware that she was still shaking her head.

But his hands turned palm up as if pressing away her refusal. "Forget what has passed between us," he urged. "Don't you see what I'm offering? I'm willing to *marry* you. In spite of your peasant status. You can become a woman of gentry when silk makes me wealthy again. Have servants of your own, Elizabeth. Several of them!"

"Mr. Cawley, I—"

"No, no!" He held up his hands to stop her. "Say no more. Not now. I know my words are a shock to you. Take time to think upon it. Take a great deal of time, and while you're doing so, you'll see a difference in me, Elizabeth. You'll discover how the *real* Thermous Cawley can act. I promise it!"

"Sir," she said quietly, "you have a wife in the other room. Such words from you are not proper."

"My wife is dying, Elizabeth. She has been dead to me for many months before now, perhaps most of our life together. But I'm a man alive. A man who *needs* a woman."

"I think I should get to my work now," she said.

He nodded vigorously. "Of course. Of course. Do that. We'll speak again later when you've had time to think. I must get to my own work as well. I shouldn't be drinking—not at all. A new interest. That's what I have now. I will succeed with my silkworms. I know I will!"

Before Elizabeth could move, he stepped around the table and placed a hand on her shoulder. "Give it good thought, Elizabeth. This could mean much to you."

He walked swiftly to the door, removed his hat from a peg beside it and was suddenly gone.

She sat for a long moment, retaining the heavy presence of his hand touching her, then shuddered and stood up. If she had experienced sympathy for him minutes ago, she no longer did. He made her ill with his talk of—and with his wife in the other room.

She hugged her arms around her. She needed to see Jason again. Needed him badly...

Sixteen

EVERYTHING HE'D LEARNED so far about being a gentleman Tom had learned from Wimberly Jones, Jones's father, or from observing the occasional gentry he came across. Most of the learning came easily because he was interested in what he learned. The manners, even the gestures of those whom he'd once considered his betters, Tom tried to understand and emulate, without at the same time appearing to merely copy. But one of the few things that didn't seem to come easily was the ability to ride a horse without flopping about like a sack of potatoes. Probably, he hoped, because his opportunities to ride had been limited.

Tom straightened his back and tried again to adjust a movement of his own to that of the horse while casting an eye toward Noble Jones riding beside him. His ex-master, now his employer, was an excellent horseman despite his portly frame. He gave the impression of being an extension of the animal he rode. But then, he was a Captain of Rangers and often needed a horse to speed himself about the colony. Practice, Tom told himself silently. Practice made all the difference.

Jones rode with a hand on his thigh, elbow bent at an angle.

Tom tried it himself, couldn't see that it helped in the riding and dropped it again.

They were on their way to Augusta, traveling over a trade road that was little more than a blazed trail through the forest. He had been pleased when Jones invited him along on this trip, pleased enough to give up for the time the study of his books. Books had become his passion, especially those of medicine that Jones had lent him. Each evening, after the tasks assigned him, he gave as many as three to four hours to his reading. He hated to break that pace, but then traveling to Augusta, a place he'd not yet been, would add to his learning. Especially if Noble Jones was in a talkative mood.

His employer, however, turned out not to be in the best of moods. As well as Tom could gather, Jones had been re-quested—nay, *required*—to hurry to Augusta and survey a large grant the Trustees had given a nobleman. Putting together bits and snatches of conversations Jones had held with various people, Tom deciphered that the grant had been requested of the Trustees from the King of England. Everyone, with the exception of the surveyor, seemed to think that fact placed the utmost urgency on the matter. Noble Jones felt the nobleman could damn well wait his turn like everyone else.

His mood had been black when they left Savannah and had continued much in the same vein the entire time they had traveled. Tom was beginning to be sorry he had come. It would be a relief to arrive in Augusta.

The settlement, the most northern in the colony, was located at the falls of the Savannah River at a trading site that had been used long before the colony was settled. Just below it on the Carolina side of the river was Fort Moore, sometimes called Savannah Town, where, he had learned, the Upper Creek Path crossed the river on its way to Charles Town. The trading site was a warehouse point for the pack horsemen who traded with the Creeks and Cherokees, as from that point goods could be transported down the river by boat.

James Oglethorpe had seen the advantage to the place early and established a town there, a settlement that quickly sup-planted Savannah Town as the main site of the Indian trade, a fact that annoyed the South Carolinians no end.

Tom was also aware from conversations with both Jones and his son that Augusta had been developed in an atmosphere nearly free of Trustee influence and, probably, without a great deal of Trustee knowledge. Thus, their restrictive regulations had been ignored. Its trade made Augusta a growing place, and its agriculture, modeled after that in Carolina rather than that of Savannah, was beginning to boom.

Too, Tom had heard, and was anxious to confirm himself, that the beginning farms and small plantations were secretly using black slaves in spite of the Trustee ban. They were brought over the river from South Carolina by Georgians who "rented" their use for the period of ninety-nine years from their original owners at the full price of the slave. He was curious to see if this use actually made the difference that many in the colony had claimed for so long.

Ahead of him, Noble Jones reined his horse to a stop and reached behind him for the leather-encased bottle of water tied to his saddlebag. Tom drew up his own mount.

After he'd taken a long draught and replaced the cork, Jones nodded in the direction they were traveling. "About ten more miles, I judge, Tom," he said. "We'll find this man we're supposed to see, obtain his writ from the Trustees and get about our business of surveying his property."

He paused and cast a glance to the sky through the tops of the trees. "We're not on my schedule for arriving. I doubt we'll have time to begin today."

"You plan to spend the night in town then, sir?" Tom asked.

Jones gave it thought before replying, then sniffed abruptly. "I think not. I've no mind for renting a part of a bed in some foul tavern and sharing it with an unwashed backwoodsman who's tried to drink the place dry. If there's not better lodging available, and I doubt it in great seriousness, I'd prefer to return to the edge of the forest and a good camp of our own making."

Tom silently agreed. It was unheard of in the colony to be able to rent an entire room to oneself. A traveler rented part of a bed and shared it with at least two others. That thought didn't appeal to him either.

What did interest him was the man they were going to meet. He had never met a nobleman. "What was the gentleman's name again, sir?"

Noble Jones sniffed again. "Sir Harold Breaksford-Pinley. He's not known to me from the time before I left England. His holdings must have been more to the north."

He cast a thoughtful glance toward Tom. "Why the devil a man in his position should suddenly decide to come here and attempt to build a plantation in the wilderness is quite beyond me. Unless it's boredom."

"Perhaps it's more than that, sir," Tom said thoughtfully. "He may be interested in building the colony. I mean, in the manner General Oglethorpe is interested. He could have stayed in England and been the better off for it."

This time, Noble Jones turned full toward Tom and shook his head. "Thomas, there are few men in this world like the general. Philanthropy is in short supply in this world and I've yet to meet a nobleman who cared a whit for any but himself. No, there's another reason this one is here."

He shrugged. "But whatever it is, it's no concern of ours. Let's be on our way."

Tom urged his horse forward to follow but continued to dwell on what the other had said. He had a great deal of respect for Noble Jones as a man who had brought himself far in life. However, it was quite obvious that Jones didn't hold a high opinion of noble blood, and he agreed. Why should the nobility be any different from other men? Surely there were both the good and the bad who shared the fortunes of birth? It made him wonder what his own ancestors were like.

The settlement of Augusta was much as he expected it to be, a goodly size, but nothing to rival Savannah. It fronted on the river and was threatened on either side by forest that seemed to have been hardly cleared enough to squeeze the raw buildings in the space. Unlike Savannah, with its well-laid out streets marching off in regulated rows, this one seemed much too rapidly put together, as if its planners had been indifferent to its plan, or didn't really expect the town to last.

The largest buildings were warehouses for goods, he needed no one to tell him that. Otherwise, there were many log cabins and wooden frame structures scattered about with no rhyme or reason that he could see. The one nearest where the two of them exited the forest was a blacksmith shop, obvious in its long, open shed and the number of carts and horses standing about it.

Jones nodded in that direction with his head. "We'll dismount there and I'll see to our horses. This one had a limp and I'm concerned about it. They'll need to be watered, fed and brushed as well. You see if you can find Sir Harold— there couldn't be many places where he could stay here—and ask if I may call on him this afternoon."

"Yes, sir." Tom waited until Jones pulled up near the black-smith's and then dismounted himself, throwing the reins over the horse's head and stepping around to hand it to his employer. Then he turned and set off up the street.

Augusta was not a busy place, there were few others to be seen walking its streets. All he did see were men who were dressed in garb more suited to the forests than a town. He felt a bit conspicuous in his well-cut coat, breeches and stockings when the most he could see was buckskin.

He walked past the first warehouse and rounded its corner. Just on the other side was a well-structured building as wide as it was long, and hanging over the entrance was a sign advertising it as BLACKTHORN TAVERN. He paused and smiled to himself. It had not been so long ago that such a sign would have had little meaning for him, but now it would have to be in another language for him not to read it.

He remembered the ache with which he stood on the London street and looked at a similar sign. Well, miracles do come to pass. He was now a long way from that lost peasant boy.

He shrugged away the thought and crossed to enter the heavy door under the sign.

The room was wide but held a low ceiling, and despite a warm day outside, there was a well-burning fire in a deep hearth midway toward the rear. A half dozen tables were scattered about, heavy oaken tables, with short, thick-planked benches pulled up to them rather than chairs. He noted, however, there was one table a bit better than the rest placed in a corner that did have chairs and decided the owner reserved it for himself.

There were only a few men in the room and none seemed to pay him more than idle curiosity in spite of his being dressed differently. Evidently he wasn't as out of place as he thought. Tom looked for the innkeeper, didn't see him and was about to ask when a short and very fat man wearing the badge of his occupation—a leather apron reaching to his ankles—hurried out from a room placed behind the hearth. He held a great bowl of steaming food before him and nearly tripped in his haste to get it to one of the tables where two of his customers sat.

Tom waited until he had placed the bowl and scurried to fetch dining bowls and wooden spoons as well before he motioned the man to where he stood.

The fat man had a wide face with cheeks like ripe melons upon which large droplets of sweat stood like rainwater on a greased paper windowpane. "Yes, yes, good sir!" The words seemed to bubble from between his thick lips. "What can I serve you? An ale? Perhaps a dollop of good rum—I've the best to be offered in the whole of the Carolinas, I assure you! Or perhaps the gentleman would care to sup? I've—"

Tom held up a hand to stem the flow. "None of those at the moment, innkeeper. Though perhaps a bit later. Right now I'm interested to know if you have a guest I'm looking for."

If the fat man were disappointed, his face didn't register it. Heavy eyebrows went up instead. "And who might that be, sir?"

"I'm looking for Sir Harold Breaksford-Pinley. He was expected to be in Augusta. Do you know of him?"

A different expression moved the wide face and Tom thought for a moment it was alarm, then shrugged the idea away.

But the man's voice did contain suspicion. "Who seeks him," he asked.

"Mr. Noble Jones of Savannah," Tom said, paused a moment, then added, "and myself, Thomas Langlee, also of Savannah. Sir Harold is expecting us."

He didn't know if the last were true or not but decided he needed emphasis. "Do you know where I might find him?"

The fat man slowly shook his head in doubt. "I do, good sir. But I had specific instructions—and I wasn't told to be expecting anyone."

Tom looked at him for a moment, then quickly made up his mind. A gentleman would neither plead nor demand, he would merely *expect* to be answered and would not be denied. "I'm quite certain you are following your instructions," he said firmly. "But you may tell me where Sir Harold can be found and I'll assume the responsibility for disturbing him."

The innkeeper wavered, doubt now large upon his round face. "But Sir Harold himself told me—"

"I *said* I would assume the responsibility." Tom didn't raise his voice but allowed a note of irritation to creep into it.

Immediately the fat man caved in. "Yes, sir. Tis a short hall to your left behind you. Sir Harold has the room at the end. I moved everyone else out of it for him, it just could not be that they share it with—"

Tom cut him off again with a gesture. "I'm sure you've done well," he said. "You say the room at the end; there's more than one?"

The other nodded vigorously. "Two, sir. But the walls are thick and I've left no doubt to the men in the first that there must be no disturbing noise. No, sir, none at all."

"Thank you." Tom turned and left before the man could say anything else. The innkeeper was obviously an excitable man and having a nobleman under his roof had put him quite beside himself.

The hall was narrow and squeezed between the guest rooms and what must serve as both the kitchen and living quarters of the tavern owner. A few feet from its end was a door and he paused and knocked.

Immediately a soft, female voice answered. "Yes?"

He was surprised. Jones hadn't mentioned that Sir Harold might be accompanied by his wife. But then, the innkeeper had said *they*. No wonder he was concerned about his guests. He had a lady under his roof as well.

He leaned closer to the wooden door. "A message for Sir Harold."

The voice from the other side was smooth and pleasant. "Come in. The door isn't latched."

He hesitated a moment, then reached to adjust his coat and remove his tricorn, before entering.

The door was weighed to swing shut behind him, otherwise it would have remained open as his suddenly nerveless hand released it; Tom stood rooted to the spot where he stood.

The young woman sitting across the room from him was the most incredibly beautiful sight he had ever witnessed. He was thunderstruck. Good Lord, she *couldn't* be real!

The vision returned his look for a long moment, a slight smile on her lovely face—the knowing smile of a woman well aware of her effect on a man. She was more than knowing of what he felt, and that increased his foolishness.

"Well?" she said at last. "And who might you be, sir?" She laughed, a tinkling laugh from between small and extremely white teeth. "Provided, of course, you do have a tongue. I believe *someone* spoke from behind the door."

It took great effort to shake himself free and nod his head. "I do have a tongue, m'lady. And a name. It's Thomas Langlee." He made a short bow. "Your servant, m'lady."

She inclined her head. Very gracefully, he thought, but then could such a creature do less? "I see," she said. "Well now. I'm delighted to meet you, Mr. Langlee. Quite delighted, in fact. You see, you're absolutely the first *handsome* man I've seen in this desolate place."

By the Furies! He had no more begun to recover his wits than she'd managed to shake him again! How do you talk to such a creature?

"I've grave doubts of that," he managed, and hated the fact that he was forced to clear his throat to do so.

Her eyebrows, already delicately arched, rose, and the teasing smile remained in place. "You've doubt that I'm delighted to meet you, Mr. Langlee? But I assure you, I never bother to lie."

She was doing it to him deliberately—making fair sport of him. There was no doubt of it. But by damn it would not continue, he'd not spent all this time studying for naught! He bent his own head a moment but left his eyes on hers. "My doubts were only of the word, handsome, m'lady," he said. "I've not regarded myself so."

"Oh? Well you are, Mr. Langlee. Quite decidedly handsome. As I said, I never trouble to lie. Were it the opposite, if you had the appearance of a toad, I would likely tell you that also."

She rose—floated up from the chair in which she was sitting, he would have sworn—and crossed the room to pause directly in front of him. One lace-enclosed hand reached out and slim fingers actually touched his upper arm and squeezed it. "And strong, too," she said quite unconcernedly. "My goodness, you do set a lady's heart apounding."

Once more she had taken the advantage. But even without her rash action, the nearness of her, the *fragrance* of her, would have been enough to win that advantage. Tom could only stare down at her.

She wore no cap, instead her long, silken hair, the color of a raven's wings and containing the same sheen, was done up in ringlets—dark, teasing curls intermixed with ribbons. The hair sheltered a finely sculptured face, a face perfectly composed of liquid, jade green eyes that reflected the light in the same will-o'-the-wisp movement as that precious stone, balanced above highly arched cheeks colored a delicate rose. Her skin was flawlessly white; she had an aquiline nose, the nostrils of which flared in gracefully tucked curves; and a full, moist, wings bow of a mouth, red enough to have been painted by the dawn.

The effect of such an angel's vision of a face would have held his attention fully were it not for the cut of her bodice, the line of which was low enough to reveal the beginning swell of high, full and softly rounded breasts, yet returned again in an arch to fasten at her delicate throat.

It required all his strength of will to return his attention to speech. He looked again into the green eyes that continued to laugh at him. "May I be so bold as to inquire if you're Lady Breaksford-Pinley?" he asked. "I . . . had expected someone older."

She nodded, keeping the sparkling eyes on his. "I'm Angelica Breaksford-Pinley. Sir Harold is my father. You, of course, will address me as Angelica, and I shall call you Thomas. That's quite decided."

His control was returning. She had been toying with him, and still was, her forwardness (inexcusable in any society, he knew enough to know that) was designed to embarrass an untutored colonist. Well, let us see . . .

"You do me great honor—Angelica. Especially since this is our first meeting."

A lace handkerchief, held between two slim fingers, came up to touch the center of his cheek for the space of a heartbeat. "First meeting?" she echoed. "Then, of course, that means I am to expect more of your company?"

He nodded, beginning to enjoy himself at last. "I can't think of a more desirable prospect, I assure you. Were I to be given privilege to witness a meeting of angels, I would readily trade for a moment in your presence." *There! Wimberly Jones couldn't have said it better!*

The small smile remained in place, but he could swear to a change in the eyes—a heightened interest? He flattered himself to believe so.

"La!" she said. "Here in the most primitive surroundings, I discover for myself a handsome man with the charm of a courtier. My, Thomas Langlee, I *am* impressed!"

"You give me far more credit than I deserve, m'lady," he said.

"Angelica."

He inclined his head and gave her a smile. "Angelica. Tis

a name that most fits. Truly, I've never met a more beautiful woman." He was surprised at his own boldness, but then she would expect boldness in a man. "Such a face could only be made in heaven."

Her green eyes brightened as she looked up at him, and Tom knew she was a woman who required such words to retain her attention at all. She was accustomed to being admired. Demanded it, in fact. But such a flaw could be easily overlooked in his estimation. Worth the cost just to look at her.

Her eyes remained long on his, probing them, then she turned. "Come," she said. "Sit with me. I must hear more of such eloquence. T'will be an enormous relief from the terrible boredom I've been experiencing this day. You've no idea how stuffy this room has become."

He remained where he was. "I'm sorry—Angelica. It would pleasure me greatly to sit with you until the end of time. But I'm afraid I've already neglected my responsibility to both my employer and your own father. I was sent here to see when it would be convenient for my employer, Mr. Noble Jones, to call on Sir Harold. Mr. Jones is the surveyor who is to lay out his property in the colony."

Angelica sat down and waved away his protest with a flip of both her head and her hand. "Nonsense. You've all the time needed. My father is away on a foolish quest, he's been invited by someone or other to view Indian artifacts. Though why he would find anything savages make of interest is quite beyond me. There's absolutely no means of discovering where he is nor when he might return. Now come and sit down."

When he still didn't move, a small frown of annoyance crossed her face, flattening the otherwise perfect lips. "I insist," she said, and the lines disappeared as the mocking smile returned. "Remember, I always get my way."

Tom wavered. He would like nothing better than to sit near this lovely vision and practice the art of conversation with a mind as quick as hers. But instinct told him that if he gave in to her, even in this small thing, he would continue to be defeated at her every whim. He would henceforth be *required* to do her bidding, a fact that would gall him. Instinct also told him that in such a case, Angelica Breaksford-Pinley would quickly lose interest in him.

He bent an arm across his waist and bowed. "Tis almost more than this simple colonial can bear, my dear Angelica," he said while matching, he thought, the mocking smile in her eyes, "but duty calls. I must respectfully decline your gracious request."

He immediately read the challenge in the jade eyes that flashed back at him.

"Tell me, Mr. Duty, why do you require my father so urgently?" she said quickly, before he could turn to the door.

"A matter of urgency for both Mr. Jones, who has pressing duties elsewhere in the colony, and for your father, whom I expect is anxious to begin building his plantation."

He thought a moment. "To begin his house, to say the least. I'm certain he finds these poor quarters as worrisome as does his beautiful daughter. Why did you come anyway?"

She tossed her head. "I was bored. That's why I was willing to come. As for my father bringing me to such a place, he could hardly help himself. The poor dear dotes on me and cannot bear to be away from me long."

"I see," he said. "Nor can I blame him." He turned to place a hand on the door. "Again my regrets, but—"

"He doesn't plan to be in the colony more than a few weeks himself," she said quickly. "He expects us to be gone very soon."

Her words had the desired effect. The thought that this might be the last as well as the first time he saw her gave pause to his pull that would open the door. He turned back. "I don't understand," he said. "I thought Sir Harold planned to build a plantation here."

Her smile was warm and friendly, but he could also read the triumph in her eyes at having stopped him from leaving, at least for the moment.

"Oh, he does. But my father is of the opinion that it will take only a short while to hire a manager, set up this plantation you speak of and do whatever else one has to do to make it operate, and then he expects to return to England."

Her smile became amused. "You see, dear Thomas, my father is under the delusion that he's *needed* at court. He thinks that fat German who rules there actually *wants* his advice."

He was puzzled. How could she speak of her own father in that light manner. Surely she wasn't serious?

Angelica laughed. "I can see by your face I've distressed you with my manner of speaking of my father. Really, Thomas, I do love the old dear quite as a loyal daughter should. It's just that I also understand him. My father is incapable of understanding the truth of the situation, that truth being that he is an *embarrassment* to the throne since he's become impoverished. King George hopes never to see him again, much less requires his presence back in London."

Tom shook his head slowly. "I must confess you've made my head swim with your talk, Angelica. You say Sir Harold is impoverished, yet he is here to build a plantation which will surely cost a goodly sum. You also say he isn't popular with our king, yet I know full well he's been granted this land by the Trustees who run the colony at the request of King George himself. Surely, you're making jest with me."

"I'll explain it to you if you'll sit with me for only a moment," she said. "No more than that. Tis a simple truth. I told you I never bother to lie, didn't I?"

His curiosity was great, but he easily saw through the game. He bowed again. "Tis not of my affair, and I would not intrude on the business of your father. Good day, Angelica."

"Wait!" It was a command, and stopped him once more. "Very well," she said. "I'll not hold you, rudely as you seem to want to rush away. But I will tell you the truth. I think it necessary for you to understand what you will be letting yourself in for when you make your decision."

"Decision?" He raised his eyebrows. "What decision?"

"Let me explain my dear father's position, Thomas," she said, quite aside from making the answer he wanted. "You see, his ancestor was a turning factor in the decision made in 1714 that brought the house of Hanover to the throne of England and that house has been grateful to my family since. Especially since my family has continued to loyally support those kings, even the one who refused to learn to speak English."

Tom raised a hand to interrupt her. "I'm not sure I quite understand. I know the king's ancestors came from a German province—"

"The elector of Hanover," she said. "At the death of Queen Anne without children, there was great disagreement as to whom would be offered the throne. My great grandfather happened to have a large amount of influence at that time and was able to lean the decision toward the German who became King of Great Britain and Ireland as King George the First."

"I see," he said. "With that background, wouldn't it have been better for your father to remain in England?"

"As dear as he may be, my father is incapable of managing anything—his money, his estate, even," she gave him a wide smile, "his daughter. He's had to trade off his holdings and really exists at all through the generosity of the crown. An embarrassing situation for the king. King George persuaded your Trustees to grant my father this land in Georgia in the fond hope it will remove him from England forever."

"I see," Tom said again. "But what if this plantation is not a success? It's a difficult task at best. A man must understand the land, choose the right crops to plant and—"

She held up a hand. "It will be a success because I will it to be so. My father might be at a loss to manage anything or to understand the use of others, but I am not. I'm quite spoiled, I admit it freely. He did the same for my mother and when she died, merely transferred his devotion to me. But I am not stupid nor simpering. I shall tell him what to do and he will do it, not realizing he's doing anything but pleasing me. Do you see?"

It was a new side to her, an interesting one. There was a hard glint to the sparkling green eyes. Fascinating...

The door behind him opened suddenly and he had to be quick to move out of its way. The man who entered was more than middle-aged and soft from far less requirement from life than would be true in the colonies. His clothes were expensive—satin breeches, a velvet coat and ruffled silk shirt. Atop the heavy but smooth face was a white powdered wig. Behind him, as he paused just inside the door, was Noble Jones, wearing a surprised and disapproving look on his face.

Sir Harold, however, showed no surprise and Tom knew instantly he was used to finding his daughter alone with men.

"Father!" Her voice was honeyed and filled with delight. It caused Tom to cock an eyebrow in cynical astonishment. "I'm so happy you've returned! I was about to lose the company of Mr. Thomas Langlee who *insisted* on going in search of you in spite of my protests. Now you can reprove him for that and invite him to dine with us."

Sir Harold looked at Tom who immediately decided he'd never looked into greater arrogance or pomposity in his life. Even without Angelica's description of him, Tom would have decided that this was a man who could do no more than bluster his way. "Why are you here, young man?" he demanded.

Tom bowed, a very short and stiff bow. "I was sent to see

if Mr. Jones could call on you, sir. But I see he found you in the stead."

Sir Harold looked at Jones and snorted. "So he did. Well, let's be quick about this, gentlemen. I require all possible haste in laying out my property, I've only a short time to spend here before I'm needed back in London. The deed must be done and I must hire a man to direct the slaves within a few short weeks."

Tom glanced at Noble Jones whose face had gone from disapproval of Tom himself to souring at his temporary employer. When Jones didn't seem about to speak himself, he asked, "You intend to bring in black slaves, sir?"

Sir Harold nodded abruptly. "The only way, the only way. Indentured servants are useless, completely useless, a foul lot, all of them. And those who work for wages are more interested in their leisure than anything else. Black slaves from Africa can stand this infernal heat naturally and work long hours without harm to themselves. I intend to purchase a goodly number."

A surprised look came over his face. "But I know not why I explain such to you, young man. Your duty is to survey the land."

He turned to Noble Jones. "The grant is in my trunks, hold here for the moment while I get it."

Jones nodded. "As you wish." And Tom could hear the edge of temper in his voice. Sir Harold, however, was oblivious.

He hardly made it across the room before his daughter stopped him. "Father, I do think you have the solution to most of your problem right before you. Do you not see it?"

"What are you talking about, my dear? What problem?"

She stood up and took his arm to turn him. The look on his face told Tom that everything she'd said about her father was true, he held the devoted look of an old dog or a child with a new toy. He smiled to himself.

"The problem," Angelica said, glancing again toward Tom but continuing to talk to her father, "that you have spoke to me a dozen times in the last two days. That of finding a trustworthy man who knows both this place and how to run a plantation. Someone to hire to develop your estate here."

She switched her gaze to Noble Jones. "You do have a plantation, don't you, sir?"

The question both shocked and irritated his employer, Tom

could read both in his scarlet face. "Why yes. Yes, I do. But I assure you, madam, it requires all my attention. That and my other duties. I have no interest in—"

"Oh, it's not you of whom I'm thinking," she interrupted him sweetly. "But the gentleman with you. Now you wouldn't be so callous nor selfish to refuse to allow my father to employ Mr. Langlee from you for his own plantation? Not when he is so desperately *needed*? And, too," the sweet smile turned on Tom, "to deny him such an opportunity?"

Jones could only stare at her.

Sir Harold recovered first. "I'm certain these people have their own interests, my dear. There are men available—"

"Nonsense." She interrupted him with a wave of her hand. "You said yourself you'd seen no one you'd trust. I know my instincts are right. Mr. Langlee is both intelligent and trustworthy. You could do no better; now be truthful."

Sir Harold swept a long look toward Tom, but the latter had fully recovered himself. He felt he already knew Angelica, and he was definitely not cattle to be bartered. He spoke before the nobleman could. "My regrets, sir. M'lady is more than flattering toward my ability, but I'm afraid I cannot make myself available. I already have a position to fulfill."

It was the wrong thing to say. Sir Harold, like his daughter, wasn't used to being refused. He frowned sternly. "I don't think you understand, young man. What was the name?"

"Langlee, sir."

"Un, yes. Langlee. Well, Langlee, I've great trust in my daughter's judgment even if she is only a woman. You don't understand that this post is one of great importance. I need someone who can manage the entire holdings, direct the overall operation, including any other white men needed. Such a position would pay to its responsibilities. You should not turn it away without serious thought. As I said, I'll be away in England most of the time."

Tom looked at Noble Jones who returned his look with one of amusement and question. He returned to the nobleman. "I'm quite sure it's a generous offer, sir. And I'm more than flattered. But I must refuse, to my regret. Thank you."

"Humph," Sir Harold said, and would have said more, but his daughter laid a hand on his arm. "Then we mustn't press Mr. Langlee to change his decision, father. However, when he's had time to reflect on his lost *opportunities*, perhaps he'll have a change of mind."

The jade eyes flashed at him. "Remember, I *always* get my way."

Tom bowed.

"Meanwhile," she continued. "My father and I insist you both join us for dinner. Don't we, father?"

And Sir Harold, true to her earlier words, couldn't refuse her.

It was nightfall before Tom and his employer could get away from the Breaksford-Pinleys and make their own camp at the edge of the forest. It had been an interesting meal. The innkeeper had fetched a table to their room rather than subject his noble guests to the roughness of the tavern and left a maid, a young but intelligent Indian girl, to serve them. Sir Harold had done most of the talking with only occasional comment from an uncomfortable Noble Jones. Tom had not followed the rambling accounts of doings around the throne, but spent his attention on the lovely girl who sat opposite him. The bold look in the deep green eyes brought him back again and again to the emphasis she'd put on the word *opportunities* that she'd said he lost. Had it more meaning than surface?

Sir Harold expected to leave the Georgia colony soon. That was obvious. But his daughter thought otherwise. Or did she? Would they leave? Or stay?

The thought plagued him more than he would admit, even to himself. Somehow, when they got back to the Isle of Hope, he would have to find an excuse in a week or so to get away. He would make the return trip to Augusta alone to see her. Why, he didn't know. Or he did know and wouldn't admit it, even to himself. But he *would* make the trip.

Noble Jones snorted suddenly and broke into Tom's thoughts. "That pompous ass," he snapped. "He serves as much chance of building a proper plantation as a sow has of neighing. And t'will serve him right when he fails."

"I would think the chances better here than near Savannah," Tom said. "Agreeing with you, of course, that Sir Harold isn't likely to succeed, but I've been studying the land since we've arrived and it seems far more rich to me. I think it more suitable for growing crops than the seacoast."

He paused and noted that Noble Jones was watching him closely over the campfire. "And, too," he continued, slightly uneasy, "you said yourself that up here you are away from the influence and spies of the Trustees and can be more free in the operation. Away from their rules with which you must admit most here in the colony disagree. I should think a man with drive and determination could readily succeed here, especially if he gets around the edict of the Trustees about the use of slaves."

Noble Jones's voice was quiet and low. "Then you're regretting your decision to refuse their offer, Thomas?"

He looked up, directly into the older man's eyes. "No, sir. I was merely thinking aloud of the advantages I saw in this area. I intend to become a doctor."

Jones nodded slowly. "Good." But then he added, "She's quite a beautiful woman. I wouldn't blame you, Thomas, if you changed your mind."

"She's beyond my reach even if she gave it thought," Tom said. "And I don't flatter myself that she had other than my service to her father in mind. She's of noble blood and I'm a b—I'm not."

Jones grunted. "She gave impression of allowing nothing to stand in the way of what she wanted. I doubt that the rules of blood society would serve any better fate to her if she made up her mind. You're probably lucky you got away, Thomas. I've a feeling that one would be more than most men could handle."

He stretched. "At any rate, I'm to bed. We've a lot of work to do on the morrow."

"Yes, sir." Tom bent to put out the fire and then turned to his own bedroll. But there would be little sleep for him this night, he knew that already. A black-haired vision would keep him awake.

Seventeen

THE EVENT FOR which Elizabeth had been both awaiting and dreading arrived at last. Sarah Cawley died quietly in her sleep, a death that hardly changed her from what she'd been in the last weeks as she lay perfectly still all the time with her eyes closed. Thermous Cawley informed Elizabeth of the death as he got up in the morning and sat down for his breakfast.

It had been a strain living with him these weeks since he made his offer of marriage to her. His change in attitude was near enough to make her want him to return to the old. He was more than polite, he was sickly sweet toward her. He tried clumsily to engage her in conversation about the progress of his silkworms, about the doings in the town and even about her own work, and Elizabeth did her best to answer. She was uncomfortable in his presence, glad of any excuse to get away. The only good thing about it was that he made no attempt to touch her. She wasn't sure she could stand it if he did.

The strain had driven her to confess to Hester, after extolling her solemn promise never to reveal the secret, that Cawley had asked her to marry him with his own wife lying near death in the next room. Hester was horrified, and sympathetic, and could do nothing, of course. No one could. But it helped to be able to talk about it to someone. She wished Tom would make one of his occasional visits to Savannah, but then knew she couldn't tell him of the problem. It would only make him feel worse about his own freedom.

And she couldn't tell Jason, for she was afraid of what he would do. She risked Cawley's anger, as well as punishment from the constables if she were caught, several times to slip out of the house at night and meet him. But Jason was tender and filled such a need for her, she couldn't resist.

Cawley brushed her words of regret about his wife's death aside. "It's a thing we both have expected, Elizabeth. The Lord did not plan for Sarah to live in this colony, nor to share the good things my silk will eventually bring me."

He paused to clear his throat and she drew up inside, waiting for him to speak again of marriage. But he didn't.

"I suppose I should feel regret—and I do, to some extent," he said. "Sarah has not enjoyed life since we left England. Not enjoyed life nor good health. But then, she wasn't a woman easily adjusting to change and depended on the decisions of her mother far too much."

He paused again, a long time. "Be that as it may, life has ended for her and I'm sure she's gone to a better one. I won't ask you to make the arrangements this time, it would be better for appearances if I did it myself. I'll go into town this morning and do what's needed. You prepare her, and we'll hold the burial this afternoon."

"Yes, sir," she said.

He drained his cup and stood erect, pushing back from the table to do so. "What's done is done," he said.

When Elizabeth didn't reply, he turned and went to the peg beside the door for his hat and left.

The funeral was a somber affair, attended by only a few persons, less really, than had attended those of the dead woman's own sons. Elizabeth stood with her hands clasped in front of her and watched Cawley as a young pastor recited the burial words over the open grave. Her master hadn't wanted this young man, he'd wanted the Reverend George Whitefield to do the services. But that famous gentleman was out of the colony, touring the northern parts to raise money for his orphanage. Cawley didn't like the young pastor, and she expected his dislike to show. But it didn't. He appeared instead as if his mind was on other things.

From where she stood she could see just over the mound of dirt to a portion of the pine box in the bottom of the grave. Sarah Cawley would sleep eternally now in peace.

She lost track of the rising and falling of the young minister's words. How terrible it would be to find yourself a wife not wanted... to lay on your death bed and possibly hear your husband tell another he wanted to marry her. Elizabeth shivered at the thought.

But then, if his words were true, Thermous Cawley had most likely never loved his wife. He'd spoken of getting her father's business—how had he done that? Was it the business he really wanted and he only took the wife for that reason? What a horrible way to begin a marriage.

Well, it wouldn't be the same for her, that was certain. She almost smiled. Jason Welburn would not be marrying one Elizabeth Langlee to acquire money nor property for she had naught of either.

What would they have, the two of them? The voice of the pastor faded away completely as she thought about it. In not too many months hence, Jason would be released from his debt to the Longfoottes and the Trustees would grant him a small plot of land somewhere outside of Savannah. He wouldn't be given a house lot and garden acre in town like the others; freed indentured servants were only given a single piece of land and that must be outside of the town. It would not be fifty acres, like the total given those who came from England or the other countries, it would be twenty-five, or at best, thirty-five acres.

But Jason was a man willing to work hard and he would do much with what they gave him; she knew he would. When she was free herself, she'd work hard beside him. No, theirs wouldn't be much, but it would be enough. Dear Thomas wanted to become a gentleman, and well enough for him, she hoped sincerely he would succeed. But for herself, all she would ever want would be to love and be loved. To be free to be mistress of her own house, with children to care for and her man to share a life.

"Elizabeth?"

She realized with a start that her name had been repeated more than once and her mind had drifted so she was unaware of being called.

"Sir?" She had to shake herself back to the present. Cawley was standing close in front of her and peering intently into her face. But his manner wasn't of anger. "Are you all right, child?"

"Yes, sir. I was just—"

He patted her roughly on the shoulder. "That's all right, Elizabeth. I understand. Mistress Cawley's death has been a shock to you I know. Even though it was expected. But come, we must go now."

Elizabeth looked about her in amazement. The service had been completed while her thoughts wandered; all the others had left the gravesite and were walking back toward the town proper. Even the pastor was gone. Only she and Cawley were left.

He patted her shoulder again. "Come. There are men waiting who cannot begin until we are away. You wouldn't want to see the grave filled."

She wanted to protest that it wasn't grief that had clouded her mind, but goodness, how terrible that would sound! She could do nothing but turn and walk beside him, back to Savannah and the house in which there would be only the two of them now.

What would she do? What would she say when he spoke again of marriage between them? Did she dare tell him she loved another man? He would likely beat her if she did. Might even become angry enough to bring her up on some charge before the town court. But she would have to refuse him marriage whether she spoke of her love for Jason Welburn or not. No matter the results, she would have to refuse. There was little doubt that he still intended it; it wasn't the drink speaking for him that day. His every word to her of late, his every gesture, led to that. Suddenly the nausea she felt so strongly this morning returned. She thought for a moment she would have to turn aside from the path and be sick.

Cawley brought her from the feeling with his words. "I must ask you to go the rest of the way by yourself, Elizabeth," he said. "Do you feel you can? You're not overcome by grief, are you?"

Elizabeth shook her head. "No, sir. I'm quite all right."

"Good. Good. You're a strong young lady, I've noted that in you for some time. Still I would walk you the rest of the way home except I must go and check on my silkworms. I feel some of them are in a critical stage and it would be dangerous to neglect them."

He cast a glance skyward to gauge the afternoon sun. "'Tis growing late I know, but if I hurry I can do what I must and still be home by nightfall. And, Elizabeth," he placed a hand on her arm, "I will want a goodly sup when I arrive. You can do that, can't you?"

"Yes, sir." She moved her arm without seeming to do it on purpose.

"Good." Cawley eyed her carefully. "Suppose this evening you set out two places at the table. I should like you to dine with me. There's only the two of us now, no need to be strict in the master-servant relationship, is there?"

Elizabeth didn't answer and watched a strained smile appear on his face. He nodded. "And after . . . I think there are things we should talk of, you and I."

Still she didn't trust herself to speak and Cawley nodded again. "Well, best we both move along."

"Yes, sir." She turned and hurried away as fast as she could without giving the appearance of haste. *God in Heaven she dreaded this eve!*

It was a great temptation to run as soon as she was out of his sight. To run to Jason, or even to the Isle of Hope where Thomas labored to build the plantation for Mr. Jones that he had spoken of to her. Or even to flee into the forest and hide there like an animal—anywhere but to the house that belonged to Thermous Cawley!

All of which was foolish. A foolish girl's fears and wild thoughts. Jason Welburn was indentured, and Thomas could not go against the laws of the colony. She would only be brought back to Cawley. Nowhere to go, nowhere to hide. . . . She was his *property!*

Elizabeth lifted her head and clenched her teeth as she walked. Property, yes. But not his wife! She would *never* be his wife!

The house gave her the appearance of a giant fat spider squatting and waiting for something to come into its maw. She had to force herself to draw near to it, to reach for the latch-string, pull it and enter the door that opened like the jaws of an abyss before her . . .

The room was the same but not the same. She was familiar with every nook and cranny of this room, she'd cleaned it inch by inch in her time here. But now it was no longer familiar to her. It was strange—and hateful. The house was *his*—and it smothered her.

When darkness began to fall and she was forced to close the shutters over the windows to bar the night chill, she had also placed her own dark fear out of her mind. Once more she was in control and didn't feel as much the child as she had in returning from the gravesite. She wasn't a child but a woman. She may be a servant, with no rights to how her own life was to be spent in terms of place and work, but she held the right of a woman to refuse to marry a man. She had no father to force her to marry according to his wishes, therefore, the decision as to her mate was hers alone. Not even the king's law could force her to marry under those circumstances.

Cawley would be angry, that was certain. Well, so be it! Hadn't she just told herself that having him angry with her again might not be worse than the sickening sweetness he'd delivered himself of these last weeks?

Elizabeth stirred the pot of cabbage she was boiling and then saw to the potato she'd wrapped in mud and placed in the hearth ashes to bake for him. Then, while her resolve was still fresh, walked to the cupboard and fetched a single plate to place on the table. She'd not sup with him either!

Such thoughts kept her occupied throughout preparing the meal, enough that when it was ready and she had to place it so as to keep it hot for his arrival, the time had slipped away before she realized it. Night had well set in before she became aware of the lateness of the hour. Cawley had plenty of time to walk to his field, to do whatever he wanted there and return. He was extremely late.

Elizabeth sat on her stool, wrapped her skirts about her legs and thought about it. Why was he late? Cawley had placed such store by his words to her of having a supper ready for him, to say nothing of what he intended after he ate, she couldn't help being surprised by his being so late. Perhaps he'd changed his mind. Perhaps he'd thought how foolish it was to expect her to want to marry a man who'd treated her so and had quite put it from his thoughts. Perhaps—

The drawbar flew up suddenly, snatched from its resting place by the drawstring she'd left out for him. A second later the door swung open and Cawley stood in the opening.

But what a change! His clothes were black from smoke, his

hat was gone, as was his wig, the short gray-brown hair stood out from his head in all directions.

Her master carried a bottle by the neck in one hand, and in a face turned scarlet from drink or heat—she couldn't be sure which—red eyes blazed at her.

"I've been cursed!" The words were slurred with rum but hurled at her with force enough to cause her to wince. "The Lord has cursed me aright now!" He bellowed the words and Elizabeth thought him more than drunk. He was mad!

Cawley stepped—stumbled—forward, and slammed the door behind him. His voice fell to a hoarse whisper. "Tis the end," he told her, leaning enough it seemed that he would topple forward. "All gone . . . everything . . . I'm finished . . ."

Elizabeth was on her feet without knowing how she'd gotten there. Her nerves were tight and strumming. "Mr. Cawley! What happened?"

He swung in a half circle, swaying, then straightened and fastened his eyes on her without fully seeing her. "Gone," he muttered. "All gone . . ."

"What's gone?" Fear was a live thing inside her now. She didn't know why. "What's happened?"

"Fire!" He strangled the word out, staring at her. Then raised the bottle to his lips and drank. When he lowered it again, some of the liquid dribbled down his neck. "Burned," he said. "All of them. My sheds, silkworms . . . even trees . . . all gone."

Oh no! She caught at her cheeks with her hands. *A fire! His silkworms burned? What would he do?*

"Mr. Cawley . . ."

"All of them," he slobbered, waving about on his feet. "All gone. Burned to death . . . the worms. No silk . . . they'll make no silk. I'm ruined."

Elizabeth moved with difficulty, her limbs were wooden. A huge bell was clamoring about her, it numbed her senses. But she took his arm and led him to the table like a child.

Cawley turned his head to see her the while, even when she sat him in the chair. The staring red eyes seared her.

Elizabeth removed the bottle from his hand and placed it on the table, but he immediately reached for it again and drank without once removing his eyes from her. He had lost his wits. She pitied him and she was frightened by him.

"Mr. Cawley. Tell me about it. Would it not be best for you to speak of it? To free yourself of it?"

He shook his head. "A fire," he said. "I know not how—yes I do! Not by accident—nothing of carelessness on my part. The Lord did it!" His voice rose to a shriek. "God Himself sent a lightning bolt! I know he did! To punish me!"

"Mr. Cawley!" She was screaming in her own fear. "That's not true! It was an accident. The Lord wouldn't—"

"Damn you!" He slammed his fist on the table. "It's true! He did it to punish me! To punish me for the lust I've held for you! For wanting that harlot's body of yours in the nights I've lain awake beside my own dying wife! It's *your* fault He's turned against me!"

The violence of his outburst sent her backing away from the table. Cawley staggered to his feet, flinging both table and chair aside, the bottle of rum flying across the room.

"Mr. Cawley, please!"

He stood, gasping for air like a fish. "It's you!"

His words were hissing out between his loose lips, like the sizzle of fat dripping on hot coals. "From the cursed day I set eyes on you—on your naked breasts—I was given over to the Devil. He took away my sons to warn me. Turned away the attention of my own wife, and still I wouldn't listen. I wanted you . . . wanted that sweet body of yours naked in my arms. I WANTED YOU!"

She was shaking her head, backing away from him though he'd made no move toward her. "No . . . no . . . it isn't true . . . I gave you no cause . . ."

"WHORE! You tempted me! You turned me from the truth of the Lord! You corrupted my flesh!"

"No!"

He staggered, stumbled and suddenly drew himself erect, taking a steady step toward her. Both his hands raised in claws poised to reach for her. "He's turned against me," Cawley whispered, his voice again in a hoarse rasp. "I'm doomed to hell. I'll burn in eternal fire . . ."

Another step, a measured step, without signs of drunkenness in it. "Then so be it. I've nothing left to lose. So I'll have you now, you harlot. I'll have that sweet body of yours to do with as I will. Tear your clothes from your back and see the nakedness of which I've dreamed."

She was hard against the rocks of the hearth. When she moved to the side, across in front of the fire, he turned to follow her. "No . . ." she whimpered to the eyes on her own.

"Come here, Elizabeth." The red eyes danced in madness, but he no longer staggered. He seemed much too much in control of himself. "Come here. Bring that tender body of yours to me so I may unclothe it. You've lain with a man before, I know that. *You're* no stranger to being impaled by a man!"

"No . . . no . . ."

Cawley lunged and she only just managed to galvanize her own limbs into action to avoid his rush. He crashed against the rocks of the hearth but whirled away as if he'd hit nothing and lunged again.

Elizabeth ran for the door, but he was faster. From somewhere he'd acquired incredible strength and speed. His hand reached past her and slammed the door shut even as she pulled it open, his other hand grasped the back of her dress and yanked her from her feet. Elizabeth sprawled across the wooden floor.

Cawley lunged for her and she was just able to roll aside before his body fell across hers.

Elizabeth scrambled to her feet, but he caught an ankle and tripped her, held to his grip and reached to snatch at her dress. She jerked away as the fabric ripped loose from a seam at her waist.

She kicked frantically with her free foot at his wrist until he was forced to let go of her ankle. Cawley screamed an oath at her.

But she was free of him now and on her feet, trembling violently and fighting the choking fear that took away her breath.

Cawley was between her and the door, blocking her escape. His face was a grimace, his red-flashed eyes jumping from his head. He climbed slowly to his feet as he watched her, pulled himself to one knee and then rose into a crouch to extend both arms toward her, his fingers curling into claws.

"Run, you bitch," he hissed. "Run all you will, you can't escape me now. I'm going to have you—have you naked on this floor . . ."

Saliva drooled from his mouth as he leaned forward. "Naked . . . wench . . . I'll have you naked and pound your pretty buttocks into the floor until you scream for mercy."

Elizabeth tried to move to her right, but he was quick to turn. Too quick. She held no chance!

Despair drained the strength from her. Fear made her teeth chatter. "Please . . ." she begged.

Cawley laughed, a guttural, horrible sound from deep in his throat. "Beg me, you slut. Plead with me to take you and mayhaps I'll not bruise that sweet body too badly when I do. Mayhaps I'll not bloody that fair face of yours that has taunted me for these months . . ."

"Mr. Cawley . . . don't . . ."

He launched himself at her suddenly and Elizabeth darted to avoid him. But he was drunkenly clever and anticipated her direction. His body struck her full force and bowled her backwards, to crash on her hip with him half atop her.

The bruising shock stunned her. Elizabeth only recovered when his clawing hand ripped away the entire front of her dress.

She fought his hand frantically with both her own, but Cawley was a madman in strength and purpose. He jerked the fabric again and bared her shoulder.

Elizabeth screamed and clawed at the contorted face rising above her. Clawed until he paused under her attack, hesitating just enough that she was able to kick free from beneath him.

She rolled, twice, three times, roughly across the floor, with Cawley crawling in rapid pursuit. Her hand struck the leg of the overturned chair and she jerked it between them. Anything to slow him!

Cawley snatched it aside. But again she was on her feet and scrambling away, without regard for her ripped clothes or the naked skin that showed above her shift. She could only think of escape. To get away from the animal that wanted to devour her. He meant to rape her—but he would *kill* her in his madness!

Cawley was panting heavily as he climbed to his feet, moving sideways at the same time to stay between her and the door. He kicked the rum bottle as he stood, paused to look down at it, then with his eyes on her, reached to fumble it into his hand.

He raised the bottle above his head and tilted it to drain the few drops that had stayed inside. Then, suddenly, he hurled it past her to shatter the clay vessel against the rock of the hearth.

"You'll be drained too, slut," he told her in his straining voice. "Empty as that bottle before I'm satisfied. You'll beg me to stop.

Her heart was hammering against her ribs, threatening to leap out from between. Her legs shook from effort and fear, and her hip threatened to collapse from the bruising it had taken when he drove her to the floor.

But in spite of all, her mind began to function, to push ahead of the fear. She had to do something. Had to stop him somehow or she was done. He was stronger, and in his frenzied state, more quick than she. It was only a matter of time before he caught her again and this time she wouldn't be able to fight herself free.

Elizabeth moved experimentally a step to her right and Cawley followed her direction. He crouched again when she paused and grinned a savage grimace at her as he licked his lips.

Quickly, as fast as she could, Elizabeth darted to her left, but then immediately stopped and whirled back again.

It worked. Cawley anticipated her first move but not the second. His headlong lunge carried him straight into the open hearth.

He saw his danger too late to stop himself; he could only throw up his hands to keep from going into the fire. His right hand managed to slap against the rock of the side, but the left plunged directly into the pot of boiled cabbage simmering above the low fire and crashed the whole of it down under him.

Cawley screamed with pain.

A second later, she was at the door and through it, running, running into the safety of the night . . .

It seemed like hours—but truth told her she had been away from the house for only minutes. She had to hold to that. Despite the horror of what had happened she must not lose grasp of truth for she would surely go mad herself. Her name was Elizabeth, and she was a woman. Not a hurt animal, as she felt, to go stumbling and whimpering forever through the night.

She had run to exhaustion before she could stop herself. Before she could gain a measure of control over her screaming consciousness. Even now, with that control of her mind, her body threatened to give way. Her legs shook beneath her; her hands were nerveless where they clutched her dress together over her breasts; and nausea churned in her throat, offering to turn her stomach out.

Then it did. Elizabeth sank to her knees and was sick. It seemed to last forever, but then, somewhere in the streets behind her, she heard a man's voice—a rough voice—and it froze her blood. *Him!*

He was pursuing her! He could be anywhere in these dark streets! *Oh merciful God, help me!*

She flung herself to her feet and staggered a half dozen steps from the violence of her effort in listening. Where? Which way to run?

No! Don't run! She would only give herself away by running! Cawley would hear her footsteps!

Quietly. She *must* move quietly!

Carefully, a few steps at a time, she crept forward, holding close to the forbidding walls of the buildings to remain away from the open street where she might be seen. It was a moonless night, but the stars were bright enough to give her away in the open spaces.

But where to go? Where was she to go? She couldn't hide in these streets all night. Or even if she could, what about tomorrow? What would she do when the dawn turned away the safety of the night?

The forest! She could hide in the forest. No, she couldn't. They'd find her there. She would be a runaway and Cawley would get them to help him find her . . .

Where? Oh dear Lord, where?

Jason. She must go to Jason. He'd protect her. *No!* Jason said he would *kill* Cawley! And he would. And they'd *hang* him!

Her chest hurt terribly, her lungs were on fire. She tightened her hands over her breasts and leaned heavily against the rough wood of a house. Her mind was beginning to weaken. It was so difficult to think!

But Jason was the only person in Savannah who would truly believe her. The only one not for the rights of a master over his servants. She *had* to go to him!

And Mrs. Longfootte! She would believe her. She'd believe Cawley was mad. They—she and her husband—would stop Jason from foolish things . . .

It was all she could think. Her tired mind would try no other. Go to the Longfootes it said over and over. Beg their help. They're good folk.

She would go. But she was terribly confused now. These dark streets, so familiar in the day hours, seemed suddenly alien. And, too, they were beginning to waiver, to pulsate as she looked down their width. Beneath her feet, the ground swayed gently.

She walked, stumbled and fell. Somehow, she didn't understand how, she was in Percival Square. The Longfoottes lived only two blocks away...down a street...which street?

Objects around her were growing fuzzy now. The night seemed blacker.

There it was. Right before her. How had she gotten here? It *was* the right house. The flowers growing in the clay pots—no one else did that—she had thought them pretty when Jason walked her by to see Alice Longfootte's flower pots...

The door was so heavy, so large, when she leaned against it. The drawstring was in, she hadn't expected it to be otherwise. It was late in the night. Decent folk were abed.

She knocked, raising her hand with the greatest of effort and hitting her knuckles against the hard wood. But even where she leaned with her face pressed against the door, she couldn't hear the sound of her own knocking. How could they inside?

It took strength she didn't know she could manage. She held herself away with one hand and slapped hard at the stubborn door with the other. "Please! Someone, please! Help me!"

The night, which had been her guarding friend until now, suddenly turned violently on her and rushed her off into a thundering blackness....

Elizabeth returned slowly, drifting into awareness and then back out again. People were standing over her, she knew that. But she couldn't hold on long enough to see who they were. Voices sounded from far away above her and she thought she heard her own name called. She couldn't be certain. Anyway, it would take so much effort to come back. She didn't want to. Better, so much better, to float here, where it was so peaceful and nothing could reach her.

Her forehead was cool. So pleasant. And her face now, it became cool as well, a delicious coolness that felt so good. She wanted to smile.

"Elizabeth." The voice was gentle, but persistent. She didn't want to answer it. Why didn't it leave her to the coolness?

"Elizabeth. Wake up."

The cool was removed from her face and her cheek was

patted firmly. She frowned.

"Wake up, dear." The voice refused to be denied and Elizabeth opened her eyes.

It was hard to focus at first. Then she could. Alice Longfootte was leaning over her, peering down at her intently. She held a wet cloth in her hand and wiped gently at Elizabeth's eyelids with it. "That's right, dear. Wake up."

Elizabeth looked beyond her, turning her head to do so. Jason was there. And Mr. Longfootte. Anxious looks on both their faces, Jason's deeply, he looked frightened. She loved him for that look.

"There." Mrs. Longfootte sat erect. "You're awake. How do you feel, Elizabeth?"

She had to moisten her tongue to reply. "I'm...I'm all right now. What happened?"

Jason let out an explosive cry. "Thank God!"

He would have said more to her, but Elizabeth saw Mr. Longfootte place a restraining hand on his arm.

"You tell us, dear," Mrs. Longfootte said. "Mr. Longfootte heard a noise and found you collapsed on our step." She glanced at the men standing beside the bed. "And your poor clothes. Have you had an accident?"

Elizabeth stared back at her. Did it actually happen? Or was this all a bad dream? It had to be true—she was here, not in her own bed.

She tried to look down at her clothes but couldn't see the top of her dress, the movement made her eyes water.

"Elizabeth?" There was concern in the older woman's voice. "Can't you talk, dear?"

She nodded. Reluctantly. If she told the truth she would be shamed before them all. Though it wasn't her fault, she would bear the shame of it. And she would be accusing her master...

Jason made the decision for her. He leaned over, his face working and tears forming in his eyes. "He did it, didn't he?" he said in a voice choked with strain. "He attacked you."

Elizabeth nodded, watching him.

"Damn!" He flung himself erect and raised his fists to heaven. But Longfootte was just as quick. "Jason! Mind your tongue!"

Tears were running down his face and Elizabeth's own eyes blurred as she saw them.

Jason moved, but Longfootte was faster and grasped both his arms. "Stop this now, Jason! I'll have no blasphemy nor threats in this house! Control yourself and let her talk."

Jason ground his teeth, his body rigid, but he held his peace at last and turned to look down on her.

"Tell us, Elizabeth," Alice Longfootte said gently. "You don't have to be ashamed. It's not your fault."

Slowly, a few words at a time, stumbling often, she told them. Told them how he had looked when he came home; about the fire; his being drunk and screaming at her; and about the attack.

Jason groaned aloud at the telling.

She told them how she had gotten away from him and Alice hissed sharply, "Serves him aright!"

Then she described her flight through the town, as much as she could remember of it. That part was dim. "I didn't know where else to go," she finished.

Alice reached a hand to touch her cheek. "You were right to come here, dear. You'll be safe now. Don't you worry."

She turned her head to see her husband. "Samuel, you must do something. This child cannot go back to that man."

He was silent a long time, enough for Elizabeth to look up at him. His eyes avoided hers as he stroked his chin. "Well, I don't know," he said slowly. "Tis a terrible thing. But there's the law . . . She's servant to him. The law's clear on that point."

"He tried to *rape* her!" Alice Longfootte's voice rose.

But her husband only shook his head. "Tis her word against Cawley's on that. And he's a propertied man."

Elizabeth closed her eyes and turned her face to the wall. There was no hope for her. She would be turned back to him. Her chest ached with the pain.

Exhaustion had been stronger than despair and she'd slept what was left of the night. With dawn, and the stirring of Alice Longfootte whose bed Elizabeth had shared, with the master of the house moving in with Jason in the shed on back, she was awake and rising to face the day. Her hip was sore, as were her legs from running, and she was more than a little nauseous. But with the morning, she was no longer afraid.

Alice stirred the fire to life and placed the pot of coffee to boil, then found needle and thread for Elizabeth to mend her dress. By the time the men entered for breakfast, her clothes were presentable.

Jason took her hand. "I don't know how," he told her, "but

I'll not allow you to go back to him."

Elizabeth gave him a smile, weak, she knew, but the best she could manage. "Go to your meal," she said. "You'll need it to work today."

Jason stared at her, his young jaw set, then shook his head in frustration and sat down at the table. Elizabeth served him and Longfootte, then stood near the fire and watched the dancing flames. Jason's eyes were on her back, she knew, and she felt more sorry for him than for herself. He was a man and it would be the greater frustration for a man to feel helpless. She could sense that Samuel Longfootte was also casting an eye in her direction. He was a good man, a fair man, she had no doubt of that. Nor could she find fault with his attitude. He believed in the law and fair or not, would serve it. But then, he, too, was a man of property.

There was a heavy knock on the door and Elizabeth turned with the others to look in that direction. Who would be calling on the Longfoottes this early?

The master of the house glanced once at his wife, then stood and crossed the room heavily to lift the bar and open the door. Elizabeth craned to see around him.

Two men stood in the doorway, one slightly behind the other, and the second was *him*. She shuttered involuntarily as she saw him.

Longfootte waited, a long and heavy pause—it seemed everyone in the room behind him held their breath—then growled, "What do you want here, Constable Fowler?"

The constable was a large man, with long arms and very large hands, a man slow to think and slower to speak. Deep-set eyes, almost disappearing in the thickly grooved face, went past Longfootte and came to rest on her. He nodded. "I come for the lass," he said in a voice like stones dropping. "It's her by the fire I want."

She was numbed. She'd expected this today—but so soon?

Dazed, she watched Samuel Longfootte sweep a gaze to her, then to his wife and finally back to the door. But it wasn't at the man of the law he looked, his stare went beyond, to the man behind him. "Thermous Cawley," he said, "you're a man to be held in contempt."

He had cleaned himself up, changed clothes and put on a wig. Now he looked the same as before, not the madman he'd been last night. Except for the bandage he had wrapped around his hand and arm, who'd believe her story?

"You're harboring a runaway servant, Longfootte," he said. "And worse than that if you but know it. Whatever the girl has told to you, she lies."

Longfootte grunted. "I believe you to be the liar," he said shortly.

"I'll listen to no such from you!" Cawley spun to the other man. "Constable Fowler, do your duty."

The big man frowned. "The lass is indentured to 'im," he said slowly. "And 'e's brought charges against 'er as well."

Somehow, she hadn't noticed him moving, but Jason was beside her and his arm went protectively around her waist.

"What charges?" Longfootte wanted to know. But again his words were directed to Cawley. "I suppose you'll claim she attacked *you*!"

Cawley flushed even redder than normal. "I know what you're thinking, Longfootte. But it's a lie. A trick on the part of that scheming girl." He looked again to the constable. "It's just as I warned you, Constable Fowler. She's come here with a wild story to try to save herself from gaol."

Longfootte was caught in astonishment. "Gaol? The lass has no more run away than I have!"

"The charge is theft!" Cawley shouted at him. "I caught her stealing from me! That's what! She was taking money from my trunks when I caught her." His chin raised and so did his finger. "And your own servant's a part of the scheme. I'm placing charges against him as well!"

Stealing! She'd never taken anything in her life!

But he didn't care she knew suddenly, it would be any charge. Cawley hated her; hated her enough to see her a prisoner for years or branded on the hand and further indentured to him. Jason! How had he found out about Jason and her?

"I'll not accept such foolishness," Longfootte told him in heat. "Jason Welburn's no thief. Nor do I believe the lass stole from you."

"They schemed it together." Cawley spoke to the constable as much as he spoke to Longfootte. "She even boasted of it to me when I caught her. They were going to take my money and escape the colony."

"Nonsense!" Longfootte's voice rose. "'Tis stupid to say

such! My servant's time is near up!"

"But her's is not!" Cawley countered. "And she's the strumpet he wants!"

He turned to Fowler again, who stood silently trying to follow the argument. "It's your duty to arrest them both!"

"I'll not have my servant arrested!" Longfootte roared.

But the constable finally made up his mind. "Tis the law, Samuel Longfootte," he said ponderously. "Mr. Cawley is of property and has the right. 'E's brought a charge and I'm bound to gaol the two of 'em. If your lad's guilty, you know the court will pay you 'is loss of time. Now I'll ask you to fetch the both of 'em out."

Elizabeth shuddered. How many times had she walked past the small gaol and felt pity for the wretches caught inside. Now it would be her. And poor Jason too!

"Samuel!" His wife's cry, against all rules of a woman's place, angered Longfootte the more. "Quiet!" he barked. Then spun to face Cawley again. "You'll burn in hell for this lie, Thermous Cawley!"

But Cawley wasn't looking at him, his eyes had fastened on her alone and even across the room Elizabeth could see the glimmer of the night before. She could read madness in his eyes.

"May I burn right enough if I'm not telling the God's own truth," he said, and smiled a chilling smile at her.

Eighteen

IT WAS NOT an extremely large room, really much smaller than
she had expected. Still it was the most important room in the
colony and surely the most important she'd ever been in. It
was used not only for the business of governing the colony of
Georgia, it was also used for town court and for Church of
England members on the Sabbath.

Elizabeth had never seen the inside of this building since
the Cawleys, for all his reading and quoting the Bible, hardly
ever attended the church. And even if they did, she wasn't
permitted to join them. Strange, as she thought about it, although she believed most wonderfully in a God above, she'd
never set foot inside a church. Briggs had not allowed her that
opportunity either.

She looked around herself, curiosity overcoming for the
moment the soreness of her limbs and the heavy discomfort of
the chains that bound her. The room was a good bit longer
than wide and most of the space was taken up by pews. At
one end, the end she and Jason occupied, there was a little
more open area. A high-paneled bench stood upon a raised
platform, several chairs and one table were placed in front of

it, and the railed prisoner's dock where she and Jason stood occupied one corner. There were two doors on this end, one of which they had entered early this morning. She didn't know where the other might lead, but the last ones, the two large doors at the other end of the room from her were open and curious spectators were already coming in to fill the pews.

Elizabeth looked at Jason standing beside her. His clothes, like her own, were dirty from his being chained inside the close, cramped little rooms in gaol. His face appeared tired and worn, but he managed a smile for her. She would have liked to talk to him, to tell him how sorry she was to be the cause of his trouble this day, but Constable Fowler had warned them repeatedly that there would be no talking between them. Prisoners weren't allowed to talk. Nor could she touch him, though she ached to do just that. They could only look. And try to smile.

Elizabeth closed her eyes for a moment. The chains around her wrists and waist were heavy and growing more so the longer she stood. She wished the trial would hurry and begin.

Closing her eyes seemed to help her. But it also brought back the memory of the three days she had spent in gaol. No one had been allowed to see her—if anyone had chosen to do so—nor was she allowed to talk to anyone else confined in the windowless log building. Jason had been there, too; it was the only place he could have been, but he might as well have been across the river for all the good it did her. She could see and hear no one but Constable Fowler and the other constable—what was his name?—anyhow she didn't like him. He looked at her when he entered her small room the same way Cawley had looked at her. At least Constable Fowler treated her as he would any other prisoner.

The worst part of it—worse even than the silence—was the continuous dark. Not being able to tell if it were day or night. She could even abide not having enough water to drink, much less in which to bathe, and the ever present rats better than she could the darkness. When at last she was let out of the room to come here, she'd nearly cried.

She sighed. At least the dried food she was given once a day had lessened her morning sickness. She hoped she was finished with that.

Oh, the tiredness! If only she could sit down for a little while! But there would be no chance of that. Prisoners were required to stand. Perhaps the trial would be mercifully short. Anyway, it should be. Cawley would be allowed to tell his lies and then the judges would pass their sentences. It was highly unlikely that either Jason or herself would be allowed to speak.

The pews were filling more rapidly now, it must be nearing time to begin. Constable Fowler's large frame blocked a good bit of the audience from her view, but she did manage to see Hester Pullam come in and sit down. Hester's small face registered shock and sympathy at the same time and Elizabeth knew she must look a fright. She wished she had been given water and time to bathe before she came here.

She watched Samuel Longfootte enter and make his way near the front, followed by his wife. Alice Longfootte gave her a smile of encouragement and Elizabeth did her best to respond.

The murmur of conversation throughout the spectators increased and Elizabeth looked for the reason. She found it in the person of William Stephens, the man who had become president of the colony with the change from the old magistrate rule, who was slowly coming up the aisle with the aid of a cane and the arm of James Habersham. She was astonished. Why would the president bother to attend a trial of no significance? Surely he had more important matters to attend?

The murmur increased dramatically as Stephens took his seat, but the heads she could see were turned again to the door. Elizabeth followed their looks and saw Thermous Cawley come in, being led by the constable she didn't like. He was dressed in his best clothes, the satin breeches and velvet longcoat she'd seen him wear only once before. His ruffled shirt was held closed by a yellow vest and he wore a powdered wig. Even the bandage on his arm was satin.

She turned her head as he advanced to keep from looking at him.

His eyes were upon her as he was given a chair at the front of the room. Elizabeth could feel his stare, but she refused to return his look, merely raising her chin to let him know she wasn't afraid.

At that moment the other door, the one she had wondered about, opened and the three judges entered, followed closely by the clerk. All three of the judges Elizabeth recognized, though for the life of her she couldn't remember their names. Why was that? These were men who were about to decide to

have her whipped and given back to Cawley or perhaps confined for a year or more to the terror of gaol. She ought at
least to remember their names!

The three of them wore purple robes trimmed in ermine and
white powdered wigs, and the first carried a strange looking
instrument in his hand, a thick stick with a ball at one end that
appeared to have jewels in it. The clerk, who took a chair at
the table in front instead of following the judges up behind the
bench, wore a black tufted robe and carried a book.

The judges found seats behind the high bench and then
seemed to her not able to suit themselves with it. Nor with
anything else, she decided, as they involved themselves in a
great fuss and bother. The clerk jumped up to listen to a whispered question from one of them and then Constable Fowler
was called over. Then the three of the judges conferred so
among themselves Elizabeth began to despair of their ever
beginning the trial. She was nervous and a little sick again,
and her arms were tired from the chains. Why couldn't they
begin!

The audience had grown quiet, watching all of the doings
with fascination, and suddenly, President Stephens cleared his
throat loudly. The chief judge—she decided he was that because he sat in the middle and wore a type of cloth over his
wig—sat up immediately and broke off his whispered conversation with his fellow. His quick look at Mr. Stephens was
followed by a gesture to the clerk.

That gentleman stood and used a wooden mallet to pound
on the table before him. "Here ye, here ye!" he cried. "This
court is now in session! Let the King's justice be served!"

The quiet was loud in her mind, a silence that seemed
suddenly to engulf her. Only the pounding of her own heart
kept her from a faint.

The chief judge looked in their direction, leaning forward
at the same time. "Constable Fowler, who be the prisoners you
have in dock?"

Constable Fowler held himself erect and took in a deep,
rasping breath. "Tis a lass by name of Elizabeth Briggs and a
man by name of Jason Welburn, your worship," he thundered.

"And what be the charges against them?"

"Tis a charge of stealing, sire. Also one of planning escape
from honest servanthood." Constable Fowler's voice was three

times louder than needed and she winced as it boomed in her ear.

The judge nodded slowly and looked at them for a long time. "Then let this trial begin," he said finally. "The King's justice and God's own mercy will deal with these prisoners this day. Who brings the charges?"

His question was no longer directed at the man who held them prisoner, but to the room in general. However, Elizabeth watched his eyes immediately go to Cawley after he'd spoken.

Thermous Cawley rose and adjusted his coattails behind him. "I do, your worship. My name is Thermous Cawley and I am a man of property in this colony. The girl is indentured to me."

One of the other judges bent to speak to the chief, but the latter shook him aside impatiently. "And the man?" he asked instead.

Cawley gave a bow. "He is indentured, but not to me, your worship. However, I charge him as well with being a part of the crime that was committed against me."

"Is his master in the room?"

"Aye!" Samuel Longfootte rose immediately, literally jumping to his feet. "And he's no thief!"

The judges, all three of them frowned severely, and the clerk thumped his table. "That remains to be seen," the chief judge said. "Tis a matter for this court to decide, Samuel Longfootte. You'll answer only what is asked, do you understand?"

"Aye." Longfootte muttered something else in a low tone but sat back down again.

The judge eyed him a moment longer then nodded to Cawley. "Tell the court the circumstances of the charges you make, Mr. Cawley. And do not spare the telling. We must have the truth here."

The man standing a few feet from her could have been speaking of someone else, someone she didn't even know. Somehow she had become detached from what was happening to her, as if she were there but she wasn't. Elizabeth hadn't wanted to look at him when he came in, but now she did and it had no effect on her at all. Thermous Cawley had tried to rape her—sent her fleeing in terror through the streets of Savannah only a few short nights ago—and he was responsible for her standing here in chains and disgrace now. But it didn't seem to matter anymore. Not nearly as much as how nice it would be to be able to sit down again.

Cawley's manner reminded her of how he had been when she first met him that long time ago in London. He was pompous and arrogant, as if he thought himself the better of those present. "If you please, your worship," he said. "I've been a patient man to have been so long wronged by the female now in dock. I made an honest purchase of her labor from her own father before coming to this colony, seeking not only to secure her services for my wife, but to offer this young girl a chance to better her circumstances. It was, however, a bargain in which I've been far the loser. I most assure you honorable judges that this girl has plagued me with laziness, disobedience and deliberate destruction of my property from the day I arrived here."

"And you did nothing about such an attitude?" the judge on the left interrupted him sharply.

Elizabeth had never seen a more pious look appear on her master's face. Cawley could have been mistaken for a saint. "I'm not a brutal man, your worship," he said apologetically. "I realize I should have disciplined the girl, but with my wife sick, as well as both my children—all of whom I have now lost—it was impossible for me to take a hard stand with her. I needed what help she would give."

"Quite right." This from the judge on the other side. "Still, Mr. Cawley, laxity toward one servant breeds discontent among them all. Discipline must be maintained for the common good."

Cawley bowed. "I stand corrected, your worship. But may I continue?"

The judge nodded. But it was as much with satisfaction at having made his point as permission.

"That wasn't the worst of her faults," Cawley continued. "She was also . . . less than chaste."

His statement drew a murmur from the listeners that swelled until the chief judge raised his head in warning.

Cawley glanced quickly at her, but Elizabeth merely stared back blankly at him. Beside her, Jason stirred.

"You had knowledge of this and you made no report of the transgression?" the chief judge asked him. "It was your bounded duty to do so, Mr. Cawley, so she could have been punished accordingly."

He bowed again. "My fault entirely, your worship. But I'm a Christian man. I thought with patience and forbearance, I could teach her the error of her wicked ways. I, after all, brought her from her home in England to a new and strange place. I felt my responsibility in the matter."

"Quite right," the right-hand judge said. Elizabeth decided he had a cruel face—a small, pinched mouth and a thin, pointed nose. Barlow, that was his name . . . or was it?

"How did you become aware of her transgressions?" the chief judge wanted to know and Elizabeth could feel the audience lean forward to hear.

She didn't really blame them. Life in Savannah was humdrum for the most of them. Except when the Spanish threatened, there was little of interest or excitement, and this was a scandal.

"It's a delicate subject, your worship," Cawley reminded him, again in his apologetic tone. "And in truth, not the charge I now bring against her."

His words irritated the man behind the high bench. "We will decide upon that, Mr. Cawley. But we must be given all the facts of this matter and the woman's morals have a bearing in those facts."

"Of course, your worship." Cawley cast a quick glance toward her, so quick she nearly missed it. "I bow to your wisdom in the pursuit of justice," he said to the bench.

He paused, as if to gather himself for a painful duty. He is enjoying this, she thought. Still, it didn't seem to anger her.

"I discovered she slipped out of my house on several occasions," he continued at last. "When I caught her the last time and chastised her for her wickedness, she admitted she was seeing the man in the dock beside her."

He turned and pointed dramatically at Jason.

Liar! I never told you his name! She looked and Jason's face was a thundercloud.

"I see," said the chief judge. "That fact will be taken into consideration in his sentence as well. Please continue."

"Yes, your worship. I do believe my discovering her sins caused her to cease them for the time being. But now I believe that to be the reason behind my present charge against her. I believe that in order for her to be with her lover, the two of them plotted to rob me of my last savings and then to flee the colony altogether."

This time there was a louder murmur and it was all masculine in tone. Since its beginning, the Georgia colony had been

plagued with runaway indentures. Some joined the Spanish to
the south, most made their way to the northern colonies although they ran a risk of detection and return, but a few took
to the forests and became bandits. Elizabeth knew that most
indentures had a reputation for laziness, and in truth there was
little incentive for them to work hard as it would make no
change in their time owed, but she hated for her and Jason to
be considered as such. The owners in the audience, however,
hardly considered that difference.

The chief judge raised his heavy frown again and the noise
subsided. When it was quiet, he nodded to Cawley. "And how
did you learn this?"

"I caught her in the act, your worship," Cawley said. "I
returned home late, having borne a double tragedy of burying
my dear wife and finding my silkworm sheds burned the same
day, only to catch my servant girl in my trunk where I kept
my money. When I accosted her, she was brazen enough to
fling the truth in my face."

He paused and drew himself erect slowly. "I confess, your
worship, I did at last lose my temper with her and struck her
with my hand."

"About time," the judge on the right muttered.

Cawley nodded. "However, she wasn't hurt, and was clever
enough to rip her own clothes with the intention that she later
carried out. She fled to another's house and accused me—a
man who had just lost the dearest wife in the world—of attempting to rape her."

This time the audience participated to the extent that the
chief judge was forced to command the clerk to pound his
mallet for order.

When he had it again, the judge looked at Cawley. "How
did you receive your injury, Mr. Cawley?"

"In the fire at my silkworm sheds, your worship. It was
through having the use of only one hand that I was unable to
prevent this wicked girl from fleeing the just thrashing I should
have given her. A fact, I believe, which she was more than
aware."

Lies, she thought wearily. All lies. But they would be believed. She could see it in the faces of all three men behind
the high bench. She and Jason were already condemned. No
one would believe the word of an indenture—even if either of
them were allowed to speak.

She had a cramp in her left leg that was beginning to ache most dreadfully. And her shoulders felt as if she were holding up the entire world.

What would it be like to be whipped? She'd watched it happen to her brother once on the ship. Could have seen it happen here in Savannah had she not refused to watch. It would be painful . . . very painful. But worse would be the humiliation. When they bared her back, did they bind her clothes so not to leave her breasts naked? Oh, how she hoped they did.

"Have you further to add, Mr. Cawley?" the chief judge asked.

"Only, your worship, that the other prisoner is equally guilty in my opinion. Not only did she admit his part, but when she fled me she went straight to his master's house. A fact that Samuel Longfootte will be forced to admit."

The chief judge turned to look full at her and his face wore a heavy frown. "Young woman, do you admit to your fellow prisoner being part of your scheme to rob Mr. Cawley?"

Suddenly the nausea returned. It threatened her throat and Elizabeth was forced to fight to keep it down. She swallowed hard. "No, sir. Neither of us sought to run away."

Her voice sounded weak to her own ears and she wasn't certain for a moment that he had heard her.

But he did, and her answer seemed to amaze him. "You are denying these charges?" he asked, his voice rising.

She'd never had to speak out before. It made her nervous. And even sicker. But she must do her best. "Yes, sir."

His face clouded in anger. "Let me warn you, young woman, there are stern penalties for those who lie to the King's court. Are you aware you're contradicting the word of a land owning citizen of this colony? A man who has no *reason* to lie?"

Elizabeth looked at him. She'd no chance of convincing him. None at all. Why didn't Jason speak up? Why was he so silent?

She cut her eyes to see his face in spite of knowing everyone else was looking at her to answer. His face was white with anger, his lips pressed firmly together, and she could feel the tension in him. But he wouldn't return her look.

"Yes, sir," she told the judge. "I understand that. But I'm not lying. I didn't rob Mr. Cawley. Nor have I thought to flee my debt of service to him."

Oh she was tired! Would this never be over?

The judge shook his head slowly and raised his hands in exasperation. Then turned to Cawley. "Do you have anything to add in the light of this woman's denial?"

Cawley shook his head sadly. "Tis of no surprise to me, your worship. The girl has such a history of lying—I cannot tell you of the times she's stolen from her dead mistress—"

"I didn't!" It was more than she could take. All of a sudden her detachment was shaken completely. "That's a lie!"

"Silence!" the judge thundered at her. "You'll speak when told, prisoner!"

Elizabeth trembled with her own anger, but his furious look bludgeoned her into silence.

The judge waited to see that he would be obeyed and in the pause, the quiet of the room was broken by someone in the audience clearing his throat loudly. The judge glanced up in annoyance, but his expression changed magically. Elizabeth looked around in surprise.

President Stephens was rising slowly to his feet. When he stood, he leaned on his cane. "If this court would permit me," he said, "I could possibly be of some assistance in this matter."

"Of course, of course," the chief judge said quickly. "We're always pleased to accept the benefit of your experience and knowledge, Mr. Stephens."

He was like a fawning dog, she thought. A moment ago, he was trying to scare me to death and now he looks as if he wants to lick the president's hand. Because he serves his position at Mr. Stephens's pleasure! The president could remove him at will and the Trustees would back the move. It made her angry all over again.

"Thank you," Mr. Stephens said. "Mr. Cawley, you've said this young servant was both disobedient and lazy, is that not right?"

Cawley was instantly on guard. Elizabeth could see it in his face. "That is true," he said carefully.

"I see." The president began to move forward slowly as he talked. "By lazy, you meant she didn't do her work. By disobedient, she *refused* to do her work properly."

Cawley nodded. "That's right."

"This being work done both in the home—your home—and outside? Errands to town, drawing water from the well, washing, that sort of thing?"

Cawley was puzzled. And wary. "Yes, sir."

Mr. Stephens stroked his jaw. "I find that very strange, Mr. Cawley. You see, I myself have had occasion to notice Mistress Briggs going about and was impressed with what seemed to me to be diligence. Industriousness, I might say."

Cawley could only stare at him.

"I took occasion to make inquiry about this only yesterday," Stephens went on. "A number of people, witnesses who are available now if needed, told me she was truly a *hard* worker."

He paused and leaned forward with both gnarled hands resting on the cane to peer at Cawley. "Do you suppose, sir, she was clever enough to only display this laxity you speak of when no one but yourself were watching?"

Cawley's face reddened. "She's a clever wench, Mr. Stephens."

"Wench . . ." Stephens drew the word out very slowly. "A moment or so ago you spoke of her as a lost child; one you were trying to lead into morality. Now she's a wench. I suppose it's natural that you should be angry at her—after all, she did flee your house in the middle of the night. The very night, I might add, that your wife was buried and only the two of you— yourself and this young girl—were alone."

Cawley's color deepened. He opened his mouth to speak, but closed it again abruptly.

The room had become so quiet it was startling. The ache in her leg, her tiredness, even the discontent of her belly, disappeared as Elizabeth watched the two men in fascination.

Stephens stirred again and walked completely to the front where he looked up at the chief judge. "May I take a chair?" he asked. "My apologies to the court, but this bad leg of mine is most worrisome to a man of my age."

The judge had to shake himself free of his own fascination in the turn the trial had taken. "Of course, Mr. Stephens. By all means."

"Thank you." The president lowered himself in one of the chairs and settled carefully back. "I would not attempt to interfere in the least in this court's capable handling of this matter," he said. "Merely to offer it my own experience. I do feel this to be a strange case—at least not as simple as it first appears."

"Please do, Mr. Stephens," the judge said. "We can all benefit. I'm quite certain of that."

Stephens nodded. "Thank you. Mr. Cawley, your wife was ill for a goodly time, was she not?"

Cawley nodded. "She suffered greatly. As did I for her."

"I see. She was confined in bed for many months?"

"That's surely true."

Stephens raised his head and his eyes suddenly stabbed at the man who stood a few feet from him. "In that time, Mr. Cawley, did you cook your own meals? Or clean your own house; sweep your yard? Or do the wash yourself?"

"Well, no...but I—"

"Who did those things, Mr. Cawley?" Stephens's voice was quick and sharp.

"I...I made the girl—"

"You *made* her do it? Then I must say you did an excellent job of it, sir. For Mrs. Habersham, the good wife of my secretary, James Habersham, was in your house the day before your wife died to see about Mistress Cawley. She made mention of how well kept it was. I believe she even spoke of how she wished she had a servant even half as willing as Mistress Briggs."

"There were times...I mean...she didn't *always* neglect..." Cawley floundered like a fish out of water and Elizabeth watched beads of perspiration appear on his forehead. Her own pain was gone. She pressed forward against the rail, afraid she would miss even a part of this.

Stephens had him impaled with a hard stare. "Mr. Cawley, were you ever aware of what your servant girl did when she was away from your house? I mean other than your statements about her *night* activities? Her washing of clothes with the other women, for instance?"

"I could not follow her...watch her all the time. I mean, I had my own work that took me—"

"But you did just that, sir!" Stephens interrupted. "You were observed on more than one occasion to follow her about town. You appeared to make great effort to know *exactly* what she was doing. On one such occasion, you were observed standing and watching this girl wash clothes from a distance, not once, but three times in the same day. Do you not consider that *strange*, sir?"

"I told you! She was lazy! I had to make sure she did the wash!" Cawley's voice rose in desperation. "What are you trying to say?"

Stephens waited...a long time. The tension in the room—indeed in her own limbs—rose unbearably.

"I am saying, Mr. Cawley, that you did not speak the truth

a moment ago when you said this poor girl neglected her duties. I believe we've proven that. And you've shown a remarkable interest in her, much more than that necessary toward a servant. Why is that, Mr. Cawley? Could it be because she is young and pretty? Because your own wife was long in her illness and unable to be proper wife to you?"

"NO!" Cawley raised his fist. "I did not! I'm a Christian man! I held no . . . no . . . *interest* in her!"

"Please be careful, Mr. Cawley." The president's voice stabbed through the tension between them. "Remember you are speaking in the King's court. Where nothing but the truth— the full and open truth—shall be said."

He leaned forward in the chair as Cawley slowly dropped his arm. "Did you or did you not, Thermous Cawley, ask this young woman to *marry* you? Asked her with your own wife dying in the next room? An honest answer, sir!"

There was a collective gasp from the straining audience. The chief judge's mouth flew open, and Elizabeth felt in a state of shock. *How could he know that!*

The audience was in an uproar and the judge made no effort to stop it, merely staring in astonishment at Cawley who stood frozen, his face a mask of horror. He had turned white.

How did he know? She'd told no one—Hester! Elizabeth looked quickly to the audience, trying to find that face. When she did, the other girl's countenance was beaming with delight. It warmed Elizabeth all over.

"Well, Mr. Cawley?" Stephens's voice was low in pitch but it immediately stilled the room again. His hard stare continued to impale his victim like a rod of iron.

Cawley's mouth opened and closed like a dying fish. But no sound emitted.

"I believe we can prove the truth of that, too, sir," the president told him.

He couldn't. She knew he couldn't. No one else was there but her and her master . . . Cawley had only to deny it . . .

Elizabeth looked in anxiety at him, and her nerves, already tight with strain, began to hum the quicker. Cawley's eyes were wide and staring in the white face—they held the same light she had seen before. The light of madness.

"Lies . . ." he croaked. "All lies . . . I didn't . . . didn't lust after her . . ."

His voice rose rapidly to a shriek. "She taunted me with it!

From the beginning! Her body . . . that young body . . . my wife didn't care for me . . . wasn't a wife . . ."

He was screaming the words now, hurling them at his tormentor. "It wasn't my fault! Don't you see that? Satan! Satan's the cause. He sent her to tempt me!"

He whirled suddenly and his good arm stabbed at the stunned listeners, his finger pointing rigidly. "And you—all of you! You hated me! I know you did! You were on her side! You're still on her side! I knew the looks you gave me! You were jealous because I am better . . ."

The madness was full upon him now. Elizabeth could see it all again—the night of terror when only she faced this creature. When he was going to *kill* her. She was afraid again, only her chains kept her from attempting to run away.

"You destroyed me!" Cawley screamed. "You burned my sheds to keep me from becoming rich! Poisoned my trees! You're on her side . . . because she's *pretty*! You tried to *buy* her from me . . ."

"Mr. Cawley!" President Stephens's voice was sharp but had no effect on the man before him. Saliva drooled from Cawley's mouth and his eyes seemed to pop from his head. He whirled to Stephens. "You got the Lord to punish me!"

He lurched forward, his hand raised in threat, but Constable Fowler was quicker. A horrified Elizabeth wouldn't have believed the large man could move so fast. He leaped forward and embraced Cawley in a bear hug from behind. Held him off the floor until only his toes touched and squeezed him breathless.

A moment later his prisoner collapsed, and Constable Fowler lowered him into a chair but continued to tower above him. Cawley began to sob, his head rolling on his chest.

"Thank you, Constable Fowler," the president said quietly. "Please remain close in case Mr. Cawley needs further assistance."

He pulled himself from his chair with difficulty, adjusted his bad leg under him and leaned on his cane to face the open-mouthed judges. "Gentlemen, I believe we have uncovered the real truth here," he said. "This man has demonstrated his own reasons for his charges against this poor girl. I think it quite obvious that Thermous Cawley, a man with a wife long sick and a desirable young woman in the house, to say nothing of his troubles with death and a failing business, has fallen victim to a temptation laid sinfully on many a man. He wanted a fair maid for his own lustful purposes and was unable to go to the Master sufficiently to remove that lust from his heart."

He paused and looked, almost sadly she thought, at the man slumped in the chair. "We have proven he lied about her work. Proven, I think, by his own actions that he was jealous of her, therefore, I think it reasonable to assume he also lies about her being a thief. I offer as proof of the last my own observations. Thermous Cawley says he caught this child with his money. That she defied him, spoke of running away with young Welburn there, and fled into the night to leave him standing. Yet, gentlemen, this same Thermous Cawley *waited until next morn* to seek help from the authorities! Only after dawn did he approach Constable Fowler to help him find her. Now I must ask, is that reasonable if he thought the two of them fleeing the colony? Or was it merely that Thermous Cawley *knew* she would go no further than to the Longfoottes? And he needed that time before morn to overcome the effects of strong drink."

Elizabeth watched all three judges turn to look at Cawley.

"That's right, gentlemen," the president said. "He purchased rum on the night in question. He was observed to be drinking heavily. His clothes were damaged from the fire at his sheds right enough and he was thought to be extremely agitated. But gentlemen, *he had the use of both hands then.* I submit to you he damaged that hand in a drunken state when he returned home. Damaged it when he was attempting, as this poor girl described to the Longfoottes, to work his lustful will upon her."

The judges were frowning again. Stern, baleful frowns. But this time they were directed at the slumping Cawley, not at her.

"I hope I have helped in this matter," President Stephens said at last. "And that the truth has been found."

"We appreciate your help, Mr. Stephens," the chief judge said. "It becomes quite obvious to me that this man has brought false charges to this court. He has attempted to use the King's justice to his own ends. And for that crime, this court will seek punishment against him."

"And the young woman?" Stephens injected gently.

The judge hesitated, suddenly aware he was caught in a legal trap. Elizabeth's hopes that had been rising so rapidly with the turn in events, swooped down again. These three men held no background in law—they held their posts only because they were appointed by the Trustees and there were no others in the colony more experienced. They wouldn't know how to deal with this for they would be unwilling to free an indenture. Not even from a man like Cawley.

She was right. The chief judge stammered. "I believe . . . the law is clear on the one point—"

"That she must remain indentured unless the debt is forgiven by her master," Stephens supplied, still in the same soft tone. "That's quite clear and I doubt we can persuade Mr. Cawley to do so even in his present disgrace. However, gentlemen, the court by its own words has been misused by this man. I should think that merits punishment in the way of a fine. A fine that also costs him the use of this servant. She could be legally transferred in indenture to the Trustees of this colony."

Elizabeth watched the chief judge's face brighten. "Quite right! That should be done. Will be done! It's hereby ordered."

"Your worship!"

The judge looked up in annoyance as a voice rang from the audience. Elizabeth turned to see Samuel Longfootte rising to his feet, looked in time to see Alice Longfootte retrieving the elbow with which she had prodded him.

"Yes? What is it?" The judge was impatient to get on with his own speach.

"If it please your worship," Samuel said loudly, "I would like to purchase the girl's contract from the court." He glanced down at his wife briefly. "The way I see it, the colony's got little use for a female indenture—she can't work at the cow-pens, nor do the farming at the Trustee gardens—it would seem best to sell her to a private household."

Again he glanced down at his wife, who smiled and nodded. "I'm in need of such services in my own home."

Before the judge could reply, President Stephens spoke. "An excellent idea. Solves all the problem."

Elizabeth wanted to run forth and hug him.

The chief judge looked to the others, one at a time, and each nodded vigorously. "Very well," he said loudly. "An excellent solution as Mr. Stephens so kindly pointed out."

He frowned heavily. "Thermous Cawley, you are hereby fined both the cost of this court—to be determined by the clerk—and the cost of this indentured girl. Furthermore, it is the intention of this court that you be banished from this colony immediately. Go ye and never set foot in the colony of Georgia again under penalty of imprisonment."

Her gaze turned to rest on the man slumped in the chair in front of her. It was over. She was free of him forever. Never would she look upon his face again . . .

Tears began to flow, to blur her eyes until he disappeared from her sight.

The rest was over quickly. All three judges left as they had entered and the spectators began to noisily file out. Cawley was led away by others as Constable Fowler came over to unlock the chains that bound her and Jason.

"Tis 'appy I am to do this, lass," he told her gruffly. "Never liked doing it in the first place. Nor 'im for that matter."

"Thank you," Elizabeth said. "You were only doing your duty."

"Aye." He released Jason, turned back to eye her for a long moment, then shrugged his massive shoulders and walked away.

Elizabeth looked up at Jason, wanting him to take her in his arms. But he couldn't. The two of them were being watched by too many. He took her hands instead. "Let's go, Elizabeth," he said softly. "Let's go home."

She shook her head. "I want nothing more, Jason. But I've got to thank him. He saved us both."

Jason nodded. "Then I'll wait for you on the square."

It was hard to let him go, but suddenly she was surrounded by well-wishers—a dozen ladies, hands aflutter and all talking at once. Hester Pullam threw her arms around her neck. "Elizabeth! I'm so happy!"

She fought away her own tears. "Thank you, Hester. If you hadn't told him—why did you do it?"

"He was our only hope," Hester said quickly. "And I knew he liked you, I'd heard him say so. I told him everything. I hope you don't mind."

"Mind? Hester, I love you!"

She had difficulty pulling herself away, but already she could see the president making his way slowly toward the doors, being held up by both age and the many who wanted to speak to him. Elizabeth murmured her thanks and apologies at the same time as she pushed through the crowd to his side.

"Mr. Stephens! Mr. Stephens!"

He spoke a last word to the man who faced him before turning to her. "Ah, Mistress Briggs. I'm happy this worked out for you."

Elizabeth wanted desperately to hug him and had to restrain herself from doing so with effort. But she couldn't check the tears in her eyes. "Thank you," she blurted. "Oh, thank you for it all!"

His eyebrows rose but his face retained its dignity. "I was merely doing what I could for the benefit of the colony, Mistress Briggs. Attempting to serve the best interest of justice, as it were. Our judges are fine citizens, but I'm afraid they lack experience in law. I feel obligated to help whenever I can."

She shook her head vigorously. "I don't believe that. You were being kind to me. You're a wonderful man."

It forced a smile to his lined face. "In that regard, perhaps I shall have to admit to a certain interest today. It seems I do hold remembrance of a young maiden who went out of her way to be pleasant to an old man. An old man, I might add, who at one time was quite unpopular with most everyone else in this colony."

Elizabeth smiled and he nodded. "I do believe it is that very same smile that sticks in my memory."

"Thank you, Mr. Stephens," she said. "Thank you for what you've done for me today."

He coughed abruptly. "Get along with you now. I'm certain your new mistress has work for you to do."

His tone was that of a father as he reached forward to pat her shoulder then turned away as someone else spoke to him.

She passed out the front doors to look gratefully at the blue sky above her, a sky she had been terribly afraid she wouldn't see again for a long time. Then she looked for Jason.

He stood halfway across the square along with Mr. Longfootte. She waved and started toward them. Before she had taken a dozen steps, however, someone put a restraining hand on her arm and Elizabeth halted to face Alice Longfootte.

"I'm so happy for you, Elizabeth," the older woman said. "I was very worried."

"Thank you. And thank you for getting him to buy my contract. I know it was your doing."

Alice smiled conspiringly. "Samuel Longfootte is master of his own house and mind, Elizabeth. But sometimes he does need a little prodding to discover what he really thinks. That, of course, must remain our woman's secret since you'll come under my roof. Samuel is a man of great pride."

"Yes ma'am. But I'm so happy to come to work for you."

Alice's smile turned thoughtful. "How long you'll be able to do that work is the real question though, isn't it?"

Her eyes remained fixed on Elizabeth's own. "That's the reason I wanted to speak to you before we joined the men."

"What do you mean?" Elizabeth was suddenly frightened again. All of this, her new found happiness, could come down quickly. She couldn't stand that.

Alice placed a hand on her arm. "Don't worry, dear. It will be all right. You see, you talked in your sleep the other night when you were so upset. You were quite out of your mind and you said what was the most worrisome to you. But even if you hadn't, it would eventually become apparent. A woman can't hide her condition forever, you know."

"I'm just so ashamed," Elizabeth whispered.

Alice shook her head. "It's nothing new, dear. You're certainly not the first. But we must do something about it. I assume it's Jason's child?"

She was immediately defensive. "It can be no other!"

"I thought not." Alice's hand closed around her arm. "It will just have to be another idea that we cause Samuel Longfootte to get into his head. The idea that since it really wouldn't be proper for two unmarried servants to live under the same roof, he should give his permission for them to wed quickly."

She smiled. "An idea that Jason Welburn will certainly approve, I'm sure. He's talked of little else for months."

I don't know what to say," Elizabeth murmured.

"Why, say nothing, love. You don't need to. Just be happy your troubles are over. Come now, our menfolk are waiting."

Nineteen

THOMAS LANGLEE, OVERSEER of Sir Harold Breaksford-Pinley's new plantation, Angel's Rest, halted his horse on the bank of the Savannah to watch the water break over some low shoals. The current seemed swift at this point in the river, as if accelerating intentionally in order to negotiate the series of deep curves below Augusta. Like his own life, he thought, the river was made of both swift and slow passages.

One great change had wrenched him out of the poor and resigned life of a peasant boy in England; informed him abruptly that he wasn't really a peasant but of noble blood; and then thrust him quickly into a great new world on this side of the ocean. It offered opportunity to him to become what he would, and he most desired to fulfill that opportunity when he had achieved his freedom. And now a second change, one which he had fought most grievously against, found him instead of free, bound to another again. Bound, not in indenture to a man, but in a tight, silken net spun by a woman. For he had no doubt that he would have refused this job of building Angel's Rest except for its owner's beautiful daughter.

Tom reached forward and patted the bay's neck and the

animal responded with a toss of her head and a snort. She was a sturdy little mare; she had to be to stand up to the use he'd put her to in these last few whirlwind weeks. He had ridden her halfway across South Carolina, moving the supplies he needed to begin this plantation; to order more supplies, including furniture for the big house; again to herd the black slaves needed to clear and till the future fields; and to secure master builders that he now had at work on the manor house.

It was an unbelievably difficult job, but one he would have relished except for the nagging fact that he must admit he was no longer his own man. Angelica Breaksford-Pinley held a lead on him, invisible as it might seem, as much so as the reins he held for the animal between his legs.

"Damn!" His explosion caused the mare to twitch a shoulder.

"And the real stupidity of it," he told the animal savagely, "is that I've no more chance of her than I have of winning a race with you afoot! My own blood may well be the match for hers, but who the hell will believe it?"

The mare wasn't interested. She merely dropped her head and tried to reach the rich green grass between her forelegs.

Tom sighed and obliged her by dismounting and pulling the reins over her head, keeping a light hold on them, however. She spooked easily, he'd already discovered that, and he would hate to be put afoot.

He really should be on the move again, there wasn't enough time in the day for all he must do. But, damn it, he'd take the time out for himself! He needed a rest. A man's body could take only so much!

He winced at the thought. Back at the Isle of Hope, Thomas Langlee was only beginning to understand the human body as a man of medicine needed to understand it, when he had flung the study aside to become an overseer of this plantation. A few weeks ago—even after he'd first met her—no one would have been able to tell him he would give up wanting to be a doctor.

Well, damn it, he wouldn't still! As soon as Angel's Rest was functioning, the house built and the first harvest in, he'd go back to medicine, Angelica or no. That was a promise to himself. He would use his year's end pay from Sir Harold to bide him over until he was able to practice comfortably.

As long as he was faithful to that promise and used his nights to continue to study the few books he'd been able to bring with him, then a year's time would make little difference. He was young yet.

He had to smile at that. Smile at himself. Angelica Breaksford-Pinley might not be completely the reason after all. Could it not be also a bit of vanity? That a man barely twenty be given the responsibility of meeting a challenge like Angel's Rest? Even Noble Jones, who had been more than a little angry about his decision to leave the island, had finally come around to a grudging approval. "It will be a large task, Thomas," he'd said. "An extremely large one. I think you quick enough in mind to realize that fact, and I'm forced to admit I admire you for undertaking it. Succeed, and your reputation will be made in this colony. Men will seek out your advice."

"And if I fail, sir?" Tom had grinned.

"Then you'll have done no more than most will expect you to do."

True enough. A man would have to be a fool to take on such a tremendous task alone. Well, that was part of the riding he'd done. He'd spent three full weeks, to Sir Harold's accute discomfort, doing nothing but riding about some of the plantations in South Carolina to observe and inquire as to their operating techniques. The owners of the plantations had been flattered enough to grant him unselfish portions of their time and advice. All invited his return. A profitable time spent, to say nothing, he thought with a satisfied grin, of making friends of a number of powerful men who would like nothing better than to see him succeed in order to prove their advice correct.

He took a couple of steps to accommodate the mare as she grazed, felt the ground soft under his feet and looked down quickly to see if he'd dirtied his boots. Then became irritated with himself for doing so. True they were fine boots, presented to him by Angelica as a "gift for being so kind as to answer her plea," but if he ascribed to ever become a gentleman, he would have to cease being vain about such frippery as that.

To answer her plea . . . his mind was forced back to the day he had received the first letter of his life. Mr. Thomas Langlee, it had said. Isle of Hope. The colony of Georgia. To be delivered by he who would travel there.

Written in her own neat hand—surprising that she could write even though she be of station—it had given him more of an emotion than he thought proper. She pleaded—begged, in a delicate way—for him to accept the post her father offered.

Sir Harold was having great difficulty, she said, in locating an overseer he could trust to do the job. Her father would agree to his having complete control if he would only consider accepting.

Still, he would have resisted but for the last line to the letter. In handwriting as beautiful as herself, Angelica Breaksford-Pinley had sweetly informed him that, "It would be most pleasant for me to enjoy your company again. I do so look forward to a new meeting."

Noble Jones may have admired him for accepting the challenge, but he left little doubt that he understood the real reason. "Go," he'd said in feigned exasperation. "You'll be of little use to me at any rate as long as you're a moonstricken fool."

Tom was far too restless to rest, even for a few moments, and he was back on his horse quickly and on his way.

The restlessness stemmed from a desire to get about a task set for him, he knew that. It was a trait he had always had. Even without Briggs's heavy hand as a youth he would have worked hard. But he was also forced to admit that his inability to remain still for long came from a nagging fear of failure. This task, large as it might be, was the first one that was his alone. Jones had said none would fault him if he failed, but Tom knew he would fault himself. He *had* to succeed.

There was no doubt that both success and failure lay completely in his own hands. Sir Harold had made that abundantly clear. He was pleased, it appeared, when Tom accepted the position; but when Tom made attempts to discuss any plans toward setting up the plantation, the nobleman had brushed him aside. "I always left details to my overseer in England, Langlee. I expect to do so here. Do as you think best."

Tom shook his head in remembrance as he rode. Sir Harold's explanation for his refusal to make decisions was that his mind must remain clear for matters of the crown. Too, he would soon be summoned back to London at any rate and wouldn't be available. His single contribution had been a quick recital of what kind of house he wanted and the name Angel's Rest for the plantation. The latter for his daughter, of course.

His help or advice was nil, but his name was magic. Tom had never understood the meaning of credit until now. It amazed him that he could order the materials he needed and never offer a penny in payment. He had only to mention Sir Harold's name and the debt was quickly recorded and the goods released. It was, he decided, because the name Breaksford-Pinley was still closely tied to the crown, and the news that King George himself had asked for the land from the Trustees was more than enough for those with goods to sell to seek that kind of influence.

Still, there would come a day when the debts must be paid and Angelica had told him her father was nearing the end of his funds. He could only hope Angel's Rest would begin to pay quickly, or his entire work might well be for naught.

The crisp sound of swinging axes mixed with many voices ahead of him echoed to his right. Tom turned the horse in that direction and rode through a heavy thicket to emerge onto an active scene. Black slaves were felling timber, trimming the logs to be used for slave cabins and piling the brush to be burned. With the logs hauled away and the stumps dug and pulled free by horses, the ground would be prepared for planting. He might even get a small crop in this year.

He spotted Farley, the man he'd hired to oversee the slaves, and moved over to where he stood. The man knuckled his forehead. "Afternoon, Mr. Langlee."

"Farley." Tom glanced around the area. "You've made good time today. I'm pleased."

"Aye, sir." Farley was a thin, wiry man with small arms. But he was highly recommended as a slave master, being both a crack shot with a musket and expert with a whip. Tom had cautioned him about the use of the latter except with extreme reason. He didn't like the idea of whipping, discipline or no, since the memory of a lash to his own back had never fully faded.

Still, one must be cautious. More than one slave had turned on his master and a full scale rebellion had taken place in South Carolina not many years before. Slaves had armed themselves and formed ranks to advance on the isolated whites, murdering and raping as they went. Only the frantic efforts of the governor and militia had managed to stamp out the uprising in time and save the colony. Slave owning was a dangerous business. He had been warned to carry a brace of pistols himself.

Tom took quick stock of those present—all males since the few females were back in camp—and missed several. "Where are the rest?" he asked.

"I sent 'em to start laying the logs we've already hauled,

Mr. Langlee. Wanted to get at least one cabin up quick and put everybody in it until the rest can be built. Easier to watch 'em when they ain't in brush huts."

Tom nodded. "You've some you can trust alone?"

"Aye, sir. Most of these are content enough, I reckon. But there's a big one named Luke that I knowed of before I came to work for you. He's the one I put in trust of the others."

Tom remembered the man. Coal black and huge in size, the slave offered a fierce appearance. But his manner was quiet and he seemed willing to do just as he was told. "Does he know what he's about in raising cabins?" he asked.

"Aye, sir. He's smart enough for a slave. I'd leave it to him to do, myself. Course, you're the overseer."

"Well enough." Tom dismissed the subject and swept his eyes over the area again. "When you reach that line of larger trees, switch to the left where it's less thick. Then move back toward the house. I want as much ground cleared as possible this year. We can fell that heavier wood in the winter."

Farley nodded, his sparse beard moving as he shifted tobacco in his mouth to speak. "You'll be planting corn, Mr. Langlee? Or mebbe rice?"

Tom hesitated. The question hastened his decision, one he'd been trying to make from the beginning. Food crops were good, but didn't produce the income that Angel's Rest would demand quickly if its debts were to be met. Tobacco was priced high in England, but there was fair competition for it out of the North Carolina colony. He couldn't get his mind away from a newer crop—one that might well dominate the region someday unless he was mistaken.

"None of those," he told the man on the ground. "I've decided to plant cotton."

Farley nodded slowly. "T'will be new to here, Mr. Langlee. New to these parts, I mean. You don't reckon—"

"Cotton, Farley," Tom said abruptly. "But that does remind me, as soon as the first cabin is up, I want two or more slaves to till some land for vegetables to feed the rest. Two to three acres, whatever is needed, near the big house. Next week I expect to bring in a few head of cattle and some pigs. Pens must be built as well."

"Aye, sir." Farley grinned a crooked-toothed grin. "Hell of a task, ain't it, Mr. Langlee? Building from scratch, I mean."

Tom didn't return the grin; he didn't feel like it. "It's a task we'll accomplish, Farley."

"Aye, sir. Right we will at that."

The manor house was to be situated on the highest rise of a short series of rolling hills. Had it been up to him, he would have located it on that part of the property he'd just left—the part that touched the river. But Sir Harold—more likely his daughter—had selected this site for its commanding view. That, and the proximity of several large old oaks that would lend the finished house a serene grace.

Tom could see the skeleton timbers of the beginning frame etched against the sky long before he could make out the men who were raising them. He shook his head at the height of what was to become a very large two-storied house. It was to be a grand structure, one to match any in the South Carolina colony. Sir Harold might not have the coin to go with his name, but it would be difficult to tell that to anyone who witnessed this building. The man was more than extravagant.

To his surprise, the owner of Angel's Rest was there in person, standing about in boots and a scarlet hunting coat. Of the two men with him, one was a woodsman, with eyes Tom didn't trust, whom Sir Harold had hired as a hunting guide. The nobleman spent most of his time now in hunting and had already gathered a number of trophies. The last man was Jonas Weber, the master carpenter from Charles Town.

"Ah, here he is now." Sir Harold turned as Tom rode up. "Langlee, we were just discussing that rosewood I'd requested for my retiring room furnishings. Have you arranged for it to be delivered yet?"

Tom glanced quickly at Jonas Weber, who returned his look with a shrug. "No, I've not, Sir Harold. It's purchased in your name in Charles Town, but it seemed a bit premature to bring it here now."

"No, no. Not in the least, Langlee. Weber here has a master furniture maker with him. I want the man to begin on that first. Right away. Then he can fashion the more conventional pieces—tables, chairs and so forth. The rest we'll ship in from Boston."

"The house is at least a year from completion, Sir Harold," Tom reminded him. "Even with this large crew you've hired, it can't be less. Furniture would only serve to get in the way."

"Normally you would be right, Langlee. But Weber and I

have come to an agreement. He's to complete one part of the house first, two large rooms on the rear, for my daughter and me to move into right away. Then he will finish the rest about us."

Tom looked at him in shock, then glanced again at Jonas Weber. The latter's face registered disgust.

"Sir, is that a good idea?" Tom asked. "Conditions are still primitive out here. There's not even a kitchen built yet, for instance. Lady Breaksford-Pinley really shouldn't—"

"Nonsense!" Sir Harold waved him off with a hand. "Decision's been made, Langlee. Up to you and Weber here to see things are made comfortable for her. Right?"

He had no choice but to agree. "As you wish, sir. I must wonder, however, how she will feel about this."

"Wonderful. Absolutely wonderful. Adventure's in my daughter's blood, gentlemen. A lady, but not one of your simpering wisps so much in evidence at court these days. Got the bold blood of her French mother in her, that one. She'll do fine."

He cast a heavy glance toward them both. "I do expect all speed on this, I should hope to move my baggage out here in two weeks. I really must have everything settled if I'm suddenly summoned back to London. Can't have things scattered from here to Charles Town, you know."

"I understand, sir." But Tom decided to try once more. "Wouldn't it be better for her if Lady Breaksford-Pinley remained in Charles Town? She'd be far more comfortable."

"Out of the question! She insists on being with her father. And I must be here for the time."

"Yes sir. As you wish. Speaking of your being here, I'd like to talk to you about the type of crop I want to plant. I've given it much thought and—"

"Your responsibility entirely, Langlee." Sir Harold waved his hand again in dismissal. "Complete confidence in your choice." He turned abruptly to Hoage, his guide, who'd spent the entire conversation staring at Tom. "Hoage, I'll not need your services tomorrow. Meet me here the following day. Tomorrow, I must see to these living arrangements."

"As you wish." The man turned on his heels and walked away.

Tom watched him go, trying to decide just what it was about him that he didn't like, then gave up and shrugged it away.

But Sir Harold had been watching him, too. "You know, Langlee, I may wish to employ that man in a permanent capacity. Angel's Rest will require a gamekeeper. I had an excellent one in England."

"Gamekeeper, sir?"

"Yes. A man to supervise the restocking of game on my land. And to keep out unwarranted hunting—poaching, you know."

Tom stared at him. "That might be a difficult task, Sir Harold," he said dryly. "The Indians could well take offense at being asked to stop their time honored practice."

But Sir Harold had walked away, ignoring him. There was only Jonas Weber, who was near doubled over in silent laughter.

She remained the most beautiful woman he had ever hoped to see, even after weeks of being near her. Here, in this yet primitive surrounding, Angelica was on display as a delicate flower among the harsh weeds. Tom was amazed that she could retain such an aura in this wilderness, with no more to aid her than the one female slave that she brought with her from Charles Town.

But Angelica Breaksford-Pinley managed that magic, and more. The carpenters working on the house she and her father had moved into stopped whatever they were doing and stared when she emerged. Even the black slaves seemed in awe of her radiance. Sir Harold's daughter noticed the looks only as the adoration she believed she deserved and otherwise ignored all, including the comments on her unconventional behavior. For she did exactly as she pleased. And what she pleased most was to ride often about the beginning estate, not in a carriage with a proper escort, but on the back of a horse, an unheard of thing for a woman in the colonies. Rides that she insisted Tom take with her.

It was both pleasant diversion and exasperating. Tom knew he hadn't the time for such, with a thousand things to watch and do, a dozen male slaves and five female slaves to account for and decision after decision to make concerning the house or the land. He had no room for the hour or so she demanded.

But he made time. For the once he refused and remained away from the house to avoid her, Angelica rode out alone, going over the protests of Jonas Weber who tried to stop her.

Tom was horrified. He would have been charged with the responsibility if she had fallen and been injured, or worse, discovered and stolen by an Indian. The Cherokees had been known to do just that and the missing white women never recovered from their mountain strongholds.

But Angelica, when he spoke to her with his temper barely curbed, merely smiled and told him that if he couldn't find the time, then what else was a poor lonely girl to do?

It was a direct challenge, and he knew he would have to respond. But even with the worry of what the delay would cost him preying on his mind, Tom had to admit riding with her was more than fascinating. Angelica had a quick mind, quick enough to hurry his own on a dozen subjects as they rode; she probed and pushed until his own study over the last years felt threadbare. And her expectation that he grant her new compliments every day stretched his imagination. She had him feel the man, but only if he kept nimbly to his mental feet and refused to allow her the upper hand.

She was spoiled, he held no doubt of that, but it seemed part of her charm. For that matter, Angelica didn't hesitate to agree with him when he told her such. She reminded him without saying as much, in every gesture and sidelong glance, that she would be disappointed with him if she did win.

Angelica Breaksford-Pinley enjoyed challenging him, but Tom realized as well that he enjoyed the challenge. The longer he remained the real master of Angel's Rest the more that power flattered his own growing assurance. From peasant lad to indentured servant to free man to man of decision—a satisfying journey indeed!

The slave cabins were up, small ones right enough, but built so that they could easily be extended in the winter months when the slaves would need to be kept busy at any rate. A kitchen had been constructed apart from the main house to prevent a possible fire from burning down the whole, and he even had his own cabin now. He could see the real beginning of progress.

He left his cabin early and spent part of the morning conferring with Jonas, wrote a quick letter for Sir Harold's signature ordering new supplies, and then went to the horse sheds to saddle up his mare.

He did the chore himself although he could easily have

ordered a slave to do it for him. The bay was high spirited, difficult for anyone else to manage, and he enjoyed the fact that she would come readily only to him.

Tom saddled her, dropped the leather bag in front of the saddle that contained his pistols and a few biscuits in case he grew hungry during the day, and trotted the mare around past the house to head out.

He got no farther. Angelica stood in front, waiting for him. Tom sighed when he saw her, but turned the mare's head.

"Good morning, Angelica."

"Good morning. I've been looking for you."

She wore a green dress, full about the hips, short enough to be daring, and light enough about her waist and bosom to be breathtaking. It closed high around her throat, concealing but at the same time revealing everything. Her high, uplifting breasts were separate and charmingly obvious.

"This," he said, looking down at her, "is a magnificent day, but I'll vow it pales entirely in comparison to that gown."

Angelica inclined her head and smiled up at him, a dazzling smile. "You're quite right, sir. At least about the day. I would very much like a long ride this morning. Away from the river, however, I want to explore some of those deep woods."

Tom shook his head. "My apologies, m'lady. Your escort simply has too much to do."

The light came quickly to her eyes, already he could recognize her signs of battle. But he was more than determined this time.

"You prefer the company of men, or perhaps only that horse, to me?" she said. "Fie! I really must be losing my charm."

"Not in the least, Angelica. You're as beautiful as the dawn, as charming as a field of bluebells wet with dew and overwhelmingly delightful in company to this poor fool of an overseer. However, as I said, I've just too much to look after today. Tasks, I might add, that will lead to Angel's Rest maintaining you in the manner you so richly deserve."

"Posh! You can spare an hour! A miserly time."

He shook his head. "I cannot in truth. Not this morn."

"Then I'm to be left again to my own diversions?" A warning note crept into her voice though she smiled up at him from under lowered lashes.

"As long as it's here, near the house and protection, yes,"

he told her. "I've taken the liberty of ordering that no horse be saddled for you to ride alone."

The lashes quivered suddenly, and Tom was looking into two green eyes that flashed at him. It surprised him that she could show anger—even for the instant it lasted. *"You* cannot do that!" she said. Then she paused and smiled the teasing smile again. "I simply won't hear of it."

Tom matched her smile with one of his own. "I do most sincerely apologize, *m'lady*. But I can. Your father agreed that I should exercise complete control over Angel's Rest and that also includes protecting its most important possession. Need I remind you that everyone here will obey me?"

"And now you expect to exercise control over me as well. I must remind you, dear sir, I once told you no one does that."

"Most assuredly so," he agreed, pleased with himself. "I only control the men and the horses. You may walk quite as far as you like."

"I've only to speak to my father," she told him, but her tone remained light.

"Yes, you can do that. He's somewhere west of here, I believe. A hunting trip of two or more days, as I remember his saying yesterday."

"I see. You seem to be well prepared this morning, Mr. Langlee."

Tom touched his hat with a finger. "My apologies, m'lady. I would surely end my own miserable life rather than disappoint a hair on your pretty head, but I must protect you."

"When father comes back—"

"He will agree with me, I'm quite sure. Even Sir Harold won't allow his daughter to ride alone out here."

Angelica surprised him by tossing her head and laughing merrily. "So I'm defeated then! Congratulations, noble sir. You've mastered my best efforts."

Tom smiled wryly. "A temporary condition, I'm certain."

She shook her head. "Oh no. I'll become quite the meek pleader, mere woman that I am. When will you ride with me? Or should I ask, *allow* me to ride with *you*?"

Tom hesitated. He'd won his point and he really had a great deal to do . . . but it was a beautiful day. "Would it please you as well to go this afternoon? Late? That is if I can finish in time?"

"Oh, I'm at your command, sir. Your mercy entirely. I shall wait breathlessly for your summons."

She turned to leave but paused to look aside at him and the green eyes sparkled again. "I do believe it will be a *most* interesting ride."

He returned for her in midafternoon and Angelica surprised him by being charmingly agreeable. An hour's ride went by before he was aware of its passage. They had ridden farther than he intended, deeper into the forest, and paused now before a shallow but wide stream. A few yards down it merged with another, leaving a point of land between the two that was lower than either bank and filled with a rich carpet of grass, due, probably, to frequent flooding by the streams. Tom stood beside her and watched the swift flowing water.

"It's charming," Angelica said. "A canvas done by a master painter."

"It is that," he agreed. Then a sudden thought struck him. "You know, you're probably the first white woman to see this place; it's well out of the travel line for even a trader's wife."

She glanced up at him. "Then I claim it for my own. Angelica's sanctuary. You must bring me here often to get away."

"To get away from what?" He couldn't help being amused. "You own wherever you trod. Everyone is at your command."

"Except the overseer," she said, still looking up at him. "My very independent overseer."

She was as beautiful as ever he'd seen her. Her riding gown was a light blue and made in two pieces, the tight fitting bodice separate from the skirt to display her muslin petticoat between. Her sleeves were also finished in soft muslin with lace ruffles. She wore a cardinal thrown loosely around her shoulders, but with the hood off her head and hanging down her back, leaving her dark hair free.

"Did not your overseer return early from his duties to escort you on this ride as you asked?" he wanted to know.

"True. But only as I asked, not as I commanded."

Tom shrugged and wondered if they would ever talk without this light edge of challenge between them. He wondered if the year he intended to spend at Angel's Rest would see him really know what lay behind those darkly lashed green eyes that looked into his own. Then decided that perhaps he might be better off not knowing. There might well be a fire there that would consume him. And she was beyond his reach.

"I want to go over there," Angelica said of a sudden.

"Over where? To that point? Why?"

"What difference does it make? I want to go. It belongs to me."

He smiled. "We're well away from the land your father owns, Angelica."

"Mine by right of discovery; you said I was the first. Take me there."

He sighed. "Very well, I'll catch up the horses."

"No." She caught his arm with her small, gloved hand. "Leave them be."

"Leave them be? Surely you don't expect to wade this stream? You'll ruin your clothes. Even you, Angelica, can't want that."

The smile she gave him was taunting. "I have no intention of setting foot to that stream, Thomas Langlee. You shall carry me in those strong arms of yours. And you are wearing boots."

He looked down at her. Another command, slight as it might be, but an attempt to impose her will over his. Her game. But by the Furies, it would give him a long desired opportunity to place his arms around that slender body!

"As you wish, m'lady. I am, as always, yours to command." He reached for her quickly, sweeping her up into his arms, and Angelica immediately placed both arms around his neck, her face perilously close to his own. The fragrance of her perfumed hair struck him like a bolt.

"Well, why are we waiting?"

She'd dazzled him for the moment by her closeness, and damn her, she knew it! He forced himself to recover. "Merely making certain you were secure, madam," he said. "And overcoming a strong temptation to drop you once I was halfway across."

Her legs, caught up in her long gown but still distinguishable across his arm, and her slender waist, caught firmly in his right, were a strong wine to his senses. As much so as the beautiful face with its red lips only inches from his own.

"Move, my great donkey," she laughed. "I desire to be transported."

He stepped into the stream slowly, aware that there were smooth stones in its bed that would betray him if he wasn't careful. He was well out into its middle, when she made a sudden movement and brushed his hat from his head. It rolled once across his shoulder and fell into the stream.

It surprised and angered him. "Damn! Why the hell did you do that!"

He spun with her still in his arms and watched helplessly as the tricorn floated swiftly down the stream, caught up in a swirl, and then was pushed against an outgrowth of twigs from one bank. There it was forced underwater by the current and soaked.

"That was a damned good hat!"

Angelica laughed merrily and reached suddenly to kiss him on the cheek. "You deserve that and more for your threat to drop me."

"A threat I shall carry out," he told her darkly.

"I dare you! Dare you!"

"You're a wench," he said. "Born a lady, but worse than any tavern wench. You tease a man for your own amusement."

He was angry...and something else. Her closeness was beginning to fire his senses...

"Then bring the wench to where she desires, lout," she commanded. "Do that, since you're not brave enough to douse her in the water as she deserves."

He hesitated, then moved forward again as she laughed, her wickedly sparkling eyes inches from his own.

But when he reached the grass and mounted it, he continued to hold her. And watched a new excitement enter the green eyes. "Well," she said, "put me down."

Tom shook his head. "No, madam. Not yet. You're quite right I won't put you in the water; I won't carry you back soaked for the rest to see. But I will collect a reward for my poor hat."

The smile was a twist to her lips, and the challenge was again in her eyes. Tom waited a long delicious moment to study the challenge, then deliberately bent to kiss her, pressing his lips against her lovely mouth.

Angelica immediately spun her head away. "How *dare* you!"

Tom dropped her feet to the ground but retained his arm around her waist and used his free hand to encircle her back. He then moved it up to her neck and held it rigid while he kissed her again. Hard.

She struggled, her hands raising to push uselessly at his

chest, and when he released her at last, she gasped and struck him hard across the face. "You *can't!*"

He grinned, the bruise to his face unable to compete with the satisfaction those now angry lips had left on his own. He caught her arm, pressed it to her side and kissed her again. A long kiss, relishing the way her lips struggled against his own, until, without warning, the struggle became different entirely— they parted and responded with a hunger that sent his mind reeling. He backed away in shock.

But the body that had so quickly and unexpectedly melted against his own in passion, was immediately rigid again. She'd tricked him!

"Who do you think you are!" she demanded. "You're an . . . an employee!"

"A witch," Tom murmured, still not releasing his grip on her arms and waist. "A beautiful, provocative witch, mercury in your changes and great in your desire to see a man crawl at your pretty feet. But you'll not have it with me, Angelica. You got no more than you deserved."

He released her then and stepped back.

She stood watching him, her breast heaving with anger. Or was it anger? By hell, he suddenly wasn't certain!

"You're a peasant," she told him sharply. "To take advantage of me like that."

"No more than you took of my poor hat," he said. "But I'll vow it was a worthwhile exchange. I've wanted to do that from the day I first saw you in that tavern."

The green eyes glinted, he'd swear they caught summer lightning the way they flashed at him, the glint increased the drumming of his blood. By damn, he'd touched beyond that challenge she flung at men this time!

"Damn you," she hissed suddenly. "You call *that* a kiss?" Before he could move, she flung herself against him, threw her arms around his neck and scalded his lips with her own, at the same time thrusting a probing tongue deep between his teeth. It took him a moment to recover, but as soon as he started to respond to the passion of her kiss, Angelica broke away from him and laughed. "You kiss like a clod, peasant! You think to impress *me?*"

The taunt sent shock waves through him, both the passionate kiss and the derision in her voice. He was angry, and he wanted Angelica Breaksford-Pinley beyond all caution. He took a step toward her and her mocking expression changed immediately.

"No you don't!" she cried. "You wouldn't *dare*!"

"Dare be damned," he muttered. His bonds were slipping fast. He could be hanged for what he was about to do, but by hell a noose would be worth it. Fire was surging through his veins and he knew there was a flame to match it in that slender, desirable body before him. A flame within his reach . . .

He grasped her quickly and Angelica fought him just as quickly.

But he pulled her to him roughly and kissed her hard, forcing her backwards over his arm and holding her quivering lips against his own until she was breathless.

Angelica fought him, pushed against his chest with her hands and writhed in his arms. But the writhing would be first away from him and then, in the same movement, forcing her hips against his in a manner to fan the raging fire within him.

He kissed her, she fought away from his lips, then returned to sear him with her own. She was a paradox—anger one second and passion the next. He didn't understand . . . but it didn't matter. He had gone far past the point of stopping.

"No, damn you!" She screamed the words as Tom leaned her over until he could drop to one knee and lay her back on the long grass.

"Stop it! I'll have you whipped for this!"

But he was across her with his own hips, pressing the writhing, twisting tempest of excitement under him into the grass as he kissed her long and hard, sliding down to taste the intoxication of her slender neck.

Angelica's mouth reached to find his, her tongue kindled him to greater heights, and then she bit him, her small teeth bringing blood to his lip.

He swore, his words muffled as he pressed his face again to her throat and struggled to bring her gown above her thrashing legs.

There was nothing beneath the petticoat, no shift, no small clothes, only the silk of her stockings held by ruffled garters. The thought of her nakedness fired his raging passion beyond belief.

Angelica freed her hands and dug her nails into the sides of his neck, raking it raw. But the devil's own claws would be unable to stop him now, he was riding the crest of a climbing wave and would feel nothing but the eagerness of his loins. Angelica was his! For this moment! And damn the rest!

She made it as difficult as she could, her hips gyrated beneath his until he had to hold her with his hands and force his way between her legs. Angelica drummed with her heels against the back of his legs, arched her back and then screamed when he pierced her.

Her screams sobered him and Tom hesitated. But then her fingers clawed at his back, like red hot irons raking through the fabric of his shirt, and her mouth closed on his as if it would draw him inside her there, too.

It was a turbulent, exploding, raging trip into a mountain of passion. He was hard pressed to remain master as the whip-lash of a body beneath him belied its size in its strength of movement. The storm increased until Tom was no longer able to hold back and the universe exploded . . .

He was drained and still she moved beneath him, slower now, a sweet symphony that lulled his senses. His arms trembled to hold his weight from crushing her.

A voice, distant to his singing senses, called softly into his ear. "You've raped me, Tom Langlee. But you're long from conquering me."

He opened his eyes and rolled free to look at her, to try to understand her. Angelica made no move to cover herself. She lay on her back, her face close to his. "You're still not my master," she said softly.

Tom nodded slowly. "I did no more than you wanted, Angelica. But you're right. No man will ever master you."

She smiled, a deep smile that rose up into the green eyes, drowning him. "Now that you have deflowered me, you must pay the price. I assure you that price will be dear, Tom Langlee. Very dear."

He shook free of her eyes and sat up to readjust his clothes. Then, when she would make no effort of her own, did as much for hers. "Deflower is hardly the word for it, Angelica. You're trying to tell me I'm the first?"

"Look for yourself," she said. "Or is it that now since your great passion has been cooled, you're once more the modest one. You're the first, Tom Langlee. The only one I've found worthy of what you took. My virginity meant nothing to me except the man who gained it had to do just that—take it."

He nodded again. "By hell, I believe you. You'd *have* to be that way, wouldn't you?"

"And now you pay the price for your lust," she said. "The high price. You will become my husband." She laughed, the green eyes boring into his. "And whenever I choose to become difficult, you'll have to fight your way through to your desire. Lust or no, my love, *I* will make the decision whether you command this body to your will easily or not."

"I can't marry you, Angelica," he said wearily. "By God I want you as bad as a man can, and I would gladly take your challenge and bend you to my will whenever I chose if I were husband to you. But you and I both know your father won't allow us to marry."

She lay looking at him until he continued, "You don't know me as well as you think. There's more to my own blood than is now apparent. Not that it makes any difference between us."

"Damn your blood," she said in a cat's voice. "You're not as intelligent as I thought, Tom Langlee, unless you know I decided to have you the first time we met. But do remember that I get *everything* I want. And I want you."

She reached up for him, drew him down atop her and began to kiss the passion alive in him again. Her lips touched his as she whispered, "I'll fight you, but if you lose, you're a bigger fool than I think, my darling . . ."

An hour later he'd barely strength enough to gather her into his arms and carry her back across the stream. In the middle of it, Tom paused and tried to ignore the small teeth nibbling still at his ear as he looked for his hat. It was gone, swept finally down the stream. He shrugged. That lost hat might well be the least of his problems now.

Twenty

ANGELICA LANGLEE WOKE as she always did, slowly, refusing to allow the world to intrude upon her until she was ready for it to do so. She slipped both arms from under the comforter and stretched. Then lay back to give thought to the night before, thought that brought a lazy smile to her face. The bed beside her was long cold, Tom as usual was up by the dawn to attend to running the plantation. She slid a hand over that part, seeking a warmth she knew she wouldn't find, and the smile increased.

Her husband was more than man enough for her, though she would never allow him to know it. He would prefer to be gentle with her in their love-making, and often she allowed him to be, giving him satisfaction enough and even enjoying it herself. But the other times . . . the times she could goad him into *forcing* her to his will . . . that was when she truly climbed the heights . . .

When she was ready, she stepped from the high bed to the bearskin Tom had provided for her in protection from the cold wooden floor, took her hooded robe from the peg on which it hung and crossed to the door. "Meggy!" she called.

The black woman appeared as if by magic. "Yes, Missy?"

"I'm ready to get up now. Tell the cook I want something good for breakfast, perhaps an egg if she has one and a small slice of beef—a thin slice, mind you. And then prepare my bathroom. I shall bathe this morning."

"Yes, ma'am."

Meggy hurried to do as she was told, but Angelica stopped her before she disappeared down the hall, "Meggy!"

The slim black woman turned, her face a question. "Yes, ma'am?"

"Has Master Langlee gone? Or is he somewhere about the house?"

"He's gone, ma'am."

"Oh, I thought I was early, perhaps he'd delayed his breakfast. He sometimes does." She was talking more to herself than to the maid.

But Meggy shook her head quickly. "Master Tom, he didn't eat no breakfast. He just left." She suddenly looked as if she wished she hadn't spoken.

"Why? What happened?"

"Nothing, ma'am." Meggy was a woman near Angelica's own age, but she could act like a small child sometimes—an irritating trait and Angelica had slapped her for it once.

"Meggy, come here. Look at me. Now tell me what happened; what's the matter with you?"

The black woman stopped again and hung her head. "Master Tom . . . he and Master Brakespin . . . they had a terrible fuss." She was frightened, and Angelica knew she was afraid of being thought of as meddling.

"I've told you a hundred times, Meggy, my father's name is Breaksford-Pinley. Whenever are you going to learn it?"

Meggy's head went even lower. "Yes'um."

"So tell me, what was the row about?" she demanded.

Meggy shook her head quickly. "I didn't listen, ma'am. Meggy knows it ain't her business and—"

"Nonsense! You have ears. Don't tell me such a lie, girl. What did they argue about? I want to know this instant."

Meggy's eyes began to water—another trait that made Angelica angry. She could be most exasperating! "Tell me. And stop that blubbering!"

"Yes'um. Meggy tried not to listen . . . but they was so loud. And Master Tom . . . he told Master Brakespin he could . . . he could just go to *hell*!" The black woman's eyes widened in surprise at her own boldness.

Angelica almost laughed but managed to hide even her smile. So Tom had finally exploded with her father? Good! It was about time that silly old fool, with his constant mouthing about returning to England, was straightened out. "What were they arguing about—oh, never mind, it doesn't make any difference. Go and prepare my water."

Meggy was greatly relieved to be dismissed. It was obvious in her black face. She had absolutely no control over her emotions, no more than a child. "Yes ma'am."

She hurried away and Angelica stepped back into her room. Then she did smile. Her father had been shocked and horrified when Tom approached him to ask to marry her. He'd fired him on the spot and demanded he leave Angel's Rest the same hour. Tom, the silly fool, had agreed, and would have done so had she not taken the precaution of listening from behind a door. He'd been as shocked as her father when she entered and took a hand in the discussion.

Her father had ranted and raved, and Tom's young face had colored scarlet with the effort of holding his own tongue. But she knew her father, knew he was weak in all things, and weak in regard to her more so than the rest. He was blusterous, but he was a coward beneath and couldn't stand up against opposition. She'd had a merry time throwing a real fit and frightening the wits out of the both of them.

Angelica crossed to the bed and sat down on it to remember. Her father had offered her everything imaginable, and Tom, his great pride damaged, had insisted on withdrawing his proposal. But neither of them had stood a chance. She could almost taste again the blood that salted her mouth as she bit it in throwing the tantrum. And in the end, she'd gotten her way, just as she knew she would. She wanted Tom Langlee for her own, and she got him. He was untamed, but hers nonetheless to continue trying her will against.

That thought brought another slow smile. He was different from any man she'd ever known, fascinatingly different. He had all the marks of a gentleman in spite of whatever his birth might have been—she'd never asked about it and didn't care. He had all the marks, and, it would seem, the training. His face held the lines of good blood, but beneath that, and she had sensed it the first time she met him she realized later, there was a freshness—a trait of peasant rawness—that had fascinated her. No man she had ever met, neither in London nor in Charles Town, with their studied grace and manners, would have had the *guts* to force her to her back in the grass that day. Beneath his air of a gentleman, there was a directness to Tom Langlee, an uncomplicated drive, that set him apart.

That drive enabled him to create this plantation from the wilderness and prevented him from becoming her slave no matter how hard she tried. And his great intelligence enabled him to understand that he could never afford to give in wholly to her. That same intelligence had also enabled him to work around her dotty father to do the things that needed to be done here.

Though Sir Harold might hate his son-in-law for taking his daughter, he stood no chance of driving him away, not as long as he knew Angelica herself would immediately turn against him. The situation did create problems at times, and she'd had to speak to her father about it harshly. Now it seems, his constant carping had gotten to Tom at last.

She giggled. It would have been amusing to have watched her father's face as he was told—and by a commoner at that— to go to hell.

Meggy returned in a few minutes to tell her the bathroom was prepared and Angelica went downstairs. She loved this bath, had been absolutely delighted when Tom designed it for her. It had originally been planned as a storage room, but Tom had come up with the idea to build into it a large wooden tub lined with copper. The tub had a high back for her to rest against but was low enough on the front for Meggy to bathe her. The two little blacks, too young to be of great use in the fields, were used for chores around the great house. They had orders to fire a pot of water each morning in case she wanted the tub. When she did, it was merely a matter of hauling the water in from outside and mixing enough cold to bring it to the correct temperature. It was greatly relaxing to sit and soak while Meggy bathed her with a soft cloth and perfumed soap.

The hot water warmed the room too because of its small size; there was no discomfort in removing her robe and gown before entering the tub. She did so, but then paused to examine a bruise on her left hip. It was long and thin, a dark purple, pleasantly painful to her exploring fingers. Angelica smiled as she rubbed it.

The water was just right, hot enough to sting her skin to life but not enough to burn her. Angelica leaned back against the high part of the tub and waved Meggy away for the moment.

The bruise was on her hip, but near enough to her buttock to remind her of another time. The time she'd been riding with him only a few short weeks after they'd been wed. She had shocked Tom Langlee to the toe of his boots by walking a little away from where he stood and suddenly stripping herself naked. He'd been horrified by the possibility that she might be seen by someone else and tried to catch her while carrying her gown in her hand. Her eyes sparkled as she remembered how she'd led him a merry chase through the woods and how he'd stumbled about in his frantic haste to catch her. She had taunted him as she ran, taunted him until, when he did catch her, Tom had forgotten the gown and turned her over his knee to blister her buttocks with his hand.

The memory of that stinging fired her now, that and the way she'd attacked him following the whipping. She'd blurred his thinking then, by heaven, and he'd exhausted himself another way... It was quite a delightful memory.

Angelica opened her eyes to see Meggy waiting patiently and languidly waved her to her task.

After the bath she was in a mood to dress and picked out soft, white silk stockings held up by handwoven garters with a red rose knitted on each, a silk shift, two under-petticoats, an outer hoop-petticoat and a brocade gown opening in front and drawn to the sides in folds. The gown had a tight-fitting bodice cut very low in the neck and sleeves that were a cascade of lace.

Meggy spent half an hour with the curling tongs on her hair before she was satisfied, and Angelica spent the rest of the hour applying just the right, delicate amount of rouge to both lip and cheek.

Lastly, she donned a pair of white kid shoes, then went down to her breakfast.

Her father was waiting for her, and she watched with amusement as the cloud of anger in his face faded immediately when he beheld her.

"M'word, Angelica. Damn if you aren't a beauty!"

It was going to be so simple she wanted to laugh—but knew better. She crossed the room instead to reach up and lightly kiss his cheek. "Thank you, papa. I'm delighted to please you."

"You do, child. You warm the cockles of this old heart, by Gad! You're the image of your mother."

"Thank you. Will you breakfast with me? I've ordered an egg."

"No, no. You know I never eat in the morning. Bad for the digestion."

"Yes, I know. But you will have a glass of sherry while I dine, won't you? It would please me much."

"If you insist." He cleared his throat. "I intended to talk with you at any rate. We really must talk, Angelica. I've reached the point—"

She shushed him with a quick kiss on his cheek again. "A moment, papa. Let me get your sherry first. Come and sit down."

She led him to one of the large chairs near her table, sat him down in it and crossed to the sideboard for a glass and a decanter. Meggy had followed her into the room and needed no direction to go outside to the kitchen to fetch her meal. By the time Angelica had him comfortable with a large glass of sherry in his hand, the slave was back with her breakfast. Angelica sat down and looked at him over her meal as she ate.

"Now what did you want to talk to me about?" she inquired between small, measured bites. "The dining table and chairs that I requested be made for me in Boston? You're not going to tell me nay, are you? You promised."

He took a large drink of the sherry, much too large, and she suspected he had had a glass or so already, though it was hardly ten o'clock. "No, of course not. You know I wouldn't go back on my promise. Although, by heaven, that furniture will cost me a pretty penny, and this plantation—"

"Is paying well for itself already," she interrupted. "My husband was right. Cotton is now selling dear on the continent."

He harumphed and took another drink. Building his nerve, she suspected, and suddenly wondered how she had put up with him all these years. Her mama hadn't, Angelica knew she had had a series of lovers before she died so suddenly. In fact, she had often wondered if she was really his daughter.

"Damn it, it's just that I've got to talk to you, Angelica.

That Langlee fellow—"

"My husband," she said.

He choked and took another drink of sherry. "You know my opinion on that."

Angelica smiled at him. "And you know my own."

"But the man's a commoner! You could have your pick in London!"

"I had my pick," she reminded him. "Several of them asked for my hand and you turned them down."

He frowned. "My mistake. I was only trying to please you."

"And you did. All of them were fancy fools. Not a man in the lot. Not like you, papa."

That distracted him, as she knew it would. He couldn't resist flattery. "Well, be that as it may," he said. "Langlee—"

"Thomas."

"Damn it, daughter. This morning—do you know what he said to me?"

"He told you to go to hell," she supplied softly. "Meggy told me. I imagine you made him angry."

"Angry! I made *him* angry? By Gad, I . . ." He could get no further.

Angelica smiled her most winning smile at him. "Papa, Tom Langlee is my husband. I love him dearly. And I think he has made this plantation grow as none other could have done. He works hard for us. Both of us. In another year or so you will be quite free of debt."

"I'll be free before then," he told her darkly. "I've made a decision concerning this property."

It was a turn she hadn't expected. What kind of decision?

"Papa, if you would only be reasonable—"

"No!" He shouted the word at her. "I've made my decision. I told him this morning! And he told me to—damn it, now I must tell you, Angelica. I'm *selling* this land."

"Selling it? You can't! It's mine!"

His eyes, almost hidden under the thick heavy eyebrows, sharpened quickly. "It's not yours, Angelica. Not while I'm alive. Tis my property and I will make the decisions upon it."

He paused, and she was intelligent enough to wait herself. He was different somehow, not drunk, and not pleading. He was being *firm*. She was both astonished and frightened.

"I'm sick to death of this," he told her heavily. "Sick of

this stupid country, this wildness around us, and sick of that man. I've neglected my responsibilities to the crown long enough. I intend to sell this place, including all my slaves, and return to London to live."

She couldn't believe he would talk like that. Didn't he know they didn't *want* him back in London? What a bloody fool!

But she said, "Papa, if you do that, what will happen to me?" She made her voice plaintive.

He shook his head. "No, Angelica. You won't play that trick on me. My mind's made up. I've already dispatched word to my lawyer in Charles Town to place Angel's Rest on the market."

He took another drink of sherry and gave her a level look over the top of the glass. "If you will not forget this . . . this commoner you've disgraced yourself with and come with me, then you must share a woodsman's hut with him after this place is sold."

His smile was ugly. "I don't think you will do that, Angelica. I simply don't think you will live in less than luxury. You've your mother's blood."

She was angry and it was difficult not to show it. "That is what you are counting on, isn't it? You think I will leave my husband for luxury?"

Her father nodded slowly. "You're not a woman to settle for less, Angelica. It has taken me a year to realize how simple it is to have you again. And to be rid of that man."

When she didn't answer, his tone changed to near pleading. "Once we are settled again in London, Angelica, I'll arrange the proper papers. The matter—this unfortunate matter—will be hushed and you'll be free to marry to your proper station. Come with me, Angelica. Don't be angry with your papa. It's only for your best."

Angelica stared at him. She was no longer angry and her mind was working furiously. He was serious! He really intended to do what he said. And what was worse, he was in a position to do it. She must have time to think.

"Papa, you frighten me. I'm so confused. I know you love me and want the best for me . . . but I must have time to think. Will you give me that time?"

He was overjoyed—but tried not to show it. She wanted to spit at the light that glowed in his eyes. "Only a short time, Angelica," he said. "I've sent word to my lawyer."

"Then stop it," she pleaded. "Hold off for a fortnight. I beg you."

"To what purpose, child?"

"Please. For me? Please? I love Tom, but you're so wise, and I've depended on you for so long..."

He relented, she could see it in his eyes before he spoke. "Well...but no more. My mind is not to be changed, Angelica."

"I'm sure I will think of a solution by then," she said in relief. "Thank you, papa."

She left her father after breakfast and spent hours in Tom's study. It was a small room in the back of the house, Sir Harold himself had the larger one where he sometimes doddled away part of the day, but this one was the heart of Angel's Rest. Tom had been delighted that she understood so much about money matters and accounts, and allowed her to go over the figures he kept about the plantation. In fact, though he never admitted to it, she was better than he was and did yeoman's work on those accounts. For himself, every moment he could spare from running the plantation he spent on his medical books. After she had time to think seriously about her father's threat, it was to those books rather than the account ledgers that Angelica went.

She raced through them with all the speed at her command, stopping often to consult the wooden cabinet Tom had built to house his herbs, roots and powders, things that before she would have disdained to touch. It was a disagreeable task, but she forced herself to it.

By late afternoon she was no closer to her solution than she had been in the morning. Angelica gave up for the time being and went out to air her tired mind on the broad veranda. Meggy came to offer her a glass of sherry, but she waved it away impatiently. However, she hid her anger when Tom rode in, swung down from the saddle and turned his horse over to one of the black boys.

She met him at the steps. "Good day, my love."

"Angelica, you grow more beautiful by the hour," he said. "I don't know if I can stand it."

She reached to kiss him, disregarding the fact that they were out in the open where anyone could see them. Tom enjoyed her being unconventional. He once said there could be no woman like her in all the American colonies. She would have held the embrace, but he moved her away with his hands. "Send your girl for a glass of brandy for me," he said. "I want to talk to you."

Angelica didn't hesitate, she turned quickly to the door and called. Meggy came and she gave the instructions, then sat down in one of the veranda chairs beside him.

She watched him as they waited for the brandy to be brought, and Tom looked not at her but across the rolling hills stretching away from Angel's Rest. The lines of his face were beginning to harden, she thought. He was handsome; as handsome as any man she'd ever known, but now the soft lines of youth were becoming sun and wind burned. He would be out of place in the stylish gatherings of London or the *salons* of Paris. He was a man of these colonies. A man both powerful in limb and will. Suddenly she wanted him with a desire that smoldered in her belly.

But there were other things to be done. Tom Langlee wasn't the only thing she wanted. Angel's Rest was hers as well. She took the glass from Meggy when she returned and gave it to her husband.

When he had sipped from it, he looked directly at her. "I'm quite sure you've heard from your father by now, Angelica," he said. "He's planning to sell this plantation."

She nodded, hoping she gave the appearance of the dutiful wife waiting to be informed.

"Do you know why he wants to sell it?" he asked.

Angelica nodded again. "He told me. He thinks I'll leave you if you don't have anything."

Tom's brown eyes were cool and level. "Will you?"

She was quite proud of the smile she gave him, especially when she saw how it softened his eyes. "Tom, you know I can have no other. I love you."

"Good. I had hoped as much—expected as much." He sighed heavily, then chuckled. "I told your father that was the way it would be. He didn't believe me, of course."

"Of course," she echoed.

His smile faded. "Angelica, he means it. I'm quite sure of that. Angel's Rest will pass into some other's hands. I regret that. I've spent a large amount of effort to see it grow. But I'll not mourn its passing long. I've learned much in this work and I'm bold enough to believe I've gained a reputation for accomplishment. As soon as I'm available, there will be several men in South Carolina who'll bid for my services as overseer. I can name a good price."

"What about your study of medicine?" she asked.

."I'm close, but I've not yet learned enough in that to want to advertise my services as a doctor. Soon. Until I can, we'll need money on which to live. Another year or so." He grinned. "You'll have to curtail your expensive tastes for a time I suspect."

"I'll do whatever you say, my husband." She allowed her eyes to challenge him. "That is in most things."

Then she quickly returned to the subject. "Wait though, will you? A few days at least. I know my father is difficult for you, but I believe I can change his mind. Angel's Rest has become so much a part of you I hate to see you lose it. If he will see things differently, will you continue?"

Tom hesitated and she had to control her nerves. If he refused it would be difficult indeed!

"Angelica, I—"

"Please!"

His brown eyes became hooded as he looked at her. Then, to her great relief, Tom nodded slowly. "I've also another idea; I don't know if it's possible or not, but it deserves the effort. I intend to be gone from here for a few days, I'm going to Savannah to see an old friend. Wimberly Jones. His father, you may remember, was the surveyor of this property. While there, I expect to see if there's a way for me to acquire land of my own. I wouldn't move back to Savannah, the land's too poor there, but if there's some way I can get land here I may well try to build my own plantation. On a smaller scale, of course."

His smile became sardonic. "A very rough life for a time. You may have to live in a cabin, my delicate love."

Angelica smiled at him.

"At any rate," he continued, "my being away will give you time to talk as you want with your father. If he decides to remain owner of Angel's Rest and wants to have me continue as overseer, then I will do so. But only because you want it and until, only until, I am prepared to go into medicine."

"Thank you," she whispered. "I know my father is difficult. But he does need you, Tom. It pains me to see the old dear make such a mistake."

"I'll leave in the morning," he said. "I should return in three

to four days—no, make that a week's time. I'll leave Farley
with instructions, there should be no problems."

"In a week," she said and lowered her lashes. "'Tis surely
a longish time. I don't know if I can stand the parting. I don't
suppose you might want to come up to our room and console
your wife for her sorrow—the rest of the evening?"

Tom laughed. "And sit lightly in the saddle on the morrow,
eh? Angelica, you may well be more wife than a man can
stand!"

Her husband was gone for a little more than a week—longer
than turned out to be necessary, for the answer came to her
with more ease than Angelica would have thought. It came not
in his medical writings, however, but in separate notes he had
made on his reading. Socrates, Tom had written for himself,
died from having been made to drink hemlock. Angelica hurried
to his notes on herbs and found, to her delight, that he had
acquired some of the drug. It had been introduced into the
colonies from Europe as a medicine. Its leaves, or stems, she
learned, held a disagreeable odor when bruised, but she was
able to overcome that by coaxing her father into drinking heavily first.

Being already drunk, he didn't really understand he was
dying. She watched without a tinge of regret as he grasped his
throat, his eyes staring, and tumbled from the chair to twitch
about on the floor.

When he was still, long after he was still, Angelica knelt
to place her ear over his heart. She was quite certain he was
dead before she screamed for Meggy and then managed a faint.

The mistake she made was in not having her father buried
before Tom returned. He took her into his arms to console her
when she told him, but then insisted on viewing the body.
Angelica knew she'd made a mistake when he stiffened and
stood up slowly.

He turned to face her. "When did he die?" he asked.

"Oh, Tom! It was only the day before yesterday. It was
horrible! I did everything I could! If only you had been here!
I mean, you know so much about medicine . . . and I . . . there
was no one who could do anything!"

His long, sober look disquieted her as she viewed him behind a mask of concern. He bent once more and placed his head near her father's.

Tom straightened slowly. "Angelica, we have to talk where no one can overhear us. Come with me."

It had worked so well! What was wrong? Her father was dead, his heart, it was so obvious! But Tom looked at her so strangely...

He led her into his study and closed the door, after first looking up and down the hall. When he turned, he seized her arms fiercely. "Angelica, what happened? What did you do?"

"I don't know what you mean..."

"By thunder, don't lie to me!" His eyes stared at her and his grip tightened on her arms to the point it hurt. "He was healthy. There was no *reason* for him to die, Angelica."

For the first time in her life she was afraid. Really afraid. She was guilty of murder—and the man she wanted above all other things was close to knowing...

"Tom, I don't know what you mean! What are you saying?"

He shuddered, an explosion of movement that shook her as well. "My God, Angelica! You killed him!"

"I didn't!"

He slapped her, slapped her hard enough to drive her across the room and into a corner, where she crouched and held her hand against her mouth. Tom was staring, his fists clenched and his eyes burning. *"You killed your own father!"*

She had to think! To gather her wits! The next few moments might be the most important in her life.

She didn't get up, but allowed herself to remain in the corner and pulled her legs beneath her. "Tom... please..."

"Damn you! Answer me!"

"Tom... I didn't *want* to! He... he... was going to *destroy* you! Angel's Rest! *Everything* you've worked for!"

"By hell, woman, not for me! You didn't do this for *me*!" He spun away and slammed a fist against the wall. Then raised both of them above his head. "Angelica... *damn* you!"

It was too late. She'd never convince him. He was too smart for her.

She asked how he knew, using a small voice in order not to trigger his anger further.

Tom turned and stared hard at her, as if seeing her for the first time. "The *smell*, woman," he spat. "There's no mistaking the odor about his lips. You poisoned him. Any doctor will know."

Angelica was truly frightened now. Her life depended on the man who stood before her—the only man she'd never been able to bend entirely to her will.

She climbed slowly to her feet, aware that pleading, or trying to tempt him, would not work. She held no choice but to deal with the truth. A great risk . . . but still no choice.

"Tom." She spoke slowly, emphasizing the words. "You're right. I did it. I killed my father. But I did it for you. Angel's Rest is for the both of us. You built it. All of it. You deserve to keep it."

"Damn you . . ." It was more a growl from his throat than words.

Angelica walked slowly toward him. He straightened, but allowed her hands to move up his chest, to stroke him, and to encircle his neck.

"For you . . ." she whispered, tightening her fingers and pulling him toward her. "Tom, I wanted both of you. You and Angel's Rest . . ."

He resisted, staring down at her bitterly.

Angelica forced him to bend his head. "Can you watch your own wife hang for the killing?"

His lips were stiff. She pressed her own against them with a hunger that lay as much in her fear as in her loins. "Tom . . . my darling . . . please don't . . . come, my sweet . . . love me. Come to my bed . . . I need you so!"

Her hopes began to rise as he responded to the urgency of her kiss. Slowly at first, but with increasing fire until his arms were crushing her to him.

When at last she felt his manhood rising against her thighs, she sighed with relief. She had won. He would not confess her guilt to anyone else. She would have both Angel's Rest, with all it entailed for the future, and Tom Langlee.

But would he continue to love her as she needed him to?

Tom helped her bury her father and accompanied her to Charles Town to the lawyers to arrange transfer of the ownership of Angel's Rest. There was a great silence between them. He was no longer the same man. Except in moments of passion, when he looked at her, his look was a dark and sober one and Angelica knew he still debated with himself over the rightness of his move to protect her from the hangman.

There was only one way, she decided at last, to assure herself that he would remain both her husband and her ally. She would have to become pregnant. As distasteful as that condition might be to her, it was the only way. Righteous Tom Langlee might consider abandoning his wife someday, but he would *never* abandon the mother of his child . . .

Twenty-One

ELIZABETH WELBURN WALKED through the woods with a light step in spite of the burden of the wet wash in her basket and the other burden, the bad news Jason had given her last night. It was a beautiful day, not many clouds—just enough for her to hope they might bring the desperately needed rain in spite of what her husband had said. The stream she washed the clothes in was a good way from the hut, but it was far easier to wash there than to haul that much water home.

She loved these woods, they were so quiet and peaceful. Jason had warned her repeatedly about going off alone, saying she could never know when she might find herself facing a bear, a wildcat, or worse in his opinion, an Indian. Elizabeth knew he was right, but in the year or so they had been on their own land, the thirty-five acre plot that butted against the deep forest, she'd seen little sign of any of those threats.

They didn't live that far from Savannah, and while their nearest neighbor was over a mile away, the presence of white settlers had driven the larger creatures such as the bear and the deer deeper into the forest. At least that's what she believed.

And she'd seen far more Indians in Savannah than she saw out here. Jason was a worrier.

There was a gully in the woods between her hut and the stream, it had been necessary to either slide down its three-foot sides or make her way around it. When she had mentioned the fact to Jason, he took a look and solved the problem by felling a stout tree across it. Elizabeth's bridge he called it back in those early, joy-filled days when the two of them were freed and came excitedly out here to their own land. She smiled as she set foot to the log. What wonderful days they were.

She balanced easily on "Elizabeth's bridge," crossed its short span and stepped to the path again. Times were hard now, that was true, and poor Jason had much right to worry. He was the man and carried the burden of supporting her and their son. Although his first crop hadn't been a total failure, it had barely gotten them through to the next. The second had fared little better, and now, last night, Jason had worried to her that unless the drought was broken quickly, this year's crop might not survive at all.

She paused to shift the basket of wash when she could see the hut through the trees. They would make it somehow, she knew they would. Jason worked too hard to allow them to fail. And if the crops did burn, then they'd find a way to get by until next year—roots and berries from the woods; she was becoming quite good in learning the ones that could be eaten—and Jason had learned how to trap rabbits and squirrels. As long as they had each other, they could face anything.

Seed for the new planting was the real problem. She considered that with a frown on her face. Credit did not exist to an ex-indenture, at least one who hadn't yet proven himself. The Trustee Store had years before been closed, indeed, the Trustees, it was rumored, had grown tired of the whole experiment of the colony and were considering turning it over to the crown before its time. Perhaps that would be best after all. She didn't know. Such thinking was beyond her.

John was playing in the swept dirt yard in front of her door, wearing as usual nothing but the short trousers she'd made for him. His small body was brown as a berry, and Elizabeth smiled as she saw him. He simply did not like to wear his shirt.

"Mama!" His chubby face lighted and warmed her heart as he spotted her and jumped up to run and meet her. "I killed a snake! A big one! By myself!"

She set her basket down and hugged him. "My goodness. You killed a snake? All by yourself? You must be very brave, I'd be too frightened myself."

He was dancing in his excitement, waving his little arms. "Here, I'll show you!"

Elizabeth took his hand and allowed him to pull her to a corner of the cleared space in the yard where he pointed to a small green snake lying, indeed dead, the whole upper part of its body smashed with a rock. A garter snake, common around the houses in Savannah . . . she hated to see any living thing killed without cause. She knelt and took her small son around the waist.

"See, mama? I'm going to be a hunter!"

"Oh, are you now?" The snake was dead and she could only make him feel bad about killing it. Better to wait and explain the harm in it later. "Wouldn't you rather be a farmer like your father? And raise things for people to eat?"

"Did I hear my name mentioned?"

Elizabeth spun, startled, and found her husband standing a few feet away with a broad grin on his face.

"I thought you were in the field?" she said. "Come and see what your son the big hunter has done."

Jason walked over. Like his son, he was shirtless, his upper body a mixture of red and brown. Brown from the sun and red from his English beginnings.

He laughed at John. "You didn't leave much of him, did you?"

"I killed him myself," John told him solemnly.

Jason chuckled again and gave him a friendly cuff behind his ear. "You'll be tough enough, I'll warrant. And mayhaps you're right at that. Be a hunter, little John. Roam these woods and live as you choose. I'm beginning to think only a fool would choose to be a farmer like your pa."

Elizabeth stood up and stroked his arm. "I like farmers, myself. Except I expect them to farm, not walk in and frighten their wives in the middle of the day."

He shrugged. "That sun is frying both my corn and my brains, wife. I decided it was a waste of my effort to continue to hoe stalks that were bound to dry up anyway."

"I think it less a worry about the corn stalks than a desire to laze about on a beautiful day," she told him and allowed her hand to encircle his arm. "But come anyway. I'll see if I can find some meal cakes and a bit of honey for my lazy husband. What in the world ever happened to the Jason Welburn I knew who was going to be such a rich farmer?"

Jason looked down at her and his smile grew thoughtful. "Sometimes I begin to wonder about that myself, Elizabeth." He took a deep breath. "Our first year out here was such a failure. And the last little better..."

"Fie!" She shoved a shoulder against him and forced him nearly from his balance. "I remember you telling me it wouldn't be an easy thing to get started, Jason Welburn. Now tell yourself the same. You were the one who used to boast to Mr. Longfootte that you would someday be the best farmer in Georgia because you knew the soil. Now after only two years—not full two years in fact—you are already talking of failure. Where's the great farmer I married?"

The look he gave her worried her, and Elizabeth had to force the teasing smile to remain in her eyes. "I don't know, Beth," he said. "I know I can do it, but sometimes I have to... well, you know no one can control the weather. If this dryness doesn't break soon..."

"It takes hard work, Jason," she said quietly, allowing the smile to leave at last. "You said so yourself. We both knew it would not be easy to get started on so little. But we agreed we could do whatever it takes."

His mood changed instantly. Jason grabbed her in his arms, picked her up and swung her around. "'Pon my word, Elizabeth Welburn, you're well right! All we need is a bit of luck and we'll bring in a good crop!"

It was wonderful to be in his arms. Even better to have him place her on her feet again and look at her—the old, proud look. "I may be out of my luck though," he said, still grinning. "Mayhaps I used the most of that in gaining you."

"Tis not luck," she told him. "Hard work and the rightness of it. I'll not have it otherwise." She smiled back at him, feeling again the sunshine she'd felt earlier. "And if this year's crop fails, we do have the great hunter behind you to do for us."

Jason glanced over his shoulder at John who had trailed behind them. "Sure," he said. "If you can eat green snakes."

They both laughed, and John, looking up at them, laughed too, although he hadn't heard what they were saying, being too interested in the kill which he carried gingerly in one small hand.

Jason slipped an arm around her waist and turned to walk again. "You know, Beth, you're the best in the world for me. I'll admit to doubts, but only when I'm by myself. With you, I know I can't fail."

He squeezed her quickly. "There's a chance of failing. We've waited too long for our beginning. Too long being at the beck and call of others. The only thing is . . . well, if I just had more land, better land. Half of this thirty-five acres they've allotted me is pine barren. I'll be years cultivating it to grow anything, even if I have the rain."

She moved against him. "It will come, Jason. I know it will. You're the best farmer there is. It will be slow, but I can wait. Someday you'll have many acres—a big, rich farm. John will be big enough to help you work it and . . . you'll have other sons." She turned to smile up at him again.

He stopped. "Is that a promise, good wife? I mean the part about more sons?"

"My promise," she told him. "But only if you cease to worry about the future."

"Then I can hardly wait to stop worrying," he said. "In the mean, how about you feeding your husband as you promised— and where did you get honey anyway?"

"I got it from Alice Longfootte when they were out here last week. I've been saving it."

"Kind of her," Jason said. "I'll thank her this afternoon myself. I'm walking to Savannah to use the town wheel to sharpen my hoe and axe."

"But you were just there a few days ago!" She was disappointed, looking forward to having him spend the afternoon near their hut if he wasn't to work in the field.

Jason shrugged. "It has to be done often, Beth. I've no money to afford a grindstone myself, we should be glad one is provided still by the Trustees. Constant use wears my tools down and I can't afford yet to buy more."

She knew he was right. Still it was a bother.

"Well enough," she said. "You must say hello to Mrs. Longfootte for me."

The cakes were already done, she had made them that morning and had only to lay them out for Jason and John. In the span of a few minutes, far shorter time than she would have wished, the meal was gone and so was her husband. John found a place in the shade to curl up and nap away his meal while she sat upon the half log step to their hut and tied new brush to her yard broom.

Halfway through the task of trimming the twigs and lacing them to the stick Jason had cut for her, Elizabeth remembered he'd been to Savannah to sharpen his hoe only the day before this one. And he'd not used it that much . . .

By the last week of June they had been forced to realize and face the worst. The corn, the crop they had concentrated on to be their money crop, had failed completely. The brown-black tassels extending from the small, knotty beginning ears was mute evidence that those ears had dried and would never produce, as was the wilted leaves of the stalks themselves. Each day Elizabeth had walked out from the hut before the dawn and prayed for the life-giving rain to come that day and each evening she had done her best to console and encourage her husband who alternated between despair and rage at his helplessness.

The half acre garden they had planted in vegetables for themselves fared no better. The green beans held only shriveled blooms, drying in the sun, and the plants were fired from the bottom by the heat in the dry soil. Only the potato mounds and the cabbage, both started in early February before the drought began could be counted on to feed them in the coming winter, and both were small crops.

She wanted no more than to go off by herself and wander in the woods to allow its leaf and needle shelter to soothe her fear and pain, but Jason needed her more than ever and Elizabeth stayed close to him, urging him quietly to go on with his work.

Jason did, but he no longer laughed at all and that worried her more than the failed crop.

She was helping him repair the roof to their hut, passing up the wooden shakes he had cut for it, when both of them heard the sounds of an approaching horseman. Few came this way and none rode horses when they did. A thrill of excitement swept through her as she recognized her brother—older, a man full grown, but still her dear Thomas. She waved, and he raised a hand in return.

Elizabeth went to meet him and waited impatiently for him to bring the horse to a halt, swing down from its back and embrace her.

"Well!" Tom stepped back and pushed his tricorn to the rear of his head to see her the better. "I'll be damned if you don't get prettier every time I see you, Beth. Marriage must be good for you."

"It's just that you don't see your sister very often, Thomas Langlee," she said in mock anger. "By the time you come around again, you've forgotten what I look like."

"You're right about the time, but not about the forgetting," he countered. "And I suffer from the neglect. I remember a time when you would have knocked me from my feet with an embrace. Being that glad to see me. Now, by heaven, a sedate young woman walks calmly out and waits for my apology. Puts me in my place, you might say."

She laughed. "You deserve a rebuke. But I didn't do it with that intent; I suppose I'm just more woman now than girl. But I do love my brother, even if he doesn't come to see me. I'll admit to being surprised that you have."

"Surprised that I wanted to see you and my nephew?" He grinned. "Now that is truly a chastisement."

He turned his attention behind her. "Hello, Jason."

"Tom." Jason stepped around her and extended a hand. "Good to see you."

It pleased her to see them together, her brother and her husband, two men she loved. For the moment her cares were forgotten; she straightened and took a deep breath. "Come and rest," she told him. "You'll spend a few days with us?"

Tom shook his head. "Sorry, Beth. I wish I could, but I've got to get back to Augusta. My wife's with child and I'm afraid not carrying well. Tell you the truth, if I hadn't had to come to Savannah for a legal paper, I wouldn't be here."

He made a gesture with his hand. "But I couldn't come this far without taking the opportunity to see all of you. Speaking of that, where's my nephew?"

She was disappointed. She'd hoped he would visit for a few days. It would be so good to talk with him. "He was playing behind the hut a little while ago," she said. "I'll find him. But you will stay the night, won't you?"

Tom nodded. "I intended that, if you'll have me. And I'll find young John myself, if you'll take my horse, Jason."

Jason reached for the reins. "Surely. Tis a fine animal, Tom. How long have you had her?"

"Almost since I went to Augusta the first time. You're right, she's sturdy stock. Tie her wherever you will, I'll unsaddle and feed her in a bit."

Jason shook his head. "No bother to me. I'll do it for you. And Elizabeth can see about feeding all of us."

"Thank you." Tom grinned again at her. "I'll talk to you later. You say this son of yours is somewhere that way?"

"I hope so," she laughed. "He's sometimes apt to wander. He thinks he's an Indian. Look in the cornfield."

She busied herself in the hut, getting a fire going in the clay and stone hearth, cleaning a rabbit Jason had trapped the day before to boil it with cabbage in the larger of the two iron pots they had brought from Savannah. It wouldn't be a great meal— from the looks of his nice clothes, her brother was most likely used to better—but he wouldn't mind. He did look so well! Good leather boots, high and turned down below the knee like a gentleman's, a fine linen shirt with a wide collar and, if she wasn't mistaken, a good coat tied behind his saddle. She let out an explosive sigh. It was so good to see him prosper!

A twinge of guilt struck her as she finished cleaning the rabbit and dropped it in the already heating water. Poor Jason would feel badly in comparison. Being a man he would look at his own worn clothes and blame himself. Well, she wouldn't allow that either. His time would come; they must be patient.

Tom entered the open door behind her, carrying John astride one arm. Her son was wearing her brother's hat, his small head nearly disappearing beneath it.

"I tell you what, sister," he said. "I've decided to take this little Indian back to Augusta with me. You may as well give him up."

"Ask me sometime when I've spent half a busy day trying to find him," she laughed. "Right now, no. How do you like your big uncle, John?"

"Ride the horse," John told his uncle, jabbing at his chest at the same time and ignoring her question. "John ride the horse."

"By the glory, you're right, sir!" Tom said. "I do believe I promised that. Excuse us, mama. We're going to ride a horse bareback."

"Bareback?" John repeated.

"Bareback. Your father has been good enough to unsaddle

her by now, I don't think he would take kindly to us replacing it after he's gone to the trouble. We'll just have to ride bareback."

"Ride the horse," John told him, returning to the part he did understand.

Tom laughed again and turned to carry him outside.

The cabin Jason had built, with the help of Samuel Longfootte on the heavier, lower timbers, but doing the rest himself, was not a large one. They planned to extend it later when the need arose. It was sturdy and tight—Elizabeth had aided herself in chinking between the logs with clay—and it held a good loft for sleeping. With three instead of two adults in it now, however, she was more conscious of its small size.

Tom didn't seem to notice. He finished his meal and leaned from his stool to rest his back against the wall of the cabin, his hands propped on the table. "Beth, that was a grand meal. I didn't know I was so hungry."

"Thank you. There's a little more—"

He waved a hand. "But no more room in me. Jason, you must work very hard, else you'd be the fattest man in Georgia."

"Hard enough," Jason said. "Though I'm beginning to think I'll never see the good of it. Has the dryness hurt you this much in Augusta?"

Tom shook his head. "No. Cotton can stand the heat better than most crops, and so far I've been lucky to get just enough rain. I'll bring in a fair crop, not a good one, but since the weather seems to have treated all the southern colonies alike this year, I'll be able to compete. The only question is whether the islands will do better and low bid us in England."

Jason asked a question, Tom answered and the two of them went on talking, but Elizabeth didn't hear what was said. It was astonishing to hear her brother speak with such knowledge of trade in England, islands—somewhere, she didn't know if he meant those off the coast of Georgia or somewhere near England—and prices of goods, both imported and exported. Her thoughts went back to those days, not all that far back in number of years but seemingly misty in the past, when the two of them were children being taken to London and thrust upon a ship bound into a frightening future.

She looked at him as he talked. He had come a long way. There was assurance—a man's assurance—in him now. Gone was the desperate look to his eyes, the look of a boy without the means to understand the world around him. Thomas had truly found himself. His gestures, the way he spoke—did she not know better she wouldn't believe he had once been a peasant's son who knew no more than his own labor and the moor that lay close beside them.

No. He was never a peasant's son. In the time she'd spent with Jason and her own son, she'd forgotten to remember that the two of them—she and Thomas—were born of the blood. Tom was of the betters of the world, it was only his misfortune to have started out in the poorness of Briggs's hut.

She cocked her head in thought. Somehow, now, their strange birth didn't seem to matter much to her—didn't matter at all, in fact. She was proud of her own name. Welburn was a good name. And kings and queens and dukes and whatever else was in titles were—

Elizabeth became suddenly aware that both men were staring at her and turned red with embarrassment. "What?"

Jason looked at Tom. "She sometimes becomes foggy-minded like that, Tom. You'll have to pardon her. If you really want to lose her attention, take her out into those woods to walk. She'll quite forget you're there."

The color was burning her face. She felt like a little girl who'd been caught doing something wrong and it didn't help a bit to see the both of them laughing at her. "I was merely thinking of what I would have to break our fast in the morning," she said, more crossly than she intended. "I heard everything you said."

"Then repeat the question," Tom said, and winked at Jason.

"I'll not be teased," she declared firmly. "Not by the likes of the two of you. If you would ask me something, you must do so again in a proper manner."

Both of them were like conspirators, enjoying the joke between themselves, until, finally, she relented and smiled in return. "All right. I wasn't listening and you caught me fair handed. Now stop those silly faces and tell me what was said."

"See what I mean?" Jason asked Tom. "The woman's impossible." He turned back to her. "Your brother wanted to know if you ever go into Savannah anymore. He said Mr. Stephens asked about you. I would have told him no, but I waited for you to be polite enough to answer yourself."

She shook her head. "I'm sorry. No, I don't go. It's really

too long a walk and I don't have any reason except to visit. Is
Mr. Stephens well?"

Tom nodded. "As well as a man his age can expect, I think.
He still thinks highly of you both."

"He's a blessed man. I'll always be grateful to him."

"So will I," Tom added. "I'm still sorry I didn't know of
the trial until it was over."

He shook off a bad memory and turned to Jason. "Listen.
I had more reason than just to see the two of you in coming
by here. I would have done it anyway since I had to come to
Savannah, but I wanted especially to see how you were doing."

Jason's expression changed. The laughter in his eyes died
as Elizabeth watched and his lips curled in resentment. "Well
you found out, didn't you?"

Tom met his look directly. "Yes," he said. "It's not your
fault. No one can control the weather. But to tell you the truth,
I'm not sorry you've lost your crop."

Her husband stiffened and Elizabeth turned in astonishment
to her brother.

Tom raised a hand. "Don't take my words amiss, Jason.
I'd be happy to see you in the best of success. If so, I'd wish
you well and keep my own troubles to myself. But the truth
is, I need help at Angel's Rest, my plantation in Augusta. I
need a man I can trust as one of my overseers. Jason, I'd be
grateful if you would consider coming there in that position."

Wonderful! Elizabeth wanted to kiss him. What an answer
to her prayers! Jason would accept surely!

She looked at Jason as he turned his head away to consider
her brother's words and tightened her fists in nervousness. Oh
he would surely accept! It would be such an opportunity for
them both and they wouldn't have to worry about how they
would get through this coming winter. He'd have a good position—an overseer—and his new wife, what would she be
like? Her mind was racing.

The men were silent, and the time grew so long Elizabeth
could hardly contain herself. Jason continued to stare at a wall
and Tom's look met her eyes briefly.

Her husband took a deep breath, glanced at her for a moment
and Elizabeth guessed his answer. It stabbed her with a pain
she had to fight to control.

"Tom, it's a most generous offer," he said. "I thank you

for the making of it. But I can't accept your charity."

"I spoke only of my own need," Tom told him quietly.

Jason shook his head. "There are many men who would do you well, we both know that. Men who are more experienced in handling slaves. No, you looked about at what I have here and you made the offer because of what you saw. Elizabeth is your sister, but she's also my wife. I'll take care of her. It may take the longer, but I'll make my land pay someday, I promise you."

Tom was silent, looking thoughtfully at him. Elizabeth wanted to cry from disappointment but at the same time she was proud of her husband. She hadn't realized the truth but Jason had. Tom had always promised to take care of her and that was the real reason he had made this offer. But Jason was a man himself.

"There's also another reason," he told her brother firmly. "I spent years of my life in the service of another man—a good man, it's true—but still my master. I must be my own man now."

Tom nodded. "I understand that. I was indentured as well. But this is a job offer, not indenture. And I believe you would handle it well or I wouldn't make it."

Jason shook his head. "There's a difference in what you offer and indenture. I understand that. But still I have to refuse. I hope you are not angered, but that's the way it must be."

"It will be as you say, Jason," Tom said. "We're still good friends, I hope. If you change your mind, you're welcome at Angel's Rest."

Jason nodded somberly, then stood up. "I've a few chores to do now, I'd best get about them. Consider this your home."

He went out the door without looking at her.

Elizabeth allowed her gaze to remain on the floor, aware that her brother's eyes were upon her and unwilling at the moment to meet them. She had wanted to go badly, but it was for her own sake, she realized, not Jason's. He was a man, with a man's pride. And he was right. Still it would hurt.

"You can't talk him into coming?" Tom asked her gently.

Elizabeth looked up at him. "No. Nor will I try, Tom. He's my husband and I respect his wishes."

"Beth, we've been through a lot, the two of us. We've come a long way from that little place on the moor where we hardly knew what life was about—a very long way. I can do well by you now. There's no more need for either of us to suffer. Please get him to come."

Her chest hurt. So much time . . . and she loved him. But there was the rightness of it. "Tom, I love you. I'll always love you. And I would be most happy to see you often. But Jason must make his decision and I think that is proper. I'll stay here until he wants it otherwise."

He allowed himself a long sigh. "If you wish it, then so be it, Beth. Remember, though, if it gets worse for you—if you ever need me—you have only to send me word."

"Thank you." She whispered the words, then changed the subject. "You look so well. I believe the wife you married must have made you very happy."

His face darkened quickly, only a flickering shadow, but enough to puzzle her. "Yes, Beth. Things are better for me though I'd much prefer it if you'd come to Angel's Rest. Your being there would give me something to . . . I'd like it very much."

"I'm grateful for your asking, Tom, but we will be well here; I'm sure of it."

Tom continued to stare at her and there was a quiet sadness in his eyes that she couldn't understand. He had so much . . . what could possibly be hurting him?

He broke the mood between them by standing. "Think I'll go and see if Jason could use a hand in his chores," he said.

A moment later he was gone, leaving her to gaze at the dying coals in the hearth. To gaze and to wonder about her brother's life and to think of what might have been . . .

Twenty-Two

LONG, DARK CLOUDS. streaked with gray on the fringes but heavy with moisture in the center, hung low above her head as Elizabeth emerged from the cabin with Jason's axe in her hand. She paused to look up at them, so close they seemed to press about her, and shook her head. Rain now came in abundance, rain that was months too late to do for the crops. It was the ending of winter but not yet time to plant again.

"Come back in another month," she muttered to the clouds. "And stay the time needed. Do some good for a change, don't bother to threaten me now."

A distant rumble, the growl of thunder somewhere behind was her answer but she ignored it. Across from her, the trees that were the beginning of the forests seemed to wait resignedly for another heavy rain, those that retained leaves or needles drawing them close about the trunks much as a woman would gather her skirts above a muddy road. The others, struck naked by the death inducing winter stood forlornly waiting for rebirth.

Rebirth . . . would she and Jason do as much as the trees? With spring the trees would begin anew and in a short time be lively and quick with green leaves dancing in the breeze. But the trees were deep rooted, reaching far down for the life-giving moisture. Life for the Welburns lay closer to the surface, within the first foot or so of soil. If the clouds left after planting and stayed away until the winter, then that foot of soil would dry and so would any hope the two of them held . . .

It was discouraging to dwell upon. Elizabeth shook the thought away and picked up the axe. The winter's supply of wood Jason had cut was nearly gone. All that was left were some thicker logs he'd not had time to split. She would have to do it herself since he wasn't at home. Otherwise there would be none to keep the fire going.

John was still asleep. She smiled to herself. The good thing that had been this winter was the health of her son. All the time he spent out of doors in his young life, time that often she was vexed to fetch him inside even when the temperature dropped, had toughened him. Sickness was something to which he had yet to be made aware.

The difference in John and the two poor little lads she had been charged with attending a few years ago was unbelievable. They had been sick almost from the day they arrived in the colony and finally gave in to that sickness. Though he ate less well than they had their first year, her own son was far healthier.

But then, was that the reason itself? She had to pause to consider. The fact that John more often than not ate food that grew naturally in the forest, could that be the secret of his good health? Did savages, who spent their entire lives in the woods, ever get sick?

The morning chill, yet in the lower temperature, got to her at last and she shivered. "Goodness, Elizabeth Welburn!" she told herself crossly. "You've work to do and you stand about in idle thought. No wonder Jason thinks you foggy-minded."

She lifted the axe and walked swiftly to the pile of wood. There she selected one of the smaller logs and stood it upright, backed a foot away and swung the axe.

The heavy blade bit deep into the wood but didn't split it as would happen had Jason swung it.

Fie! But it would have to be, she must have the wood. She pushed the log over and heaved against the axe handle. It took three tries to remove it, working the handle back and forth, but when she had it free, the log upright again, and swung the axe once more, to her surprise it struck true to the cut she'd already made and the block split asunder.

Well! She was certainly getting better, and so she continued, choosing an easier log for her next effort. Soon she was already breathing hard from her exertions and had to pause to rest.

She wished Jason would return. He'd promised to be back from Savannah last eve, it was only to be for the day. He must have taken longer than he expected in town and spent the night with the Longfoottes rather than come back in the dark.

He was a worry to her. The long winter had been hard on him, more so than the little they had to eat. She could see him sit and stare into the fire and know he was thinking of what would happen to them if this year's crop didn't make it. And worrying if he would be able to plant a crop at all. If he could get the loan of money for seeding to begin with . . .

She placed another log upright and heaved the axe. Jason was different now, sometimes almost a stranger to her. He talked little to her throughout the winter and never mentioned his plans for the future at all. There had been a time when he could talk to her for hours of what would be. But now he spent far too much time lying on his back and staring at the roof.

He was worried. Else he wouldn't be of a mind to neglect his work as he did. That wasn't Jason. Not the Jason she had married. Somehow she would have to bring the other back in him.

But then, with the spring arriving, with the time for planting and hoping upon them again, he'd become as the trees, ready to unfold, to grow and to be happy. She knew he would!

In an hour she had a fair-sized stack of cut wood for the fire. Enough to last the day and the night as well in case Jason didn't make it home. He had stayed away for two nights once, but only because he'd drunk too much and was ashamed to let her know it.

She was warm from her exertions, not enough to perspire, but warm enough to push back her shawl from around her arms. Over the top of the forest the sun struggled with the clouds and she waited to watch for the winner. The woods seemed to support and encourage the sun and Elizabeth smiled at them. They were beautiful to her in spite of the damage of winter. She loved those woods.

What would it be like beyond the small part that she knew? How deep did they go, and what was beyond them? In the far distance were there mountains? Steep clifts, lofty peaks? Or did the forest go on and on forever?

She suddenly remembered Cawley's tales to her while they were still aboard the ship. She had been young then and ready to believe whatever was told to her. Elizabeth twisted her lips in a grimace. Cawley had known no more than she at the time, it was only his own stupidness that believed the tales of monsters and cannibals. There were no more than more Indians and bears and such, she was quite sure of it.

If she were a man, she would just gather a pack for her back and start walking west to see what she would see...

The cabin door opened behind her and the sound flooded Elizabeth with guilt. A yawning John stood in it and looked out to her. The son who, like his father, required her attention. She ought not to be daydreaming about roaming through the forest like a savage. She leaned the axe against a log and bent to gather the wood she'd cut.

Jason was home by midmorning, but his mood was dark and he had little to say to her. "It was late when I finished; I decided to stay in town. You had no trouble being alone, did you?"

"No." She busied herself with the repair of her weaving frame, replacing the broken pegs. He had turned away from her attempted embrace when he entered the hut, but not before she had sniffed the rank smell of rum on his breath.

Jason had no coin when he left, only a pack of animal skins he'd hoped to trade for salt. But then he may have been given the drink when he visited Samuel Longfootte, she told herself.

But she didn't remember Longfootte ever drinking rum during the time she stayed there.

He sat down by the fire and began to clean his shoes of the mud from the road. Elizabeth watched him from the corner of her eye. He really looked as if he'd slept the night out of doors. She thought suddenly of the night Thermous Cawley had returned drunk from the fire at his sheds. But he'd looked much worse than Jason—and this was *Jason*, her husband. It wasn't the same...

The warmth from the fire seemed to revive him. Jason rubbed his hands together, stretched out his stockinged feet and heaved a large sigh.

It gave her courage to ask what she'd been dreading. "Did you have success in getting the money for seed?"

His mood changed instantly and she regretted the question. His lips pinched inward bitterly. "Twas a stupid question, Elizabeth. Near as stupid as my own quest in going to Savannah. Who would loan money to me?"

"It's not that at all," she said quietly. "You're well known in Savannah, Jason. All of them know how hard you work. And they know as well the weather has been—"

"They care little for that!" He glared at her. "Like everyone in this world they care only for profit that is immediate to them! Why should they risk their money on the likes of me?"

His hands became fists where they rested on the insides of his knees. The muscles along his jaw were rigid.

"Mr. Habersham knows you well, Jason," she said. "Did you go to his mercantile store?"

"Aye, damn. I went there. And every cursed other place I could think to go. None of them would even talk to me. James Habersham or his partner could have seen me just off a ship from England for all they cared. No one would consider a loan."

His voice dropped off from its anger as he spoke, the last words were no more than a mutter.

It was frightening. Without seed there would be no money crop. She'd saved enough to plant a few vegetables, eye cuts for new potato mounds, but there had to be seed for corn. Without the corn to sell they would eventually be lost.

But she had seen hard times before. She'd known cold and hunger most of her life on the moor in England, far too much to fear it now. "Jason, we'll find a way. We've weeks yet before it's time to plant and—"

"Damn it, woman! Don't you even *care*? That's all you ever say—we'll find a way! But it's not you who must find that way! *I'm* the one who must beg the help!"

His eyes were red and angry. He looked as if he wanted to strike her.

"We have yet to beg," she said with a calmness she didn't feel. "And we will not. What we do, we do together."

"No." He shook his head slowly, eyeing her closely. "We don't do it all together. You were here, away from all who could know you. Hiding away out here and not willing to face the people who know us in Savannah. *You* won't go to town. You didn't have to go to Samuel Longfootte and beg him to give you the seed to plant one more crop. Don't say *we*, Elizabeth!"

"Jason—"

"Begged him!" He stood erect and raised a fist. She was glad John had gone outside.

"I had to go to him and tell him I couldn't make it on my own. Don't you realize that? Do you know what that did to me?"

"I'm sorry," she said. "But I'm certain Mr. Longfootte—"

"Oh yes!" He turned and slammed a foot against the stool he'd been sitting on, driving it flying against the wall. "He understood! He understood his *indentured* servant was too poor a man to make it on his own! That he must come crawling back and ask for help. Oh he was happy to give it. Happy for he thinks he still owns me!"

She bit her lip and held her silence. He was in no mood for her words.

"Do you know what he said?" Jason demanded, crossing to stand above her. "Do you know what he really wants?"

"He wants success for you," she said, straining her neck to look up at him. "I think no more than that."

"No, by damn! He wants me to come back and work for him! To work together, he says!"

"I'm sure he misses you, Jason," she said. "He thought of you as a son, and he's getting old. Perhaps it wouldn't be such a wrong idea—"

"No! I'll not be another man's lackey! Not ever again!" He caught her face in his hand roughly. "Not even if we starve!"

He waited, and when she didn't move, turned and stalked back to pick up his stool and resume his place by the fire. It was a long time before he spoke again, but when he did, the bitterness was still deep in his voice. "You think I'm being foolish, don't you? That I'm blaming everyone else for my troubles."

"No, I don't. I think it weighs heavily on your mind and you've not yet given yourself a chance."

Jason turned to look at her and there was more than anger in his look, there was resentment. "You know I've had the same chance as your brother," he said. "And you know he's become successful. He has a big plantation. Slaves—"

"I don't compare the two of you," she cut him off.

"Like hell you don't!" He got up and stalked from the room.

Elizabeth looked at her hands. They were trembling. But she didn't compare them, she told herself. She'd never even thought of such!

Jason had. That was now obvious. How could she make him realize otherwise?

The Indian glided through the woods at a fast pace, his moccasins making no more than a whisper across the pine needles, a whisper that was cousin to the snake. No harm could threaten him here, this was Creek territory and there was not an enemy within five days' journey. Nor could he be threatened by the bear or the wolf, for he was Creek and more than a match for either. It was only the habit of long training that caused him to move so silently—a part of his nature as an Indian.

The cold time still held its sway, clinging to life as all living things did, but soon it would die its natural death and the young freshness of a new time would come. These trees would become green and breathe with new life. The forest would shake itself, much as the beaver shakes its coat free when it emerges from the water, and all would be happy again. It was good to know that was coming, good enough that he anticipated it and shrugged free from his deerskin coat, tossed it over one shoulder along with his pack and allowed his bare skin to challenge the still sharp bite of the dying winter.

Half a day's walk from his last camp site, he paused and debated with himself for a moment. The sun found its way through the bare-limbed trees and highlighted the coppery sheen to his face as he twisted his head in thought. Then he nodded and turned aside from the path he'd been taking. The task to which he was assigned lay several days before him, and this turning aside would delay it. But life itself was short, and neglecting the small things that pleased him was also a waste.

By late afternoon he had reached the place he sought. He squatted by a rotting log, still deep enough in the trees not to be seen from the white man's home, and waited in patience.

There was only the man, his small son, and the woman who lived in this home. The man was young, a few moons less than himself. But he owned a musket and the Indian had seen him shoot it reasonably well. To be caught watching his home might mean he could face death, or face the need to kill the man.

Why do it then? He knew enough of the white man's ways to understand they were easily frightened by such. And the laws of his own Creek Nation spoke against taking another man's woman. But he had become fascinated by the young white woman who walked so bravely alone in the forest. Only by accident did he first find her, and that time he had crouched for a long time to watch.

She was different. He'd been enough in the towns to observe that white women were a noisy lot, constantly moving about and talking all the time to each other. Chattering as much or more than Creek women. But this one, perhaps because she was alone, seemed more serene. She looked, and walked, as if she loved the forest, often raising her hands to the tops of the trees. And it was that, as much as her beauty, that made him content to watch.

This time he was rewarded quicker than he was prepared to wait for. The woman with the beautiful hair emerged almost as soon as he waited, carrying a bucket of water. She poured it carefully around a piled mound of dirt then set it aside and placed her hands on her hips.

She was wearing a long dress in the manner of the white women. It hid her shoes. But she didn't wear the white cap so many of them wore, her long brown hair was free as nature intended. He liked the way it fell about her shoulders.

To his surprise, she didn't turn and go back into the cabin, but walked directly toward him, as if she were coming into the woods to meet him. He glided backwards, keeping low, aware there was little cover in the winter woods to prevent his being seen.

She came on and he was forced to move again. Even in his awareness that she might discover him and raise the alarm, he had to appreciate her beauty. The clothes she wore, white man's clothes, covered far too much of her. The Indian could see her in his mind's eye wearing hand rubbed buckskin, no lower than to her knee, to leave her legs free for movement. In all, since he was gifted with the ability to picture things in his mind, he saw her with no hindrance at all, beauty as nature intended, poised to plunge into a hidden, deep pool . . .

His tongue moistened his lips. What he was thinking would be enough to set the whites against the Creeks as much as some of them now were against the Cherokees. There would be war between those some day. It was part of his task to see that the Creeks did not become a part of that war.

But this woman. Would he give up all to have her for himself?

She came even closer and he stretched out on the ground to keep from being seen. The woman was searching for berries, and he suddenly knew she was hungry. His own pack was more than enough for his journey, suppose he stood and offered it to her? What would she do?

But he waited, still as his brother the eagle, and watched as she finished and made her way back to her home. It took a long time. But not enough for him to be filled. He would come back this way after he finished his task.

The thought of what it would mean if he gave in to what would please him the most and took her for himself gave a twist to his lips. That had been done by the Cherokees more than once. And the men from the South Carolina colony were already speaking of war to eliminate those tribes. But the Creeks—until now—had left white women alone.

He shook his head. No, he could not take the woman from her man. But he would return to watch her. He believed that what was destined to be, would be. Fate had decided that he would have this beautiful woman who walked so freely in the forest or his heart would not have been so moved by her.

His father, the Mico, had become angry with him because he had not yet taken a wife. But none had moved him until now. This woman, this white woman, had moved him more than he would have believed possible, therefore, Fate had decided he would have her.

Somehow, the white man with whom she lived would have to be removed. It was only a matter of when and how. But Como-tan was patient . . . and would wait.

Twenty-Three

COMO-TAN, SON OF CHEKILLI, Mico of the Creek Nations, stood in the bow of the packet boat and watched with dark eyes as it approached the dock in Charles Town. He stood erect and alone because the rest of the passengers had left him alone, quite obvious in their intention. His copper face was impassive, but amusement lay hidden just below the surface. These white men who shared the journey from Savannah aboard the packet boat would speak to each other later of the sinister countenance of the red man, of their inability to read his thoughts, as if it was some strange trait known only to those of a different skin. These, the men who dwelt in the towns and never went beyond, built up in their own minds a mystery about Indians. Then allowed that self-created mystery to awe themselves. It was amusing. For if they ever made an attempt to know the Creek, they'd find him as open and friendly as a man could be—in fact, more as a child than not. Except for those like himself, who had spent most of his life dealing with the white man and had learned from necessity the need to hide his thoughts, the Creek could not be less a mystery.

But the white man built up his own images in his mind and

the Indian became something entirely different from his true self. And there lay more a problem than just amusement. The thought banished the humor from his mind as suddenly as it had come. More and more of the whites were arriving at the shores of this colony of South Carolina and the one called Georgia as well. New men, coming both from England and the other places on the continent where they spoke languages that he did not understand, arrived each week. These new men knew nothing about the Indian. Nothing about the treaties made between James Oglethorpe and Como-tan's great uncle, Tomochichi. They knew only that they wanted the virgin land for themselves and the red man stood in their way. It would someday become cause for war; he was convinced of it.

A sailor moved past him with a coiled rope in his hand and shouted to a man on the quay. The man answered and made ready to receive the thrown rope. In a moment the boat would rub its long bow against the wood of the quay and be drawn tightly in place for its passengers to step ashore before its freight was unloaded. Como-tan bent to retrieve his pack and loft it to his shoulder. He cast a glance toward the others, saw the returned looks and knew they would wait for him to step onto the short boarding plank first. None would take the chance of touching him by moving at the same time. His amusement returned, but only briefly.

The sailors, and the men who worked the docks, seemed far less interested in him than in their own work, he walked along the quay unhindered and made his way into the streets of Charles Town. He walked with assurance, but his dark eyes were alert for danger, as much so as when he walked through the forests. Perhaps more, for this end of town was replete with grog shops, where men of lesser character spent what idle time they could garner drinking spirits.

This time he had no trouble and emerged into the better streets of the city unchallenged. This town was full of bustle, a far cry from the slow, indolent style of Savannah. These were the industrious people, the whites with the drive to take over all the land—and therefore, the ones to be more greatly feared. It was that fear, as much as the need to make trade agreements between the leaders of South Carolina and the various tribes of the Creek Nation, that brought Como-tan more often than he would prefer to this place. Chekilli and the other Micos were aware that only by communication could the misunder-

standings between the races be countered. Combine those mis-
understandings with greed and temper, and war could quickly
result.

Therefore, Como-tan, and others like him, came often to
Charles Town and talked of rights as well as trade.

In a short span of time he was clear of the wealthier area
and passing smaller houses, neither mean nor pretentious, but
well built, their wooden sides neatly painted. Halfway down
a street he turned in a small gate and knocked on the door of
one of the houses.

He waited patiently, aware that if the owner was in, as he
usually was, he would hear and come as soon as his age would
allow him.

His knowledge was correct, the door opened slowly and a
white man, advanced in years, peered out at him above small
round glasses propped across his large nose. It took no more
than a second for the Reverend Thaddeus Miller to recognize
his visitor. "James! How good to see you!"

Como-tan nodded and smiled. "Reverend. It's always my
pleasure."

Of all the things he'd acquired from the whites—the education he'd received from the man who stood before him; the
ability to judge and measure them by their own standards learned
in debate with the leaders—Como-tan took the greatest pride
in his use of their language. It was disconcerting to those who
met him for the first time that he spoke it so well and usually
gave them doubt as to their preconceived notion that all Indians
were simple.

"Come in, come in!" The preacher stepped back and swung
the door wide. "You don't know how much I look forward to
each of your visits, James. What a delight it is to see you! You
know, I sit around staring at these walls until I find myself
talking to them."

Como-tan stepped inside, took the door to close it and allowed his smile to broaden as he placed a hand on the frail
shoulder of the older man. "Then the walls should learn a great
deal, Reverend. But I doubt that you do as much talking inside
as you do to those flowers you grow in the rear. Tell me, what
new types have you created since I was here last?"

Thaddeus chuckled, a thin sound from high in his throat.
"It's winter still outside, James. Hadn't you noticed? My good-

ness, I wasted years on teaching an Indian boy only to have him grow into a man who doesn't recognize the seasons."

"You taught me better than you realized," Como-tan told him. "You taught me to study men as well as books, and I used that knowledge to study you. I know full well that you have been conducting experiments with seeds through this winter. And I know you are experimenting with pieces of glass to make your own summer for your flowers. I can see through you, Reverend."

The old man chuckled again. "And so you can. Perhaps I didn't waste my time after all. Though I'm not sure I want my own flirtation with the Devil by wasting God's good time over the growing of flowers known to all. You do keep my little secret, do you not?"

"A sworn promise," Como-tan said. "But I'd hardly call it a waste of time, your God's or anyone else's. There's never enough beauty in this world."

Thaddeus nodded. "That much is true. But I do feel guilty at times. I've been a preacher of the gospel too many years not to be so."

"You did what you set out to do," Como-tan said. "You've earned your rest. Let younger men take over."

"They have, they have!" Thaddeus's eyes glinted over his spectacles in amusement. "These young sprouts are marvelous at waving their arms over a congregation and gushing forth with words that most of the people in the pews can't understand, but I wonder just how well they accomplish the task of making God's wishes known."

"You, on the other hand, were very good at it," Como-tan said.

"Except for one Indian I know," Thaddeus said, still peering at him.

Como-tan shrugged. "An uncivilized savage," he said, and grinned. "Hopeless."

"But I haven't given up yet. Nor will I as long as you continue to come and see me."

"I don't expect you to," Como-tan said. "But may I have a cool drink of cider first before I must defend my unchurched ways?"

"Good heavens! My manners!" Thaddeus reached to clap himself on the head. "Did I not tell you I so thirst for words

I mumble to these walls? Here I am fencing with you when I should be recognizing you've traveled over night or more. Come, come. I keep your clothes ready in the trunk by your bed as always. And I'll fetch you a pitcher of water for refreshing yourself. Then when you're ready, we'll have the cider and our talk. I'm anxious to know what you've been doing since the last time."

He was as good as his word. The water in the pitcher was cool and welcome. Como-tan poured a portion of it out into the basin and bent over it to bathe his face. Thaddeus had also fetched a small cloth and he wet it to rub over his chest and upper arms after he removed his shirt.

When he was finished, he went to the trunk, opened it and took out the clothes.

They had been hand cleaned—the white shirt with its wide collar had been washed and pressed with a hot iron, the wool breeches rubbed with a brush to remove any trace of soil and the woolen stockings were wrapped around a piece of birch to give them a good odor.

He dressed quickly, then combed his long black hair and tied it into a bagwig. He grimaced at the exchange of his moccasins for the stiff leather shoes, but that was necessary for where he was going as was the split-tailed coat he would wear. He glanced around, didn't see it hanging and decided Thaddeus had placed it elsewhere.

The old man enjoyed taking care of his "civilized clothing" as much as his presence, and visiting him for the time before he went to meet the colony trade leaders was the only enjoyable time Como-tan spent among the whites. His uncle, Tomochichi, had been wise to know the Creeks needed members of their tribes who understood the white man's ways and had been the reason behind a young boy being sent to live with the Reverend Thaddeus Miller to receive that education. He was glad he had been chosen, for it was good to know books, to have a knowledge of the world that many—no, most—of the white men he met did not. But Como-tan had long ago come to understand himself. He may be educated to the white man's ways, but he was, and would always remain, a Creek. The forest was his home; he would have it no other way.

It was soothing to his spirit to shed the tight-fitting clothes of the whites and don the loose freedom of buckskin and follow his namesake the eagle to whatever whim he chose.

Discipline was necessary, including discipline of the mind. But freedom was his winged soul, and though he was earth-bound of foot, his mind soared with the eagle when he was alone in the forest.

Thaddeus had a small fire going in the front room, necessary, Como-tan realized for his host's old bones. It would be uncomfortable for himself, but a small price to pay for their talk. The preacher also had two large mugs of apple cider, cool from his cellar. Como-tan picked up the one meant for him from the table and chose the chair furthest from the fire.

Thaddeus looked at him in pleasure. "It's been what—eight or more months since I saw you last? I've missed you, James."

"As well for myself," Como-tan said, and sipped the cider. "How've you fared?"

The old man made a gesture. "Well enough. The stipend I receive from the church is quite enough for my needs. I don't require a great deal as you know. I do miss the pulpit, I must confess to that."

He nodded, but remained silent.

Thaddeus smiled into the fire. "You're the cause of it, you know."

He was surprised. "The cause of what?"

The other glanced up and the twinkle was back in his eyes. "Why, the cause of my being retired before I had mind of it myself, of course. You didn't realize it?"

He was wary. Aged or not, the man opposite him had a mind quite unshackled, quick to dart and probe. He had been a professor of learning before he took up his religion at a late age and came to the Americas. Thaddeus Miller enjoyed nothing more than to lead his former pupil into a verbal trap. "Just how did that come about?" he asked at last.

"By your own teaching, of course." Thaddeus was laughing at him now, a soundless chuckle.

"I see." Como-tan watched him over the top of his cider mug. "It seems in my own remembrance that I was *your* student, sent here to learn the ways of white men. You taught me to read and to think, with, I also remember, sometimes a short temper at a boy's summer day's restlessness. How did it get turned the other way?"

"But I taught you not of my God, did I?"

"I believe that Spirit exists, but not in your churches wearing stiff clothes and ready to punish any who happen to smile at the wrong time. I also believe, as do most Creeks, that it is a Spirit not very concerned with what we do in this world."

"Yes," Thaddeus nodded. "I'm quite aware of all that. We've spent many an hour debating it. I don't agree with you, obviously. I believe in the Lord, but . . . a little too much of you rubbed off on me. You're an excellent debater and I'm far too good a listener for my own good. That was eventually my downfall."

He took a long draught of cider. "You see, dear James, I didn't remain quite rigid enough for my church leaders. I was sent here to preach hellfire and brimstone—to, in effect, *scare* the Devil from my parishioners. You taught me your Creek forbearance for the foolishness of man and I allowed it into my practice. Fortunately, my leaders decided I had merely become addled with age rather than come under the influence of the Devil, and pensioned me off."

"I never knew why you stopped."

"Well that's the truth. I taught a boy; I learned from a man. God does care what we do on this earth, James. But I do believe you're right in the fact that He's forgiving of our mistakes."

He sighed loudly. "Be that as it may, I'm left in peace by both my church and the good Lord. We've reached an agreement, He and I. I serve Him as best I can, but I'm no longer required to go forth and bang Him over the heads of unwilling listeners." He looked directly at Como-tan. "Why don't you give up that forest and move to Charles Town?"

Again an abrupt change. "I'm an Indian, not a white man."

"But more civilized in your thinking than most men I've ever met," Thaddeus said quickly. "You could do a great deal of good here."

"I couldn't, even if I wanted to."

The old man smiled softly. "I taught you much, but I never succeeded in removing the barbarian from you. You'll always be a child of the woods, James."

Como-tan returned the smile. "I wouldn't call it barbarian. More the naturalness meant for man. There in the forest I'm brother to the eagle, and feel as he must in flight."

"Yet you can come here and fit in with our civilization quite comfortably. Perhaps I do envy you, James, after all."

"No." Como-tan shook his head. "Not you. You envy no man. I know that because you tried too hard to civilize me, Reverend. For you to want my life in the forest would be to deny your own—to deny the meaning you gave to yourself."

"Ah, you know me too well, James. But tell me, out of curiosity, is there *anything* at all that would change your mind? Anything that would bring you to this world to stay?"

He was silent, thinking. A vision of her floated before his mind; lovely, graceful creature, but with a skin different from his own. . . .

"Perhaps, Reverend. For some things a sacrifice would be a price worth paying. But only if there were no other way."

Thaddeus was interested. He leaned forward in his chair. "What things, James?"

He shook his head. "I can think of none at the moment. I was only speculating. But tell me, how does a white man separate himself from his mate? It's a subject we've never talked about."

Thaddeus frowned and shifted quickly in his chair. "Because it's an evil subject; that's why we never discussed it. It's a sin in the eyes of God. A man should never divorce himself from the woman he married in God's holy church."

A sudden suspicion crossed his face. "Why do you ask that?"

"But is it ever done?" Como-tan ignored the question to pose another of his own.

Thaddeus nodded reluctantly. "Yes. Tis a matter for the courts and the church frowns heavily upon it. But it is done, more's the pity."

He watched, and when Como-tan didn't reply, continued with even more suspicion in his voice, "You're not . . . *involved* with a white woman, are you, James? I would hope you would not consider coming between a man and his wife. T'would be a terrible thing. A terrible thing indeed."

Como-tan shook his head. "No. I would not come between a man and his mate as long as she wanted her man. But often among the Creek, two people come to know they are not good for each other and agree to go their separate ways. A woman having the right to make that decision as well as a man."

But Thaddeus was shaking his head violently, now very agitated at the conversation. "James, don't even consider such a thing! You must not . . . become involved with a *white* woman!"

A short feeling, the same as he had felt on the boat, crossed his spirit, but he brushed it aside. "A moment ago, Reverend, you were urging that I give up Indian ways and become a white man," he said quietly.

"No, no. You misunderstand me, James. I only meant that a white woman couldn't live as you do in the forest. If you came here . . ."

"I would still be a Creek," he said. "But suppose there was a white woman who loved the forest, would it not be better for the both of us if she lived there with me? Indians do not object to those of another race living among them."

The old man gave him a pleading look. "James, don't consider it. Please do not."

He smiled at him. "I was merely making conversation, Reverend. As of this moment, I know of no white woman who would care to live as an eagle."

The meeting with the trade negotiators appointed by the governor went far more slowly than he had hoped. There was a new man in charge, a young man, full of his own self importance and unwilling to concede that an Indian could converse on his level. He insisted on explaining everything in slow, carefully spoken syllables. It delayed the talks and took Comotan half of the three days he spent in the trade headquarters to convince the man. The fact that he could also read with ease seemed to irritate the other and he had the bad taste to inquire if there wasn't some white blood in his background. All in all, this session had required a great deal of patience. So much so that he was nearly rude himself to Thaddeus in his haste to leave Charles Town.

But he spent one last night in town, partly at the old man's insistence and partly because he wanted to buy a large amount of food staples to take back with him. Food that was more suited to the taste of whites than Creeks. His pack, when he left, contained white milled flour, dried beans, salted pork and even a small packet of sugar.

Once more in Savannah, he skirted the town itself and took the road west immediately. As soon as he could, he left the road and entered the woods, making a half circle to avoid the few huts occupied by whites enabled him to approach the one he wanted from the side nearest the forest.

By early afternoon he had reached it. Just through the edge of the trees he could see the small log cabin clearly. There was no sign of activity, not even a trace of smoke from the chimney.

This was the fourth time he'd approached the hut, counting his last stop on the journey to Charles Town he'd just completed. The first time had been a full year ago when he had seen the woman and paused to watch her. Between that time and now, he thought as he watched, a subtle but apparent change had come over what he now saw before him. Some things, things a woman could do, remained the same. But the labor of the man had fallen off. Como-tan could see signs of neglect. Winter had left damage that wasn't yet repaired and if it continued in that state the spring rains would increase that damage.

He watched long enough to make certain he wouldn't be seen, then, keeping at least one tree between himself and the hut, moved to the very edge of the forest and placed his burden on the ground. It was a spot he knew she would be certain to cross when she went again into the woods. He separated his own few possessions from the other then spread the food on the opened pack so that it could not be mistakened. Lastly, he crossed two evergreen limbs over the offering in the traditional Creek sign of friendship. When he was satisfied, Como-tan turned to leave . . .

And found himself looking directly into the large eyes of the woman.

He stiffened, afraid she was going to scream in fright. How had he missed her? He was a hunter, used to the forest. He had learned from the lynx how to stalk game. But somehow he had moved past this white woman in the forest without seeing her!

She stood as still as a startled deer, her brown eyes stretched wide. But her hands were not raised to her face in great fear, they pressed instead against the trunk of the tree that partly concealed her.

He must be careful. Move very slowly. Or he would frighten her and forever she would be lost.

Slowly, ever so slowly, as if he were truly facing a deer, Como-tan straightened, watching her for response. When he stood erect, he raised his right hand with the palm out. The other he kept free of his body so she could see he held no weapon.

The woman's eyes followed his movements with fascination.

"Please," he said, loudly enough so she could not fail to understand him, but still in soft words meant to soothe her. "Do not be frightened. I come in peace."

She didn't move her hands from the tree, but her eyes flicked beyond him. Como-tan thought first of her man and braced himself, then bent his head to look and realized it was only that he stood between herself and the safety she sought in her home.

"I wish you no harm," he said, spreading his hands wide. "Please do not be frightened. If you are afraid of me, I will leave. I promise you."

He turned back slowly and made a gesture with his right hand. "I will leave in that direction, not toward you. You will be able to watch me go."

It was a good choice of words. He watched some of the tension leave from her hands. The woman followed the direction in which he pointed with her eyes for a moment before bringing them back to his face. Finally, she dropped her hands and stepped a pace from behind the tree.

Her clothes were more worn than they had appeared from a distance. The long skirt was carefully mended in a number of places, but it was very clean. Como-tan thought of the good cloth of his own clothes left behind in Charles Town.

"Do you wish me to leave?" he asked.

"What do you want here?" Her voice was soft, pleasing to his ear. Just as he had imagined it would be.

"I want nothing," he said. "I came as a friend. Behind me I have left a gift for you and your family on the ground. Please take it in friendship."

His care with his voice as well as the fact that he hadn't moved more than absolutely necessary seemed somehow to reassure her. Her brown eyes were honest and therefore easily read. He watched them change to more curious than afraid.

"You've brought a gift? Why? I don't know you—are you a friend of my husband?"

He was still holding his hands away from his sides. He lowered them and relaxed himself. "No. I do not know your husband."

Her puzzlement grew. Como-tan was very glad she no longer seemed afraid.

"I don't understand," she said. "You said you came in friendship, but you didn't come to our house. If you leave a gift out here in the trees how are we supposed to know who gave it?"

"Does it matter who gives a gift?" he inquired. "Those who

receive have the pleasure of its use and the one who gives has the pleasure of giving. That is enough. Why should it matter that each is known to the other."

She shook her head quickly. "That isn't fair. You give no chance to the saying of thanks for your gift. Is that the way all Indians do?"

Como-tan smiled. "If I tell you my name will it make the gift the better?"

"It might make me accept it," she said.

"You would refuse? Only because you didn't first know the giver? But that would be—"

"Bad manners," she interrupted. And suddenly smiled herself. "Bad Indian manners I suppose, but no worse than what we would see in doing the giving in secret."

He enjoyed her smile. It made her even more beautiful. Suddenly he was glad he'd been caught. "You're right," he said. "I am wrong and you are right. My name is Como-tan and I am of the Creek nation."

She seemed fully relaxed now. "Then why is Como-tan bringing gifts to the Welburns?" she asked. "We don't know any Creeks either."

He was right, she'd lost all fear of him. That was good. He was afraid to move for fear of disturbing her new mood.

"Is it good manners to ask the why of the gift?" he wanted to know as she took a few unconscious steps in his direction. "I would not think so. For either Indian or white."

She paused and stretched to her tiptoes to see beyond him. "No it isn't. But I truly believe I'll burst from the wondering if you don't tell me. And tell me as well what it is."

He moved aside so that she could see. "It's no great gift. Only a little extra food. Some I didn't need. I was passing by here and thought you might use it so it wouldn't be wasted."

"Food?" She suddenly walked swiftly past him and stood looking down. When she turned, her smile was gone. She was angry. "Why do you think we need food?"

It had been a mistake. He knew it. The pride of the whites. An Indian would have happily accepted such a gift and then done the same for someone else if the occasion arose.

"I'm sorry," he said. "I didn't mean to offend you. It's just as I said, these things were extra to me and I didn't want them to be wasted. Your home was—"

He stopped, for she was shaking her head. "No," she said.

"You're an Indian. I don't know much about Indians, but I do know they don't eat salt pork. Nor, do I think, do they use flour that has been milled white. You got this in Savannah."

He shrugged. "Does it matter?"

"Yes." The brown eyes stared directly into his own. "You had an honest face and I was beginning to believe you before. I was frightened at first, but then I wanted to believe you. Now you're no longer honest with me."

"You are right," he said carefully. "I didn't speak the truth. This food comes not from Savannah as you think, but Charles Town. I bought it in one of their stores. Not for myself, but for you."

"Why?" The question was hard and direct.

"Because I had seen that your husband did not do well with his growing. Because I had watched you gather berries from these woods to have enough to eat."

"You *watched* me?" She was astonished. "Why would you do that?"

"Because you are the most beautiful woman I have ever seen," he said levelly. "You walk in grace and your fairness pleases my eyes greatly."

She colored. "You were spying on me!"

"No. Not spying. I stopped to watch you much as a man would stop to gaze at a waterfall that soothed his spirit. As he would pause to look upon the pleasing flowers."

The color in her cheeks deepened. "I'm not like that."

Como-tan nodded. "And now you are not being honest. You're too wise not to know of your own beauty. Has it not ever been said to you before? Have you not seen your own reflection?"

"Yes." She spoke slowly, reluctantly. "I've been told I was pretty, but . . . not in the way you just said."

"You asked me to be honest, and I spoke the truth as I see it. You are beautiful. In your face, and in the way you feel for the forest. I stopped to watch you and I learned you needed what I have brought. I'm sorry I made you angry."

She took a deep breath and her eyes fell. "It's the truth that we are hungry and I've no right to be angry." The eyes came up again. "Thank you for your gift, Como-tan."

He smiled, as gently as he could. "I had to give my name for you to accept my gift, now I think you should give me yours."

Her smile came back, but it was a timid smile and he knew she was still unsure of him. "My name is Elizabeth. Elizabeth Welburn. My husband's name is Jason."

"And your small son?"

A mother's pride, quick in response. "His name is John."

He nodded. "A fine son."

They stood. There was no more to be said. The gift was hers and they knew the names of each other. He should go.

He had no choice. "Goodbye, Elizabeth Welburn. Perhaps I can come again?"

"Yes, but—"

He waited.

"I only thought . . . if you wanted to be friends with us. . . . Will you come and eat? Now?"

"Your husband will not mind?"

"No, he's—" She stopped suddenly. "He's not here."

"Then I will come another time." He nodded to her. "Thank you."

She continued to look at him in embarrassment over her mistake in forgetting her husband was away and Como-tan sought to relieve her by leaving. But she allowed him only a few paces. "Wait!"

He paused again and looked at her inquiringly.

"My husband will return in a few hours. He promised me so. It will be all right if you want to come and visit. I'd like for you to come."

"Then I will be happy to do so," he said.

He walked back and gathered up the food he had laid out only a few minutes before and waited for her. Elizabeth walked beside him toward the cabin.

"I've not known many Indians," she said as they walked. "You speak English so well. Do most?"

He glanced aside at her. "No. Very few. I was taught your language in Charles Town where I lived as a boy."

"You lived in a town?" Her look told him she was having even more trouble in understanding him.

"Not from choice, Elizabeth Welburn. It's the truth that I much preferred the forest where my people live. But I was sent to learn your language so that when I became a man I would be useful to the Creeks. It's not as strange as it sounds."

She was watching him so intently she nearly stumbled. He wanted to take her arm as he'd seen them do in Charles Town, but decided against it.

"I go to Charles Town, and sometimes Savannah, to talk of trade and other things with them for the benefit of my people. But most of the time I live back there." He indicated with a wave behind them. "And that is much more to my liking."

They were approaching the hut and she put a hand on his arm to turn him toward the front, then dropped it. Its presence remained bright to his skin after she removed it.

"I don't blame you," she said. "I love the forest." She paused and faced him, causing him to stop as well. "Tell me," she said earnestly. "What's beyond the forest? What's on the other side? I've always wondered."

Her eyes were a pleasure to look into, they were wide and deep, like softly shadowed pools. "Beyond?" he said, forcing his mind to think on her question. "There are more forests. Rivers. And open land at times where you can see for more than you can walk in a day."

"Mountains? Are there mountains?"

Como-tan nodded, puzzled now himself. "There are mountains. I've seen them myself."

She sighed. "Oh I would love to see a mountain. I've never seen one."

Then she laughed suddenly. "And there aren't any beasts a hundred feet tall, are there?"

He laughed with her. "No. Did you think so?"

She shook her head, still smiling. "Once someone told me that, but I really didn't believe it. He also said there were—" She stopped.

He nodded. "He told you there were Indians who ate their children. I heard that often enough when I lived in Charles Town. Most of the time it was from those who had just arrived. But that is untrue as well. It comes, I think, from white men first hearing about the practice of *huskanaw*. It was a way some tribes treated their children to teach them to take care of themselves. It was sometimes cruel, but they did not *wish* them harm, only that they grow to be strong."

She cocked her head. "You know so much. You know about both the whites in places I've not been and about Indians, too. I'm glad you're coming to eat with me. I have a lot of questions. Do you mind?"

At the moment, there was nothing he would mind less. He hoped her husband was late in returning. "I'll tell you anything

I can," he said. "Would you like me to start with the mountains?"

"Oh yes! But come first and meet my son. I want him to listen, too."

This time he did take her arm, catching it just above the elbow. "Aren't you afraid he'll be frightened of an Indian?"

She turned her head again, the little tilt that he liked. "No . . . I don't think so. He's never seen an Indian that I know of. We have lived here most of the time since he was born."

Her look became apologetic. "We don't meet many at all, I'm afraid. I don't go into Savannah very much and . . ."

Her voice trailed off, leaving him to wonder. But they were at her door and he followed her inside. Only after they had entered did he remember the poorness of her dress and realize why she did not go to Savannah.

Twenty-Four

THERE WERE TIMES, Elizabeth decided, pausing to gaze at her home, that she truly felt she'd come full circle and had returned to living as she'd lived the first years of her life with Lyman Briggs. This hut was built of logs and clay, that one had been sticks and mud, but they were the same—small and mean—and rotting away, along with her life. She looked at the corner of the square building that had sagged nearly half a foot and felt herself wanting to cry. Then clamped her teeth together. They had been so proud of this home, Jason and she, when it was first built. Now it was aging and she could not keep up with the repairs it needed. And Jason no longer cared.

She was weaving a basket, using thin strips of bark from a birch tree she had cut down herself, and sitting outside to take advantage of the spring sunshine. As well as, she admitted to herself, to get out of the cabin and the man who now wanted to do little but lie about inside. That, and make his way into Savannah to drink.

The bark strips had soaked for three days to become pliable. Now they bent easily in the direction she formed them as she wove a rounded basket. It would serve many a purpose when she finished it, as had the large one she'd made before this. Jason had thrown that one in the fire in a fit of temper and a second one, given to her, had fared no better when he staggered home and fell full across it on one of his early morning returns from Savannah.

Como-tan had shown her how to make the baskets. Elizabeth smiled as she thought about it. In the year now that she had known him, the tall Creek had taught her many things. She'd first believed he knew all of them himself and marveled at his knowledge, until she learned by accident that for some, like the art of basket weaving, he'd sought advice from the women of his village before telling her. Como-tan had given himself away quite unintentionally in one of their conversations and became embarrassed when she teased him about his pretense. Indians, she discovered, have their great pride, too.

Her smile lasted but a moment. Como-tan had become more than a friend since that day they first met. He'd become . . . a provider. If it hadn't been for him, for what he brought her both in food from town and game he'd killed himself in the forest, they well might have starved in the winter. She was ashamed to have accepted so much from him.

It shouldn't have been necessary, she told herself crossly. This last season wasn't as dry as the others before it had been. But Jason's crop had failed once more—as much from his neglect as any other cause. He just didn't seem to care!

She snatched at a piece of bark, it slipped through her fingers, and the rough edge left a trace of blood. Fie!

But she was right. Jason could have made at least a portion of that crop had he only attended it closely. She'd done far more of the hoeing and thinning herself than he had. It seemed that after he'd been forced to accept the loan of seed from his old master, Jason Welburn had felt nothing but anger. He had taken no joy in watching the beginning corn grow. And when the critical times had come, when she herself lay awake worrying for the rain, he'd gone off to Savannah each night and staggered home drunk!

Fie indeed! She'd wanted to fetch a stick to his back at those times. What with him feeling so sorry for himself he couldn't work properly. Even Lyman Briggs had done his labor in the fields! Jason Welburn certainly wasn't the first to fall on hard times in this colony!

The anger faded as quickly as it came. Poor Jason. She was

truly being too hard on him. A man has his pride and Jason's had been beaten to earth when he was forced to go to Samuel Longfootte for seed. If only this year they could—but what about seed this time?

Perhaps Como-tan could advise her. He knew so much, both of matters in Savannah and of his own Indian ways. He might be able to suggest a means of gaining seed that Jason had not yet considered.

There she went again! It was becoming so easy to depend on the Creek. But he was so quietly certain of himself His assurance was so . . . so assuring.

She finished the row and fastened the end smoothly. Then noticed her finger was still bleeding and sucked it in her mouth.

If only Jason liked Como-tan as much as she did. He could be of such help. But the one time the Creek had come to visit when Jason was at home, her husband had been barely civil. Como-tan never seemed to arrive again except when Jason was away and she wondered how many times he'd passed the cabin in his travels and refused to stop when he saw her husband.

Her son, on the other hand, adored him. Almost from the day they had met, John and Como-tan became friends. The Creek had given him a breechcloth made of doeskin, moccasins that fit his little legs and feet and a grass woven shirt that was John's great joy. He would wear little else. She had, she realized, a little Indian on her hands. Much more so than she was willing to admit, for John wanted already to learn to hunt and Elizabeth knew Como-tan waited only her approval to begin to teach him.

But Jason was her husband and John was *his* son. She had watched with even greater worry the splitting between the two of them. Jason now ignored his son for the most part, and John in turn had begun to save his childish interests and triumphs for either herself or for Como-tan.

She had paused to reflect on the problem when the little Indian himself suddenly gave a loud whoop behind her and startled Elizabeth half from her stool.

"John!"

He squatted on the ground before her and laughed with glee. "I caught you, mama! I creeped up and you didn't see me. Just like a lynx would do!"

"You creeped like a little snake, you mean," she grumbled, gathering her strips back to her lap. "Or better, like an Indian.

I should take one of these strips to your backside, and I would this minute except I don't want it broken."

His merry little face beneath the wild brown hair regarded her without the slightest belief that she would do as she threatened, and Elizabeth struggled to hold a serious countenance herself. "Don't you ever do that again!"

"Yes, mama." But his attention was diverted to an itch on one leg. After it had been fully and vigorously scratched, he turned back to her once more. "When will Como-tan come again?"

Elizabeth began her weaving. "I don't know, John. He didn't say. Perhaps in a few days; it's been a long while since he was here last."

"He promised me a whip."

"A what?" She cast a quick eye at him.

"A whip. Como-tan said he'd make it from the skin of a snake. I can make a noise with it." His face became thoughtful. "I don't know how, but that's what Como-tan said I could do."

"And you believe anything Como-tan says, don't you?" She smiled down at him.

"Como-tan says a man does not have to lie," he recited. "I'm never going to lie when I'm a man."

"I should hope not. But you know, John, you really shouldn't—" She stopped. How could she explain it to him? "Is your father still inside?" she asked instead.

The earnest look on his young face immediately disappeared and it became blank. It was that look that worried her the most. Her son was drifting away from his father in his own way as much as Jason was leaving his family behind. She had to stop it before it became too late for all of them.

John looked at the ground.

"Well? Is he?"

"He went to the fields, I think," the boy said at last. "He was sick while you were gone."

Jason was often that in the morning. It was the cheap rum he got in Savannah. How did he get it? They had no money, no way for him to buy it. Yet somehow he managed it. If he would only put that effort into his land . . .

Perhaps he would! If he'd gone into the fields like John said, it would be the first time since before winter. And it was spring again! Jason might be—

She stood up quickly. "Which way did he go?"

Her son pointed and Elizabeth was even more encouraged. It wasn't his best field but the worst. Jason had said in the early days he'd have to build up that part of the land slowly. That without it he'd not succeed as he wanted. Perhaps he was thinking in that manner again!

"Did he take his axe?" She shadowed her eyes with one hand to look.

"I don't know." John got to his feet himself. "I'm going to the woods."

Elizabeth nodded absently. "Don't go far."

But he was already scampering away, and she turned to walk rapidly toward the field.

She found her husband easily. This field had been a pine barren when they first came here and Jason had felled the stunted trees and cleared most of the brush away. But he'd not come back to haul away all of the downed trunks. He was crouched beside one as she walked up.

"What are you doing?" she inquired to his stooped back.

Jason spun. "What're you doing out here?"

His eyes, as usual, were red-streaked. He'd not shaved in several days, nor would he allow her of late to cut his hair.

"I came to help," Elizabeth said. "John told me you were out working in this field and I thought I might help."

She looked around, avoiding his hard stare. There was no axe nor saw, only a rough stick cage at his feet. "What is that?"

"It's a trap," he said shortly. "I've no money for musket balls, I've got to trap what we eat."

Elizabeth looked at him in puzzlement. He'd not brought a single piece of game, large or small, into the house in months, what in the world—suddenly she knew where he was getting the coin for his drink. It made her angry.

"I see you aren't working," she said shortly. "Do you ever intend to again? It's almost time for planting, you know."

Jason shrugged and looked away. "So what's the use?"

"The use is, Jason, that you have a family. You've a son to raise."

"He's doing all right. Better than I did at his age, I'll warrant. I began to work when I was no more than him."

She forced her temper down; it would serve no good to make him as angry as she herself felt. "John would do whatever you ask him to do," she said, more shortly than she intended.

"But there's precious little to do these days. Why don't you show him how to plant?"

He turned back to glare at her. "Because I've no intention of breaking my back again on a crop that's doomed to fail," he snapped. "I've had my fill of that!"

It was as much as she'd feared. Without even the planting there was no hope at all. "Jason, you've got to plant again. This time we'll—"

"No, damn it! It's ended, Elizabeth! Don't you see that?"

"Then what are we to do?" she asked with a calmness she didn't feel. "Are we to sit here and starve?"

His eyes were still hard upon her, and Elizabeth wondered if he cared at all for her now. He looked as if he hated her—but it was only his hating himself. She knew that.

"I'll tell you what we'll be about," Jason said harshly. "It's what I should have done two years ago when I had the offer, instead of thinking I could do for myself."

He waited, and Elizabeth searched her memory. "What offer?"

"Don't tell me you've forgotten, woman," he sneered. "You dragged about long enough with a pulling face after I refused your brother that time."

Her brother! Tom had made him an offer to come to work for him. Oh no! Not now! Jason couldn't be serious!

He watched the look of alarm on her face in triumph. "Aye, dear wife, that's exactly what I intend. The both of us know he didn't want me for what I could do, he merely wanted his precious sister close. Well I'll tell you: he can have his sister close to him, close enough to pat her dainty hand the whole damn day if he wants."

His mouth tightened. "The two of you and your *noble blood* you're so damnably proud of. Well you can have that cup of tea! But your royal brother will pay me well for the privilege."

"No! I'll not have it, Jason. We won't go to Tom and—"

"*You'll* not have it? Damn you, I'm still master of my hearth! I'll make the decisions as to where we go!"

"Jason, please!"

"It's what you want, isn't it? It's what you wanted all the time. You thought all along your brother was successful because he had better blood, didn't you? That your stupid husband was a peasant who didn't know his backside from the red dirt he stumbled about in trying to raise the corn? Well, you'll get your wish, Elizabeth Welburn—or Langlee as you might better want—but I'll gather the spoils along with you. Your brother can damn well provide for the both of us."

"Provide the bottle for you," she said with both rage and fear edging her voice. "If you do this, Jason, you'll prove yourself not a man to me. I'll have no part of it."

"You'll do what I say." He raised a fist and shook it at her.

Elizabeth backed a step away. "No. It will not be. And you can't make it so, for my brother will take you only if I come. You're right about that at least. He made the offer because of me but at that time you were a man, Jason Welburn, and turned him down. If I don't go with you you'll get no job. And I won't go."

He stepped threateningly toward her, but she shook her head doggedly. "If you beat me to make me go, he'll kill you. So what are you to do?"

"Damn you, Elizabeth!"

She was cold all over, as if it were winter again. He was her husband—but what had happened to the love between them?

"You've only this farm, Jason," she said slowly. "Only the farm and a wife who still cares for you. Who's willing to work it beside you if you'll try again."

Elizabeth paused and made her last play. "If we fail then we will starve. Or . . . we will become indentured again."

Jason stared at her, but his fist slowly dropped.

"Give it your thoughts," she said, turning to leave him, but looking over her shoulder. "But give it thought without the rum to aid you in thinking, Jason." Then she walked away.

He was long in the field alone, long enough she began to hope. But the sun had hardly broken its height of noon and started its descent before he came to the hut, gathered his coat without speaking to her and walked away down the road to Savannah. Elizabeth watched him go and it was only after he was well out of sight and wouldn't know, that she allowed herself to cry with the hurt of it.

The afternoon seemed to take forever to wear itself away and the evening, the time between the sun disappearing beneath the trees and full night, almost as long. She was relieved when it became dark. Jason wouldn't be home, Elizabeth was sure of it, and not unhappy that she would be alone. Somehow she didn't want to lie beside him this particular night. Didn't want to lie and share the heavy silence of the cabin. To smell the stink of rum. Tomorrow, or the day after, Jason would come home and after he'd spent his time to recover from the drinking she would talk to him again. What words it might take for her to convince him he couldn't give up she didn't know. But she would have to try. She would have to try again and again. Tonight, however, she didn't want to face it.

In the middle of her cabin she paused and took a deep breath, lifting her shoulders and then dropping them again in an explosive sigh. That was tomorrow, or the day after, depending on when he came home. Tonight she would prepare a good meal for herself and John. Then the two of them would sit before the fire and talk.

Elizabeth glanced toward the corner of the cabin where he sat on the floor playing with some chips of wood he'd gathered from around the chopping stump. He was her joy. The one pure pleasure she retained. "Are you hungry?" she asked.

John looked up and grinned. "Yes, mama."

"Humph," she said. "A foolish question that. You're always hungry. Well I tell you what, young sir, tonight I have the intention of filling you up. I'll stretch that small belly of yours until it pops. What do you think of that?"

His grin widened. "Good!"

She laughed and turned to the hearth. She would make a thick soup with plenty of potatoes in it, and she'd make enough to feed a room full of boys. For once in her life, she wouldn't be sparing.

She went busily about her task. Being busy helped her not to think, and the time passed quickly. Almost before she knew it, the soup was ready. She placed two wooden bowls on the table, fetched her good metal spoons instead of the everyday wooden ones Jason had carved that had begun to splinter from use, and was about to call him to eat when a knock at the door startled her.

John looked up, first to the door and then to her.

Elizabeth was frightened, but hid it from him. No one ever came here even in the day—a knock at night could only brood ill. Nevertheless, it was there and she would have to answer.

Still she hesitated. But then, staring at the door, she could see the latch string was left out. Whoever was there could enter as they pleased anyway. She braced herself and crossed to lift the bar and open the door.

"Como-tan!"

She was never so happy to see anyone in her life!

"Good eve, Elizabeth," he said. But got no further than that as a small bundle of energy shot past her and hurtled into him. Como-tan grunted with the blow.

"Did you bring it? Did you bring my whip?" John had the tall Creek's fringed buckskin breeches firmly grasped in both small fists and was swinging from side to side.

Como-tan bent to pick him up and sat him on one arm. He looked at Elizabeth. "Could I enter?"

She had a brief urge to hug him herself she was so glad to see that it was him. "Of course, come in." She stepped back and held the door open. "You startled me."

He entered and turned as she closed the door behind him and replaced the bar. "I'm sorry, Elizabeth. I know it's late."

"It's no matter," she said. "We're happy to see you at any time."

"Where's my whip?" John demanded from his position on Como-tan's arm.

"John! Your manners!"

Como-tan crossed to sit down in a chair and held her son on one knee. "I don't have it, little John," he said gravely. "That is, I don't have it with me now. I've made it, but left it in my village. I didn't know I would come by here or I would have brought it with me."

John's face fell. "You promised."

Como-tan nodded. "Yes I have promised. And it was not my intention to break my promise. I'll leave here tonight and go to my village, then return immediately with your whip."

"Goodness no," Elizabeth cut in. "You don't have to do that. It would take days!"

He shook his head. "A promise must be kept. Is that not right, John?"

"A promise must be kept," John said.

"Como-tan—"

He held up a hand to forestall her. "It is decided."

Elizabeth shook her head. "You and your Indian ways. What brings you by here this late?"

"I had business in Savannah that came up very quickly. A

man from there wounded a Creek in a disagreement and I was asked to speak for the man who was hurt."

~ "My goodness. He shot him?"

Como-tan nodded. "The man will be tried. I'll have to return again then—as soon as the wounded man is well enough to come to Savannah."

"You're very important in such matters, aren't you," she said.

He shrugged. "Keeping the peace between us is important. I do what I can."

He glanced at the simmering pot hanging from a hook in her hearth. "You were about to eat?"

"Yes. You'll eat with us? There's plenty."

"Thank you."

Elizabeth got another bowl from the shelf, and since she had only the two metal spoons, a wooden one for herself. Then she served the soup.

Como-tan ate slowly, but with enjoyment, complimenting her on the soup and asking for a second bowl. John, as she expected, ate like a starving puppy. It was an enjoyable meal.

She left the two of them to talk as she covered the pot and set it aside for the morrow, then went outside to wash the bowls and spoons. By the time she'd finished, Elizabeth could see the lateness of the hour and a full belly was having its effect on her young son. His eyelids drooped.

Despite his protests she ordered him to bed and Como-tan carried him up the ladder to their sleeping loft. A few minutes later he rejoined her before the fire.

The few minutes had given her time to think. "Como-tan, why did you come tonight?" she asked as he pulled a stool close.

His dark eyes turned into hers and held steady. "I have explained that," he said.

They were magnetic eyes. She suddenly knew why they fascinated her so—it wasn't just that they were black and deep, unlike any white man's eyes—it was that looking into them gave her the same feeling she got from walking alone in the forest. Elizabeth forced herself back to her senses.

"This morning, John and I were talking about you," she said. "He said you told him a man must never lie."

The dark eyes continued to draw her against her will. He

nodded slowly. "And now you believe I lie?"

"I don't know. I'm certain the part about being in Savannah because of the shooting is right. But I don't believe you're telling me all the truth as to why you came here tonight. You never come at night. You never come when Jason is here either."

Again the slow nod without releasing her eyes. "You're able to look inside others, Elizabeth," he said. "To know them perhaps better than they know themselves. No one can hide from you, I think."

"What are you hiding?" She was very conscious that she was alone with a man other than her husband. Not just a man, but an Indian. Despite his ability to speak so well and his long experience with whites, most would still consider him a savage. It was a strange feeling.

"I was hiding the truth that I saw your husband in Savannah," he said after a moment. "I saw him and I knew he was drinking a great deal."

He paused again, a very long time for her. "I knew he would not come home tonight, Elizabeth."

The feeling grew. Not fear—or was it? She'd never felt this way before when she'd been alone with him. But those times had been outside in the light of day. Not close, in the smallness of a cabin, with only the light of the fire between the two of them...

The glow of the flames increased the copper sheen to his face. His cheekbones, high already, gave shadow to his long jaw and his black hair, lying loosely about his neck, glistened like a raven's wings. "I see," she said, much quieter than she felt.

Como-tan turned his palms up. "If you are afraid, Elizabeth, I will leave. I've no wish to make you even more unhappy."

"No." She looked away from him into the fire. "There's no need for you to go."

There was a long silence between them, a dark, heavy silence that seemed to press down upon her. The fire became uncomfortable until Elizabeth realized it wasn't the fire at all, the heat was inside herself.

"Why do you think I'm unhappy?" she managed at last.

"Now it's you who hides the truth," Como-tan said gently. "I have known from the beginning."

"He's my husband," she said. "Jason is doing his best."

"Your good heart makes you lie even to yourself, Elizabeth. He is not a man. A man does not leave his wife and son to drink in the town. To drink with strangers to him."

She shook her head, wanting to cry. "You mustn't say that," she said. "Not to me."

"There is the truth between us, Elizabeth," he said. "He is your mate, but he is not a good man. He dreams, as all men dream, but he cannot succeed in his dream because he is afraid inside himself. He does not believe in himself as a strong man must."

"Don't . . . please," she whispered.

"It's the foolish rules you force on yourself," he continued in the same soft voice. "An Indian woman would be free to put an end to it. To go away and live a better life."

"Please stop . . ." She knew she was going to cry and clenched her fists to prevent it.

"I will say no more about it," Como-tan said. "It is not for me to speak for you. Only you can decide for yourself."

The tips of her eyelids began to burn. She was going to cry in spite of herself.

"I won't speak for you, Elizabeth," he continued after a moment. "But I will speak once for myself. Look at me."

She shook her head and clenched her fists tighter.

"Look at me, Elizabeth."

Slowly she turned and met his eyes.

"I have a great love for you," he said from beneath the black, pulling eyes. "I have wanted you for myself since the day I first saw you walking alone in the forest. You are the beautiful dream with which I spend my nights. Someday, you will come to me. I know this."

The desire to cry left her as Elizabeth looked at him in growing astonishment. Why hadn't she known? Or did she just not admit it to herself? He was in love with her and that was why he came here; why he brought them food. The answer was really so simple it should have been easy for her to see from the beginning. She had wanted a friend and . . .

Como-tan regarded her silently and his direct look forced her eyes away from his, to drop instead to his arms with the smooth, strong muscles apparent under a copper skin. Arms that were bare because he had removed his buckskin shirt, leaving only a vest.

His bareness reminded her that he was considered a savage.

Jason would consider him a savage. Suppose those who thought so were right? What prevented this silent Indian from doing what might seem the more natural to him—that is, seizing her now?

A gradual tingling began in her limbs and quickly expanded throughout her body. It was a strange tingling—a singing fear. Fear that he might take her into those powerful arms against her will. Singing . . . because she was suddenly not certain at all that it would be against her *want*.

"That can never be," she whispered hoarsely. "I have a husband. You must not speak of such."

"There will come a time, Elizabeth," he said. "I will wait."

He got up then, causing her singing fear to heighten. But Como-tan reached for his shirt from the peg. "I will go now," he said. "But I will come again in four days to bring the whip to John."

He crossed to the door and put his hand on the bar, then turned to regard her. "I will come often, Elizabeth, while I am waiting. If you decide at any time—"

"I won't," she said quickly. "I can't."

Como-tan nodded. "I believe it is meant to be. I will wait whatever time it takes. Goodnight, Elizabeth."

He went out and closed the door before she could answer.

Twenty-Five

THE LATE JULY sun was growing hot overhead although it was barely halfway into the morning. Elizabeth paused to wipe perspiration from her head and glanced at Como-tan. The Creek was stripped to the waist and his back muscles stood out with the strain he was placing into lifting the whole corner of her cabin with a long pole. Little John stood beside him with a shorter timber, ready to brace the cabin when Como-tan told him.

The Indian's muscles were smooth and long, and didn't knot as a white man's would. She also marveled at the complete lack of hair about his upper body. Were all Indians that way?

The object of her study grunted loudly and gave a short bob of his head to John, who immediately shoved the fat pole he held into place. Como-tan eased off his, a measure at a time, and the cabin stayed in place. He kept both hands on his lever and turned to her. "Get another brace."

He'd cut three prior to starting the repair and had laid them close. Elizabeth retrieved the second, looked to him for instruction and placed where he pointed with a nod of his head.

"No," he said. "Over a little. There. That's right."

He leaned across his lever to see. "Good. Now back away and I'll move this. Then we'll see if your cabin falls down."

He grinned at John who immediately grinned back.

Elizabeth stepped away and he joined her in a moment, dropping the long pole to the ground. The cabin stayed in place, just as she knew it would.

"Well," he said, "what do you think?"

"I think it did just what you said it would. You're always right. But I would have never thought of lifting the whole corner of the cabin."

"With enough men and long poles, you can lift a whole house," he said. Then smiled at her. "I'm not the first to think of such."

Elizabeth laughed. She was comfortable in his presence again, and happy to be so. After the night he had told her he loved her, Como-tan had never mentioned it again. It was as if it hadn't happened. Nevertheless, it had taken several visits before she could relax and feel the same as she had before. He came often now, but he came only when Jason was away and neither of them mentioned the fact. She wondered how close an eye he kept on the cabin to know when her husband was away. And wondered, too, if he were living somewhere close by in the woods.

"Well, what do we do now?" she asked.

"Put in the other brace with some big rocks behind each, then we'll place more under the floor logs and pile dirt around them. By the time the braces rot, the rocks and dirt will have settled into hardness."

"All right," she said. "Let's do it. Then at least I can get my clay to stick between the logs. I've grown tired of replacing it only to have it fall out again. At least I won't have to shiver next winter."

His face clouded. "It is not a good house—" He stopped and shrugged. "John and I will gather the rocks."

He walked away with his hand on John's shoulder and Elizabeth turned back to look at her home. Como-tan was right. Although the corner that had sagged so badly was now in line with the rest, she could see the hut was deteriorating. The base logs were still good, they were thick enough to last for years longer if the wood eating insects didn't get into them too badly. But the upper logs, made of smaller timbers and exposed more to the wind and rain, were rotting enough to leave shards about on the ground. Another winter and she and Jason would have to begin to think of building a new cabin.

She smiled a bitter smile, drawing down the corners of her mouth. A great chance she had of getting him to build a new cabin when he would not even plant the crop they needed to make any success at all. If she had not done it herself, they would not even have a garden of vegetables to feed them next winter.

Como-tan would not allow them to starve, she knew that. But how long could she depend on him for charity? How long before he grew tired of waiting—waiting for what? Only once in her life had she ever heard of a woman leaving her husband. In Savannah a woman had left with another man and gone into South Carolina to live. It was talked about for months among the women in Savannah and she was roundly condemned as her husband went to the Magistrates and received permission to place a notice of divorce in the paper and immediately found a new wife among the widows. A woman's place was considered to be beside her husband, no matter what their life. The Church insisted on that point.

No, she couldn't even consider that. Then how long would Como-tan wait before he tired and left for good?

He and John had not gone far, they didn't have to, there was a wash not too distant where deep rocks were available. Como-tan carried three large ones and John two smaller, much smaller. She smiled at her son.

The Creek placed them all where he wanted and started back for more. Elizabeth went to the shedhouse for a shovel but on the way back decided to detour by the food cellar for a jug of water. She kept a fresh jug there to stay cool.

When they came back, she motioned. "Let's take a rest. Wouldn't you like some water?"

She led the way to a pair of oak trees in front of the cabin and sat down on the ground. When they joined her, she poured the water and passed a gourd cup around.

"Como-tan, where do Indians come from?" John asked suddenly.

The Creek leaned his back against a tree and looked at him. "Do you mean where did they begin?" he asked.

The boy nodded. "Mama told me we came from England— that's some place on the other side of the ocean—but I don't think Indians come from there, too."

"I didn't say that all came from England," she corrected him. "I said that your uncle Thomas and I did. Some people came from other countries. They don't even speak the same language that we do."

John nodded as if he understood but Elizabeth knew he didn't. She wished she understood more about the world herself so she could teach him. She listened carefully as Como-tan recited magically the legends of his people.

Elizabeth leaned against a tree trying to pay attention, but her mind soon stopped following the Creek's words as he talked. Instead, she watched him. He was a strange man, unlike any she had ever known. He was an Indian—he reminded her of the chief, Tomochichi, who came to Cawley's house in the way he walked, and he was more than at home in the forest. But he knew so much about the white men as well. If he didn't have skin the color of copper, and dressed himself in English clothes instead of buckskin, he would be at home in the best of places. He could speak as well as any she'd ever heard, even Mr. Stephens. And he could read books—her brother had said that was the most important thing a man could learn.

She watched his hands with their strong fingers as he made imaginary things out of the air for her son. Those hands were powerful. He would have to be a fighter to have lived as he had, she knew that without asking. But he was also gentle.

Who had she known that she could compare him to? Her brother? No. Tom was strong and brave. And he was gentle, at least with her. But Tom had a temper and he sometimes grew very excited. Como-tan was always calm.

She allowed her mind to play freely over all the men she had known in Savannah. None could compare to him. Before that she had hardly known anyone, so there was no comparison in England. She gave it up suddenly and listened again.

"I'd like to be an Indian," John said.

"When you are a man you can live the way you choose," Como-tan told him. "But there will be many ways for you to choose from. If you choose the way I live, I would be pleased."

"You have everything, don't you?"

Como-tan smiled. "No. Not everything. The thing I want most I can't have."

"Why not?" John asked. "Why can't you get it?"

"Because it belongs to someone else and it would be wrong

to take what belongs to another man even though he no longer wants it."

Elizabeth felt the color rise to her cheeks and looked away.

"If he doesn't want it, why would it be wrong to take it?" John persisted. "I don't see what difference it would make."

"Because if I took it away from him, then it wouldn't belong to me," she heard Como-tan say. "So I must wait."

"I don't understand," John said loudly.

Como-tan laughed. "When you become a man, young John, you will understand. Now I think it is time we went back to work."

He stood up and Elizabeth moved to place a cob in her jug and rise too when she saw him stiffen. He was looking above her head toward the road.

She turned and saw a man in the distance, walking unsteadily in one of the twin wagon paths. Jason . . .

"I was wrong about the work," Como-tan said to her son. "I remember it is time for me to leave. Will you dig the dirt for me?"

"Sure," John said. "I can do it."

"Then goodbye, John. I'll see you soon." He turned to Elizabeth. "Goodbye."

She nodded. "Goodbye, Como-tan."

He went quickly, walking swiftly across the short field between the hut and the forest. In minutes he had disappeared inside the trees.

Elizabeth looked back to the road and could see that Jason was having difficulty in walking. "If you want to go and play before you finish that, John, go ahead," she said. "I see your father coming."

John looked up quickly. "I can dig the dirt later," he said. Moments later she was alone and started walking toward her husband.

The ground was uneven under her feet and she bent her ankles sharply more than once before she reached him because she held her gaze on Jason rather than where she walked. The man she was approaching was her husband; only a few years ago the person she loved more than anything else in the world. What had happened to them? Those early days, the times she had slipped away from the Cawley's house and met him in the square, had been both terrifying and the best moments of her life. Jason Welburn had loved her and he had been the man who made for her the dream of the future, of the time when they would be free. But now the two of them were more a prisoner than they'd ever been before . . .

What had happened to his dreams—and to her own? Comotan said Jason only dreamed, that he was unable to make his dreams real. Why? What made the difference?

He saw her now and made an attempt to wave, but the effort made him stumble and nearly fall. Elizabeth closed her mind against the feeling his action caused in her.

Jason had loved her once, and once his love made her feel whole. But it had been months since he'd touched her in love. Months since she had known more than the dead feeling of his body as he lay beside her either in drunkenness or cold indifference to her need to be held.

He didn't love her; he no longer wanted her. In a few more steps she would be beside him.

Como-tan wanted her. She must push that thought aside. She had no right to think of that . . .

But the image persisted. *He* would take her in his arms and hold her the minute she went to him. He would—*Oh please! Put such thoughts from my mind!*

"Elizabeth." Jason's voice was slurred, as if he spoke with his mouth full of pebbles. "I've come home to . . . I've decided to . . ."

He could get no further. He stumbled and nearly fell into her and Elizabeth caught him, bracing herself in time.

"It's all right," she told him. "Come in the house and I'll fix you something to eat."

He shook his head and pushed away from her. "No, no. I'm all right. I've got to get to the fields. Lots of work to do . . ."

Elizabeth took his arm and put her own around his waist. "You need to lie down for a while, Jason. Then we'll talk."

The stink of him was enough to make her stomach turn. He smelled as if he'd fallen into the hole under a privy. That and the odor of rum. "This way," she said patiently.

It took great strength as well as patience to get him into the cabin. Jason was so unsteady she wondered how he had made it home at all. He must not have slept in the two days he was gone—or he'd slept passed out along the road.

When she had him inside the cabin, she sat him down on

a stool and removed his coat, then took off his shirt and bathed his face, neck and shoulders. She would have to wash all his clothes, she'd not be able to stand him otherwise.

Jason sat, weaving about on the stool, his red-rimmed eyes following her every move. "You're good...Elizabeth." He spoke with great effort. "You're..."

She'd not be able to get him up the ladder to the sleeping loft, he'd have to lie on the floor. She only hoped he wouldn't be sick.

Jason's hands came up and caught her around the waist. He buried his head against her breasts. "I'm sorry, Elizabeth....So sorry..."

She tried to pull away but he held her tightly, desperately. "Elizabeth...I've not done for you as I should..."

She strained away from him and closed her eyes as she lifted her head. "Jason, it's not the time for this."

"Aye..." His voice was muffled against her stomach now, his head pressing close under her breasts. "I must tell you, Elizabeth...I'm so sorry. But it will be different...I promise you..."

"Jason—"

"No, no! He shook his head violently, bruising her with his straining against her. "I know it now, Elizabeth!"

He pulled his head back and looked up at her, and the tears were streaming down his face. "I've made a new decision. No more drinking! I promise!"

Elizabeth reached to hold his head in her two hands. "You need to rest now, Jason."

"No! Not until you say you believe me! I'll quit. I promise! I'll work...no matter what they say, I can do it! It's just that..." He pulled her close again, forcing her close. "It's so hard, Elizabeth...so damned hard..."

"Jason, stop."

"Elizabeth, please..." Suddenly his sobs began to wrack his body until she was afraid he would shake from the stool.

"Stop it, Jason," she said.

"Elizabeth, please..."

Then she could no longer resist and pulled his poor head close to her body again, bent over him and held him tight. "Jason, it's all right. It's all right, darling. Don't be frightened. You can do it, I know you can. I believe you can, darling."

"Elizabeth!" he wailed.

"Shush now. Don't be frightened. It's all right. We're together. We'll be together."

He tried to get to his feet and Elizabeth had to force him
back down. "I'll plant late," he slurred. "Fall corn...It'll
work...We'll have a good crop..."

Gently, but with force, she made him sit on the stool. Then
felt his body lose its stiffness and become limp. She caught
him before he fell and eased him to the floor.

Because there was no other way and she was not str ng
enough to lift him, she picked up his feet and dragged him to
the corner where he could sleep away his drink.

It was more than she could stand. She left him and walked
out to the front of the hut. To breathe, and to look, against her
will, toward the green of the forest.

It was cool and quiet there. Somewhere beyond were the
mountains Como-tan had described to her. Somewhere beyond
was a river—a river so wide you could hardly see across...

Elizabeth fought back her tears.

In the weeks following his last return from Savannah, Jason
surprised her by remaining at home and sober. The work he
attempted, however, didn't seem to go well. His strength had
fled with the long period of drinking and he was forced to stop
and rest often. Elizabeth watched him chopping wood, saw the
effort it took from him and felt a renewal of the leadness in
her heart. He was not the same man and now she had to wonder
if he would ever be again.

She made herself angry because she couldn't bring herself
to encourage him more. Jason was attempting to do as she had
begged him to do for so long. He was staying away from the
rum and paying an interest, however feeble, to working his
land. But with all her effort, she could be no more than quietly
civil to him, and the thought of his touching her—attempting
to make love to her—made her ill. He tried it only once and
she stiffened before she could stop herself. Jason immediately
turned away in the bed and was silent.

He was still wrapped in a cloak of sorrow for himself, but
he was trying. And she wasn't giving him the help he needed
if he were to succeed. She had to change!

The woods were several degrees cooler than outside them,
reason enough to walk there even without her excuse to pick

berries or persimmons. Her real reason, Elizabeth admitted to herself, was to get away from the hut for a while. Away from Jason Welburn with his drawn, apologetic eyes that constantly followed her.

Walking slowly and looking for new thickets where she might find the berries to finish filling her pail, Elizabeth felt a breeze cross her face—the zephyr was gone as quickly as it came. She stood at the brink of a shallow gully that extended through the trees, its needle- and leaf-covered sides fading softly into nothing in the distance. It did, however, create an opening in the trees and she wondered if that natural break had been the source of the small wind.

Then another thought struck her as she looked—more a sense than a thought. She wasn't alone in the trees. Someone, or something, was watching her. It was a feeling that slid across her shoulders and raised the skin to a prickle.

Elizabeth turned slowly, looking at the brush and trees, trying to pick out the eyes she knew were there. A fox, she hoped, or at least a bear. The bears were usually not dangerous to humans unless they too were frightened. Wolves were another thing, there would be more than one of them, and Como-tan had said they sometimes excited themselves through their own curiosity.

She found nothing. Nothing at all. But now she was fully aware that something was there. It was another thing the Creek had taught her, that when the mind or eye cannot be trusted, then one must allow instinct to rule.

Slowly, without permitting a sudden move to betray her beginning fear, Elizabeth walked toward the source of her feeling. If it were an animal, that move of boldness would probably decide it to leave.

She had taken no more than a dozen steps before Como-tan appeared from behind some brush.

"You've become more aware of the forest, Elizabeth," he said calmly. "I think you have begun to understand it."

She took a deep breath and allowed it out slowly. Allowed out the breath and her fright with it. "You were spying on me again," she said.

He nodded. "I've often done that. But I can no longer. I taught you too well."

He was still partly in shadow, standing in a small glade

that, as she approached, turned out to be feather soft with pine needles and guarded by the brush behind which he'd been standing.

"Why?" she asked curiously. "Since we're friends, why would you do that?"

"To enjoy you," he said simply. "All people are different when they know others are about. Even you. But when they are alone they are true to themselves. I enjoyed seeing you alone."

He stood motionless, tall, strong and relaxed in that inner peace of his being. Peace—without thinking, she took three quick steps toward him, reached up her arms to encircle his neck and kissed him fully on the mouth.

His was a beautiful mouth—firm, but warm in its softness. The lack of beard around it, even a shaven beard, was a pleasant sensation.

Como-tan's arms went around her quickly, even as she realized in shock what she had done and tried to get away. He held her in his powerful hands and kissed her again. A long, mind numbing kiss. It set her to reeling.

When he released her at last, Elizabeth took a step backwards, her face aflame. "I'm sorry," she stammered. "I didn't . . . I shouldn't . . ."

Como-tan gazed at her steadily. "I'm not sorry," he said quietly. "I've wanted to do that for a very long time."

She didn't know what to do. She felt so helpless. It was an eternity before he moved, an eternity of drowning in his dark eyes before he took her hand. "Come," he said. "We will walk together.

The presence of her hand in his increased her inner turmoil. This was wrong! She should not do this!

"Como-tan . . ."

He turned his head. "Yes?"

Elizabeth struggled to gather calmness to her shocked senses. "I should not have done that," she said. "I'm sorry."

"Why are you sorry?" The hand that held hers tightened. It was a slight increase of pressure, but it set her nerves afire again.

"Because it isn't fair," she said. "Not to my husband. And not to you. Especially not to you."

"You no longer love your husband," he said as if he were discussing the weather. "I know that."

He turned her with the pressure of his hand and guided her into a natural path between the trees.

"No," she said and the word seemed to emerge of its own. It was the first time she'd admitted it fully, even to herself.

"Then it is ended between you?"

"No," she said again, and was surprised at the pain it caused her. "It's not ended. I cannot let it end. Jason needs me. I think he needs me more than ever now."

Como-tan stopped and turned to face her. He held her arms in his hands. "I need you, Elizabeth. And now I believe you love me. Not your husband."

She shook her head, unwilling to meet his eyes. Not trusting herself to meet his eyes. "I don't know that, Como-tan. I can't be sure. It could be that I just *want* someone—that I need someone. That was what happened when I first met Jason. I'm not sure I know what love is. That I will ever know."

"Elizabeth—"

"No." She shook her head harder. "I can't allow it. I can't love you, Como-tan. Jason is my husband. It wouldn't be right."

"Foolishness," he murmured. "Foolish rules that bind a woman to a man she does not love. Rules that keep her from the man who could bring her such happiness..."

She closed her eyes for fear of looking into his.

"Elizabeth." His voice came from far away, outside her tightly closed eyes. "The fire inside me is bright," he whispered. "It burns sometimes so that I must rise from my bed and walk through the forest to cool it. Beautiful Elizabeth, that fire is for you."

"Como-tan... please don't..."

She felt him relax. The pressure of his grip on her arms softened. "The rules," he said gently. "I understand the rules, though I do not believe. The preacher told me often enough of your foolish rules of life."

"The preacher?" She was glad of any diversion. Anything to slow the whirling of her senses.

"The man I lived with in Charles Town," he said. "I spoke of him to you."

"Yes," she said. "I remember."

He moved, caught up her hand once more and began to walk through the woods. "We discussed many things," he said. "Discussed them in the manner of men who are willing to listen to each other without anger. Of course, that was after I had become a man. When I was young I did all the listening."

"He must have been a nice man," she said, then corrected herself. "Is a nice man."

Como-tan glanced down at her and this time she was able to meet his gaze. "He called me James," he said. "Did I tell you that?"

"No. Why did he do that? Is that Como-tan in English?"

He chuckled softly. "No. The translation of my name into English would be, I think, eagle flying. Or, the eagle in flight would be better. That's what it means."

"I like that," she said. "Eagle flying. It seems to fit you. But why then did that man call you James? Where did he get the name?"

"He is a good man," Como-tan said. "But like all men he has his own small devils. He could not use my Indian name, so he invented one for me. It was from his bible."

"I don't understand," she said.

"For him to use my Indian name would be for him to admit, even in that small way, that the Indian culture was equal to that of the white. Though he tried in words to say it was, much more than any other man I've ever known, in his heart he could not admit it. To do so would be a denial of his right, his *requirement*, to convert me from a child of the forest to those rules that now bind yourself, Elizabeth."

"I see," she said quietly, then paused to look up at him fully. "They may seem foolish to you, Como-tan, but they're the rules I grew up with. I cannot deny them."

"Then we must abide by your rules," he said. "Come, I will walk with you to the edge of the forest. Then I must go."

It was early in a cool morning, well before dawn. Time when the air was moist and pleasant to walk about in and the darkness gave her no problem in setting her feet to the soil. She seemed to float as she approached the woods. Even in the darkness, she knew he waited there, and went gladly to meet him.

Como-tan stood, shadow among shadows, but solid and wonderful as she went into his arms. He held her close and kissed her until the fire of her passion grew to consume her.

Then she was lifted and held next to his naked chest, and carried deeper into the forest to a place where he found a glade of pine needles to lay her upon.

He stretched beside her, the touch of his breath soft against her cheek and one strong hand closing to stroke her breast.

"The fire burns bright," he whispered. "It is a fire that consumes me. Only you, my beautiful Elizabeth, can quench the fire."

"Yes . . ." she felt herself murmuring. "Yes, my darling . . ."

He kissed her again, softly, but with a growing demand that brought her straining against him. Beneath his loving hand, her clothes melted away until she pressed unhindered against his smooth skin.

"Elizabeth, my love," he whispered. "Come and fly with me."

"Yes . . . yes . . ."

And she did, as their bodies became one in a pulsating, cool searing flight that rode her on the billowing crests of passion until desire burst forth like an opening flower and scattered the clouds beneath her into scuttering streams of rain . . .

Elizabeth woke, near trembling in the realness of her dream, and lay beside her sleeping husband in horrified guilt. She would, she knew, lie awake the remainder of this night in both guilt and fear. For her inner self had surely betrayed her.

Twenty-Six

NATHANIEL HACOX, "Axe Nate," as he was known to everyone within miles of Augusta, was sprawled in all of his six-foot-four size on a bearskin rug thrown across a wooden frame facing the fireplace as Dr. Thomas Langlee entered the cabin. His large head, beard and all, was swathed in a piece of Indian blanket and he held both hands to it in misery.

His Cherokee wife paused and indicated her husband with, Tom thought, a slight smile to her lips, then stepped back to fold her arms and watch.

He pulled up a stool, aware that the suffering man didn't yet know he had entered, and placed his bag of instruments and medicine on the dirt floor beside him, then leaned forward to tap Nate on the shoulder.

A muffled voice rumbled from beneath the cloth. "Get the hell away from me, woman. I've had a bellyful of your unholy concoctions."

"'Tis not your wife, Nate," Tom said, chuckling in spite of himself. "Dr. Langlee. What seems to be your problem?"

The giant slowly unwrapped the bandage and turned to peer up at him. The whole side of his face was swollen, his neck as well, and his lips protruded like fat slices of melon. "Good God, man!" Tom exclaimed, touching the neck and finding it hard under his fingers. "Have you been bitten by a snake?"

Nate's words seemed to bubble beyond the lips, painful even to hear. "Ain't the snakes, doc. I could do for that meself. Slice it open with a knife and have that useless baggage there suck the *pizin* out quick enough. Tis me tooth. Mayhaps the whole damn bunch, I'm thinking."

"A toothache! By all the fires of hell! You caused me to ride thirty miles because you had a *toothache*?"

The big man, for all his size, whimpered like a babe. "It *hurts*, doc! So much I can't see me hand in front of me face!"

Tom was angry. The messenger had told him Axe Nate was near to dying and he had dropped everything he was doing to ride a good stallion hard to get here. He knew the propensity of these backwoodsmen to exaggerate, but he also knew their strengths. He'd seen men cut nearly to ribbons, their flesh hanging in shreds, walk calmly into Angel's Rest and ask if he could do for them. Axe Nate had a reputation for being among the best of them.

"How long have you felt the pain?" he gritted.

The big man whimpered, "At least a fortnight, doc. I figured it to become better, but it didn't."

"Nate, you've the brains of a donkey! If you'd come to me when it started, we could have saved you all this misery. Not to say in the least saving me a long ride and perhaps a good horse in rushing out here. You're a damnable fool and I ought to leave you to your suffering!"

"Doc! Please!"

"All right," he told him. "I'll do for you. But I promise you, my friend, you'll come first to me the next time."

"Doc!" Nate wailed. "I can't live with more of this pain!"

Tom turned to the Indian squaw. "Does he have any whiskey?"

She nodded and this time he was certain her black eyes were bright with amusement. Tom decided that she'd stood for more than one blow from the big man and was laughing at his loss of courage.

"Then fetch it."

He turned and pressed against Nate's forehead to lay him back, knocked his protesting hand aside impatiently, and forced open his mouth.

His patient's jaw was so swollen it was a task. And true enough, most of the teeth were decayed, or at least were streaked with black. He reached into his bag for a probe.

Nate's eyes were swollen, but not to the extent they couldn't focus on his instrument. "Gawd a'mighty, doc! What you gonna do?"

He had sat bolt upright, it took all of Tom's own considerable strength to force him back again. "I intend to find the one that's causing the trouble and remove it," he told the other grimly.

"Ohhh . . . Give me the whiskey first, doc! I can't stand the pain . . ."

Tom laughed. "I'll wait for the whiskey, right enough. But I'll tell you now, friend Nate, it'll do you little good. What you're about to feel cannot be quelled by whiskey, I'm afraid. All it'll do for you is put you out of your misery after."

The big man groaned again, a long shuddering sound that shook his huge frame.

His mouth closed and Tom forced it open again. Then, ignoring the shudders of fright that shook his patient, began to tap, one at a time, upon the teeth on the more swollen side. When he hit the right one, the second from the rear, the giant erupted and nearly knocked him from his stool.

"Damn it, Nate! You'll have to hold still!"

"Awww," was the only answer he got.

The woman came into the cabin again, carrying a jug. Tom reached to take it from her hands and pulled the cob from its top before laying it to Nate's lips. The big man sucked greedily upon it, then jerked it from his hands to tip it up and allow its contents to pour down his throat.

Tom stopped him after a moment. "Hold, man. You'll kill yourself."

"One more, doc. Please," he begged.

Tom reached to tip the jug himself, held it as Nate drank, then pulled it down again firmly. "Enough," he said.

He glanced at the Indian woman as he placed the jug aside. "Fetch me some rope."

"Rope? Gawd, doc! You ain't gonna pull it out with a rope!"

Tom laughed. "No. But as soon as I touch that tooth of yours, you'll be flailing about with those great logs you call arms. I'm damned if I'll be struck with one of them."

He pushed his patient back against the frame again. "Now lie still until I'm through."

"Doc..."

"You want an end to this or not?" Tom demanded.

The giant subsided. A moment later the woman brought him a rope and between the two of them they tied Nate to the floor, using wooden pegs she drove in the ground with his own axe.

Helpless to move, the giant's one good eye, the one not swollen, followed their action with fear. Tom ignored him as he dug his iron forceps from the bag.

"Come here," he told the woman. "Take hold of his head and hold it back until I tell you to let go."

Her grin was well in place now, the Cherokee made no effort to conceal it as she placed a strong brown arm across her husband's forehead and bent his head back. Then Tom set to work.

Had his mouth not been full, Nate would have screamed. As it was, the ropes holding him, and his Indian wife as well, were hard pressed to stay his fierce struggles. He was near to strangling with the sounds coming from his throat.

Tom tightened the forceps, braced his knee against Nate's chest, rocked his hands back and forth quickly and then yanked with all his strength.

The tooth, already loosened with the rotting gum around it, came out whole, to his great relief.

Nate came straight up, jerking the stakes from the ground and sending his wife flying to her back. "Awrrr!" he screamed. Then suddenly grabbed his jaw and stared at Tom. "Damn! What a relief!"

Tom rocked on his heels and looked from the tooth, still locked in his pliers, to the man with blood and pus dripping from his chin. "I should think so," he said. "That could well have killed you; you know that?"

Nate was shaking his head in wonder. "It don't hurt now, doc. Not like it did!"

"The pressure's gone," Tom told him. "Makes all the difference. It'll ache for a day or so but it'll be all right soon. Don't get so drunk you can't spit the blood out. If it doesn't quit bleeding, have your woman pack it with a piece of cloth."

"Aye, doc. My thanks to you." Nate was already mumbling from the effects of the whiskey and his relief from the tooth.

Tom looked to the Indian woman. "If he passes out, don't let him lie on his back. You understand?"

She nodded.

"And tell him he owes me a bearskin for my ride out here," he continued. "Then the next time he has a toothache, he'd damned well better come to Angel's Rest when it starts."

She grinned. "You will eat?"

Tom smiled back. "No, I've not the time. I'm long enough away as it is."

He went outside and caught the stallion who was contentedly munching away on some sparse grass it had found in the woods. It would be a slow trip back to the plantation, and he'd have to walk the animal most of the way to keep from overtaxing it. He swung in the saddle and turned its head to leave.

Tom arrived back at Angel's Rest as tired as his mount. He retrieved his bag from behind the saddle before walking slowly to the house. The front room was empty as he expected, but walking down the hall toward the back stairs, he passed a sitting room and heard his son crying.

The baby Charles lay in his cradle, alone in the room. Tom bit his lip in disgust. His son's color didn't look as it should and he knelt and touched the side of his finger to the small face. Charles wrinkled and cried the harder.

Tom pulled back the blanket, much too warm in the first place in this weather, and ran his hand down across his son's chest and belly. At his hips, his hand became wet.

"Damn," he muttered. "Is it too much to ask they keep him dry?"

He ignored the problem for a moment and forced open one of his son's eyelids. The eye that stared back was wet with crying, but otherwise clear, and the heat in his face, he realized, was more from the crying and the blanket than any fever. He sighed with relief, then stood and bellowed, "Meggy!"

His wife's maid appeared in seconds. "Yes, massa?"

"Where in the living hell is this child's nurse?" he demanded. "Why is he left alone?"

"I don't know, massa. Missy Angelica, she was with Baby Charles the last time I was here."

"Then where is my wife?"

"I don't know, massa." Meggy looked at the floor.

It wasn't this black woman's fault. He turned to stare hard

out the glass window. Angelica acted mother to this babe only at whim. One moment she was adoring of it, and the next hardly knew it existed.

"Either find the nurse or change his bunting yourself," he ordered in a quieter voice. "And do it now."

"Yes, massa."

He strode from the room, his boots hitting hard on the wooden floor, and went down the hall to the rear stairs. At the top, he glanced once at his wife's room, then turned to his own instead. He was both hot and tired, better to rest a bit before he spoke to her.

Inside, he removed his hat and coat, turned back the collar of his shirt and plunged his face into the basin of water he poured from a pitcher on the sideboard. It was refilled thrice daily at his order, one of his few luxuries.

When he'd dried his face and hands, he moved to a chest, opened the top and removed a bottle of brandy and a small glass.

The bed was tempting after his long ride, but he chose his chair instead. Angelica—she had been wife to him for a goodly time now, but he knew her little more than he had that day he walked into the tavern at Augusta. One minute loving—with a flame that set him ablaze for her—and the next cold as a winter wind. Who was she? And could she really love him— or for that matter love any but herself? Hell's flames, did she even love herself? It seemed at times as if she were bent on self-destruction in her rages.

The brandy warmed his insides. He leaned his head back against the headrest of the winged chair and closed his eyes.

His wife was a murderer. The worst kind—she'd killed her own father. How cold a blood had it taken for her to do that?

Yet, to his knowledge, she'd never shown the least remorse. No regret for the killing of the man who sired her into this world.

No, she'd shown only fear. Fear that he would give her over to the law to be hanged for her crime.

And himself, Thomas Langlee—*Doctor* Thomas Langlee— had become party to the crime. Was he any less guilty?

He'd not been able to bear to tell the truth. Not able to stand and watch her hang like a common strumpet—the rope around so lovely a throat...Or was that the real reason? That was what they would ask. Did not Thomas Langlee *induce* his wife to do the deed so that he would become master of Angel's Rest? After all, it was a producing estate. Producing now beyond his wildest beliefs. Would not a man kill for such land—especially a man who had been born with nothing?

In all truth he had thought of that as well as her being hanged during those first terrible days. Thought long of it. And in the end, he'd done just as she expected him to do. He had buried her father and accompanied her to Charles Town to the office of the lawyers.

And that was the real marvel of it. He'd expected a hue and cry to arise over the death of a nobleman, a man who'd received a large tract of the Georgia colony at the request of the King himself. He'd waited, braced, for the inquiry to come back from England after they had sent the news. But there were no questions. None at all. Almost as if the crown had been relieved.

He had gained Angel's Rest with no quarrel from the lawyers. With Angelica's request, the title had passed into his name easily. He'd controlled its management before, but now with no one at all to answer to, he had begun to experiment, and had become lucky. Cotton grew in trade by the year—he had stumbled upon a rising crest—and within a few more years he would own the wealth this land was capable of producing.

But to what end? All he'd wanted from the beginning was to be considered a gentleman and to be called doctor. That . . . and Angelica.

The first two he had. He was accepted in South Carolina by most of the plantation owners and even by some of the older names in Charles Town. He also had a building reputation as a physician. Angelica, however, was another thing. He loved her . . . and he sometimes hated her. She could at times drive him near from his senses in passion. Other times she could be the sweetest of flowers to hold and to touch.

Tom drained the glass.

But there were times as well when she could goad him into a near rage with her tongue and then laugh at him, daring him to strike her, and knowing that he knew she wanted him to do so. At such times, he thought her mad. Mad enough, he must admit, to kill. That was how she had done the deed that damned them both. There was no other explanation.

Tom rose from the chair and placed his glass beside the

basin and pitcher. The other maid, the very young black whose name he could never remember, would soon find them and wash the glass while refilling the pitcher. He crossed the hall and tapped on his wife's door.

"Yes?" Her voice, like the rest of her, the part the world was able to see, was soft and lovely.

Tom opened the door and stepped inside. Angelica sat before a half chest that had a mirror hanging on the wall above it. Her black hair was free of ribbons for once and she held a brush in one hand poised above her head as she turned.

"Well," she said as he entered. "My doctor husband has returned. Did you save the poor peasant's life? Whomever he was?"

"He'll do," Tom said shortly. "T'was not the emergency I thought it to be."

"I see." She lay the brush on the dresser and placed both hands on one arm of the chair as she twisted to face him. "But it *was* necessary, of course. I mean, you really *had* to go and save him. You *are* a doctor, after all."

Tom recognized the signs. She was very angry with him. Her eyes were too bright, her voice too sweet.

"I had no choice, Angelica," he said.

He closed the door. "I'm quite certain you had no trouble entertaining the Watlingtons by yourself."

"Not in the least." She laughed without humor. "Gerald Watlington was simple, he spent the entire evening entertaining himself by gazing at my breasts. While his wife occupied herself with jealousy."

"No doubt he had ample to look upon," Tom said shortly.

She nodded, and smiled sweetly. "I'd thought you'd forgotten."

"They're the breasts of a mother," he countered. "You've a child downstairs who has an interest in them as well as your stupid friend."

"Your son takes his milk from a cow now, husband," she said. "I've fed him all I needed."

"Or all you wanted. Did you not know he was crying downstairs when I returned? Or didn't you care? I'll not have you neglecting him, Angelica."

"I've more to do than forever holding that child!"

Tom crossed the room. Her danger flags were all up—the

green eyes were far too bright, her nostrils too flared and the red mouth too thin, but he suddenly didn't care. He was tired and cross himself.

"Damn it, Angelica, there's more than yourself in this world. If you can't see to the child, at least see that the servants do!"

"Damn yourself!" She shocked him by rising to her feet quickly and raising two clenched fists. The blood disappeared from her face. "I'm not a cow to nurse that child! And I'm not a peasant wench to jump about at your demand! You *hear* me?"

"Angelica, stop this!"

Her raised hands opened into claws, the long fingernails scratching toward him. "You don't *own* me! No one *owns* me! I do as I please! Do you *hear*?"

Her eyes rolled wildly, and suddenly he was afraid. She was worse than he'd ever seen her become. "Angelica—"

"Damn you!" She hurled herself at him and Tom managed in time to grasp her wrists and halt her plunge. But she shook about in his grasp until he was afraid she would be injured. "Angelica!"

She screamed—a piercing shriek that stretched his already taut nerves. Tom crossed her wrists into one hand and put his other around her body to bring her close to his chest. "Angelica, stop it!"

She writhed like a snake in his grasp. It was all he could do to hold her. "I'll *kill* you!" she gasped. "You're not my master—no one owns me!"

He had no choice. He squeezed her breathless, picked her up and moved toward the bed. When he reached it, he flung her across it and held her in place with his own body. "Angelica," he said hoarsely into her ear, "calm yourself. It's all right. There's no reason to—"

She screamed again, the scream of the damned it seemed to his ear. And Tom leaned forward to muffle it with his face. "Angelica . . ."

His wife's body undulated beneath him so violently Tom was hard pressed to hold her. What had caused it? One minute she was normal, the next she was beyond control! Good Lord, what was wrong with her?

"I'll kill you," she hissed from beneath him. "You'll not make me do as you want! *He* couldn't make me. And you shan't!"

"Angelica," he gritted. "It's all right. No one is going to make you do anything."

"Massa?" Tom became aware at last of the third voice above him, a voice masked by the panting of his wife in his ear. He turned his head to look.

Meggy stood beside the bed, her eyes stretched wide and her hands to her face.

"Meggy! Get my bag! My medicine bag! Hurry!"

Angelica screamed again and tried to bite his face. "Hurry, damn you!" he yelled as the slave didn't move.

She left, moving backwards toward the door and keeping her eyes on them. Tom renewed his struggle to hold Angelica.

It took an eternity for her to return, an eternity in which his strength was taxed and he was faced with the choice of releasing Angelica or choking her into unconsciousness.

Meggy stood by the bed, the bag in her hand.

"Hold her," he gasped. "Hold her arms!"

At last she understood. She leaned across him and took the arms of the woman struggling on the bed, pinning them back above her head.

Tom kept his weight in place as he turned and plunged his hand into his medicine bag. He found the vial he wanted, it was separated into a cloth pocket in the bag, and withdrew it. He'd no time to mix it with water, he would have to be very careful not to give her too much.

Angelica struggled the harder. But with Meggy's now willing help, he held her face in his hand and forced her mouth open to drop a tiny bit of the liquid into it.

She immediately flung her head aside to spit, but he anticipated her action and held her mouth and nose closed until she was forced to swallow.

Angelica's struggles increased, but quickly diminished again and then ceased altogether. At last she relaxed under him. Tom drew back, looked up at the black servant and then removed her hands from Angelica's wrists.

Quickly he bent his head to his wife's chest and allowed a sigh of relief at the steadiness of her heartbeat. Her eyes were closed, but her breathing became regular, and he knew he'd judged rightly. Only enough of the drug to make her sleep. Not enough to kill her. Still . . . it had been a near thing.

"She's asleep now," he told Meggy while still sitting on the bed. "I want you to stay with her for a while. You can leave in an hour or so, as long as she's sleeping normally. If she has any change, call me."

"Yes, massa." The black woman looked at him. "Missy, she sometimes do get the *debil* in her!"

Tom glanced at her sourly. So it was obvious even to the house servants. "Your mistress is merely ill," he said. "She'll be all right in a few days."

"Yes, massa." Meggy turned to look down at Angelica.

Tom crossed to the door. "I'll be in my room, Meggy," he said. Then before he lifted the thumb latch, "I expect you to be silent about the illness of your mistress."

She nodded vigorously. "Yes, massa."

He went out the door, knowing full well the black woman would not be quiet and suddenly wondering what the rest of them thought.

That had been a near thing; he'd come close to injuring Angelica in his attempt to restrain her. His wife was ill, and growing worse. What was he to do about it? He was a doctor, but this was beyond his learning . . .

She slept calmly enough, he checked on her twice during the late afternoon that he spent seeing to his duties of the plantation. Afterwards, he took his sup in his own room and then spent the evening studying. All of his books, however, dealt with the diseases of the body, the workings of the internal organs—none spoke of the intricacies of the mind. It was late in the night before he had exhausted himself enough to go to bed.

His head had hardly touched the pillow when his door opened and then closed again, its movement disturbing the blackness of the night with only the softest of sounds. Tom raised to one elbow. "Who's there?"

"Tom, it's me." Angelica's voice, like the night, was soft and low. "Please, may I come in?"

He sat up swiftly. "Of course. Wait, I'll light a lamp."

"No, don't. Please don't. I've been bad. I only want you to hold me a little . . ."

She was moving somewhere in the darkness, he couldn't be sure where. His curtains were drawn and there was only the faintest of light, that of starlight, filtering between them, a light no broader than a string.

"Let me get the lamp, Angelica. You'll injure yourself in the dark."

"No, no. Please don't." Hers was a small voice, near that of a child. The voice she often used to wheedle him.

He waited. She would be nearly nude, wearing only the flimsiest of nightwear. Silk, and bare of shoulder. Awareness of her being close in the darkened room, of being so dressed, and so . . . desirable, put his problems with her from his mind. He loved her. Damn, how he loved her!

She moved to the side of his bed, between it and the curtained window, and Tom felt her presence. "Thomas?" she whispered.

The thin shaft of light saved him. That, and instinct. He caught the glint of steel in the smallest instance of light, realized instantly what it meant and flung himself away from her even as she slashed at the bed where he had lain. "Angelica!"

She came after him, stabbing at the bed even as he left it. Tom could hear her grunting with the effort. He had to have light!

He bent quickly and grasped the thick feather mattress in both fists, straightened and rolled it and Angelica away from him. His bed lamp was to her side, he'd never reach it even with her thrashing about to clear herself of the mattress. Better the door!

He reached it after stumbling once against the furniture in the room and running his hands along the wall. He didn't have her cat-like ability to find the way in the dark. Outside, the hall was nearly as dim, but there was a gleam of light in her room. She'd left a lamp. He crossed the hall in two strides and flung open her door, then turned.

Angelica appeared from behind him, a knife—his own hunting knife—in her upraised hand. Her black hair was flung wildly about her face, and she wore a silken nightgown. But the look she gave him was murder.

"Stop it!" he cried. "Angelica, don't do this. You're sick. I can help you!"

Her beautiful face twisted. "You'd let them hang me," she said, spitting the words at him. "I know you would. You want to get rid of me. I'll kill you!"

"Angelica, stop it." Tom tried to force his own voice to steady, to be calm. "I'd not do that. You know I wouldn't. You're upset. Put down the knife. Please."

Her eyes were wide; they seemed to stare beyond him. "You tried to poison me!"

Tom placed his hands up, palms out. "No, darling. It was a drug to make you sleep. Only to make you sleep and rest. I wouldn't harm you, Angelica. You know I wouldn't."

She was beyond reason. He knew it with a coldness that spread down across his shoulders. She was mad. And she fully intended to kill him.

He took a step toward her and watched the knife in her hand lift. "Angelica, put it down," he said softly. "I'm not going to hurt you. You don't want to hurt me. You don't really want to hurt me."

The green eyes lost a little of their wildness, only a small amount, but he was encouraged. "Put down the knife, darling," he said again. "Come, let me hold you close. Let me take you to bed with me and hold you."

"Thomas . . . I . . ." Her voice seemed lost inside her, and the knife dropped a fraction.

"I know, darling," he murmured. "It's all right. You'll be all right."

Angelica lowered the knife to her waist. "I don't know what . . ." She lifted her other hand to her face. "What am I doing, Tom . . ."

He was almost to her, moving slowly, a step at a time. "It's all right," he whispered. "Angelica, give me the knife."

She looked at him. And smiled. Then slashed at him with all her strength, lunging forward at the same time. He had only time to lean away from the stroke, to dodge its flight by a whisper.

With both despair and fear tearing at him, he smashed his fist to her jaw. Then caught her as she fell.

The knife dropped from her hand as he caught her, and Tom kicked it savagely down the hall where it came to rest at the feet of a startled Meggy who had appeared with a lantern.

"Massa?" she said. "What you doing? What's wrong with Missy?"

"Get the hell out of here!" He screamed the words at her. "Go back to bed, damn you!"

She disappeared as magically as she'd come.

Tom carried his wife into her room and lay her across the pillows. Her face where he'd struck her was red and beginning to swell. He examined it closely and was relieved to find the jaw wasn't broken, but she would have a terrible bruise for days.

He covered her carefully and then softly stroked the bruised jaw. What was he to do? What the hell *could* he do?

There were two white field overseers now at Angel's Rest, one married and sharing a cabin with his wife and children, and the other living alone. Both were rough outdoorsmen, but both were intelligent enough to leave him alone. If they recognized the trouble at the big house, they kept quiet about it. When he gave orders or discussed the running of the plantation with either, their attitude remained respectively the same.

But Tom knew the two men had to wonder. The slaves did and were too much like children to hide their interest. Wherever he went, he felt their eyes follow him and knew that Meggy had not restrained herself. He could only wonder to what stretch her imagination and tongue had taken her.

Angelica had been subdued when she awoke. He spent the night beside her bed to make certain she'd be all right. After that, and with her refusal to talk at all with him, Tom had stayed away from her room. But he gave strict orders that she not be allowed to leave it herself for any reason. He nailed a bar latch to the outside of the door and promised the black servant that he would have her whipped within an inch of her life if her mistress left the room.

It was all he could do. No drug that he was aware of would help to calm that twisted brain; no knife would cut out her unreasonable suspicion. It was, he decided, after sitting up most of the next two nights in his own room, the murder she'd committed on her father that had finally eaten away at her until she had lost her reason. Time would numb her senses, sitting alone in her room would give her time to think and then, perhaps, he would be able to talk with her.

He went about his duties with half a mind, made two short trips, one to deliver a baby and the other to treat a fistula. Both were nearby and didn't take him away from Angel's Rest for long. The third request in as many days was a different matter. It would take him half a day's ride to get there and half to return, to say nothing of the time spent. Tom started to refuse, but the man who stood before him was speaking of his child, and there was no question but that he had to go.

"I'll fetch my bag," he told him. "Go to the stable and tell them to saddle two of my best horses. We'll leave immediately."

The man's face was a study in relief. "I don't mind the walking, Dr. Langlee. I'm fair used to doing it."

Tom merely glanced at him. "Do as I say, man. The horses are because I haven't the time to wait for you to walk."

"Aye, sir." He turned and went quickly out the door and Tom got up to get his bag and to leave instructions for Meggy.

The child, a girl, suffered from the dry gripes, less dangerous than it appeared. He treated her, left a drug and mounted one horse to lead the other back to Angel's Rest. Traveling that way and swapping from the back of one to the other, he made better time.

The minute he rode up to the house he knew something was wrong. Both female house servants stood on the veranda with their arms folded across their breasts and looks of fear on their faces. Farley, his chief overseer, stood in the yard.

Tom jerked his stallion to a halt beside him. "What's wrong?"

Farley had an expression of fear and anxiety on his own bearded face. "It's Mrs. Langlee, sir. She's gone."

"Gone! What the hell do you mean, gone? Where's she gone?"

The man on the ground shook his head. "I don't know, sir. I just found it out. She gave orders to have a horse saddled and rode it out not more than a few minutes ago."

Rage clouded his vision, he could see only through a red haze for a moment. "Damn it, man! I gave orders for her to stay in her room. How the hell did she get a horse saddled?"

Farley took a step backwards. "I didn't know until she was gone, Dr. Langlee. I swear I didn't. And the black boy in the stable didn't have the courage to tell her nay."

His hands gripped the saddle ridge until they hurt as he looked furiously to the veranda. "Meggy! How did she get out?"

The black woman sank immediately to her knees. "Please, massa! Meggy couldn't help it! She just done it! I swear I didn't leave the door unlatched!"

Unlatched. The stupid slave had done just that. Wait! He had to think! Where would she go?

He looked down at Farley who was watching him with wary eyes. "Do you know the direction she took?"

The man nodded quickly. "I was just about to get a horse

and follow her. The stable boy said she rode in that direction."
He pointed with a long arm.

Tom turned. Across his fields the forest loomed like the
silver web of a spider. Angelica loved to ride through the forest,
loved to ride too fast for the narrow passages between the
trees . . .

He knew the path she'd most likely take. He jerked the
stallion around and dug in his heels.

"Wait, sir!" Farley called from behind him. "I'll come and
help search!"

But the stallion was already pounding into a gallop. Tom
leaned over its back and urged it on. In a moment they were
racing through the cotton, smashing clumps of dirt and plant
from their passage.

The big horse seemed to sense his need and kept its furious
pace well inside the trees until Tom was forced to slow its
speed himself. He'd serve no purpose in aiding Angelica if he
struck his own head on a limb and was knocked senseless.

Still, he traveled at a speed that nearly caused him to miss
her cape. It hung from a limb well in the direction he was
taking—the way he expected her to go. Tom jerked the stallion
to a halt, turned him and urged him over to where he could
retrieve the cape.

She had left it there deliberately, it hung too cleanly to have
been snatched from her shoulders in passage. He held it in his
hand and considered the fact.

For all her madness, Angelica was intelligent. This was no
mad flight to nowhere. She knew he would follow her. She
expected him to follow her. And she wanted to make sure he
chose the right direction. But why?

He shrugged the thought away. No time to reason it out.
These woods were dangerous for a woman alone. He tapped
the stallion in the sides. "Let's go, fellow."

He rode at a slower pace now, more alert for the signs he
knew she would leave, and found the second minutes later.
She had turned up an old wash, thick with pine brush but still
passable, and her stomacher, complete with bows and lace,
was draped across one of the bushes at the end.

Good Lord! He'd expected a broken limb or twig to lead
the way. What the hell was she doing? Undressing?

The stallion pushed through the wash and up the other side.
And there he found her dress.

Tom gathered it in with a sinking heart. She was mad and playing a wild, incredible game with him—a game understood only in her own twisted mind.

Farther along, he found her shoes. Then her petticoats, three of them, and a half mile more, her stockings. These last were hung side by side about the height of a horse, as if to form a gateway. Angelica could be wearing no more than a shift now. The thought sent his nerves to screaming.

She was deeper into the woods than she'd ever before ridden. He wondered if she truly expected to return. But then, she was daring him to follow her . . .

Her horse appeared ahead of him; Tom sighed with relief, then realized it stood with empty saddle. Angelica was nowhere in sight.

He swung quickly to the ground and tied the stallion. She couldn't be far, she was bare of foot and nearly naked.

"Angelica!"

The silence of the trees mocked him. Tom swung slowly in a circle and stared at them. "Angelica! Where are you?"

A flutter of white caught his eye, thirty yards distant and only an instant's flash, but he started toward it immediately, his boots kicking aside the long undisturbed needles of the forest floor. "Angelica! Wait!"

He reached the spot and looked frantically about. Nothing . . . "Angelica!"

She laughed, a trilling, insane laugh, nearly at his back.

Tom spun . . . still nothing.

He hesitated, then took a few slow, deliberate steps. "Angelica, come out. Please come out and talk to me."

The low brush surrounding the trees made seeing very difficult except through the few open spaces. She could well hide from him for hours. He had to convince her to come out.

"Angelica," he said calmly, "you must come out. At least allow me to see you."

"And why should I do that?" The voice was directly in front of him and not too distant. Tom peered intently into the brush.

"Let's talk, Angelica. That's all I want to do, I swear. I won't harm you."

"You don't love me," the voice said. It had moved somehow to his right. He turned.

"I do love you, my darling. I love you more than anything. Please let me see you."

"You loved me at first," the voice said, moving again. "You liked to make love to me in the forest. I remember."

It was frustrating that she could move without his being able to find her with his eyes. She was like a cat!

"Angelica, I still love you," he said, turning slowly in the direction he thought she might be going. "I'll make love to you now, if you want. Right here. Come to me and find out."

"You're lying." He was wrong, she had gone the opposite direction and now the voice came from behind him again. Tom spun.

But he caught and held his urgency. Kept his voice very calm. "Angelica, I want you," he said slowly. "I want you most badly. Come to me, darling. Let me hold you. Let me hold your sweet form . . ."

"Will you make me do it?" Her old voice—the teasing one.

Tom nodded his head. "I'll take you—the way you want. You can fight me and I'll force you to submit. Do you hear, my darling? I'll make love to you here on the ground. Just as we once did. All you have to do is let me see you."

She appeared directly before him. Angelica stepped out from behind a thick bush clad only in a thin shift that reached hardly to her knees and was held up by two thin straps which allowed most of her breasts to show.

He swallowed hard. Her long black hair was loose, her form more beautiful than ever. She was a woodland nymph . . .

"Angelica," he said. "Come to me."

She laughed and shook her head. "You think I'm mad, don't you, Tom? You think I'm mad and I'm angry toward you."

He shook his head. "No. Right now all I can think of is how much I want you. Come to me."

She lowered her head and smiled at him. "No, my lover," she said. "That's not the way it must be. You must catch me. You must force me to make love. You promised."

"Angelica—"

But she laughed again and turned to run. Tom knew it even as she did and ran himself, full tilt toward her.

She was quick; he was clumsy. But this time she made sure he could see her as she darted just beyond his reach.

Tom crashed through the branches, grasped for her, only to have her slip away again. It seemed an eternity of movement.

Then she was gone. He stopped, panting, and listened.

"Over here, my lover," she called. "I'm waiting for you."

The last word broke high with her laughter—then suddenly turned into a scream. A horrible scream, followed by more, each reaching a higher peak of fear. The sounds shocked him into immobility.

But only for an instant. He ran, harder than he had before, toward the screaming.

He broke through brush and found her on the other side. Angelica had slipped into a natural pit, a bowl-shaped opening of rocks in the forest floor, lit brightly by a shaft of sunlight through the trees and shared with her by an endless amount of snakes.

Rattlesnakes! The dry, angry clatter of their warning tails made a background to her screams as Angelica thrashed help-lessly among them, her head jerking in fear. Even as he found her, she fell to the ground where she pitched and bucked in horrible madness while the serpents struck at her rapidly.

Tom screamed her name—a choking scream. Then crashed among the snakes himself, stamping madly with his boots.

He had only sense enough to keep his hands high, to allow his squirming enemies no more than his boots at which to strike. He killed more than one, stamping its head into the rocks, treaded on the backs of more, until the rattlesnakes had enough and retreated from her frantically writhing form.

Tom bent swiftly, gathered her into his arms and fled.

Fifty yards away from the hell of the pit he paused and knelt to lay her on the ground. "Angelica! My darling!"

The green eyes stared up at him without seeing; she was still screaming, but in a meaningless screech. Tom gathered her to his chest and held her. "Oh, God, Angelica! Don't die!"

Quickly he examined her. Scrapes and bruises from her thrashing about on the ground he ignored. But he couldn't ignore the dozen or more black pricks in her white skin—in her belly, her arms, her breasts, and one even on her face. Twin black holes of death.

Medicine! He had snake antidote in his bag! But even as he started to rise, to run for his bag, he knew it was useless. Too many strikes, she had no time left. No antidote would be swift enough, as quick as the poison she'd absorbed. He had struggled for years to become a physician, and now he was as helpless to save her as if he'd never begun.

Tom knelt again and took her into his arms. She was merely

twitching now, her mind already gone and only her body re-acting. He held her tightly.

Slowly, the movement within his arms quieted. Then ceased altogether. Tom pressed his face against hers, felt the stillness, and raised his head to the treetops above him and screamed in anguish. "Angelica!"

But she was gone and all the racking sobs that shook his body now would do nothing to bring her back to him again.

Twenty-Seven

THE CABIN SURROUNDING her was oppressively dark, illuminated treacherously by the faint light of a false dawn. Elizabeth Welburn lay and listened to the soft sounds of her son in sleep, a whisper of wind crossing the wooden shakes of the roof just over her head, and the thin rustle of an early rising ground squirrel as the tiny creature scampered across the seam of a log.

She was restlessly awake, had been most of the long night. Lying alone under the blanket she felt the solitude of the cabin acutely in spite of the presence of her son. It was like a weight pressing against her chest, weight enough to make her move under its discomfort. Finally, because she could stand it no longer, she rose and pulled on her dress. On the cabin floor beneath the sleeping loft, she draped her shawl around her shoulders against the morning chill, then crossed the room to try to rebuild the fire in the hearth.

There were still faintly glowing embers under the ashes as she expected and Elizabeth placed some dry moss about them. She knelt close and blew gently until the moss was ablaze, then added twigs to it until it grew in size. Lastly, she added larger sticks and finally a good-sized log.

Soon the firelight was bouncing brightly on the walls and partly dispelling her mood, but she knew it would be a time yet before the room was warmed. She went outside.

It had rained during the night and the freshness of the wet combined with the lateness of fall caused her to draw the shawl close about her shoulders. Too cool to be outside this early, still she was too restless to want to return inside. There was so little to do now and . . .

She felt alone. So very much alone. Como-tan had not appeared for a good number of weeks, her son spent most of his waking moments in the forest or wandering about on his own and Jason . . .

Her husband was a very sick man. Sick in his mind to the point she had lost hope for him. He was as often now in Savannah and drunk out of his senses as he was at home. Even if he wanted to work he was no longer capable of it, not without long rests to rebuild his strength. Elizabeth felt she was waiting, each day was merely a lengthly measure of time—waiting for what? They would never have a farm now. Jason would never recover.

She was, she was forced to acknowledge, waiting for what would surely be. The two of them would eventually face indenture again. The colony would not allow them to remain here and starve, but without the effort to make his own living, Jason would finally be reported to the Trustees and the two of them would be forced back into indenture. And poor John would be sent to Mr. Whitefield's orphanage.

She closed her eyes against the thought, then opened them again. It was always coldest at the beginning of dawn. She shivered and tightened her arms across her breasts as she watched the first streaks of light probe the mists that mingled with the trees. A red glow was building in the east—there would be more rain. Perhaps even a storm. Elizabeth sighed. A storm would keep her inside the cabin and like as not Jason would choose to return home and she would have to care for him.

The blur of the forest was beginning to lighten. Individual shapes were forming against the mists and the dark, and she could distinguish a tall, straight pine she liked. The dawn was winning as she watched, it rolled across the ground, chasing the mists, and coming toward her. Elizabeth slowly turned, fascinated, as the unknown became familiar under the probing light.

Strange . . . one tall stump near the road wasn't familiar. What was it doing there? She bent her head and peered hard at it, still partly obscured by the mists. Peered until she did understand. It wasn't a stump, but a man. A man standing perfectly still, and watching her in return.

Who? Why? Jason . . . no, Como-tan! No doubt of it!

But he acted so strangely! He was so still. His arms were folded across his chest and she had the eerie feeling he had been standing so for a very long time. Waiting. But waiting for what? Her?

A chill pressed her in spite of knowing him so well. Elizabeth began to walk slowly toward him. But stopped after only a few paces. The light was growing, the mists losing the struggle, and she could see more clearly. Como-tan stood with his feet apart, and lying before them was a long black bundle. A bundle much too big and too long to be his pack . . .

The chill became a shiver of fear. She knew suddenly what the bundle was, knew without a doubt. Had he killed him? Had Como-tan, the Indian, finally grown tired of waiting for her and allowed the savage in him to take over? The bundle was Jason. Had to be Jason. She knew it.

No . . . he would not kill her husband. Not Como-tan. For he would know he would destroy her if he did . . .

She couldn't move, wouldn't move, and he realized that. Como-tan knelt and lifted Jason into his arms so that she could see the truth of it. It *was* Jason, and he was dead. His arms hung too limply and his head drooped too much to be other.

Jason Welburn was dead. Her husband was dead. And lying in the arms of the man she loved . . .

It was a shattering feeling—an icy clash that froze her. The two acknowledgements should never have come at the same time. She should not admit she loved another man in the same moment she knew her husband was dead.

But it was the truth. Elizabeth raised her eyes under the truth and looked at him. She was in love with this tall savage who stood now so patiently waiting for her to understand her husband was no more. Loved him with an overpowering feeling. The one truth had triggered the other, she realized. She could not admit, could *never* admit, she loved him until poor Jason had released her with his death.

There was a brilliant light about her. She wasn't conscious of the earth beneath her feet, no longer felt the cold except that which was inside herself. It was as if one of her dreams were being repeated, except never before had Jason appeared in them.

Como-tan watched as she approached him—watched her with his copper face impassive—but when she stopped to face him, Elizabeth could read both compassion and triumph in his dark eyes. He was sorry for her, but he knew his long wait was over.

"What happened?" Her voice was distant to her own ear, hollow sounding, echoing in the stillness of the morning around them.

"I found him so." Como-tan's words, like his face, betrayed no sign of the emotion she could see in his eyes. "He had walked nearly to here. Only a short distance away."

"How did he die?" The hollow sound seemed to come from somewhere else.

"The cold," he said. "Too much of the drink to remain warm. He fell asleep and did not wake." He held her husband with the ease of holding a child as he spoke.

"I don't know what to say," she said, looking up into his eyes. "I should be—I only feel sorry for him."

Como-tan nodded.

"I loved him," she insisted. "At one time, I mean. We wanted to be . . ."

"The dreams are always there," he told her gently. "But there must be strength as well. You gave all of yourself. Now it is over and you can give him no more."

"Poor Jason," she said.

"We will give him back to the peace of the earth. Go and bring a shovel. It is all you can do now, Elizabeth."

"But he has friends, Como-tan. I must go to Savannah . . ."

He shook his head. "It is ended. Did he have a digging tool?"

"A pickaxe. It belongs to Mr. Longfootte. Jason borrowed it to dig stumps."

"Bring it as well."

Still she didn't move. "Como-tan, I can't. Not without telling someone in Savannah."

"You have not been there, Elizabeth. They no longer like your man as they once did. He makes them angry."

"You were there? You know what happened?"

He nodded. "Bring the tools for digging. We must bury him together. It will be better that way."

Elizabeth turned slowly, but stopped as he spoke to her again. "Do not wake the boy if he is asleep, Elizabeth. He no longer has love for his father and to watch will only make him feel his guilt for that lack of love."

He was right, she knew. John had nothing at all to say to his father for many weeks now, and avoided him whenever he was at home. He was too young to have to bear that burden. She began to move again.

A sudden picture took her back to years before when she had been present at another burial. Only a cloth over her mother's poor face—"The dead don't feel the cold . . ."

"I'll get a blanket," she said without turning. "I want to use my best blanket to wrap him. The warmest."

"Good," the voice said from behind her. "A warm blanket. But do not wake the boy."

He followed her carrying her husband until she reached the shed where Jason had kept his tools. She went inside and found the shovel easily, but had to search for the pickaxe. It was buried under a pile of wooden staves Jason had been cutting last year to build a rain barrel.

She left both at the door of the cabin and went inside where she first added another log to the fire to warm the room for John when he woke. Could it have been no more than minutes ago that she had built this fire? It seemed a lifetime.

She shook away the feeling and climbed to the sleeping loft to retrieve the blanket. John was hard asleep, curled into a ball on his own small bed. Elizabeth looked at him for a long moment before she moved back down the ladder.

Como-tan was waiting near the edge of the trees. He lay the tools she brought aside and helped her place Jason in the blanket, waited patiently as she held a last look at her dead husband's face, and then led her aside where he took off his deerskin shirt and placed it around her shoulders.

Elizabeth stood and watched as he cleared the ground of brush and leaves. Watched and felt the first stroke as he heaved the pickaxe over his head and sunk it to the haft in the earth. Then she was forced to turn her head to the rising sun over the top of the trees.

Its rays were cold to her in spite of the warmth of his shirt over her shawl. The coldness was in the sound of his digging. The heavy thud of the pickaxe, and then, shortly, the scrape of his shovel, seemed to draw away any warmth the sun might offer.

Morning . . . the rise of a new day. It would be her first day without Jason. What now?

She knew. Knew it without doubt, and turned back to watch the rythmic movement of his strong arms, the flattening of the muscles of his bare stomach, as Como-tan bent to drive home the tools of his digging.

Some would call him a savage. He spoke of himself as a child of the forest.

She looked at the endless trees before her. Now she would become, like him, a child of the forest.

It was a sweet, sad feeling.

Como-tan paused. "You are all right?" he asked.

Elizabeth nodded, not really trusting herself to speak, not at the moment. He went back to his digging.

The news of what she did would horrify those in Savannah who knew her. Hester, Alice Longfootte, others who had been her friends. Some would despise her and call her names for going away with an Indian. But none of them would understand.

They didn't know him as she did. Didn't know his gentleness, his strength. They could not understand that he was a child of the forest—the peace and contentment of the forest. And that he was the man she loved. That knowledge was overwhelming, an entirely different thing from what she had ever known before. Como-tan was a man. Different from what she had known in that she could have no doubts in her love. No reservations. She could love him and receive his love in return.

He was finished before she was aware of the passage of the time. When he spoke, Elizabeth turned to find him on one knee beside the body. "Do you wish to speak?" he asked.

She moved to kneel on the opposite side. "Goodbye, Jason," she whispered. "You're with God now and needn't be afraid anymore."

A moment later he lifted her to her feet. "Go and look to the new day beginning," he told her. "Do not watch as I bury the past."

Numbly, she did as he directed, standing to watch the morning and listening to the first sounds of the shovel behind her. After that, she didn't listen anymore.

She still experienced an air of unreality as she walked back to her cabin with him. Except for the presence of the tall Creek walking beside her and holding her arm she would have believed she was dreaming. But Como-tan was there. And life was real.

The door to the cabin opened as they approached and John emerged. He looked about, spotted them and waved. Then ran to meet them.

"Hello, Como-tan. Are you going to stay long? Can we go hunting? What've you been digging for?"

A flash of pain—the first real pain she'd felt—and then it was gone as quickly as it came. "John, I have to talk to you," she said. "Let's go inside."

"Why?" His young face turned at her tone. "What's the matter, mama?"

He spun back quickly as a thought hit him. "You're not leaving, are you, Como-tan?"

"No," the Creek said from beside her. "But listen to your mother."

"What's the matter?" he demanded. Alarm was spreading quickly across his young face.

"Come inside, John," Elizabeth said, placing an arm around his shoulders.

He became silent but continued to twist his head first to her and then to Como-tan. The Creek placed his tools beside the door and opened it for the two of them to enter.

Inside, Elizabeth paused, not really knowing how to begin. John stopped, too, his young eyes now grown large. He looked for a moment as if he were going to cry.

"Elizabeth," Como-tan said, "John and I are good friends. Perhaps it would be better if we talked as friends. Would you mind?"

She shook her head, her eyes on her son.

"Then perhaps you would make us some coffee," he said. "It would be good against the chill of the morning."

She turned away and fetched the pail she made the coffee in, filled it with water from the water barrel and hung it over the fire to boil. Then she reached for the sack of coffee beans she kept on the shelf and removed enough to pound for coffee.

Como-tan drew John aside and sat down on a stool with the boy beside him. "John," he said, "we have talked, you and I, of what happens to a warrior who reaches death. Do you remember?"

John nodded, but his eyes strayed to her. "Yes. They go to live with the Great Spirit, you said."

"Or God." The Creek's voice was low. "That is what white men call the Great Spirit."

"I know." John turned back to him.

"It is a time of great peace for the warrior who goes," Como-tan said. "He is never troubled again."

Again her son nodded.

Como-tan placed his arm around the small shoulders. "That is what has happened to your father, my young friend. He has gone to live with his God."

John watched him for a moment as she held her breath. Then he turned to her in question, and Elizabeth nodded.

"It is a sad time for those who are left behind," Como-tan told him, and John returned to looking at his face. "But a good time for those who go."

"My father didn't like me," John said in a weak voice.

Elizabeth closed her eyes.

"No, that is not true," Como-tan said before she could speak. "Your father loved you. But he was very sick at heart. It was only that sometimes his troubles made him forget that he loved you."

"How did he die?" John asked abruptly.

"He was tired and lay down to rest on his way here," Como-tan said. "Then he became so sick he did not wake up."

"He was sick a lot," John agreed solemnly.

Como-tan nodded.

Elizabeth remembered to add the ground coffee and stirred the pail of water.

"I hope he's happy now," John said, looking at the floor.

"I'm certain that he is," Como-tan said. "He is at peace. But now we must talk of other things. There is much to be decided."

"What things?"

"You and your mother must find another place to live. This would not be a good place to remain."

John looked up quickly. "I don't want to go no place else," he protested. "I don't want to live anywhere but here."

"Are you certain?" Como-tan asked him. "You said that you liked the forest. You like to hunt with me, don't you?"

"Yes, but if I leave here I can't do that anymore."

"You could if you came to live with me in the forest," Como-tan told him. "Wouldn't you like to do that?"

Elizabeth watched as her son's eyes grew wide with interest. "You mean it, Como-tan? Could I go and live like an Indian?"

The Creek glanced at her quickly. "Not all like an Indian, but some. I would build a house—larger than this one—and you would live much as you do here except it would be near an Indian village."

He smiled. "But there would be much time for you to learn to hunt. Time for you to learn as much the ways of the Indians as you do your own. Would you not like that?"

John nodded quickly. Then shot a look to her. "Can we, mama?"

Before she could answer, Como-tan spoke again. "There will be other things to learn as well, John. I will teach you to read books as well as to read the forest."

"That'll be all right," John assured him. "I won't mind learning to read."

Como-tan smiled. "Good. Then that is settled. Now will you do something for me?"

"Un huh."

"There are things your mother and I must talk of. Would you go outside for a while? Perhaps you might like to think about going to live in the forest. In a little, your mother will call you for some of the coffee when it's ready."

"Sure." John started for the door.

"Get your coat," she reminded him. "It's cold outside."

"Yes, mama." A thought struck him and he crossed the room to put a small hand on her arm. "It'll be all right, mama," he said, looking anxiously at her. "You'll like it there. Don't worry."

Elizabeth squeezed the hand on her arm. "Yes, I know," she told him.

He got his coat and went outside.

Como-tan waited until the door was closed and then moved to her, reached down and lifted her to her feet. His hands held her arms and Elizabeth looked up into his face, measured the strength she saw there and felt most of the tension that had built up in her this morning drain away.

"It is time to talk," he said. "I have waited for this time because my heart told me it would come. You have waited, too, Elizabeth. But you didn't know it."

"I know it now," she whispered. "I love you."

His strong hands moved up her arms to rest just below her shoulders. "I knew that as well, my beautiful Elizabeth, and it pained me greatly that you could not admit it to yourself."

"Jason was my husband."

He nodded. "And you honored him. By your rules you did as you must. But now he is the past and we are the future."

He waited, holding her, then asked, "Are you afraid?"

"No," she said. "I'm not afraid. I want to be your wife and I'll learn how."

Como-tan smiled. "There is nothing for you to learn. You have only to be yourself."

His smile became deeper. "You won't live as a savage, Elizabeth, if that is what you're thinking. I intend to build you a house in the forest not unlike the best in Savannah. I can give you clothes as well, the finest in the colony. I can easily acquire wealth in trading, but until now I had little need for it. You can have whatever you want."

"That doesn't matter," she said. "All I ever wanted was someone to love me."

"You have that and more. For as long as time for us exists, I will love you. You will have no more pain, no more suffering. I want to show you the mountain."

His arms slipped around her, drew her to him, and he kissed her. It was a long, comforting kiss, full of love and promise.

Elizabeth responded, putting her own hands up to encircle his neck and pressing into his strength. He was right. She understood his being right as a peace grew in her that she had never before known. Como-tan was not a sapling to bend to the force of the winds. He was an oak. Her long search for happiness was over.

She lay her face against his broad chest, transported by the comfort of being in his arms. "Tell me of the mountain," she whispered.

Como-tan bent his head until his lips brushed her hair. "The mountain belongs to us, Elizabeth. We will build it for each other and live atop it like the eagle. Flying whenever we like. The wind will be our friend; the sky our limit. The long years will be kind to us and when we have had a great number of them together, you will still remain my beautiful Elizabeth. My eyes can never tell me differently."

She closed her eyes.

"Soon we will leave," he continued softly. "We will go to my village where they will welcome you gladly. Then we will begin to build our mountain together."

He kissed the top of her head. "Take nothing from here, Elizabeth. Especially not your memories. Let the past be forgotten."

"I'm ready," she said into his chest. "But hold me just a little longer first."

His arms tightened about her.

Twenty-Eight

THE DEEPER THE three of them traveled into the forest, the more Elizabeth could sense she was sloughing away a depressed state that had been years building in her. She felt clean and light-headed. Walking beside Como-tan took no effort at all and she wanted to keep moving. She protested when he insisted she stop and rest. If she had a regret at all of leaving, it was the fact that she had not been able to speak to some of her old friends in Savannah. But then, she had hardly seen any of them in the last year or so anyway, perhaps it was really for the better. Como-tan had promised he would write a letter for her and deliver it himself to tell Hester Pullam what had occurred. He would also write one to Tom and see that it got to her brother's plantation. That would be done, she was sure of it, but now it was not a thing for her to think about. She was free for the first time in her life, free to be herself. And the man who walked beside her was wise enough to understand her need.

She glanced at him in her joy, caught his return gaze and smiled.

"How are you feeling?" he asked. "Tired?"

"No. Not at all. I don't think I can ever feel better than I do at this moment. I could run the rest of the way to your village."

Como-tan chuckled. "I don't know if that's true or not, but your son could. He's run most of the two days we've traveled."

Elizabeth looked for John. Como-tan was right. Her son had been unable to hold his excitement and constantly darted ahead or to the side of their path to investigate the forest. She had worried about his becoming lost or hurt, but Como-tan had assured her on both counts. He would, he told her, have no trouble knowing where John was or what else was near. John was safe and they should allow him to enjoy himself.

The Creek moved closer to her and placed his arm possessively around her waist as they walked together. The very few goods she owned that he allowed her to bring were in a sack thrown across his left shoulder, leaving his right arm free. It had seemed a shame to leave some other things behind, but he had said they would be replaced with better. The pride in his eyes when he spoke had told her not to argue. And in truth, Elizabeth wanted little to remind her of the last bitter years.

"Is it far now?" she asked him.

"I thought you weren't tired."

"I'm not. I just want to hurry and get there. Don't you?"

The arm around her waist tightened. "I've waited a long time for you. I can wait another mile or so."

Elizabeth placed a hand over his and pressed. "Will your people really accept me, Como-tan? As your wife, I mean?"

"They will not only accept you, they will love you as I do," he told her. "My people have their faults, as do all people. But dislike for others because of the color of their skin is not one of those faults. They are willing to accept all who accept them."

He took a few more steps in silence and then said, "There is one exception, of course."

She glanced at him in alarm. "What's that? Some of your family?"

Como-tan gave her a very serious look. "No, I'm afraid it might be worse. It will be some of the younger women. They will be envious of your beauty and your success. The fact that you have captured the heart of a most desirable male from them will make them very angry."

He couldn't maintain a straight face and laughed at his own joke.

Her sudden alarm vanished. "Is that so?" she said. "You certainly do not think lightly of yourself, sir."

"I speak only the truth, madam," he said with a broadening smile. "I'm considered quite a catch. Handsome, wealthy, in good health . . . many a Creek maiden has cast an eye—*oof!*"

Her elbow had sharply ended his words. "There will be no more of that," she told him. "I'll share you with no other, handsome or not."

Como-tan stopped and turned her to face him, drew her into his arms and looked down at her. "That is the truth," he said softly. "For me there is no other."

Then he kissed her.

"Hey!"

They both turned to look. John was thirty or more paces ahead of them and seemingly impatient with their dawdling. "Is this the right way, Como-tan?"

"Bear to your left a bit, John," Como-tan called. "Look for a ridge to rise on that side and follow it."

The boy waved and immediately disappeared in the trees.

"How is he able to find the way himself?" Elizabeth asked. "He doesn't know anything about the woods."

"He knows more than you think," Como-tan said, guiding her into following the direction John had taken. "Your son has as much a feeling for the forest as you do, you just haven't noticed. But it really doesn't matter that much, as long as he is going in the right general direction. I've just been following whatever path he takes."

"You mean we've been wandering about? Wasting time?"

Como-tan replaced his arm around her waist. "What's the difference, Elizabeth? We've plenty of time—the rest of our lives. And John's enjoying himself."

"But—"

He squeezed her waist. "Remember, my love, you have changed your life. Time is not the driver it was. It is to be enjoyed. To be savored. There's nothing that must be done today. Enjoy yourself."

The idea was a strange one to her. All her life she had been conditioned to do at once and it would be hard to change. But, as she walked and thought about it, the idea pleased her greatly.

The Creek village shocked her with its huge size. Elizabeth had expected a gathering of small huts, or even smaller skin tents—*tipis* she'd heard them called in Savannah—and a number of open campfires. But when she and Como-tan emerged from the trees at last and joined John at the edge of the clearing, she couldn't believe her eyes.

There was open land as far as she could see and most of it was under cultivation of some kind. She could see evidence of fields harvested of corn, peas, squash and other plants she didn't even recognize, and even empty fields, seemingly waiting the hoe or plow. Nearer to her were pens—large wooden pole fences for horses, cattle and sheep. Even—she had to rub to clear her eyes—pens for swine. She had thought the Creek Indians only hunters!

The village wasn't a village at all, she realized. It was a town. A large and busy town. Como-tan waited as she looked.

Once it had been palisaded just as Savannah was, Elizabeth could see the remnants of the upright-placed logs. But those fences of protection had long been overrun with growth, the town spread far beyond their restraint.

Now, wattle and daub huts, few of them small as she had expected, abounded. They were laid out in orderly and straight rows with wide streets between. Many more homes were larger structures, and some were as much as fifteen to twenty feet in height she judged from where she stood, and they were as long as three townhouses in Savannah.

The wattle and daub houses were far the majority, but certainly not all the construction of the Creek village. Elizabeth marveled at the half dozen or so wooden houses, not log constructed as her own cabin had been, but made of sawn timbers like the better of Savannah. Two that she could see near the center of town even held broad verandas across their front!

She turned to Como-tan who was patiently watching her. Turned in unconcealed amazement. "I can't believe it," she said.

"You expected to see only savages," he said. "Primitives who exist only by the hunt. I assure you, my darling Elizabeth, my people had been farmers—successful farmers—for centuries before the white man came to this land."

He swept an arm. "Corn is our major crop, but we've long ago learned it exhausts the soil after a while. That's why if you look you'll see some empty fields. We move around and allow different sections to recover with nature's help. Before we plant again, the earth will be refreshed. That's something the white man has yet to learn. But they will, and the lesson will be a bitter one, I'm afraid. For now they see only the virgin land to the west and continue to move as they use what they have until it will no longer produce and—"

He broke off suddenly. "That's another thing. We'll speak of it another time."

"Who owns the cattle?" she asked him.

"They're owned for the common good of the village," he said. "At least that's the idea. Actually they are owned by the upper class."

He smiled down at her. "Yes, we too have our class levels. Some are poor and some are rich. But here, no one starves if others have food to eat. And everyone works."

"The rich own those houses?" she asked.

Como-tan nodded. "The largest, the one near the center of the village, belongs to my father, the Mico. His name is Chek-illi. You'll meet him shortly."

"He's the leader of everyone here?"

"Within the limits of his power, yes," he said. "I'll also explain that to you later. But I can tell you now he is the man who will marry us. If you don't object to Creek custom."

His mouth twisted. "I didn't think of that, getting a preacher from Savannah to marry us."

Elizabeth reached quickly to touch her lips to his cheek. "I don't object to anything," she said. "As long as it brings us together."

John, impatient to get down the hill into the village, again interrupted the kiss he gave her.

But for all his excitement and interest, her young son began to walk closer and closer to her as the three of them entered the village, Elizabeth noted. Indeed, she was more than a little nervous herself. The pressure of her hand in Como-tan's was a reassurance, however, and she walked with her head up.

The Creeks were curious, but friendly. They spoke to Como-tan as the three of them passed, but most of the eyes, both of men and women, were on her until Elizabeth became very self-conscious.

Como-tan noticed. "There have been many white men here," he told her. "But you're the first white woman. Don't be alarmed, they're merely curious."

"I'm not," she assured him. "It's just that I suddenly feel very clumsy. I'm afraid I'm going to trip over my own feet."

He laughed. "I know how you must feel. I was the same way the first time I went to Charles Town."

"But you were a boy then. I'm a grown woman."

"A very beautiful woman," he said. "That's why they're staring at you."

He addressed a dignified appearing Indian with gray hair who spoke to him, then turned back to her. "We'll be at my father's house soon. He and my mother will be waiting there for us."

"Oh my," she said. "That does frighten me."

He tightened his grip on her hand. "Don't worry. He will like you. Being a Mico, he will have to retain his dignity when he speaks to you, but underneath that he's a kind man."

"I hope so," she said, now feeling a bit less nervous. "How do you know he'll be waiting. How does he know we're coming?"

Como-tan smiled. "It is his business to know who approaches the village at all times. We've been watched since early this morning, I assure you."

"Oh."

A group of boys, still half naked in spite of the cold, crowded together to observe them. Elizabeth watched her own son eyeing them in return, his head revolving as he walked. Had she done right by him to bring him here? But then, what other course could she have taken? The thought of John, with his love for the forest, being trapped inside the orphanage quickly dispelled her worry. John would be happy with the Indians once he became accustomed to them. She believed that. And too, Como-tan had promised to teach him to read.

She turned to look over her shoulder and was surprised to find that a large number of people had followed them at a distance. When they reached the Mico's house and went up on the veranda, the crowd circled the front silently. Como-tan turned and raised an open palm in their direction and spoke briefly. When he finished, Elizabeth watched many smiles and nods of agreement.

The door opened behind her and she turned at the sound. A man stood there, but a different man, he didn't look like any of the other Creeks she had seen. His skin was darker, his forehead sloping. She glanced in curiosity at Como-tan.

"He is Apalachee," he told her. "One of my father's slaves."

"You have slaves?"

He nodded and spoke to the man in Creek. The other answered and stepped back to hold the door for them.

"Come," Como-tan told her. "My father is waiting."

He had released her hand when they mounted the veranda and now took her arm. Elizabeth felt a small hand creep into her other and looked down to smile reassuringly at her son as John crowded closer to her skirts.

The room they entered was well furnished, as good as any she had seen in Savannah, but it was empty of people. The servant crossed it quickly and opened another door, stepping back to hold it for them with his head bowed.

The second room was much larger, but Elizabeth had no time to examine it. Opposite the door, at the far side of the room, two people, a man and a woman, sat in large carved chairs. A half dozen others stood about and all were watching her intently.

Como-tan guided her into the room and stopped. She was hardly conscious of the door being closed behind them.

The seated man was as large as his son, indeed, his face was an older, more lined version of Como-tan's. He was richly dressed in a silk shirt and velvet breeches that didn't end properly below his knees with stockings, but extended fully to his feet. Over his shoulders was thrown a cape made of rabbit fur entwined with bright feathers, and on his head was a wrapping cover of silk.

The woman who sat beside him was dressed in soft fawnskin that had somehow been turned white. Moccasins of the same material reached halfway up her calves.

Como-tan bowed and spoke respectfully from beside her as Elizabeth wondered desperately if she should bow, too. When he finished, the Mico inclined his head gravely and replied at length. Afterwards, his eyes moved to her face, remained for what seemed an eternity to her and then he spoke again.

"My father gives you his welcome," Como-tan told her when the older man had finished. "He says he is happy for your arrival and hopes you will be comfortable."

Elizabeth looked to him and the ghost of a smile tugged at Como-tan's lips. "He's probably happy that this wayward son of his has finally chosen a wife," he added. "Although he didn't say that."

"Please tell him I'm happy to be here," she said. "But don't tell him he scares me to death."

Como-tan spoke and the Mico nodded. After another long look at her, he turned his head and spoke briefly to his wife. She replied and stood up.

"My father has asked my mother to show you the hospitality of his home," Como-tan told her. "She wants you to go with her now."

Elizabeth looked quickly at him, but he only smiled and nodded. "I must stay here and give my father a report of what I've been doing for our people in the last weeks. After that, he will plan our marriage celebration."

"I won't see you again today?" she asked.

"There are things I must do," he said. "You will be fine. Tomorrow I'll show you my village and then the wedding feast will take place tomorrow evening."

He reached to take John's hand from hers. "Don't worry about young John here either. I'll see that he is in good hands. Right, John?"

Her son nodded reluctantly, his eyes moving up to hers.

Elizabeth wanted to protest, but realized she could not disagree with him in front of these people. And, too, she had made the decision to place herself in his hands. "All right," she said instead.

The Creek woman moved as Elizabeth's eyes turned to her and she had no choice but to follow. Two other Indian women, servants she imagined of the Mico's wife, followed them from the room.

Outside the door, in the first room, the tall Creek woman gave her a smile, the first expression that had appeared on her face. "Welcome to my home," she said to Elizabeth's surprise. "My son makes a good choosing."

"You speak English?"

The woman nodded. "I have my son to teach me. I tell him of my interest and he teach me to speak your language. My name is Takoa. I think we will be friends, Elizabeth."

She was flooded with relief. "I know we will . . . Takoa— do I call you that or . . . ?"

"I would be pleased, Elizabeth. Now you come. You have traveled much. I will have water made hot for you to wash and then food . . . to bring. Do I say that correct?"

"You said it very well," Elizabeth told her. "I hope I can learn to speak your language as well as you do mine."

Takoa's smile increased. "We will have much time to talk

after you become wife to my son, I think."

The smile turned into a twinkle. "And you must not fear Chekilli, my husband. He likes you, I can know that already."

Elizabeth smiled ruefully. "I had forgotten I said that. I hope *he* doesn't speak English."

Takoa laughed. "No, he does not. But come now and I will tell you of him and how we live. And in our talk you can tell me if I speak wrong. That is good?"

"That will be very good," Elizabeth said. "I think I like you very much."

"Then I am pleased." Takoa reached for her hand and took her into the rear of the house.

Elizabeth spent a very pleasant night in the rooms belonging to Takoa, taking a leisurely bath in water heated for her, being fed a delicious meal and then sitting on a cushioned chair to talk with the wife of the Mico. It was, however, difficult for her to adjust to having others wait upon her. The two slaves bathed her and even helped her to dress.

With morning, after rising from a pillow soft bed and being served breakfast, she was taken outside to meet Como-tan. He nodded his approval of her new dress of doeskin and moccasins, and then took her on a walking tour of the village as he explained it to her. There were large kitchens set aside to cook for many at one time, storehouses full of grain, cool underground caves shored with timbers where more food, including meat was stored. Como-tan showed her a mound with a decorated clay walled hut atop it where, he said, the planting rituals were held each year to insure a good harvest.

To relieve her mind, he also took her to see her son and the Indians with whom he was staying. But John, having lost his fear completely in the presence of several Creek boys near his own age, had little time for his mother. He was, he told her breathlessly, learning a new game they played with a leather ball and sticks. And would she mind if they hurried back to it?

With her agreement he was quickly gone and Como-tan had noticed the worry on her face. "He will do well," he told her. "Like all boys he will have his disagreements, but he will learn very quickly, I think, to defend himself. Do not worry about him."

In mid-afternoon, she was returned to the house of Chekilli

and given over to Takoa's maid servants again. Once more she was bathed and rubbed with a sweet smelling lotion, then dressed for the wedding ceremony.

The dress she was given was sky blue silk and reached in wide pleats to her toes. The bodice was high and threaded with white lace and the sleeves puffed at the shoulder and close about her wrists. A stiff lace collar swept outward from about her neck. Elizabeth felt like a queen in the dress in spite of the beaded soft white moccasins she wore beneath it. She stood and admired herself in a long looking glass while one of the servants carefully brushed her hair into place.

Both the dress and the single muslin shift she wore beneath it bore the soft scent of flowers, and Elizabeth wondered how that had been accomplished. But neither of the handmaidens could speak a word of English, she discovered, and she hadn't seen Takoa since morning. She sighed and stood still while one of the servants adjusted a very small, beaded headband of silk around her forehead.

Then they left her to wait to be married.

It was growing late in the afternoon when her future mother-in-law came for her and led Elizabeth through the house to the veranda where Como-tan and Chekilli waited. She looked at the man she was about to marry and knew without a doubt that she was making no mistake. He was more of a man than any she'd ever known.

He was dressed simply—buckskin trousers like his father's but made white and containing a fringe down the side of each leg. His shirt, however, was made of cambric and cut in a European fashion with a wide, long pointed collar open at his throat. His tall frame was as handsome as she could have wished, but it was the light in his dark eyes that caught and held her attention.

Como-tan reached for her hand. "Lovely," he whispered. "The vision I have waited so long for."

"I love you," she whispered, having difficulty with her own speech.

"Then come," he said. "The celebration is for us."

Chekilli, wearing an even more elaborate cape of feathers, stood beside his son and Elizabeth bowed her head to him. His face could have been made of stone, but when she straightened and looked him directly in the eye, she was certain she saw a twinkle.

She had been so nervous upon exiting from the house and then so taken with her husband-to-be that Elizabeth had failed to notice the four of them were certainly not alone. As Como-tan took her hand to guide her from the veranda, she was astonished to find the street before them aswarm with silently watching people of all ages. The faces were smiling, but the silence was startling. It lasted only as long as it took for Como-tan to raise his free hand above his head in a sign of victory. Then the shout deafened her. They were suddenly like school-children being freed from their classes, jumping about and clapping each other on the back or shoulder as they parted to allow the four of them to pass down the street.

When the din subsided enough so that she could be heard, she asked him why they had been so quiet at first.

"They waited to see if you would accept me," he said. "They knew you had a choice. But when you took my hand and started to walk beside me, they knew you had agreed."

Elizabeth smiled. "I could have told them that before," she said.

If she had not already been the happiest she had ever been in her life, the infection of the wide smiles and merry laughter around her as she passed down the street would have made her so. These were wonderfully kind people, and she felt as if she were walking on air.

He held her hand and turned toward the square in front of the ceremonial mound with its decorated hut. Elizabeth suddenly realized that she and Como-tan led the party; that the Mico and Takoa followed behind. "Shouldn't the King be leading?" she asked.

"Not at this moment," Como-tan told her. "For this evening I am the King and you are the Queen of this village. All have made themselves our subjects. Even my father."

She returned the smiles around her with a glad one of her own. "It feels good to be a queen," she said.

The square before the Indian temple had been changed for the festival. To one side, pits had been dug and whole steers roasted slowly over low burning fires. Masses of low tables were set about and loaded with dishes of food, and in the center of the square, a huge pile of wood awaited only the starting flame to become a bonfire. Every wattle house or hut around the square was bright with color, either in cloth waving from it or dyed ears of dry corn. Caught in the beginning dusk, it was a beautiful scene, made even more so as the chattering, laughing people behind them crowded into the square and seated themselves on the ground in a huge circle.

Como-tan led her to a mound raised about a foot from the earth that had not been there that morning. It contained four chairs, and as soon as they were seated, slaves quickly brought them bowls of food.

The celebration meal was a mixture of things she recognized, and some she didn't, but Elizabeth could barely taste the food. She looked at the faces around the circle before her and searched for her son. She found him seated eating busily with a Creek and his wife and two other boys.

Como-tan caught her search and leaned toward her. "The man is my cousin. I chose his home because of his two sons. John will do well there until we have established our own home. Don't worry," he assured her. "But you are not eating, is something wrong?"

She shook her head quickly. "None but excitement."

He smiled. "Then try some of this to drink." He motioned to one of the slaves who quickly fetched a clay bottle and real glasses.

Elizabeth took the filled glass gingerly. She had never drunk from real glass before. The Cawley's had owned a pair and she had washed those often enough, but never had she drunk from one herself. It was a beautiful goblet, curved in the body and long in the stem. Only after she had admired it at length did she realize that Como-tan held one himself and was patiently waiting for her.

He smiled again when she looked up in guilt and raised his glass to touch against hers. "To our future, dear Elizabeth. May it be as sweet."

Her first glass and her first experience with wine. The drink was red, light red in color, and deliciously sweet in taste. She took another small drink. It was as if she were inhaling soft clouds, perfumed clouds; the wine was as good to her nostrils as to her tongue.

The wine relaxed her quickly. It was wonderful to be sitting beside him, occasionally reaching to touch his hand on the arm of his chair, and watching the people enjoying themselves around the circle. As dusk fled before the night, men came to torch the wood and the quickly climbing blaze brought a new and different cast to the scene. Darting shadows masked the people into a pulsating sea to match the throb of their voices.

The people ate, and then, starting with a few at a time, both boys and maidens began to dance rythmically around the bonfire. The movement of their young bodies was a pleasure to see.

"The dance is also for us," Como-tan said from beside her. "It's a dance of fertility. My people always hope that with the beginning of any new marriage more sons and daughters will be born to strengthen the tribe."

She closed her hand upon his.

The dancing, however, ceased abruptly when Chekilli rose. As did all other sound. A second later, the leather-skinned drums that had provided a beat for the young dancers rapped out a quick tattoo and a great shout went up from the crowd. Elizabeth looked quickly at Como-tan and he nodded. "It is time, my love. Are you ready?"

"Yes," she said. And she was.

Chekilli gestured toward the fire and several more logs were thrown upon it, causing the blaze to brighten the square. He raised his arms above his head, and once more the silence returned to the crowd.

The Mico descended from the mound and walked slowly to a place several paces away from it. There he raised his arms again, extended them as far as he could reach and held his head back to the sky. He dropped them after a moment, turned a half pace and repeated the gesture.

Como-tan leaned close to her. "He is appealing to all the spirits on our behalf," he whispered as the Mico continued to turn slowly and repeat the raising of his arms. "He asks the Wind, the Sky, the Earth and the Rain not to stand in the way of our happiness."

She was about to reply when Chekilli stopped and faced them. He stretched out his arms in their direction and Como-tan took her hand and guided her from the mound to walk to his father.

He stopped and stood before the Mico, still holding her hand by his side. Chekilli asked a short question.

Como-tan's voice was strong, loud enough for all to hear as he spoke in Creek. When he had finished, he bent his head and spoke in a lower tone to her. "I have declared to all here that I want you for my wife. That I will care for you and provide for you as a good husband should. I have also promised that I will protect you from all danger and," he permitted himself a small smile, "that I will not beat you unless you deserve it."

Elizabeth smiled back at him as he continued. "I have also made a promise for my future children that when you become old and can no longer do for yourself, that they will be kind to their mother and provide for her needs. Now you must speak and I will translate."

"What do I say?" she whispered. "I want to say it right."

"There are no special words, my love," he said. "You are expected to say whatever is in your heart."

She gave him a long look, feeling the love welling up in her. Then slowly turned to look at the solemn-faced Mico who stood before her. She was happy and her voice was strong. "I love this man who stands beside me," she told him. "I will love him forever and be a good wife to him. It is my greatest wish that I can make him as happy as he has made me."

She paused, not knowing what else to say, and Como-tan squeezed her hand. He spoke loudly in Creek and when he finished, a great shout went up and Chekilli nodded.

"What did I tell them?" Elizabeth asked without looking at him.

The pressure on her hand increased briefly. "You said just what you said, my darling." He hesitated a moment, then chuckled under his breath so that only she could hear. "But you also said you would give me many strong sons."

Chekilli made a gesture and immediately a man ran to his side to hand him a short piece of rawhide. The Mico took it and reached forward to grasp his son's hand. He moved his hand up before him with the palm down. Then he reached for her free hand and placed it atop Como-tan's. Elizabeth felt the strength beneath that hand as well as the pressure on her other.

Chekilli wrapped the rawhide string around their hands and tied it into a knot. Then withdrew the cord and slowly released their hands to their sides. He spoke gravely, first to Como-tan and then to her. Afterwards, he held the circle of rawhide before him as Como-tan translated.

"My father has tied the knot of our marriage to each other," he told her. "We are to keep the cord with us as long as we love and respect each other. If either of us decides that is no longer possible, he or she has only to untie the knot and leave it across the door to our home."

"This knot will never be untied," she said. She wanted very much to kiss him.

"Never," he nodded, and reached to take the cord from his father and hold it aloft for all to see. If the cheering had been loud before, it was deafening now. Mixed with the sudden heavy beat of the drums, it seemed to make the earth beneath her feet throb.

The shouting increased the more as the Mico made a gesture and suddenly she and Como-tan were surrounded by six fiercely painted warriors carrying long spears. The men provided a shield for them as Como-tan led her through the crowd, where everyone made great effort to touch them.

Como-tan held her tightly and guided her through the clutching hands, bending his face close to hers. "Don't be frightened," he shouted into her ear. "They consider it good luck to touch you. Some of our happiness this night can be transferred to them!"

"I've enough for all!" she screamed, but knew her voice was lost in the din about her.

The warriors did their job, trying not to injure those whom they forced aside. In minutes they were through and the happy crowd allowed them to go in peace. Elizabeth found herself walking swiftly through the dark streets being guided by Como-tan's strong arm around her. The silent guards moved with purpose, swiftly, and she had to walk rapidly to keep up.

"Where are we going?" she asked breathlessly.

"To a special place that has been set aside for us," he said.

It was fully dark around them now and she had no concept of where she was. Only the grip of his arm around her and her hand in his kept Elizabeth from stumbling. But in less time than she expected they saw a light ahead. Two lanterns hung from poles and behind them was a rounded hut. Como-tan led her between the lanterns and stopped at the door. He spoke to the warriors briefly, and four of them moved aside to go around the small building. The last two turned their backs and stood rigid.

He looked down at her. "They will remain here all night and leave as the dawn breaks."

He smiled at her. "The purpose is to defend against any evil spirits that might want to sneak into our marriage house and destroy the beauty of our first night together."

His smile broadened. "There's also a more practical side of

it, however. They will prevent our being disturbed by any curious young people from the village."

"Then I have you alone?" she asked.

"Tonight is only the beginning," he told her. "Come."

The inside of the hut was quietly beautiful. Its rounded walls were completely covered with woven mats dyed in soft colors. On one side was a raised mound covered first with skins and then a casing of sorts—a huge pillow more than six feet in size. Across the bottom of it was a soft blanket, folded neatly, and at the top, two head pillows. On the other side of the room was a wooden table with a glass bottle and more drinking glasses arranged beside it. But the real beauty lay in the shallow pit in the center of the clay floor that was lined with stones and guarded a small cheerful fire, the only light in the room.

Around the floor, covering most of it, were soft skins for them to walk upon.

"It's lovely," she said.

Como-tan took her into his arms. "A setting for the true beauty," he said. "The beauty of Elizabeth, who at last belongs to me."

He held her close to him and kissed her. She melted against him, felt the hunger of his lips . . . the joy of his lips.

His voice was deep, a murmur beside her ear as he brushed it with his kiss. "I've waited so long for this night, my lovely Elizabeth . . ."

"Love me," she whispered. "Don't ever allow this to end."

He kissed her again. Gently, but long in its lasting and growing in its demand for her. Elizabeth responded, the excitement of the wedding fading with her sense of now being alone with the man she loved . . .

He released her lips but not her body, holding her close to him, his hands against her back. "There is a special wine for us," he said softly. "A gift from my mother. We must drink it together."

"Whatever you wish," she whispered. "My husband . . ."

Como-tan released her reluctantly, crossed to the small table and poured the wine. He returned and gave a glass to her. "Drink, my sweet Elizabeth. Drink to the happiness we shall know forever."

The wine was light, so light she seemed to taste only of its essence, but it was nothing compared to the look in his eyes above her. Como-tan took the glass from her hand, set it on the table along with his own and then turned to show her another object. He spread his hands to present a string of perfectly matched pearls, a necklace beyond belief.

"For you," he said. "My father's gift to his newest daughter."

Elizabeth couldn't speak as he placed them around her neck. It was beginning to be a dream...the wine...the beauty of the pearls...Como-tan. She began to cry softly in fear she would awake.

He held her and kissed her. "Elizabeth..."

Her fear vanished with the strong presence of his arms around her. Then, gently, without the least hint of clumsiness, he began to unhook the dress at her throat. Elizabeth reached to stroke the backs of his hands as he continued down the front and then slowly drew the dress aside.

He freed the drawstrings at her waist, raised his hands to her shoulders and dropped her dress from her completely.

He kissed her again, a long, gentle kiss.

"I have dreamed many times of this moment," he whispered, his lips barely apart from hers. "I would see you as in my dreams..."

Elizabeth reached to kiss him in return, then moved her own arms up to pull her shift from her shoulders and allow it to drop to the floor.

For the first time she felt a tremble in his strong hands. "Elizabeth..."

"I belong to you, my husband," she murmured, reaching to brush his lips with her own. "Whatever I am is yours."

Como-tan picked her up and carried her to the bed where he lay her atop its softness. Then quickly removed his own clothing and Elizabeth could see his hard muscled body in the dancing glow of the firelight. Could see, and know of his great desire for her...

He stretched beside her, this man she loved more than she had ever thought possible, gathered her into his strong arms and kissed her with a passion that drew her senses alight.

"My lovely Elizabeth..."

"Take me," she whispered, covering his face with her kisses. "Love me, my husband..."

He kissed her throat, the hollow below it, and moved gently across to the end of her bare shoulders as one loving hand began to caress her breast, his fingers creating a fire in her.

"The mountain belongs to both of us," Como-tan whispered

as his lips moved back to touch the lobe of her ear. "It is not for me but for the two of us together. Fly with me, Elizabeth. Fly with me to the mountaintop."

He held her close to him, his gentle hand stroking her body from breast to thigh, and Elizabeth began to experience a response that was new and startlingly strange to her. Her body, loving him in the beginning, became alive with its own needs. She began to throb within herself, stirred impatiently under his gently probing fingers, and pulled him to her fiercely. "Como-tan," she gasped. "My darling . . ."

"The mountain is ours," he whispered, his firelit lips now searing the other side of her throat and his moving hand bringing her more and more to quivering life.

She was breathing harder now, unable to still her restless body; unable to slow the building *need* for him. "Como-tan!"

She had never known it could be like this. Her body was now her senses . . . she wanted him with a desperation that set her aflame.

He moved; Elizabeth was no longer aware of what was his being and what was her own, only that the two of them were now a single moving together. She was rising in a rapidly building cresendo of experience . . . moving, and holding to the man she loved as the mountain carried them to its heights.

"Como-tan!" Her loud cry was not her own. It echoed from a distance below the mountain.

Clouds of love for him rushed in, gathered her and whirled her upward and upward until her senses reeled, and Elizabeth struggled to retain the warmth of his body next to hers. She felt she was being rushed upward into a vortex that would whisk her forever away along with its rapidly disappearing smoke. "Como-tan!"

His lips touched hers, seared them with desire, and suddenly the clouds that bore her burst around her. Elizabeth's body quivered, then flooded with great release.

She clung to him as Como-tan hesitated. Clung to him with all her strength in fear that both the sensation would cease and that it would not.

"Elizabeth . . ." His loving voice echoed distantly beyond her exploding senses. "My darling Elizabeth . . ."

She began to float downward with the ceasing of his movement, float with a giddiness of no longer being herself. But

Como-tan kissed her and began to move and bring her back up and up . . .

It seemed to last an eternity, an eternity of being beyond herself, until, when she thought she would certainly explode forever into the universe around her, he hesitated for a moment and Elizabeth felt his trembling release.

The clouds closed in upon her again, she shook violently with their movement and again rushed off with them into the vortex.

The weight of his body, his strong, protecting body, was all that prevented her from becoming hopelessly adrift on a languid sea of tranquility.

Elizabeth woke slowly, drifting back a little at a time and feeling as if her body still floated. Como-tan . . . her husband . . . held her close to him. He had drawn the blanket around them as she slept and encircled her with his arms, resting her head against his broad chest.

When she stirred, he kissed her on the forehead.

Elizabeth pulled closer to him and slid a hand around the back of his neck, enjoying the strength she found there. "Will it always be so on the mountain?" she whispered into his chest.

Como-tan raised her head with gentle fingers against her chin and kissed her. He moved until his dark eyes probed her own in the low light of the dying fire. "We have this mountain forever, my lovely Elizabeth," he said. "We can never lose it."

She brought her face back to his chest and closed her eyes again. He was right. Her struggle was ended at last. She had found the mountain she so long sought. They had found it together.

Twenty-Nine

BY THE TIME he was forty years old, Doctor Thomas Langlee' had become a wealthy man. The Trustees of the young colony of Georgia had given up their "noble experiment" and turned it over to be ruled by the crown under an appointed governor. Therefore, the binding restrictions set by the Trustees no longer applied and Dr. Langlee had been free to acquire all the virgin acreage he desired to enlarge his plantation. Cotton was growing in demand and his slaves were carefully chosen and well treated. Year after year the income of Angel's Rest had doubled.

His reputation as a surgeon nearly rivaled that of the most famous doctor in the colony, Dr. Noble Wimberly Jones, and his afternoons set aside to treat his patients always found him working well into nightfall.

His friends in both Georgia and South Carolina, however, thought of him as a lonely man who broke his guarded reserve only in the presence of his two sons. Understandable, they said, for the man had been misfortunate enough to bury two wives after only a brief marriage to each. The first, Angelica Breaksford-Pinley, went quite mad, they whispered, and perished from snakes bites while actually running naked through the woods. The second, young Faith Wellingsly Langlee, had already been in poor health when he married her and died in struggling to give him his second son.

His hard luck did not, however, prevent many other ladies in both colonies from yearning to become the third Mrs. Langlee. But the doctor had withdrawn himself into his work and his sons. He was polite and correct at the occasional social events he could be persuaded to attend, but definitely, the longing ladies discovered, no longer agreeable to marriage.

The amount of cotton he was now exporting to England finally became great enough to force him to make a voyage he had long thought about but had delayed. In late spring, he took ship to return for the first time to the country he had departed as a mere youth. A youth trapped by both indenture and ignorance.

The necessity of his going was to solidify his connections with the Import House of Wainwright, Hallmore and Bray of London, a contract readily negotiated by that old and honorable firm. Afterwards, the directors of the firm were more than pleased to extend the use of an expensive carriage along with driver to escort their valued customer on whatever excursion he cared to make into the countryside.

Dr. Langlee leaned back into the luxurious cushions of the smart coach as he rode and smiled wryly to himself as he watched the passing scene through the window. None of it was familiar to him now although he had once traveled this way on foot going in the opposite direction. He had been a callow youth then, steeped in ignorance, when Briggs led him and Elizabeth to London. How much, he wondered, would those eager directors have done for such a youth?

He wished suddenly he'd gone to see Elizabeth and invited her to come along with him on this trip. That would have heightened the pleasure of it—to retrace their steps together. But he quickly shook his head to dismiss the wish. His sister would not have come. Not have been willing to leave her husband and children nor, he suspected, that great forest in which she took such pleasure.

Only once had he persuaded her to visit Angel's Rest, and at that time he had extended himself to be the best of hosts to her Indian husband. He had found Como-tan to be a gentleman, and truly the two of them had been comfortable in each other's presence. But Elizabeth was far too content with her life to travel again and he was forced to go to her to see her. If she wouldn't come to Angel's Rest, how could he hope to persuade her to spend months on a visit to England?

Dr. Langlee shook his head and smiled. No, that would have been wasted effort on his part. Elizabeth cared little for the past.

The coachman brought him back from his musings by leaning over to shout around into the coach. "We'll be there in less than an hour, sir, if I'm right about it! Is there somewhere you prefer to be taken?"

Tom leaned forward to make himself heard over the rattle and rustle of the coach. "Find a comfortable inn if you can, driver. I plan to spend no more than one night in this place."

"As you wish, sir!" The driver straightened and Tom was alone with his thoughts again.

It had been years since he passed this way, but his beginnings had never been far from his mind since he learned of his birth from Elizabeth on board that ship—what was the name? *The Grace*, that was it. How could he have forgotten?

Anyway, he'd promised himself that someday, if at all possible, he would return and discover all that he could of their strange beginnings. He would pay a visit to the Langlee estate if he had to—under another name, of course. It would be preposterous to announce himself the bastard child of—who? He didn't even know his mother's name.

What had happened to Lyman Briggs? Probably drank himself to death in London, or when his money ran out was forced to return to that hut on the other side of the moor. He might even be there still. No matter, he had no interest in seeing the place of his mean youth again. He was interested only in the Langlee estate on this side.

He shifted to a more comfortable position on the cushions and closed his eyes.

"There's the town you want, sir!" The coachman's voice roused Tom from his doze.

He leaned out of the carriage to see. The town was small, hardly different from dozens of others in the English countryside except that this one belonged to his own ancestors.

"Find an inn," he called.

"Yes sir."

To his surprise, he became more than a little nervous as

they entered the town. His palms were moist and his pulse quickened.

The inn was the first large building they reached and contained an enclosed courtyard with a stable to one side. Tom stepped stiffly from the coach, his bones were not accustomed to riding most of the day, and glanced up at the driver.

"Stable the horses and find yourself accommodations, driver," he said. "I expect to be here one night only."

The man knuckled his forehead. "Yes, sir. You'll be wanting the carriage early?"

"I don't know. I'll send someone for you when I'm ready."

"Very good, sir. I'll fetch your luggage to your room, Dr. Langlee. Right away."

The carriage moved away and Tom entered the inn.

A room was readily available—the innkeeper was anxious to please his well-turned guest and was quick with both a hot meal, which he brought to the room himself, and information.

"Yes, sir," he said to Tom's careful inquiry. "Sir Barton Langlee, it is, sir, who's master of the estate. Master, I might add, sir, to all the land for a day's horse any direction you would take from this spot."

Tom nodded and inspected the glass of wine the man poured for him, lifting it to the light and then sniffing it. "How is Sir Barton's health? Do you know? And does he have a wife?"

The innkeeper was thin, unlike the usual innkeeper in the colonies who waxed fat on his own victuals, but otherwise he was of the same manner of innkeepers everywhere. Whatever his guest's business, it was not *his* business, except to be of the best service he could. He shook his head. "I'm not aware of what goes on at the manor, sir. Tis no one bothers to come to my humble inn who visits there, you see. There would not be the need. But I do know Sir Barton has had no wife these many years. He lives alone in the manor. I could direct you though, I'm thinking, to a man who could answer your questions completely."

He paused and shrugged. "That is unless you expect to visit the manor house yourself. Then there'd be no use, of course."

Tom hid his excitement in an indifferent nod. "I was merely curious. As a landowner myself, I can appreciate the care I see about me."

"Yes, sir. The Langlee land is well looked after, I'll tell you that."

"Who is this person?" Tom asked the question as casually as he could.

"Pardon, sir?"

"You mentioned a man familiar with the Langlee estate."

"Oh yes, sir. That would be old Giles. He was coachman to the manor until he grew too aged to serve. He lives in a hut at the end of this village. I could send for him if you like?"

Tom shook his head. "No, that won't be necessary. As I said, I was merely curious. I might stop by this hut tomorrow, however, if I have the time. Can you identify it for me?"

"Yes, sir. Tis a stone hut hard by a very large oak. It's set apart from any other dwelling by a hundred paces or more. You can't mistake it."

"Very good. Thank you, innkeeper."

"Will there be anything else, sir?"

Tom dismissed him with a wave of his hand.

The stone hut was tiny, its interior could not possibly be beyond a single small room, judging from its vine-covered exterior. This Giles obviously lived here alone.

He had been unable to wait, and unwilling to rouse his coachman to drive him here. It was still early in the evening, plenty of daylight left, and he was used to exercise. The walk through the town had been enjoyable in spite of the stares it invoked from the people.

But now, standing before the home of a man who could well unlock the truth of his birth, a man who might have known his mother, gave him pause.

He shook away the feeling and stepped close enough to rap on the thick wooden door with the head of his cane.

The sound echoed in the stillness of eve. Tom waited, a long time, and was about to rap again in impatience when the door swung open.

The man who stood there was gray with age, but Tom had long studied the human form as a physician and could readily see the remnants of what had once been great strength. He was stooped with his years, but his wide shoulders and large chest were that of a giant. Deep-set eyes, under heavy and gray brows, peered out at him. "Yes?"

"You are Giles who was coachman to the Langlee manor?" Tom asked.

The man stepped through the door, necessary in order to be

able to lift his head erect. "Yes, sir. I am he. What service could I be to you, sir?"

Tom hesitated, then decided to plunge ahead. If this man were unwilling to talk, so be it. There was no use in wasting time about it. "I would ask you some questions, Giles, if I may. You're under no obligation to answer, of course."

To his surprise, the old man moved closer and peered directly at him for a long moment.

"Might I ask your name, sir?" he said at last. "I mean no disrespect."

"None taken, Giles. My name is . . ." he hesitated only briefly, "also Langlee. I am, however, not from here, from the colonies."

The old eyes held him for long minutes, exceedingly long; Tom felt every pore of his face was examined thoroughly. He began to grow irritated, but held his peace. The man, after all, was old.

Finally, when he suspected he could bear the inspection no longer, the old man nodded very slowly. "Aye," he said in a low and strained voice. "You would be a Langlee. You've the eyes . . . and the jaw of it."

He paused and his voice trembled when he spoke again. "You would be the boy . . . you would be *her* son."

Tom felt a chill run down his back, icy fingers that touched even the muscles of his arms. He started to speak, and stopped.

"You are him," Giles murmured, half to himself. "I've no doubt of it." He slowly shook his head. "After all these years . . ."

Tom found his voice with difficulty. "Then you know why I'm here," he said.

"Aye. You'll be wanting to know who you are." Giles rubbed a large and knotted hand across his forehead as if to brush away something. "I've often thought of you . . . sire. You and your sister."

"Not sire," Tom said gently. "Merely Dr. Langlee. Dr. Thomas Langlee, Giles."

"No." The old man shook his head. "Dr. Langlee it may well be, but in truth it should be Sir Thomas."

He closed his eyes briefly, as if in pain, then opened them again. "Will you honor my home, sire? Methinks I've a deal to tell you."

Before Tom could speak, Giles shook his head again in wonder. "Once the telling would have been worth my life. But now, with me already feeling the cold of death's opening door so to speak, it doesn't seem to matter. I'll tell you all, sire, if you care to listen."

"I want to hear it all," Tom said. "Especially that of my mother. You knew her?"

"Come," Giles said. "T'will not do to stand out here. I was about to brew my evening tea. Will you share it, sire?"

"As you wish."

He followed the old man into the hut, a home with bare walls and only the simplest of furniture. A raised stone ledge to one side with a straw-filled mattress atop it, a small table, a pair of wooden stools and a recessed fireplace made the bulk of it. The rest was a small chest, a worn cupboard, a greatcoat hanging from one peg in the wall and a long, coiled whip hanging from another.

Giles indicated the bed. "Sit there if you will, sire. T'will be more comfortable than my stools."

Tom crossed to the bed, only four steps, and sat down. "As I said, Giles, you needn't address me as sire. Dr. Langlee will do nicely."

The old man shook his head stubbornly as he picked up a brass teakettle. "By the right of it, sire, you are both heir to the manor and a knight of England."

Tom sighed. "I'll settle for the truth of my birth, Giles. Tell me all you know of it."

Giles glanced at him. "I know all of it, sire. It was meself who fetched you to the peasant. You and your sister."

He felt the cold chill again and shook it from his shoulders. "Tell me," he said softly. "Start at the beginning."

"Aye." Giles slowly added his tea leaves to the kettle and hung it over the small fire. Then he sat down to watch it, not looking at Tom.

"She was the most beautiful soul this side of heaven," he said in a low voice, a voice that shook more than a little. "Beautiful in both face and her kindness to others. The servants, all the household without exception, would have given their lives for her at the asking."

Tom watched the large old hands shake. "Meself, I would have been glad to die for her. I thought her the sweetest . . ."

Giles shook himself free of the memory. "Never was she known not to smile, sire, or to have any but a sweet word for those fortunate enough to be in her presence. And when she

laughed . . . I tell you, it was enough to make your heart jump
with the pleasure of it."

"What was her name?" Tom asked, when the other fell
silent.

Giles glanced at him in brief but honest surprise, then nodded. "Lady Edythe. I forgot you wouldn't know." He shook
his head as he returned to watching the flames in the hearth.
"Not know your own mother's name . . ."

Tom leaned his back to the wall. "The beginning, Giles."

"Aye, sire. Sir William—your grandfather—was killed by
the French," Giles said slowly. "He was taken prisoner, but
somehow before the ransom could be paid, he was killed by
them. Murdered, Sir Barton said, and none could say why.
Not that it mattered, the act was enough to make Sir Barton
rightly hate the French."

"The same Sir Barton who is lord of the manor now?" Tom
asked.

"Aye, sire. One and the same. He has been a bitter man for
the most of his life. He was brother to your grandfather and
after Sir Edmund, father to the both of them died, he became
master of these lands in right."

Giles took a deep breath and reached to stir the tea, and
Tom was forced to wait.

"Sir Edmund was not in good health," the old man continued
after a pause. "He took the death of his oldest son most hard.
Following, as it did, the death of your grandmother from sickness. Only the cheer Lady Edythe provided for him kept him
from his own sick bed. He loved to sit with her and to sup
with her in the evenings. Most of all he loved to ride about
with her in the carriage I drove. She was, methinks, all that
kept him alive. Then Lady Edythe met the Frenchman."

"This was following the war?" Tom asked.

"Aye. England and France were no longer at each other's
throat. Lady Edythe met him on a visit to her friends in London.
Met him at a ball there, I understand."

Giles glanced at him again. "He was a marquis, sire. I never
knew his name though. I'm sorry."

Tom brushed it aside with a hand. "What happened then?"

"The Frenchman was invited to the manor by your mother.
She was already fair in love with him, so much, she surely
glowed with it. But Sir Barton went into a rage at the news
and sent a message to forbid his coming. "T'was himself who

convinced Sir Edmund to agree to it. But he also threatened to lock Lady Edythe away forever if she ever saw the Frenchman again. Nothing she could say would change his mind."

"She was bad hurt and begged her uncle." Giles smiled a hard little smile. "And when he still refused, she slipped away to see him. She had the steel in her, too, that one."

He paused to rub his forehead. "But far better she had not, for it caused her death."

"He killed her? Sir Barton, I mean?" Tom sat erect.

"No, sire. Lady Edythe died of a broken heart. I watched her pine away after you and your sister were taken away from her."

"Tell me about that," Tom said, lying back against the wall again.

"Aye. She loved the Frenchman. Loved him so much she birthed his children. He was your father but he never knew it. When Lady Edythe found she was carrying the two of you, she kept herself to her rooms to avoid her uncle. She knew if the truth were discovered, he would have you murdered. And then he would keep her under lock forever."

Giles fell silent and Tom thought for a moment, then asked, "Who took us away?"

"It was Authur Massengale. He was chamberlain to Sir Edmund and therefore in charge of the household. Like the rest of us, he loved Lady Edythe. And he knew if the truth were discovered, it would kill his master. T'was no more than a few days after the two of you were born that he came to me and swore me to an oath of silence I've kept to this day. He told me Lady Edythe knew she couldn't keep her babes, not and see them live, but she would not give them up without his swearing to her that they would not be murdered by others. Massengale was caught between that promise and the need to get the babes beyond the reach of Sir Barton for her sake."

The tea began to boil and Giles removed it from the fire, set it on the table and went to fetch cups for them.

Tom was impatient, but held his tongue until the tea was poured and Giles sat down again.

"Authur Massengale remembered Lyman Briggs who had been a soldier under your grandfather. Knew only that the peasant was awarded his place to live because he could carry out orders without question. That he would do exactly as he was told. He decided to take the babes to him and frighten him into forever being silent about it."

Tom watched as the large hand removed itself from Giles's cup and slowly turned into a fist. The old man stared down at it.

"Authur Massengale didn't believe you would survive long, for the two of you were not strong babes. He hoped you would die of your own in the hands of the peasant."

His head came up slowly. "T'was all I could do, sire, to leave you with the likes of Briggs. The thought of his foul hands placed upon the babes of her . . ." He took a deep, rasping breath, then shook away the thought.

"But we didn't die, as Massengale wanted," Tom said quickly. "Was he aware of it?"

Giles shook his head and smiled the hard smile again. "Only I was aware, sire. Tis so bad I felt for the deed and my part in it, and so much I loved Lady Edythe, that I made occasion to cross the moor more than once and see for meself how you fared. But I told Authur Massengale that you had died."

"I see," Tom said. "What happened to my mother?"

"A broken heart, sire, just as I said. She was denied the man she loved and then her babes were taken from her breast. T'was more than her tender heart could bear. She pined away slowly and Sir Edmund was not long in following her into death."

"And no one but yourself ever knew we lived?" Tom asked quietly.

"No, sire. I knew if Sir Barton ever found out the truth he would have the two of you killed and stretch my own neck for it."

The old eyes looked directly at Tom. "I hoped hard that would not happen, sire. Not as much in fear for my own neck as . . . well, you were all that was left of her, you see. In you she was still alive, I thought."

He nodded slowly. "In truth, I watched sometime from a distance and saw your sister working in the field. She looked so much her mother it near broke me heart. She belonged not in such work. She had the right of a lady denied her."

Tom smiled. "Then you will be happy to know, Giles, she has that life now. In a manner of speaking she is the wife of a prince of his people, with maids to serve her if she chooses."

"I'm most glad, sire."

There was a long silence between them as Tom allowed his thoughts to carry back over the years. The story had been true then. He was born of noble blood. Born to a gentle and lovely lady.

"Giles, is there chance I might see her grave?" he asked, breaking the silence. "Without, I mean, the knowledge of my great uncle?"

"Aye, sire. There is that. I could take you there in a manner we could avoid being seen by anyone. The Langlees are buried in a glade that is apart from the main house. But I'm afraid these old legs of mine won't stand the walking."

"We'll go by carriage," Tom said. "I'll have it here first thing in the morning. I'd like to pay my respects to my mother."

Giles nodded.

Tom sipped his tea, now grown cold, and a thought occurred to him. "Giles, did Lyman Briggs return to here—the other side of the moor, I mean?"

The old eyes flashed. "Nay, sire. Had he been fool enough to do that without the two of you with him it would have been worth his life. I would have beat the truth from him and then strangled him with these two hands. T'was only that I never knew where he had taken you that I didn't follow. You say you went to the colonies?"

"Yes," Tom said. "I'll tell you about it if you wish."

Giles nodded, but he was thinking of something else. "I remember the night, sire, remember it as though it were but yesterday. I almost killed Briggs that night. It was bad I wanted to strip the flesh from him for the mere touching of his foul hand to her babes. When I left, I was that sick at heart I wanted to die."

"It turned out for the best, under the circumstances," Tom told him. "But I thank you for the way you felt toward us."

Giles stared at him. "It might not be too late, sire, to correct the wrong. Are you certain you would not like to call at the manor house?"

Tom raised his eyebrows. "That wouldn't appear wise, Giles. Besides, I don't really care to see my great uncle. Only my mother's grave."

The old man shook his head, his eyes suddenly grown wide. "Things have changed now, sire, the thought occurs to me. You see, Sir Barton has become of late most aware of his own growing age. He never gained an heir, so when he dies, the Langlee lands will return to the crown and the name itself will die."

He jerked erect in agitation. "Bitter he has always been, sire. But he is also a man of pride in his own name. I am of great suspect he would certainly prefer to recognize a bastard, even one with a French father, than see the end of the Langlees. Let us go to him, sire. I'll tell my part of it and I also know an old woman who was once maid to your mother. She will swear to the birth."

Tom held up his hands. "No. I thank you, Giles. But there's no point to it."

"But sire!" Giles climbed to his feet. "You could claim your rightful title! You would become Sir Thomas! Master of these lands!"

Tom rose and reached to take the other on the shoulders and reseat him. "There was once a time when that title would have had great meaning for me," he told the anxious old eyes looking up at him. "But I was young and foolish then and had little else to sustain me. Now it no longer matters, Giles."

He smiled. "I came here to seek the truth of my birth, that's all. I've land and wealth enough of my own in the Americas, and that is where I prefer to be. As for the title, it too has little meaning. You see, Giles, as an American, I believe titles to be of short use. It's what a man is worth inside that counts."

He patted the old man on his shoulders and picked up his cane to leave. "I'll call for you in the morn to visit her grave. After that, I'll be going home."

Then he went out the door.

She was an American made three-master, one of the incredibly swift sailing vessels for which the northern colonies were becoming famous. He'd had the choice between her and a British merchantman leaving two days earlier. It had been difficult to wait in London for those two days but all the time he waited he knew he was right. The urgency had grown in him hour by hour to depart these shores for his home in Georgia and that urgency would have been relieved for the moment to board any ship. But the merchantman was slow, would have lumbered through the Atlantic on its passage like one of the huge sows at Angel's Rest wallowing through the mud of its pen. The

American ship, sleek, trim-lined and sharp of bow, would cut through the water like a knife and complete his journey in less than half the time. The two days would be well worth the delay.

Still, his nerves were on edge while he waited aboard *The Northwind,* out of Boston Harbor, as her crew hurried to finish the last minute tasks before casting her lines free of the London quay for the trip down the Thames and into the open sea. Tom stood near the bow, for she was headed aright and that would be the first away. It wasn't a good day for setting out on a voyage, whatever the distance. Yesterday the sun had been warm, the clouds few, but today was a close-set, foggy one; common, he was told, to London this late in the year. The dampness in the air promised more than fog ere the morn was well begun.

"Excuse me, sir."

He turned to find a ship's officer at his elbow. "Yes?"

"The captain has ordered brandy sent to your cabin, Dr. Langlee. He suggests you'd be far more comfortable there as we leave. The weather's apt to be unruly."

Tom nodded. He wasn't the only one who thought it about to turn nasty. But the weather was not a thing to consider at the moment, something else was far and away on his mind. At least it was now that his impatience had been curbed by boarding a vessel for home. Standing on the deck of a ship at a London quay had brought the memories rushing back. Perhaps it was his visit to Giles, the man who unlocked his birth for him, that brought on the clear vision of his youth, but more than likely it was being on the quay itself and then boarding this ship. At any rate he was suddenly in touch with himself in those early, early years, sensing full the innocence of his youth, and he didn't want to let it go—not yet. Plenty of time later for brandy, and the comfort of being Dr. Langlee of Georgia.

"Thank you," he said. "I believe I'll stand here for a while. I'll go below shortly."

"Yes, sir."

The man waited a minute longer, as if he would add to his words, but Tom kept his face away, discouraging further conversation. In a minute he was alone again.

He moved closer to the rail and looked across where the ship's fore hawser was looped around a post. Had there been this few people on the quay when he left here those long years ago? It seemed not; he had blurred visions of there being many— a crowd. Hard to remember. He'd been so concerned with Elizabeth, frightened for her being left alone with that family, he'd had no time to experience the rest of it. He'd expected her to be terrified.

A smile crossed his face. Foolish of him to worry so. That slip of a sister of his had other things on her mind than being frightened. She was bent on making life miserable for Lyman Briggs and she had succeeded.

The smile became a chuckle. It hadn't been too many months ago that he had spent time with her and Como-tan, sitting on the shaded arbor at the rear of the house and speaking of earlier times. Elizabeth had repeated to him what she had done that day they departed England, and of how Briggs had turned white in the face and nearly fainted. Whatever the sum he'd gotten for selling the both of them could not have been worth the fear he'd held the rest of his life of Sir Barton Langlee discovering the existence of his niece and nephew and of Briggs's own part in rearing them.

A shout sounded behind him and Tom turned to see. The aft hawser was released from its mooring, lifted and tossed into the river by two stout men and pulled toward the ship by equally strong-backed sailors. He turned again, knowing the bow rope would follow shortly.

Years ago a very young and very unsure peasant lad had boarded a ship in this self-same river, boarded it with worry for his innocent sister, and then sailed away to a new land. But now that land was his own. It had given him heartache enough to break a man, but at the same time it had given him opportunity . . .

The mist was more than that, suspiciously like rain, and he pulled the high collar of his coat closer. *Be honest with yourself, Thomas Langlee. The wetness in your eyes is not all caused from outside it.*

Elizabeth was happy, obvious in the peace in her face when she looked at him, more so when he watched her speak to her children. She too had known a hard life in the beginning, harder than his. But all of that was behind her now. His sister had all she could want of life.

The bow rope was tossed as he watched. Shouted commands rang from behind him and he knew without looking that men were scrambling aloft to loosen the top-gallants under which the Northwind would make her way down the river. He'd done that once, clumsy in the rigging through lack of experience. A peasant lad, knowing only the working of the land, and suddenly sold like a piece of cattle, given no choice but to try and adjust to a new life.

He turned slowly as the ship moved, watching the dock—this last bit of English land—slipping away. Lyman Briggs had thought only to be rid of him and Elizabeth that day so long ago. Cared not a whit for their future. But in truth his callous act of selling them had been the greatest boon he could have offered. Without that act, he, Thomas Langlee, would have forever remained an English peasant, tied to a poor tract of land in the service of others. And Elizabeth would never have known the peace she now knew.

The rain began to pelt down and he nodded into it. *Thank you, Lyman Briggs, wherever your evil bones may lay. Thank you for making us Americans.*

He turned his back on England and made his way down the short passage to his cabin.

Bestselling Books from ACE!